MW01504660

From the Ashes

Jessica K Mckendry

Copyright © 2013 Publisher Name
All rights reserved.

ISBN: 1-4802-8707-5
ISBN-13: 9781480287075

This story is a work of fiction. Any resemblance of characters to persons, living or dead, is coincidental.

For you.

Prologue

Altair raced through the jungle trees. His heart pounded so hard against his ribs it hurt and his legs threatened to give out. Every breath he took was strained, but he forced himself forward. He only had a little ways to go.

The edge of the jungle came into view, and he charged out into the open. White Tarnoshian marble buildings surrounded the courtyard. They towered over him like giants.

A bell rang and students rushed into the courtyard. Altair made his way through the crowd to the fountain in the center. The setting sun made the water look gold.

Altair touched the cool stone of the fountain and stopped to catch his breath. As his opponent ran into view, he smiled.

"I won!" he cried.

"Only because you're two years older," Liam protested between gasps. "I bet you weren't as fast as me when you were six."

Altair giggled. "I was way faster."

Liam kicked at a rock on the ground. "I'll beat you in something, someday."

Altair took a seat on the side of the fountain. "Good luck with that."

He dipped his fingers in the cool water and twirled it around, watching it twist into a tiny whirlpool.

"Shouldn't we get back to the dorms?" Liam asked.

Altair shook his head. "I have to wait for Jaina."

"Oh, right. Shouldn't she be here by now? She usually gets here first."

A starship flew overhead and the two boys looked up in awe. Altair wondered if he'd ever be able to fly something like that.

"I dunno. Maybe I should go look for her," Altair replied as the ship passed out of their vision.

Liam took a step back. "Well, I should be going to the dorms. See ya tomorrow." At that, he left Altair alone.

Altair waited at the fountain feeling the cool water run over his hands. As time dragged on, he began to worry. Where was Jaina?

His stomach churned. She'd never been this late before. Being the same age as Liam, she got out of class at the same time. It wasn't a very long walk from her classroom. She usually beat them here. His muscles felt tight and it became difficult to breathe. The cool water felt ice cold to his touch and somehow, he knew she was in trouble.

He bolted to her classroom. Although tall for his age, he was still too short to see through the window on the door.

Master Nara glided out of the room, and Altair's heart skipped a beat. Everyone was supposed to be headed to the dorms now. He didn't want to get in trouble for this. He jumped behind a bunch of bushes to his left and waited for her to pass. She paid no attention to the soft shuffling of leaves and wandered into the courtyard with a silverscreen in her hand.

He moved quickly to the open doorway when she was nowhere in sight and took a tentative step inside.

The black desks sat empty. The walls and floor of the classroom were made of standard, silvery Galla steel.

All the holographic projectors and lights were off, leaving him mostly in darkness.

Roshiva Korr stood tall next to Ana Sonn near a locked supply closet in the back of the room. The two were known troublemakers. Altair's hands felt cold and clammy at the sight of them. They looked at Altair as he took a step closer and their devilish grins faltered.

"What are you guys doing?" he asked.

The two looked at each other like they didn't fully understand. A soft whimpering filled his ears and his body went cold.

"Who's in the closet?" he demanded.

Korr flashed him a toothy smile, then pointed to the closed door. "She punched me!" He tapped against the metal.

Ana Sonn twirled her black hair in her fingers and turned toward the door. "Not so tough now, are you, Jaina!"

"Please, let me out!" Jaina begged through her sobs. "I-I won't do it again! I'm s-sorry!"

Altair's heart felt heavy in his chest, yet it pounded faster now than when he was running. He knew better than anyone how afraid she was of the dark. Jaina was so small and innocent...how could they do this to her?

He grabbed Roshiva's shoulders and pushed him backward. "Open the door or I'm telling Master Nara."

"Master Nara," Korr spat, "said it was okay. She didn't care."

Cold darkness raged in Altair's blood. No longer afraid, he clamped his hand around Korr's arm and shoved him to the ground. A strange energy filled him and he focused on Korr. The boy on the ground began to scream and writhe in agony, flailing his arms and clutching his throat as if someone were choking him.

Ana shrieked and brought Altair out of his concentration. He jumped back from Korr.

Korr stopped screaming and gasped for breath. His grey eyes were filled with tears, and dark rings lined them as if he'd been awake for days.

"What did you do to me?" Korr cried.

Although Altair had no idea, he said, "Unlock the door or I'll do it again!"

Korr stood, unlocked the closet, then bolted for the door with Ana close behind him.

Altair opened the closet, letting what little light there was fall over the tiny girl huddled in the corner. Jaina hugged her knees to her chest. She looked up at him, and her trembling slowed, but she didn't move.

He stepped inside, took her hand, and pulled her into his arms.

Tears streamed down her face, and soft sobs wracked her fragile body. She wiped her dark brown eyes, but it did no good. She couldn't stop crying.

Altair's chest felt tight. He was supposed to protect her. Prevent things like this from happening. It was his job to keep her safe. How could he have let this happen?

"I'm sorry," he said. Each tear that fell made him feel more like a failure. "I'm sorry, I should've come sooner. Why would they do that to you?"

"Th-they said I ins-sulted them in front of the class," she managed between choked breaths. "But I d-didn't do anything, I promise! I said I had to meet you at the fountain but they didn't believe me. I'm sorry I couldn't–"

"Where was Master Nara?"

She didn't answer at first.

"Kira," he said, softer this time, using her nickname to soothe her. "Where was Master Nara?"

Jaina shook her head, and wiped away her tears. "She said I had to be strong and if I was too weak, I'd get what I deserve. I'm so weak, Altair. And it was so dark..."

"It's okay," he reassured her. "You're not weak. I bet you'll be one of the strongest fighters here, someday."

Her tears began to slow, and she smiled. "I don't know what I'd do without you."

He squeezed her tight. "Don't worry. I'll always be here for you."

"Promise?"

Altair nodded. "I promise."

chapter

ONE

TEN YEARS LATER:

Kavi taps me on the shoulder. "Jaina, you've got to stop moving around. I can't concentrate."

Master Ijani's weary eyes bore into me as if I'd broken a law. My first warning. Two more to go before I get a detention. Her attention shifts back to the class and she continues her lecture.

I glance at Kavi. "Sorry."

"You're not nervous, are you?" she whispers.

"Of course not," I lie. I shift around in my seat, unable to get comfortable.

Master Ijani pulls something off her desk. "Jaina, since you can't focus, why don't you deliver this message to Master Aron?"

My classmates 'ooh' disapprovingly. I shake it off and take the memory chip containing the message.

"Be back before the bell rings," she warns.

Relieved to be missing class, I exit the room and wander the empty halls of the school. A soft breeze rushes past me, and I take in the tropical air. I like how the Masters leave the windows open during training season. It relieves the stress of everything leading up to the Trials.

Peering into Master Aron's class of seven and eight-year-olds, I smile. It was only eight years ago that I was in this class.

I slowly open the door, hoping not to interrupt. He glances at me with his soft, blue eyes, but continues addressing the class:

"After the fall of the Galactic Alliance, the galaxy fell into one hundred years of darkness. There was starvation. Death. Destruction. Do any of you know what time period I'm talking about?"

A boy in the back raises his hand. "The Century of Darkness?"

"Very good!" Master Aron says. "That was the Century of Darkness. After that, came the Great Stellar Wars, which lasted for seventy five years. There were many power struggles, but in the end, the Imperial Alliance and our wonderful leaders prevailed. And exactly four-hundred and twenty-six years later, in the year 426 ASW," he writes the year on the silverscreen at the front of the room, "here we are. Our people can be strong. But for that to happen, we take the children who have promise and train them at Gifted Schools.

You're all here because we believe you can become part of the Superior society our Emperor has created. You hold a great responsibility. Never forget it. Now, do you have any questions?"

"Is this planet part of the Imperial Alliance?" a girl asks.

Master Aron nods. "Yes, Lea. The Earth is part of the IA."

"How many planets are in the IA?" she asks.

"Thousands." Master Aron smiles and then turns to me. "Jaina, you have something for me?"

"Yes, sir. Master Ijani wanted me to deliver this message to you." I hand him the memory chip.

He scans it, nods, and then places it on his desk. "Thank you, Jaina." Master Aron shifts attention back to the class. "Children, this is Jaina Indera."

A few of the kids gasp in awe, while others stare blankly at me, not sure what 'Jaina Indera' is supposed to mean.

"Jaina is one of the most experienced students in the school. She'll be trying out for the Trials this year. Right?" Master Aron asks me.

"Of course."

A little boy in an orange shirt wrinkles his nose. "Ew, a *girl* in the Trials?"

I stifle a laugh. Well, that was blunt.

Master Aron nods his head. "Yes, Ian. There have always been girls in the Trials."

One of the girls raises her hand. Master Aron nods.

"Why are the Trials so important?" she asks.

Master Aron looks to me.

I answer, "The Trials are like tests. If you pass, they let you into the Crystal City."

"What's the Crystal City?"

"The Crystal City is the most perfect place in the galaxy. Only Superiors are allowed there," I reply.

"I want to live in the Crystal City," another girl murmurs dreamily.

"So do I," I agree. "But the only way to get in is to study hard in your classes and do well in the Trials."

Master Aron pats my shoulder. "Thank you, Jaina. You're dismissed."

"Thank you, sir." I bow to the class then exit the room. The bell rings just before I make it back to class. Master Ijani glares at me, but I think I've escaped punishment. For now, anyway.

I grab my textbooks and leave the classroom in search of Kavi. It doesn't help that she's not very tall. Pushing my way through the crowd, I finally spot her shiny, black hair and dark purple shirt in a small mass of classmates. I make my way to her before I lose her again.

"What'd I miss?" I ask.

She grabs my arm and pulls me along the hall on the way to our next class. She sighs. "Her long, boring speech about how wonderful the IA is, as if we didn't already know. Then she started talking about the Trials and how the only way to improve society is to live in the Crystal City."

"Sounds fun."

"Yeah. If you call sitting around doing nothing, *fun*. Anyway, are you ready for the exam?"

"I've been preparing for it all month. Rock climbing isn't one of my strong suits, but I think I'm ready. What about you?" I ask.

"I think I'll be okay. It's only eight meters."

"Of unassisted climbing," I remind her pointedly.

She shoots me an amused glance. "I never thought you were afraid of heights."

-4-

"I'm not afraid of heights, Kavi. It's the idea of dropping I'm not fond of."

She rolls her eyes. "We'll be fine."

"Students listen up!" Master Rhan bellows. "You've got ten minutes to climb eight meters. You think you can handle it?"

The rocky wall doesn't seem so big until we're only moments away from climbing. Plants jut out of the rock face and roots drape the sides. I scan the area for footholds and crevices that I might end up needing.

"Now, I'll be assigning partners. Once you've got your partner, line up near the wall, and wait for me to start the timer."

Master Rhan goes down the lines of the class, saying 'you and you,' pointing to people here and there. "Liam, you're with Jaina."

Liam shoots me a seductive smirk and raises an eyebrow.

I look at Master Rhan, horrified. "Sir, I really can't work with him." I shudder at the thought. How could he do this to me? He knows Liam and I have a history!

"Jaina, who knows who will be on your team if, and when, you make it into the Trials. Whether you like it or not, you'll have to work with people such as Liam," Master Rhan replies.

Liam and I make our way toward one of the many bright red X's taped to the ground in front of the wall. "Of all the people in class, I get stuck with you," I mutter, forgetting my vow never to speak to him again.

"You don't have to act this way, you know," Liam says, his voice soft and low.

"I don't want to talk to you," I shoot back.

"You don't have to be so harsh."

Master Rhan moves near us and Liam falls silent.

"Is everyone ready?" Master Rhan asks. When no one answers, he smiles. "Good. Begin!"

I reach for the first crevasse but Liam brushes my hand away.

"Me first," he snaps.

He begins making his way up the wall and I follow close behind. After climbing high enough to make looking down extremely uncomfortable, I check my surroundings. We're halfway to the top, but the other pairs are swiftly gaining altitude. Much faster than we are.

"Could you go any slower?" I grumble.

"Don't tempt me."

I look up at him, and wish I'd been partnered with someone else, anyone else.

"How much time do we have left?" he asks.

My eyelids grow duller with every word he says. It's the involuntary effect he has on me. "Four minutes and ten seconds."

"Come on, we can still make it," he says.

I reach for the next crack then look up. Only three meters to go. Liam slips, and I gasp. A few rocks tumble down the wall, but he manages to catch himself before losing altitude. I can't be sure he'll make it the rest of the way. He's so clumsy, he shouldn't even be in this class.

"How're you doing, Jaina?" he calls to me. As if *I'm* the one about to fall off the rocks.

"Let's just get this over with, okay? I'm doing fine." At least he's being nicer. Before, he was worse. Much worse.

"We're approaching the last two meters. I heard the Masters did something different to the climbing course for this class," he says.

I sigh. "And what might that be?"

"I don't know. Maybe there's a trap."

"I doubt it." I wonder how he came about *that* information. He could be right. I glance down at the ground and can't help but cringe. The coarse sand at the bottom would do little to soften a fall. In the best case scenario, one might not break anything if they landed right. Of course, that doesn't mean it wouldn't be painful. I look back at Liam. Traps or not, odds are he's going to fall.

My arms start to cramp. The tropical sun beats down on me, tempting me to let go of the wall.

"In the name of the Emperor, it's hot out."

I roll my eyes. "Maybe it's because Virana is in the South Pacific."

"Virana is an island in an archipelago once known as Indonesia over 1500 years ago. And strictly speaking, Indonesia was a part of *Oceania*. You should know that," he says smugly.

Shaav, I hate him.

As he looks down at me, the blood drains from his face.

I try to keep panic from surfacing. "What? What's wrong?"

"Um, Jaina? Don't move, okay?" Worry creeps into his voice.

My heart skips a beat. Frantic thoughts shoot through my mind. What does he see? I can't let go of the wall, or I'll hit the ground. He could be trying to pull a prank on me. I hope. But that look in his eyes tells me otherwise. I try to stay calm.

"What's wrong, Liam?" My arms quiver from the stress of holding me up on the wall.

"Jaina, please. Just don't move. I'll, uh, get rid of it, okay? Stay still."

"*It?*"

He climbs down so he's next to me and I realize he's not joking.

"Um, hold on," he mutters. He comes closer and brushes my shoulder with his hand.

"What was it?"

"Just a spider," he replies.

I sigh in relief, and shiver. "Thanks. I hate spiders."

My hands are unsteady as I search for another crevasse. My fingers brush against something soft. Before I have time to think, I jerk my hand away. The furry, hand-sized spider appears out of the darkness. I jolt backward and start to lose my balance.

"Liam, help!"

Even before it happens, I know I'm going to fall. The spider disappears, but my shaky hands grasp only air. Liam reaches out toward me, but I've already lost altitude and he's too far away. A sensation of falling takes over, and the top of the wall rapidly recedes into the sky. I hit the sandy ground with a thud and everything fades into darkness.

I know this place.

The night is cool, yet a warm breeze sweeps across the island. Ocean waves crash in rhythmic harmony. Palm trees sway back and forth, the only dance they know, as leaves brush against each other, adding to the lullaby.

Yet the serenity doesn't last.

Fear envelops the island like a raging fire. The dark grey clouds on the horizon are approaching. Something terrible will happen; I can feel it.

The world becomes cold. The storm has arrived. Lightning flashes overhead. The sun shines brightly to my right, while the moon is shrouded in darkness to my left. Shadows fall like raindrops from the clouds, and burn my skin with their touch. They form figures on the ground and claw at my body.

A cry rises up my throat, but no sound escapes my lips.

Voices fight within my head and the shadows pull me down.

"I have found you," one whispers.

"You should have left," says another.

"You're mine."

I try to tell them to leave, but the searing pain is too great. Rage, anger and agony pulse through my body, and the strength to scream fills me.

Tears stream down my cheeks and I shout to the sky. "You lied to me!" I sob. "You lied!"

The shadowy voices drown and suffocate me. Everything dissolves into the sea, yet their voices haunt me in the waves.

"He can't save you from the Dark."

I'm ripped from my sleep, panting and shaking uncontrollably. Their voices still echo in my mind.

A cool breeze slides past the columns between my open windows. I twist to the side. A dull pain radiates from my shoulder, and I can't help wincing. It's still sore from being dislocated.

I run my fingers through my long, wavy hair as my feet brush the cold marble floor. Today was my fifth day of skipping training because of my fall.

Cool blue moonlight washes over me as I stand and step on a platform that lowers me to the ground. Beads of sweat stream down my back.

The platform slows to a stop and I make my way toward the fountain in the courtyard. Palm trees sway in the breeze to the rhythm of the ocean waves. Stars gleam like tiny gems in the sky. It isn't raining tonight, as it usually does. I miss the constant soothing sound of the raindrops caressing my bedroom windows. Tonight, there is only the occasional crash of the waves.

I try to find peace in the serenity of this place, but my thoughts can't stop returning to the dream. The dark shadows won't leave my mind. I know how dangerous dreams are.

It's why they took him.

That night remains clear in my mind, despite how they tried to help me forget.

How he screamed my name when they tore him from his bed. How he fought them with every ounce of strength he could muster. But it just wasn't enough.

My fingers brush the marble bowl of the fountain. I touch the cool water and smile sadly.

"I miss you, Altair," I murmur.

They told me he was weak. And that being his friend made me weak, too. I was only six, he was eight. No one ever saw him again. I pull my thoughts from the painful memory. My mentors did a good job keeping my waking moments free from the past. But in the darkness, I can't help the scenes that flash across my mind from that night.

He was thrashing about in his sleep. Calling my name. It all scared me, and if the cameras caught him...I wasn't sure what would happen. So I woke him.

His eyes were dark and clouded with agony. I won't ever forget his cold merciless stare. Yet as he said my name, it all faded.

Altair reassured me he was all right.

I wanted to believe him. But he'd lied. He'd told me his dreams no longer bothered him. Obviously, he was wrong. And I felt betrayed.

Then, the door burst open.

Three bulky Imperial Guards surged into the dorm room. He tried to fight them, but it was no use. I'd never seen him look so small and weak.

The tallest guard caught his arm and pinned him to the ground.

Altair called out to me.

Screamed my name and begged me to help him.

Yet I could only stare in horror as the guard pulled out a syringe and injected a clear fluid into Altair's arm. His screaming became weak, his body went limp, and just like that...they took him.

He was gone.

They said Altair was tormented by his dreams and could no longer ignore them. That's why they took him. Because he was weak. He was Inferior. He wasn't worthy of the Crystal City and the Imperial Alliance.

But he wasn't weak.

He was strong.

Much stronger than I was.

"You promised," I breathe against the darkness.

If only he were here with me today...

It doesn't matter. He's gone, and I'm still here. If he was taken away because of his dreams, who says I won't be? I can't let this distract me. Not when I only have two more months to prepare for the Trials.

I head back to my room, trying not to let it bother me. My voice bounces around in my head, telling me over and over it was only a dream. The shadows weren't real. The screams were only memories. The dark hasn't consumed me. Once I reach my room, I climb into bed and shut my eyes. *Only a dream.* My inner voice trails off, but another part of me finishes.

You're not fooling anyone.

chapter

TWO

A digital screeching pulls me from my sleep. I block out the sound, rejecting the thought of waking so soon. Finding that impossible, I open my eyes and slam the "off" button on my alarm clock. The awful sound stops, but I won't be getting back to sleep anytime soon.

Staring at the ceiling, I take in the fresh morning air. My shoulder isn't hurting as much anymore. Thank the Emperor for that. Before I can stop myself, I get up and force myself to dress.

I snatch my small, paper-thin silverscreen off my desk and make my way to the dining hall, only a minute's journey from my dorm. The tall, green, glassy doors open after I press my index finger to the scanner and my fingerprint is confirmed. The large white room I step into is crowded, as usual.

Kavi smiles when I see her. "Jaina! Over here!"

After grabbing a tray of food I take a seat across from her. A silvery cup of freshly chilled ginger tea sits waiting on my tray, along with a small plate of sweet bread and Vava honey. The best honey in the galaxy.

She takes a bite of her bread as she studies the small, hand-sized silverscreen on the table. "I didn't know you were coming back today," she says. She doesn't look at me, but she smiles.

"I got tired of lying around all day," I laugh. "How was training yesterday?" I sip the cool ginger tea. It's sweeter than usual and I'm grateful for that.

"It was all right. Mostly physical combat. But Liam kept asking the Master questions he obviously knew the answer to. He wasted so much time. I can't believe you used to like him." She sighs in disgust and brushes a strand of her black, shiny hair behind her ear as she looks at me.

Chatter fills the dining hall and my eyes automatically search to make sure Liam's not anywhere near. He's not, so I reply, "Kavi, it was last year, okay? I don't like him anymore. Why do you keep bringing it up?"

"I just think it's funny; of all the guys here you chose Liam. I mean...yuck." She shudders. Her eyes flicker to the surrounding tables as if she's searching for someone. "Anyway, what did the doctors say? I wasn't allowed to visit because the Masters kept talking about how I *have enough on my schedule already*."

"That's okay. It's healing quickly, but I'll be lucky if I qualify for the Trials." That better not be the case. I have to make it in.

"Well, you took a really hard fall."

"It was a pretty big spider," I retort taking a bite of bread. It's sweet and sticky with a little bit of tanginess. Delicious.

"I saw," Kavi murmurs.

"I'm still going to try out."

She looks at me like I just said the IA is about to be overthrown. Her eyebrows are raised high and she smiles like she's not sure if I'm joking or crazy. "You haven't been at practice for five days, and you have to be in *perfect* shape to participate."

"Your point is?"

"The Masters might not let you enter if you haven't shown up," she says. "You know how it is. Missing class is missing class. Even if it's because you dislocated your shoulder."

"But I've been training my whole life for this. I don't want to stay here until I'm twenty and get thrown into a...you know..." I lower my voice. "Reconstruction Camp on some remote planet."

"We've all been training for this, and only eight people from each school can go each year," she pauses, "but you *are* at the top of the class. I'm sure the Masters won't dismiss that fact when you try out."

"Thanks."

"I just don't get it," she says, taking a silvery stretchy band from her pocket to tie up her hair. "The Masters always tell us we don't want to go to Reconstruction Camps but they never really say why. Except it means you're weak."

"They're terrible places where you're forced to work for hours rebuilding fallen cities for the Imperials. It's a life without reward."

"But the Trials are violent and–"

"I'm trying out, regardless."

She smiles sadly and takes her cup of cold ginger tea in her hands. "All right, I'm just trying to warn you." She takes a sip then gobbles down her bread.

"Are you going to try out?" I ask, finishing off the last bit of my tea.

"I haven't decided yet. I don't think I'm ready. Being sixteen we should have a good chance getting in. But I'm not sure I trust myself to survive them. You have to be fifteen to enter, right?"

I nod. "We could try out together. It might be fun."

"I don't think *fun* is the right word for it. I'll tell you when I've made up my mind."

I sigh. "Okay, fine. But you should. We're both good enough to go. I mean, you don't wanna be stuck here taking these classes until you're twenty then be kicked out, do you?"

Her lips twitch into a frown. "No, not really. But, speaking of classes, Master Sharan's preparing a test on the Cora language and told me to make sure you were going to take it."

Oh, no. "You're kidding, right?"

"Unfortunately, no."

I run my fingers through my hair and sigh with discontent. This won't be a fun week. "Okay, fill me in later. We should get to class."

We finish breakfast and head outside when the bell rings. An ocean breeze sweeps across the courtyard and tosses beads of fountain water above me. The droplets sparkle in the hot tropical air. I pull out my silverscreen and turn it on. The inner part of the screen turns a dark blue and I check this week's schedule.

Monday: Basic Combat Training, Prehistory, Terrain Exploration, Mathematics, Weaponry, Music, Science.

I look at the time on the screen. 8:20 a.m. Standard Time. I've got to hurry if I don't want to be late for class.

"Master Ijani, I've missed class for the past few days. Could you postpone my test on World War III?" I ask as politely as possible.

"What's your reason for missing class?" She doesn't look up from the hologram hovering over her desk. Her beady eyes flicker over the images before her, her long blond hair pulled back in a tight bun so it looks like she's got an octopus on her head. She touches one of the images and moves it into a holographic trash bin on her right.

"I lost my grip in rock climbing and was in the hospital for five days."

She nods, making her pointy nose and chin bob awkwardly up and down. "The test is tomorrow," she says. "You can take it Friday."

That's more than I'd hoped for. "Thanks."

"Have Kavi help you study for it."

I take a seat while Master Ijani waits by the door, waiting for the final bell to ring.

"Well, this is wonderful, isn't it," Kavi whispers from her desk.

I follow her gaze to a bunch of boys, attempting to get attention from some girls across the room. Finding Liam amongst them I avert my eyes.

"Seriously, why do they have to act so immature?" she asks.

"Stop staring. You're going to catch Liam's attention," I shoot back.

Too late. Liam saunters over to us from the other side of the classroom. "Hello, Jaina," he says, taking on a flirtatious tone.

"What sort of trouble are you up to now?" I moan.

"You know, I remember when you actually used to like me."

"That was last year," I remind him. "But you clearly didn't feel the same, so I moved on. And seeing that you kind of made me fall off that wall the other day–"

"Whoa, I didn't make you fall. You touched a spider in the rock wall and screamed like a little girl. If you recall, I *saved* you. At least, the first time I did," he says matter-of-factly.

Oh, wonderful. Now I bet he expects me to repay him. "What do you want?" I ask, dully.

He crosses his arms. "A *thank you* would be nice."

"Well, thank you, Liam. I really appreciate that you saved me the first time." I study him critically, hoping he'll get self-conscious and leave, but he doesn't. "You know, I think it's weird how, suddenly, after six months you're chasing after me."

"Very funny, Jaina but I'm not *chasing after you*. I'm merely showing you what you're missing." He stands up a little straighter and pushes out his chest, as if trying to prove to me how tough he is.

I raise an eyebrow, scanning him up and down. His arms are crossed inelegantly over his chest and he keeps most of his weight on his right leg. He's not skinny, but he's not muscular, either.

"And what might that be?" I ask.

Liam's mouth drops open and his grey-blue eyes widen. He gestures to himself and says, "Are you blind? How about all of my seductive cuteness?"

I shake my head, disgusted, and turn away. "Uh, huh. That's what I thought."

Realizing I'm serious, he sits in the chair next to me and places a hand on my shoulder. "Jaina, just listen to me, please." He scoots closer to me.

I brush his hand away but listen.

"Jaina, how many times do I have to tell you? I'm sorry. Honestly, I am."

"You don't have to apologize, Liam. I only regret that I didn't realize what kind of person you were before I started liking you. I can't believe I wasted so much time." My voice sounds bratty, even to me, but I can't help it. After all I went through for him, I have a right to feel the way I do.

Liam takes a deep, frustrated breath. "There's nothing I can do?"

I shake my head. "I'm sorry, Liam. But in the Crystal City, when they assign our perfect genetic matches to us, I need to be ready. I can't become attached to things I know I can't have."

"Yeah, sure," he mutters and picks at a black flake of paint in his desk. "I bet you'll find someone else before we get to the Crystal City."

I feel the blood drain from my face. "*You're* trying out for the Trials?"

A grin splashes his lips and he flips his shaggy hair out of his face. Clearly he's enjoying my reaction. "You bet I am."

I put my head in my hands, resting my elbows on my desk. If he's on my team, I think I'm going to kill myself. "You're not even at the top of the class! What skill do you have that would contribute to the Trials? Do you even *have* a skill?"

"Oh, I'm full of surprises," he reassures me. "And that's why you'll be *very* mad when I outscore you." The bell rings, and his cocky grin fades. He moves back to his seat in the row behind me and one desk to the right. "Just watch, Jaina," he mouths.

Everyone is quiet, but I can feel Liam's gaze on me.

Master Ijani slowly makes her way into the classroom and starts talking, but I hardly listen to what she's saying.

Why can't Liam just leave me alone? I shouldn't have wasted my time on him in the first place. That's probably why I couldn't focus on anything last year.

Master Ijani inputs the word America onto the large silverscreen behind her. "Can anyone tell me what modern-day country America is?"

A few kids raise their hands, but I stare forward, not in the mood to participate today.

"Amarija?" a girl asks.

Master Ijani smiles. "Very good. And, during which war did this country come to an end?"

"Wasn't it right after World War III?" a boy suggests.

"Yes, good. Today, we'll be learning about what happened after those two important events. It was called The Great Flood. You've probably heard things about it, but this week we'll be going into a lot more detail," Master Ijani says. "Someone tell me what they know about The Great Flood."

There's a short silence.

"Yes, you, sir." Master Ijani points to the boy behind me.

The class turns to him to listen to his answer and I do the same.

He clears his throat. "The Great Flood began in the year 1425 Before the Stellar Wars. I think it was nearly seventy-five years before the formation of the World Wide Federation and about seventy-five years after the beginning of World War III. I'm not entirely sure what the causes were, though."

"You are correct. Now the causes have remained to be a controversial topic, yet many suspect..." her voice trails off somewhere in my mind.

Words don't process, and I only see him. I can't pull my eyes away from him.

Sandy-brown hair, olive skin, and perfect lips...

His broad, sturdy chest and muscular frame send my heart into a panicked frenzy. His deep, aquamarine eyes meet mine for a fraction of a second. An electric sensation fills me as if he'd reached out and shocked my soul. My senses no longer receive information and the only sound is my heartbeat.

Thump...

    Thump...

        Thump...

"Jaina?"

I whip around with a start, regaining sensation.

"Yes, Master?" I try to keep my voice under control, but it trembles as I speak.

The eyes of the entire class are on me. I glance at Liam. He rolls his eyes and drops his head into his palms, running his fingers through his dark hair. Oh, how I hope he didn't see that. My cheeks start to feel warm.

"Is there a problem?" Master Ijani asks, glancing from me to the boy.

I look back at him and his perfect features. He stares down at his desk, hardly noticing me. "N-no, I'm sorry," I stammer, tearing my gaze from the beautiful boy once more. "Forgive me."

Master Ijani nods then continues speaking.

I sit up straight and try agonizingly hard to concentrate on Master Ijani and the words I'll need to remember for the test, but my back prickles with sensation, begging me to turn around. I want to see him. I must see him. In addition to being the most attractive boy I've ever seen, I can't help but feel that somehow I know him.

Of course, I couldn't have seen him before. I definitely would have remembered if I had. He's in the seat directly behind me.

I run my fingers through my hair, pulling it back into a higher pony-tail instead of the saggy one it is. The bell rings, and for the first time, Prehistory ends much too soon.

"So, how were you after missing five days of practice?" Kavi takes a seat at the dining-hall table for dinner, and sets down her plate of food.

It's similar to mine, but of course, the meat on her plate is substituted with vegetables. She never liked the taste of meat, so she says she may as well be saving animals.

"Pretty good, actually," I reply, then remember the new guy from Prehistory. My stomach twists, nervously, and I suddenly feel like I can't swallow.

"Are you still thinking about entering the Trials?"

My fork stabs a juicy piece of chicken and I bring it to my lips. "When they choose the team of eight people, I want to be one of them."

"Jaina, the Trials are dangerous. Some people get killed."

"I know, but...they're the whole reason why we're here at the Gifted School of Virana," I say. "And there's the Crystal City to look forward to."

She shakes her head and itches her arm nervously. "But if we don't win...Jaina, I'm just scared. I really don't think it's my time yet."

I take another bite. "I think it's worth a try. People can still go to the Crystal City, as long as their DNA is strong enough. You don't have to *win* the Trials."

"We'll see. I'll think about it." She twists around as Liam strides into the dining hall. "What was all the fussing about in Prehistory this morning?"

"I think he's still mad that I'm over him. He implied that I'm a heartless nobody who will move on to some other boy before the Trials." I glance at Liam and the people at his table. Just looking at him makes me want to roll my eyes.

With a start, I realize the handsome boy from class is sitting only two tables away and is talking with a few other boys. The feeling that I know him, somehow, somewhere, returns. He finally looks away from his table, and his eyes meet mine.

I wait for that spark of recognition. The explosion in my mind that'd make me want to shout "I remember you, now!" but it doesn't come.

He turns away like he'd never seen me before in his life.

If we'd met, surely one of us would've remembered. I'm not sure whether to be completely hypnotized or nervous.

"Jay. Jaina." Kavi snaps her fingers in front of my face.

My eyes snap to her with a start. "What?"

"Don't stare at him."

"Who is he?" I can't take my eyes off him.

"Come on, Jaina. You've got to look at me first, okay?"

I turn my head to her, but can't help glancing his way every few moments.

Kavi scoops a forkful of vegetables and stuffs them into her mouth. When she's mostly done chewing, she says, "People call him Dragon."

"You're serious?" I laugh. "His name is *Dragon*?"

"Yes, people call him Dragon. But that's not his real name. No one knows what his real name is. How did you not hear about his return?"

"I don't know...I'm not exactly the 'social' type. And I was in the hospital for nearly a week," I snap defensively before I go back to gazing at him. "I feel like...I know him."

"You might. He used to live here."

I shoot her a skeptical glare. She's known for making her own versions of the truth.

"That's what I heard! Apparently, he's been through a lot. He's only eighteen and has been in the hospital for more than half his life. At least that's the rumor."

"So is he a...defect? An Inferior?" How could someone so dazzling be a defect? He's the most beautiful defect I've ever seen...

"No! He's just different. The Masters wouldn't have brought him back if he was a defect. To tell you the truth, no one believes there's anything wrong with him." She smiles wryly. "Anyway, I saw you staring at him in class today."

"I wasn't staring," I murmur, completely neglecting my food now. How can I eat when my stomach's knotting and churning the way it is? Why bother when I can feast my eyes on him?

"Well, if you weren't staring then, you are now."

"I'm not staring! I'm just trying to figure out who he is." We both know that's only partially true.

"I think you just proved Liam right. You found a guy before the Trials." She giggles. "Didn't you tell him you were done with relationships for a while?"

"Oh, Kavi, stop it! I meant what I said."

She rolls her eyes. "Uh huh, sure. You realize you're saying that while you're staring at a very handsome boy?"

"Shut up."

"You hypocrite," she mutters glancing from me to him. "So, when are you going to talk to him?"

"Who ever said anything about talking to him?" I'd probably make a fool of myself.

"You should see the way you're looking at him. It's hilarious. I think he's trying out for the Trials, too."

"There's another good reason for us to try, right?"

She giggles and finishes her food.

Only once the final bell rings and dinner is over, do I stand with the rest of my classmates and lose him in the crowd.

chapter

THREE

Thoughts swim around my mind like tiny fish in an unknown ocean. Light streams into my room, and it's time to get ready for training. Today, the Masters are choosing our training classes. The higher the level we're put in, the better chance we have at making it into the Trials. My stomach churns, and my heart flutters with the thought of where I might be placed.

At breakfast, I sit with Kavi, anxiously waiting for my silverscreen to vibrate and tell me my class placement. We're silent. The whole room is silent. Everyone is waiting...

The clock on the wall ticks, and the faint buzzing of the lights fills me with unease. I can almost hear the beating of my heart drumming out a rhythm in slow motion.

In a burst of excitement, everyone's silverscreen vibrates.

I don't want to look. Kavi gets hers out and reads.

Finally, anxiety overrules my fear. My eyes are glued to the screen. I can hardly read the words: *Congratulations! We're pleased to welcome you to Class Alpha. You have brought great honor to yourself by making it into the highest level. Meet your Master in the Centerpoint Arena.*

"What does yours say?" Kavi asks.

"Th-they put me in the top. I'm in Alpha!" I cry. "What about you?"

"Me, too!" She jumps up and wraps her arms around my shoulders in excitement. "By the stars, we made it!"

Laughter fills my lungs, bubbling up my throat and popping into jolts of joy. My body trembles as excitement tickles my stomach. Is this actually happening? My whole life has depended on the Trials, and now I have a chance. I can hardly sit still.

I finish breakfast as fast as possible and rush to the Centerpoint Arena. There are nine others waiting, and I search for people I know. Thank the stars Liam isn't here.

Garr Aldon, a fifteen-year-old boy with short blond hair, stands next to Roshiva Korr, a tall boy about my age, with dark olive skin. Korr and I haven't shared classes for the past five years, so I'm hoping our previous animosities are forgotten. If either of us got injured this close to the time of Trial selections...we definitely wouldn't be chosen.

Xana Devyn and Maria Solam stand next to each other, looking almost like twins with matching blond hair and lightly tanned skin. Even their eyes are the same, sparkly grey color. A younger girl, maybe only thirteen or fourteen with long black hair, stands in the back of the group, while Seth Onan stands across from me.

And there he is. Again. Dragon stands near the edge, alone. It doesn't surprise me he's here.

I move to the back of the group. Something about him makes me nervous.

An older woman with silver hair approaches us at the center of the group. She wears a dark yellow shirt decorated with green swirls. To be honest, it looks like an ugly curtain someone turned into a shirt. Wrinkles sag under her sunken, blue eyes and her long, grey hair is pulled back into a large, tight bun. She smiles, but it's clear it's not genuine. More like an "I'll enjoy torturing you" sorta smile.

"Children of the Galactic Imperial Alliance," she begins. "Congratulations for making class Alpha. I'm your only hope if you wish to become Superior and enter the Crystal City. You cannot make it without me. Up to this point, you have all been petty creatures. Not ready for the world outside this school. For the next month and a half, you must do whatever I say." Her deep booming voice echoes throughout the depths of the jungle as if commanding the entire world to listen. "I am Master Zoma."

We bow gratefully to her.

"Students, assemble in a circle," she orders.

We do as we're told. I try to stay away from Dragon but end up standing across from him.

"You call yourself warriors?" Master Zoma asks. "Well, I'm telling you that you're only beginning to understand what the word means. When these four weeks are over, you will be changed. You will be strong.

"Our parents were Inferiors. They were weak, as are you, but you can rise above the commoners of the IA.

You were born with the perfect combination of Inferior genes and it will make you strong. As long as you are willing to fight, you'll live. You'll be merciless. If you should decide to try out for the Trials when these weeks of training are up, I wish you the best of luck." She pauses. "Now, I'll call two of you into the ring, and you'll duel." She studies us all then snaps, "Kavi Agni! Seth Onan!"

Kavi's face goes pale and she shoots me a horrified glance as she walks to the center of the ring. Seth approaches her. His short, sandy-blond hair seems to glisten as he walks. He's tall and muscular and keeps his chest out, like he knows he's got it all. His jaw is tight with determination. Very handsome, I'll admit. But Kavi's reaction isn't quite what I expect. She glares at him, and he mockingly smiles back.

There's something between them I can't quite make out. I've never seen her like this. She's usually pretty good around guys, but all of that has vanished.

Seth enters the ring and stands, facing her, staring at her. She meets his gaze, frustration flickering across her face.

"Kavi? Seth? Are you ready?" Master Zoma asks.

"Yes, Master," they say in synchrony.

Kavi looks at him like she can't stand being on the same planet as him. His smile suggests he would like nothing more than to kill her...or kiss her...I can't tell which.

Master Zoma hands them each a wooden practice sword then backs away. They bow and face each other.

When a bell rings, they hardly move. They stand still, staring deep into each other's eyes.

Kavi sprints at him and jumps only a moment before smashing into him. She tries to kick him, but he ducks and easily pushes her away.

She falls to the ground but is up again, faster than a plasma bolt and she glowers at him. They move around the circle, both in defensive stance, ready for attack. Kavi fakes a charge, but he doesn't flinch.

Seth makes his way to the center of the circle, keeping an eye on her so as not to let his guard down. Kavi does the same. Seth jabs his sword at her, but she's completely ready and bats it away.

She grabs his sword arm and kicks him in the stomach, making him fly backward. Seth takes a hard fall but not hard enough to quit. He doesn't look too badly hurt, and I fully expect him to get up. He shoots Kavi a devious grin, then trips over himself, falling in front of Kavi's blade. Kavi looks at him, dumbstruck. He let her win.

Master Zoma nods. "Very good, Kavi. Seth, you're terribly slow. I don't want to look at you until you've run a lap around the South side of the island."

Seth massages his palm, but nods.

"Jaina Indera!" Master Zoma calls out.

I make my way toward the center of the ring and breathe deeply. How can I fight with everyone else watching? It's nerve-racking! I don't do well when I'm put on the spot.

"Dragon Kasev!"

I freeze. The words don't make sense. That can't be right. My entire body trembles in anticipation.

Dragon steps confidently across the ring and stands before me. He bows.

I don't have time to think, so I only nod stupidly in reply. How am I supposed to win now? If I defeat him, will he hate me for it? And if I lose, will he think I'm weak?

Pulling at my fingernails, I try not to look into those deep, piercing eyes. I'm miserably failing. I can hardly move and I can't tell if it's from exhaustion or nerves.

"Dragon? Jaina? Are you ready?" she asks, handing us swords.

No way. I'm not ready for this at all.

"Yes," we reply.

The bell rings.

A sudden burst of energy gives me the strength I need. The familiar feel of the wooden blade in my hands and adrenaline rushing through my veins makes me surrender to my instincts. Maybe he's good looking, but I can't lose. I run and swing at him, but he jumps out of the way.

He kicks my feet out from under me, and I hit the ground, hard. I grit my teeth in pain and jump up, but I can hardly breathe. He waits for me to stand, not bothering to finish me off yet.

With a flurry of blows, I try to knock him off balance. I attempt to kick him in the chin, but he backs away, and takes the blow in the chest instead. He stammers back but hardly looks surprised. Lifting his sword high, he comes at me with tremendous strength and I barely have time to block.

Another bell rings, and we stop.

Master Zoma stops us. "Fight with a sword."

I stagger back with confusion. We've been fighting with swords the entire time. When I look at her, she holds up two *real* swords and shoves one into my hand.

The metal is heavy. Much heavier than what I'm used to. We've trained with real weapons before, but not often. I struggle to keep the sword in the air. My mind wants to shut down. This isn't going to be good. I don't want to fight him. Not for real.

My reflection is distorted in the polished, silver blade. Does she really trust us not to kill each other?

This is my chance to prove myself. If I could say with certainty that anyone was going to make the Trials, he'd be on my list. And if I'm going make it, I want to be his equal on the team. I have to show him I'm not going to let him win. At least, not without the fight of his life.

I keep my eyes down, trying not to look at him.

The bell rings.

Dragon shifts his body toward me; his lips pressed together, and his eyes devoid of emotion.

It's easy to be afraid of him. He could knock me out with a single punch or kill me with a sweep of his sword. The point of his blade touches my own, tempting me to strike him.

I don't take my eyes off of him, aware of his every move. Every ruffling of his black t-shirt against him. Each calm breath he takes. The flexing of his biceps as he strains to hold his sword. His focused gaze doesn't once break from my own. Maybe he's stronger and more powerful than I am, but my strength lies in my speed. I have to win quickly if I want to win at all.

Without warning, he jumps into motion. I block his offense without hesitation, but his raw power scares me. My sword weighs me down and my muscles strain from the stress of holding it up.

There's a pause, then I lunge forward with a swift downward stroke, but he stops me mid-swing with a powerful counterattack. I swing my sword to my left, and he blocks to his right. He lunges forward, and I manage a much-less-than-perfect somersault back keeping my sword in my hand.

With every breath, my heart feels like it could explode, and the heat begins to suffocate me. Sweat drips down the back of my tight shirt. My energy is draining. I can't go on much longer.

Dragon makes his way to attack me, and I brace myself for the next blow. My hands are numb. Dragon's blade falls on mine, and the vibration rings through my entire body. Our swords are locked. I squeeze the hilt so tightly I'm afraid my hands will bleed. I'm losing.

Staring into his focused eyes, warm energy flows through me. I loosen my grip and move my sword in the same direction he's pressing. He stumbles to the right and I jump left. My arms are shaking and I'm gasping for air, yet I lunge forward to make my final move.

Flinging myself through the air at him, I land then spin away from his defensive swing. I turn back toward him, my sword pointed at his throat. Lowering my eyes I see his sword is at mine. Neither of us move.

Silence engulfs us.

He smiles.

With a swift flick of his wrist, he twists his blade around my own, prying it from my hand and forcing it to the ground. I step back as he advances, then crouch low to grab my sword. Before I can close my fingers around the hilt, he kicks it to the side and keeps his sword at my throat. The tip touches my neck, lightly grazing my skin. I raise both hands in surrender.

His eyes are calm despite the anger infused behind them. He backs away and the fire fades.

The bell rings.

"Dragon Kasev wins," Master Zoma says. "Jaina, you may stand."

I get off my knees. Unable to meet his eyes, I glance at the ground. "How..." I pause, "how did you do that?"

Dragon smiles slyly. "Basic skills, Jaina. It's all in the early books."

"Very good," Master Zoma continues. "Unfortunately, we're running out of time. Training will resume at six. You're dismissed!"

"See you around." Dragon nods then leaves the arena.

———

"Master, I'm looking for books on basic fighting skills. Can you point me in the right direction, please?" I ask the head librarian.

She furrows her brow. "Aren't you a little old for that sort of thing?"

"It's for a friend," I add.

"Ah, of course. Right this way."

The library is a large open building, like most on Virana. A soft breeze sweeps through the aisles of glassy, silver shelves. Large areas of the wall have been removed to keep the place open to the outside and I can see the soft sandy beach from here. The floor is some sort of black, polished rock, maybe imported from a volcanic planet like Hefezta.

I follow her down a few aisles of books, then she stops. "Here they are, my dear. I hope you find what you're looking for."

There are a few hundred books in this single section. I barely know where to start. "Thanks," I say, not exactly meaning it. That wasn't helpful at all.

Not that it matters, but the technique obviously works. I don't care how distracting his looks are. The next battle between us, I'm going to win. I'm at the top of the class, and I lost to the 'new guy.' How embarrassing.

Time to focus.

The bookshelf is flat, and not really a shelf. It's a screen that stands taller than me and when I touch it, a digital list of books and their covers appear. Swiping my finger across the glass, the books move and disappear off the screen. I start my search and tap a book by the author Aliah. The book loads on the screen and I skim to the first page. Instantly know I can't read this. Way too boring. Alorze hardly talks about combat at all. Amiria is a little more understandable, but upon reading the first page, I have to stop.

I close the book, frustrated.

A dark figure stands a few meters away. I let my gaze drift to him, and I stumble backward, realizing who it is. A cool wave of anxiety washes over me. A part of me says *walk away*, while another says *go talk to him*.

I'm unable to do either.

My feet are planted into the ground, so I pretend not to notice him.

From the corner of my eye, I watch him turn around, and face me. Should I make a run for it? That would look ridiculous, now that he sees me.

"Jaina...?"

My heart stops at the sound of his voice. I shift toward him pretending to act surprised. "Oh, hey," I say nervously, trying hard not to hyperventilate. Of all the things I'm bad at, why does talking to guys have to be my biggest weakness?

A gentle grin parts his lush lips, revealing his sparkly white teeth. "Sorry about what happened in the arena today. Are you all right?"

I finally squeak out a reply. "Oh, yes, I-I'm fine." I stand a little straighter and try to act more composed than I feel. I'm not short, but next to him, I feel completely insignificant. He's so tall...

I'm not exactly sure what else to say so I nod. Sprinting out of here sounds so good right now...

"What are you doing here?" he asks.

"I'm just, um, looking for something to read. What about you?" What a stupid thing to say. We're in a library.

He holds up his silverscreen and shows me the cover of a book with foreign letters on it, as if it told me everything I need to know. "Studying for Cora," he says.

"That's always fun."

"Yeah." He studies me for a moment then continues, "Well...I should probably be on my way."

"Oh, of course. Good luck."

Good luck? Did I just say "good luck?" What am I talking about?

He shifts uncomfortably, and laughs. "All right, you, too." With that, he leaves.

Na'lav, I'm so stupid. I roll my eyes and look back to the shelf. The book by Amiria is still selected, so I close it and continue scrolling through the covers without any luck.

Maybe this trip was a waste of time. *You got to talk to Dragon again.* Yeah, and I made a fool of myself.

This is too much work.

The librarian stops me on my way out. "Did you find what you were looking for?"

"Yeah, thanks."

She looks at me skeptically but doesn't reply. I pass her and head back to my room.

Of all people, why am I so interested in him? How could I let myself make such a fatal mistake? He must think I'm crazy. I'll be surprised if he has the courage to look at me tomorrow without laughing.

I want to be more positive, but how can I?

The last time I lost that badly to someone was...

Was...

Ten years ago.

chapter

FOUR

ONE MONTH LATER

Pain. I'm used to it now. Blood oozes from a fresh cut above my left eyebrow. I lie on the ground in agony and watch as Seth approaches to make the final move. But I still have one more trick up my sleeve.

He raises his small practice dagger as if he were going to really kill me. I lash out, and my heel makes contact with his knee. Seth moans and grits his teeth, but his shock won't last long.

I spring to my feet, punch him in the stomach, twist his arm, and catch his dagger as it falls to the ground. The tip of the dagger brushes his throat as I hold it to him. There's nowhere he can go from here. I've won.

Master Zoma smiles. "Very good, Jaina! You've improved!"

Seth stands, his shoulders slumped in exhaustion. He grumbles a few words to himself and bites his cheek, as if holding back from snatching the dagger out of my hand.

"Seth, I thought you were going to win. What's the first thing we learned here?" Master Zoma asks.

"There's a weakness to every move," he replies mechanically.

"Correct. Never let overconfidence be your downfall." Master Zoma rests her gaze on me. "Jaina, you may lower that dagger. I'm starting to think you might kill him."

Kavi and a few other classmates laugh. I lower the small knife, and hand it back to Seth. "Sorry."

Seth lowers his head respectfully and fakes a smile. "It's fine."

He seems nice. But after hearing what Kavi told me about him last week, maybe I don't know him well enough to make that judgment. Why would he ditch her after being friends with her for eight years? Even worse, he hardly spoke to her after that. Kavi likes to exaggerate, but there's obviously a conflict between them.

Master Zoma waits for us to quiet down before speaking. "I'm going to assign you into groups of four to a certain training plate on the island. Since you need to learn how to fight in a group, you'll go two against two. Maria Solam and Garr Aldon, you'll remain with me to continue your hand-to-hand combat.

"Avan, Roshiva, Xana, and Cindra, you will all go to the Desert Terrain Training Center." She stops and looks at us. "Jaina, Kavi, Seth, and Dragon will go to the Training Center on South Beach. I trust you to play fair and return in one piece. Move along!"

On the way to South Beach, Kavi and I walk together. Dragon and Seth trek a few meters ahead of us through the thick jungle foliage. There are stone walkways all over the island from one arena to another, but it's never the fast way to go.

I suck in a gulp of ocean air. "This is going to be awkward," I say loud enough for only Kavi to hear.

"No kidding," she replies, eyeing the boys. "We're going to be on the same team, right?"

"Of course," I laugh. "It's not like I'd ask Dragon to be on my team."

Kavi shudders. "Dragon scares me."

"I still can't believe he beat me in that duel," I mutter. "I mean, I could tell he was going to be good. But not *that* good."

"Yeah, that's not something that happens every day."

"To tell the truth, I'm a bit scared of Dragon, too." A twig snaps under my feet and the two boys glance back at us nervously.

"We're fine," Kavi manages, and the two carry on walking.

"Virana is the top school in the world," I say, quieter this time. "Where could he receive such high quality training?"

"It's weird," she ponders. Her long black hair floats down her back in long, beautiful waves and I can't help being a little jealous. "But you've always been the best," she continues. "Being second for a while might do you some good."

Shaav, I don't want to be second! I haven't worked this hard for so long to be second. My chest constricts as if a snake were wrapped around my lungs, trying to suffocate me.

I can't fail.

Being second wouldn't only mean I've failed myself, but I've failed *him*.

Altair.

He said I'd be the best one day. And I won't let him down.

We approach the arena and show the coast guard our Identification Numbers. Once we step onto the large training plate, he raises it about three meters off the ground. If we fall, it's guaranteed to hurt.

Moving to the center of the training circle we take out four, lightweight suits of armor. The fights can be brutal on occasion so it's good to have some form of protection. We strap on the armor, equip ourselves with practice swords, then take up position.

"Jaina," Dragon says. "Do you want to be on my team?"

Whoa, that was unexpected. I look at him, feeling hypnotized, and distantly remember telling Kavi I'd be on her team, yet I find myself saying, "Of course, I'd love to be on your team."

"Okay, good. Let's get started." His lips curl into that smile of his I could never get tired of seeing.

Kavi furrows her brow and shoots me a glare as I take sides with Dragon. I shrug and shoot her an apologetic smile, but she turns away. Dragging her feet across the ground, she takes up position next to Seth.

"Dragon," I whisper, "how do you want to do this? Shouldn't we have some strategy?"

He shrugs. "I dunno. How do you do it?"

"I usually have some sort of plan. Don't you?"

"I make it up as I go," he replies. "Besides, there'll be times in the Trials when we won't have time to come up with a plan."

He said *we*.

I nod, but I can't help smiling. Does he think I'm good enough to make it?

I can hardly think with him so close, so I try not to. *Just fight like you've been trained to do.*

We begin.

My eyes are trained on Kavi and Seth. I wait for them to make the first move. We rotate around the center of the circle, keeping our distance from each other.

Kavi lunges forward, startling the rest of us into action. She comes for me, probably because she doesn't want to be stuck fighting Dragon.

She swings her sword left then right, and I block her blow for blow. Even through the white, fingerless gloves that extend to my forearms, my hands sting from the force of her blows. Kavi's sword skims my arm. If this were a real fight in the Trials, I'd have a gash of red where her blade had been.

Matching her next attacks blow for blow, I gain ground. I don't want her to fall off of the training plate, but scaring her into making a desperate move could work to my advantage. My sword skims her belly, giving us a point. If the wound could prove fatal in the Trials then it counts.

"Damn it, Jaina," Kavi curses.

"What? Am I moving too fast for you?" I ask, slyly.

She raises a finger and glares at me. "Shut it."

We set up again.

I glance over at Dragon and Seth. They're fighting furiously. Seth finally scores a point on Dragon. A glimmer of frustration etches itself into his expression.

Kavi's sword lightly touches my neck.

"*Shaav*, I didn't say go," I snap.

She shrugs. "Pay attention and maybe I won't totally crush you."

"The only way you could *crush* me is if I let you."

Kavi smiles. "You may be at the top, but that doesn't mean you can't lose. Now go."

I curse under my breath. Now she and Seth are in the lead.

After I hit Kavi again, I realize we have to switch. Since Seth doesn't know my style as well, it'd make an easier win. Dragon backs off while Kavi and Seth switch places. Seth stands across from me with determination in his eyes. He's really going to kill me for beating him earlier. I wait for him to make a move but he doesn't, so I take a quick step forward. Our blades clash too many times for me to count.

He gains ground with such speed I hardly have a chance against him. Seth forces me to the edge of the training plate. I struggle to keep my balance, but my foot slips off the edge. It's too late for hope, and I start to fall backward. Not again!

Someone catches my hand. Seth pulls me back then moves into his 'ready' stance. My breath catches in my throat, and I choke out a surprised cough once I find my footing. He saved me from another year on Virana; if I'd taken that fall, I wouldn't be ready for the Trials. He nods to me, gesturing for me to attack. Despite feeling a little guilty, I assault him again.

With a final sweep, my sword brushes his chest. A bell rings. The four of us stop at the sound. The battle is over.

"Who won?" Kavi asks.

"Four to four," Seth replies. "We tied."

Kavi throws down her sword and begins taking off her armor. "*Na'lav*, what are we going to tell Master Zoma?"

Seth raises an eyebrow. "Aren't you supposed to be the smart one?"

"Shut up," Kavi shoots back angrily.

Dragon drops his sword and pulls off a wrist guard. "Can't we tell her the truth?"

"She'll probably have us rematch," I say. "Remember what happened to Xana and Roshiva the last time there was a rematch?"

"Yeah, I'd rather not go through that," Seth agrees.

My lips form the most innocent smile I can manage. "So...we'll just tell her that we won."

Kavi and Seth turn to me, their faces contorting in exasperation and disbelief.

"What the *shaav*, Jaina?" Kavi protests. "We're not going to just let you win!"

Dragon's lips press together, a sorry expression in his eyes. "Well, it *would* be more believable."

Kavi puts her hands on her hips and scoffs. "Are you saying you're better than us?"

"I've won more duels than the two of you combined," Dragon replies. "So I think it's safe to say that if we continued this fight, we'd win."

Kavi's mouth twists into a sneer. "We could beat you."

Dragon smiles, amused. "Wanna bet?"

Seth steps in front of Kavi and glares at her. "No, we don't want to bet. I think we can live with letting you two win."

"No," Kavi objects. "We've got to tell Master Zoma the truth."

"I don't exactly like fighting either of you," Seth continues.

"Why can't we say that *we* won?" Kavi's voice is soft and whiny, like she's been ignored far longer than she can tolerate.

Seth grabs her wrist, but she pulls away. He turns to us and raises a finger. "Lemme just talk to her for a minute, okay?"

The two of them move to the other side of the training ring. She argues viciously with Seth, but I block their words from my mind.

Dragon grins at me. "Good job."

Despite the simplicity of his comment, my mind struggles to keep up with the conversation.

"Thanks," I manage. "You, too."

Kavi stalks over to Dragon and me, raising her hands in defeat. "Fine! But you owe us."

chapter

FIVE

It's the day of the tryouts and the training grounds are completely full. I'm standing next to Kavi in the sea of our classmates, under the wispy palm trees and bright blue sky. Birds flutter overhead, singing playful songs to each other without a care in the world. I only wish I could feel the same. There are only two groups left to test before the tryouts start.

Three judges sit on tall, silvery chairs before a long metal desk, making notes on their silverscreens. They're all wearing the official red and black robes of the Virana Master Trainers.

The kids testing now will be placed in different levels, depending on their scores. They're not old enough to participate in the Trials yet, being younger than fifteen standard years. The real tryouts for the Trials begin once the last few fourteen-year-olds are finished.

My innards slowly churn into soup as my nerves eat away at my resolve. What if I don't make it?

I glance to my right, enough to see Dragon out of the corner of my eye. He looks toward the arena with a strange sense of peace about him. I wonder how he stays so calm.

In the arena, the two kids have finished their duel. All the judges have to do now is write down the score.

Then it's our turn.

With this new realization, I start fidgeting and feel like I'm falling down a waterfall. My stomach shakes and quivers as adrenaline flows through me.

The judges nod.

The students bow to each other and leave the ring.

"All students entering the Trials, proceed to the center of the ring," says the judge in the center.

Kavi and I inch to the center. There are about sixty kids, and we're divided into groups of thirty. The opposite team is given red markers to put on their clothing below their shoulder. We're given blue.

Thank the Emperor Kavi's on my team; I'd hate making it into the Trials without her or vice-versa. I recognize Seth; Hiro, one of Kavi's friends; and Xana Devyn who was in our training class. Garr Aldon is standing next to a girl from another class.

I spot Liam, looking overconfident, as usual. He glances at me every few minutes until I shoot him a glare and he stops. Finally, there's Dragon two meters away from me, next to Luci Adelina. At least I won't have to fight him.

A man in his early forties hands me a small electric pistol, then moves on to the next person without one.

"What's this for?" I ask no one in particular.

Liam approaches me. "Hey, Jaina. Have you ever tried out before?"

I shake my head. "No, but the times I've watched, no one had any *pistols*."

He fidgets with the pistol in his hands. "Are you nervous?"

I'm afraid he might accidentally set it off, so I snatch it from him and turn on the safety. "Of course. Are you?" I ask numbly, handing it back to him.

He scoffs, and takes back his gun with a little extra force. "Very."

"You're lucky we're on the same team, or I'd stun you without a second thought," I shoot back.

He glowers at me, and stalks away.

The crowd becomes silent as Master Zoma strides into the center of the arena. "Younglings, Juniors, and Contestants. Welcome to the Imperial Trials. You have been chosen because of your Superior DNA. Today, eight of you will prove yourselves as worthy candidates for the Crystal City.

"Your first challenge is to reach a checkpoint placed somewhere in the arena. You may use the stun pistols against each other. They're set for a low electric pulse that will do nothing more than shock your enemy. You'll have five minutes to come up with a strategy for your team. When the gong sounds, the challenge begins," Master Zoma concludes.

Our team gathers in a large circle.

"Okay, so what's the plan?" Liam asks.

"Does anyone know where the checkpoint is?" Kavi asks.

"I do." Avan's voice is a higher pitch than the rest of the boys in our group. I recognize him from Alpha, but I'd never heard him say a word.

"Really?" Dragon asks, his eyes hopeful with surprise. His deep voice contrasts so much with Avan's I almost laugh.

Avan nods. "I saw them setting it up a few hours ago to the northwest. Almost a kilometer from here."

Dragon glances at me, and I look down at my feet, then at the rest of the group.

"We'll have twenty people distract the other group," I suggest. "And a team of ten to find the checkpoint?"

"Good idea, Jaina!" Liam cries, a sarcastic cadence in his voice. He scoffs.

I cross my arms and feel like a whiny toddler, but I can't help it. "Do *you* have a better idea?"

"Yes," Liam snaps, "I do. Send a group of four to go find the checkpoint while the rest distract the other team. That way it won't be as noticeable."

"We'd have a much higher chance of failure," another girl cuts in.

Liam rolls his eyes. "That's only if the people searching for the checkpoint don't get their job done!"

"So who do we send?" Kavi asks.

Liam gestures to the four of us as if the answer is obvious. "Jaina, Dragon, *you* and Seth."

Kavi and Seth shoot each other a glare. "We don't work well together," Seth reminds him.

"The four of you were in class Alpha," Liam says. "You're the best four in the school. It's our only chance."

"Um, what about me?" Maria Solam's face goes red with anger. "I was in class Alpha!"

Liam waves his hand at her, as if to shun her from the group. "No, not you, Maria. You'll just mess people up. So yeah, you guys go. It's the best way to get things done."

"I don't think we have another choice," Dragon agrees. "We'll split off of the main group after the battle has begun."

The gong sounds.

My teammates charge into the forest. I sprint, quickly picking up speed. The red team gets closer to ours as we tear through the trees...too close. Their strategy isn't to get to the checkpoint first. They want to be the only ones there.

All hell breaks loose. The boy leading the red team trips the girl at the front of ours. Avan is there and catches her fall. He retrieves his stun pistol and fires at the boy. I don't have time to watch what happens next, because Kavi grabs me by the wrist and pulls me away from the battle.

We take a sharp right turn and take cover behind a cluster of trees. "Where's Seth and Dragon?"

"I couldn't care less. Now, come on, let's go!" She drags me behind her.

We continue on through the forest at full speed, dodging trees and boulders. Something catches my eye.

I pull back on her grip and stop her. "Whoa, did you see that?"

Her hands turns cold on my wrist as we search for whomever or *whatever* it was. With a snap of a twig, I swing around and high-kick him in the chest. He falls but springs to his feet just as fast and pulls back his fist, getting ready to punch me.

"Dragon, don't!" I shout, closing my eyes and bracing myself for the blow. I can't believe I just kicked him!

"*Shaav*, Jaina, don't do that!" Dragon relaxes and takes a step back. "That was *way* too close."

I let out a breath of relief and see Kavi standing over Seth.

"Really, Kavi?" Seth groans through clenched teeth. "Really?"

A dark smile parts her lips. "Sorry. You looked Inferior to me."

I turn to Dragon. "Sorry about that."

"It doesn't matter, now we're even. Come on, let's find the checkpoint." He helps Seth up off the ground.

We pick up the pace, but the forest looks the same in every direction.

"Seth, Kavi," Dragon calls.

"Yeah?" they both return breathlessly.

"Head slightly north. Avan said it was to the north-west. We'll keep on this trail, just in case."

Seth grins and says, "Got it."

Kavi's face remains stern, and I can tell she's holding back from tripping Seth. Still, she moves off with him.

"Dragon, where are we?" I ask nervously. He's only been on the island for a month. How does he know his way around so well? Maybe he doesn't and I'm just blindly following!

His eyes meet mine and every muscle in my body tenses. "Almost there," he assures me.

No more than a minute has passed when he stops abruptly. I try to stop in time, but crash into him, almost knocking him over.

I regain balance then smile sheepishly at him. "Sorry."

He curses under his breath. "It's all right. Just try to be more careful." He continues searching the area.

Wonderful, Jaina. Just wonderful. I'm sure he's going to want you on his team. I roll my eyes at myself.

He breaks into a run. "Jaina, come on, this way!"

We jog a little further into a circular clearing. In the center lies a touch sensor, and the two of us move toward it. A crunching sound makes me stop. I whip my head around and find Roshiva Korr with his pistol aimed at me. I jump out of the way and he misses completely. Now it's my turn.

I aim and pull the trigger. He falls, stunned.

Dragon finishes off three other students effortlessly. I'm dazed, watching him fight. Every move is... flawless.

We run to the center of the circle. I touch the sensor before anyone else has the chance to show up. As if by magic, a helitransport appears above us. Dragon and I climb the ladder into the transport and are taken back to the main camp. After about five minutes of awkward silence, the doors open.

Master Zoma greets us. "Ah, my dears! Congratulations! You've won your team and yourselves a great opportunity!"

As she speaks, the other transports arrive and our team comes together.

"Very good, blue team. I admire your strategy. A less violent approach than the red team, but a good plan." She dismisses the red team then returns her attention to us. "Now, I'll split you into two groups. If I call your name, you'll be on the blue team. If I don't then you're red. Xana Devyn!"

Xana steps forth and is fitted with a blue marker then stands behind Master Zoma.

"Liam Rodan, Taryah Asavaah, Hondo Adom, Evelyn Crymzav." The four approach her and receive their colors. "Isabel Cerem, Kavi Agni, Yuza Lynn, Seth Onan, Qin Xia...Luci Adelina, Avan Sirius, Chanya Ozar, Dragon Kasev, and Jaina Indera."

I let out a long breath of relief and move to the other side of Master Zoma.

Kavi grabs my arm and pulls me to her side. "I was starting to worry you wouldn't be on my team."

Unable to hold back a smile, I say, "You think I'd let you enjoy the glory of the Trials alone?"

She grins and shakes her head, her long black hair tossing back and forth as she does.

"Now," Master Zoma says, "you'll fight in the Digital Arena. You've not done this before, which makes it a wonderful environment."

An older woman hands us each a black suit.

"What are these?" Seth asks, examining his.

"It's a device to track your movements," Master Zoma replies. Her face is as expressionless as ever. "You'll still feel pain when you're hit, even if you aren't physically hurt. Your weapons are digital as well, but you'll be able to feel them in your hands. Your opponent will be a projected image of their real selves in another room."

A rush of excitement shoots through me.

This is really like the Trials.

As we put on the black suits, Master Zoma continues her explanation.

"A fatal wound counts as 'game over.' Your image will stop being projected on the other screen, and you will have no influence on the other team. The first entire team to fall will lose. The winning team has the greatest chance of participation in the Trials. Eight will be chosen to enter. Good luck."

Master Zoma steps out of the ring as a large, black barrier rises out of the ground. Darkness engulfs us as the ceiling closes us in. We're in some sort of spherical room. The walls are screens, the tiny bumps on the walls are projectors.

The room becomes bright with the digital image of the world. An image of the red team appears in front of us. A bell rings, and the fight begins.

I draw a holographic sword as my first opponent comes at me with an ax. He strikes hard, but I block his powerful attack at the last moment. Backing away to regain balance, I shift the heavy sword in my hands then strike, concentrating on the moves that have been hammered into my mind over the years.

With a powerful kick, I knock his feet out from under him and stab him in the stomach. His image evaporates into the air. I look over my shoulder in time to see Ana Sonn slit Liam's throat. His suit shocks him with a jolt of electricity. He flails about, clawing at his suit, attempting to rip it from his body, but ultimately fails. When the electricity stops he curses and steps away from the battlefield.

Xana is attacked by three others, and I rush to her aid. One of her attackers slices me across the arm. A burning heat shocks me, and I jolt back with the sudden pain. Before she can finish me off, I pull a dagger from my belt and throw it. It strikes her in the heart, and her image fades away.

Now it's two to two. Xana strikes at the boy on her right while I attack the girl to her left. She's faster than I expect. Her sword skims my knee. Another jolt of electricity shoots up my leg and I grit my teeth, doing my best to overcome.

I block another hit with a powerful push, then swing my sword across her belly. She moves back, just in time. Sweat drips down my forehead and runs like rivers through my hair.

The girl lunges at me, and I can't back up far enough to evade her attack. *Shaav*, this is it. At the last moment, Luci gets in the way and stabs the girl, but gets herself stabbed as well.

Luci cries out as the strong electric jolt pulses through her. She stumbles backward at the force of the impact. The image of the girl disappears, and Luci leaves the training circle.

"Jaina!" Dragon calls.

Without hesitation, I swing my sword around and slice through another image. The projection of a boy flickers then dies.

The only people left on the training plate are Xana, Dragon and me. The dark walls recede into the ground to reveal the piercing light of day.

Master Zoma approaches us as our holographic weapons evaporate from our hands. "Once again, the blue team takes the prize. Congratulations!"

My stomach tingles with what little joy I can muster after wearing myself out fighting this long. Xana's eyes are furrowed in concentration, but a slight smile lights her face. Dragon shows no sign of emotion at all. He doesn't smile, or sigh or even look relieved. His blue eyes are cloudy, and he stares forward as if he expected this all along. Can't he look happy for once?

The rest of our team surrounds us, and we're now spoken to as a group. The red team stands together, breathing heavily and swearing between gasps. One girl stomps her foot loudly and leaves the arena.

Master Zoma smiles. "The fifteen of you have managed to survive this long. Seven will be removed from your group by tomorrow, and the remaining eight will continue their journey. Let's hope you aren't one of the seven! Blue team, you are dismissed for the remainder of the day."

The judges nod in approval as we hold hands and bow before them. A sudden rush of awkwardness shoots through me. I'm holding Dragon's hand. My heart starts racing, and I really hope he can't feel my pulse through my fingers. His hand feels familiar and strangely good around mine. I look at him, and he smiles, his eyes now full of mischief, as if hinting at some shared secret between us.

In the back of my mind, I can't help feeling that something's slightly off. Like it wasn't supposed to happen this way. Like things may be going a little too perfectly...

Of course not. I made it into the final round because I've been training for sixteen years. I tell myself it's nothing, and try to ignore it. Yet another, deeper voice responds:

You're not fooling anyone.

Anxiety rises in me, like magma in a volcano until it's too hard to contain. The scores won't be ready for another hour. I sit on my bed and can't help glancing at the clock every few minutes.

6:05 a.m.

The clock glares at me, mocking me. Ever since last night, it's as if time has intentionally frozen to torture me.

There isn't a coherent thought in my sleep deprived mind. It's as if all common sense has left me. Once I get my thoughts sorted out, I begin to fall asleep again, only to be awakened by excitement.

Soon, I'm awake enough to recognize the rising sun. At first, there's only a purple lining of the Eastern sky. There's nothing significant to it yet, only faintly brighter than the deep black of night. Yet as the minutes pass, the purple grows and becomes lighter and lighter near the edge of the Earth. It bleeds pink, then a red and orange. Finally, the golden sun peaks over the horizon.

The view is breathtaking. A feeling of freedom and joy spreads through me, mimicking the rising sun; it's small at first yet grows into the most beautiful thing conceivable.

The moment doesn't last. The clock now reads 6:45 a.m. Time to go. A tidal wave of excitement washes over me.

I quickly change out of my loose garments into tight black pants and a fitted, red shirt. The sky brightens with amazing speed, and I find myself having to rush to get downstairs.

After riding the lift into the courtyard, I search the area for Kavi. She's near the front of the large crowd that's gathered to see off the chosen contestants. I push through the mass of people chattering and whispering to one another.

"Kavi!" I try to get her attention.

She turns around, her eyes scanning the crowd. When she sees me she waves me forward with urgency. "Jay! Hurry, get up here! Master Zoma will be here any minute!"

Forcing myself through the last line of people, I'm finally able to take up position next to Kavi in the front row. The fourteen others who were on our team yesterday stand in a semicircle around a silver platform in front of the dining hall. Only eight will walk up onto the stage and be congratulated.

What if I don't make it?

Master Zoma opens the door and steps up onto the stage, a silverscreen in hand. "Students of Virana," she begins, "I'll now present to you the eight that will participate in this year's Trials." She looks down at the list, and it's all I can do to keep myself from begging her to call out my name. "Xana Devyn!"

Seven to go. It's possible my name's not on the list. Xana walks up onto the stage and is greeted by Master Zoma. Fear floods my veins like cool water.

"Luci Adelina! Liam Rodan!"

Oh, no.

This is terrible. *Liam* made it?

"Jaina Indera! Kavi Agni!"

For a moment, the words don't process and I'm dumbstruck. The crowd claps loudly, and Kavi pushes me up onto the stage. I did it. I actually did it! I can't believe I made it. Standing on stage, I look out at the rest of the crowd, cheering and shouting for us.

"Seth Onan! Avan Sirius!"

Only one more name.

"And finally, Altair Kasev!"

chapter

SIX

The name doesn't make sense in my mind, as if it's been forbidden to say. The crowd cheers as Dragon makes his way onto the stage and takes his place next to me.

My heart stops dead.

By the stars.

My body feels numb. "Altair?"

He doesn't look at me, but whispers, "Hey."

As if nothing's wrong.

As if I shouldn't be surprised.

"I present to you, the representatives of Virana!" Master Zoma shouts. The students shout our names, but I hardly hear them.

"It's really...you?"

He faces the crowd, but replies. "Yes. It's me."

My head is spinning. The cheering crowd and Master Zoma's compliments become echoes in the distance.

"Why didn't you tell me?"

"Meet me in the jungle. The place we first fought."

"I can't. I've got a lot to do before we leave."

"Jaina," he says sternly. "Please."

I look up at him and see that little boy from long ago. How hadn't I known it was him? As his eyes peer into my own, I know no matter what I feel, I can't say no to him. I take a strained breath. "All right, I'll go. But not for long."

He nods.

I don't know why it changes anything. He's still the same person he was before. He's back. My Altair, who was taken from me...

I snap out of my daze to hear Master Zoma shout to the crowd, "You're dismissed!" After they leave, she faces us. "You have the rest of the day to pack your prized belongings. Tomorrow you'll meet me at the island caves at six. I'll see you there."

———————

We're dismissed and I leave the arena with Kavi. I try to lose Dragon–Altair–in the crowd, not wanting to be near him until we can talk. A shiver runs through me. He's back. *He's back.* The words fill my mind but don't completely process. My body trembles with fear, not knowing what I should feel. There's a deep rooted knot in my stomach, but I'm not sure if it's from excitement, anger, or the intense sensation of betrayal. It was their fault he was taken away. But he promised.

It hurts more that he didn't bother bringing it up. He obviously remembers me! Otherwise, he wouldn't have asked me to meet him. Why didn't he say anything?

Kavi steps in front of me, stopping me in my tracks. "Jaina, are you all right?"

"I'm fine," I snap then try to move around her.

She puts her hand on my shoulder, forcing me to stop. "No really. What's wrong?"

"Nothing," I insist.

Kavi raises an eyebrow, a fiery look in her eyes. "*Shaav*, Jaina, tell me. Clearly, you're not fine."

I hesitate. There's no way she'd understand. She wasn't there when they took him. "It's...It's him."

Kavi furrows her brow. "Who? Dragon?"

"You wouldn't understand. It was so long ago–"

"Jaina. What the hell happened?"

I swallow hard. "Dragon is Altair. The-the boy who was taken."

Kavi looks at me as if I'm crazy. "What? I thought he was executed or something."

"We all did, Kavi. But it's him," I cry. "You heard his name called."

"Yeah, but I'm sure there's more than one guy named 'Altair' in the galaxy."

"Stop it, Kavi!" I feel like slapping her. "It's him. I know it. There's no doubt now. And I don't *shaavez* know why he didn't tell me before!"

Her shrug infuriates me, but I hold in my anger and push past her.

"It doesn't matter. I need to talk to him." I make my way through the jungle. All of the arenas are closed today. Hopefully security won't catch us.

I find him standing in the center of the training ring. He isn't facing me. That makes things easier.

"Dragon?" I choke. "Altair?" Despite my doubts about him, I suddenly feel the need to surge forward into his arms. To hold him close and cry in relief that he's alive.

He turns to face me. "Listen. I'm sorry about... everything. I can't tell you much, but if you ask, I'll do my best to answer."

His blue eyes remind me of the sea when it's still. How could I have looked into those eyes and not known it was him? No one else in the galaxy has eyes like him... those eyes which can reveal his deepest secrets, yet hide the world all at once.

I glance down at the ground and gently kick a pebble from my path. "Why didn't you tell me?"

His eyes meet mine with such a pleading desperation that I can't bare being angry at him for this. "The Masters... *discouraged* me from talking to you. They didn't want my presence to be a distraction since you're at the top of the class."

His presence distracts me anyway.

"I wanted to tell you. I would have told you if I'd gotten a chance to speak to you alone, but...they never let me out of their watch." He takes a tentative step closer. "You don't know how hard it was for me to stay away."

The voice of my Master echoes in my mind. They constantly reminded me how "he was such a bad influence."

"They still don't trust you?" I ask.

"I don't blame them," he says, softly. "I'm not a trustworthy person."

"That's just what they told you," I insist. "You were never a good liar."

His gaze falters to the ground. "I might have changed a little since then."

How can he stay so calm after what he's been through? "Why are you back?" I ask, trying to mask the bitterness beginning to seep into my voice.

"For the Trials." He cuts himself off, like he's considering saying more, but can't bring himself to do it.

There's a long, awkward silence. The only sounds are the crashing waves and the palm trees dancing in the wind. My fingers find their way to my forearm and I pinch my skin, trying to feel something, anything, other than numb. I'm so lost, I need time to think. "I should go pack."

"Yeah me, too," he pauses then adds, "I missed you, Jaina."

A weak smile lifts the corners of my lips as I uncomfortably back away. "I missed you, too."

Dragon's expression tenses and he reaches out toward me, closing his fingers around my forearm. "Jaina, wait." His grasp is gentle, yet the simple act of touching me makes my heart sprint into action.

I stop, and look at him, struggling to breathe.

He lets go, seeing my confusion. "I'm sorry I didn't tell you sooner. I really am. I just...didn't know how to bring it up."

"It's okay," I manage. "I'll see you tomorrow, Altair."

He flinches at the use of his name as if he's been hurt. "You can stick with Dragon. Everything bad about me is associated with Altair."

I almost protest, and say that no matter what they told him, he was always a good person. Yet somehow by that sad, pained look in his eyes, I can tell it has nothing to do with the Masters.

"All right, Dragon," I breathe.

He nods, and I turn, stepping out of the training circle. I feel his gaze follow me as I leave, but I don't look back.

The sky is dark and I'd like nothing more than to go back to sleep. But by the stars, how can I? Sleep was easy at first. But after the initial shock faded, the numbness was replaced with everything else.

It's all my fault. My fault he was taken away. If I wasn't such a weakling back then, he'd never have saved me so many times. He was my weakness.

And he had dreams. Nightmarish dreams that he'd sometimes describe to me. Ones with lurking shadows, knives, and screams.

I stand up and throw on some clothes, then take a seat on my bed.

All my fault.

I could have tried to stop them. Tried to save him, as he'd done a thousand times for me. But no. I stood there, frozen with fear, unable to do anything but watch them take him.

"Knock, knock!" I'm jolted out of my thoughts as Kavi opens the door. "Can I come in?"

My body relaxes. "You know, it doesn't help to ask if you've already come in."

She rolls her eyes and presses herself through the doorway. Her tough, bony fingers clamp around my wrist and she pulls me off my bed. "Come on, we have to go," she says.

I free myself from her grasp and pick up my backpack. Stepping through the doorway, I turn around and take one final look. Sixteen years were spent in this room. Memories flash like a movie in my head. Like the time Kavi and I stayed up the whole night with some friends, talking the hours away. The teachers were furious when we fell asleep in class the next morning.

There were other not-so-great memories. Like the time our good friend Sanara was sent away to a Recon

Camp because she was pregnant. They kicked her out of her room on her last night at the school, so I let her stay with me. Could that have only been last year?

"Let's go." Kavi tugs my arm and I shut the door behind me.

We walk through the courtyard in the dark and approach Xana's room. I knock, and before I have time to blink, she's at the door.

"You ready?" I ask, startled by her quick appearance.

She grabs her backpack then smiles. "Yep, bring it on."

We head out to the jungle. A guard paces back and forth around the boys' dorm. The door opens behind the guard and the boys approach us. I look at Dragon, and his eyes meet mine. He smiles, acknowledging me, but says nothing.

"Does anyone know where these *caves* are?" Kavi asks.

Seth points to a small, holographic map on a silver-screen. "Point X is the center of the island, so probably around there."

"Would you mind leading the way?" Kavi sounds frustrated for no apparent reason.

"My pleasure, my lady." He smiles awkwardly and exaggerates a bow.

Kavi looks disgusted at his remark as he heads to the front of the group.

The jungle is much stranger in the dark. Little drops of rain fall from leaf to leaf, glittering like diamonds in the moonlight. Crickets chirp, and the birds are loud enough to hear from kilometers away. Other than the occasional snapping of a twig, we are silent.

"Look up ahead," Seth whispers to the rest of us.

A large cave juts out of nowhere. What could possibly be an inspiration to begin the journey here? It can't be safe. Streams of lava light up the cave, surrounding the only path.

We enter, careful to stay on the dead center of the trail. Strangely, the air doesn't feel hot. Not hotter than usual on this tropical island, anyway. I wonder if the glowing red along the path is lava at all. Maybe it's just there to light the way?

My footsteps crunch the stones on the gravel path as I walk directly behind Avan. The path is too narrow to safely walk side by side, yet up ahead I notice that it widens.

"Look out!" someone ahead calls.

A plume of fire shoots out of a hole in the ceiling, fast enough to fry anyone standing in the area.

I duck. My heart pounds in my chest. When the fire dies away, I swallow the fear building in my throat.

"What was that?" Liam shouts.

Seth shakes his head, wide-eyed. "Probably a security check."

"Some security system," Liam grumbles.

We make our way slowly, ensuring every part of the ground is stable. We find the source of the lava where it bubbles from a fissure in the ground. The path widens and the reddish glow fades, leaving us in near darkness.

Liam examines a skeleton on the side of the trail. "Check this out."

"Don't touch it, Liam. That thing's gotta be a trap," I warn.

"Are you sure?" He jabs his finger at it.

"Stop!" My voice echoes through the caves, and the rest of the team looks at me oddly.

"Calm down, I didn't touch it!" He laughs. "I was just kidding."

I let out a breath. "Do *not* do that again."

We finally reach a chamber in the cave where water has collected in pools, and artificial lights brighten the room.

Dragon analyzes the cavern. "We're here."

A figure approaches from one of the darker tunnels. "So you found me." Master Zoma's voice is clear. She steps into the light, and I relax. "I'm glad you made it in one piece. I assume you didn't touch the skeleton on the way?"

I shoot Liam a glare. He snarls with disgust, then turns away, pretending to ignore me.

"I'll take you to your ship. From here, you'll drive to the Western edge of Virana then fly to the Uncharted Lands where you'll meet your trainer. He'll help you get through the Trials. Any questions?"

Everyone is silent.

"Good. This way." She gestures for us to follow her.

The tunnel is long and dark. It's hard to see my own hand in front of me, and I wonder how Master Zoma can navigate it. The air is cool, and I shiver. I hear the faint plops of water, dripping from stalactites into pools on the hard, rocky floor.

"Here we are," Master Zoma says.

A click sounds and a set of lights bring the room out of darkness. A large black transport stands in the center of the room on four leg-like metal spires. Heavily armored, it looks more like an army vessel than an ordinary transport.

We climb the ramp at the back of the ship.

"Whoa, this thing is awesome!" Liam remarks.

There are eight seats, four on each side. They look uncomfortable, but I've sat on worse. The inside looks something similar to what I'd imagine a hollowed out bird to look like, except with windows near each seat.

"Strap yourselves in. Your captain will take it from here. Good luck." Master Zoma steps away from the ramp and leaves us alone in the passenger hold. The ramp shrinks and disappears beneath the floor and a door slides shut, closing us in.

I'm probably never going to see this place again, even if I make it out alive. I thought this would be a hard moment for me. But I was wrong. There is no fluttering panic in my heart, or fear of what's to come. That, I'm sure, will come later. But for now...for now, I'm strong.

"Good morning everyone, this is your captain speaking," says a husky voice over the speakers. "The weather's supposed to be nice today and tomorrow, but the trip may get a little rough. I suggest you remain seated. We're about to begin moving, so if you're not in a seat yet, you should get to one immediately."

Liam sits next to me, fidgeting with some sort of plastic device that changes colors depending on the arrangement of a few squares. Kavi's next to him, putting her next to Seth. Dragon's in the seat directly across from me, and I wince.

I realize how stupid my behavior toward him is. He was my best friend, and I'm *wincing* at the sight of him?

We're jerked into motion as the transport begins its drive from the cave. The world around me brightens, growing lighter with each passing second. There's a blinding flash of light as we exit the darkness of the cave. For the first time, I'm able to view my island of Virana with new appreciation. The palm trees are suddenly so much greener, and the rich, brown soil looks so much softer. The flowers are more vibrant, the sun even brighter, and the ocean is that much more blue.

"I never realized our island was this beautiful," Luci says, dazed.

I nod. "It seems more peaceful. It doesn't look like a training camp anymore."

"I don't know. It doesn't seem much different to me." Liam looks out the window with us, but quickly turns to me, his eyes full and clever with that seductive stare. "Mind if I join the conversation, sweetheart?"

"Yes, I mind quite a bit, *sweetheart*," I shoot back.

"Hey, don't get too excited. I'm officially done with you, Jaina."

I raise an eyebrow. Yeah right. "You are? Well, congratulations. I'm really happy for you, Liam. Now, since we're done, would you kindly mind your own business?"

"Fine. *Sweetheart*." He shifts his attention to talk to Avan.

There's a long silence as Luci and I stare out the window. Kavi and Seth argue in the background like children.

"I never said that!" I hear her say.

"I'm pretty sure you did. I honestly can't believe we used to be friends," Seth snaps back.

My gaze rests on Dragon, who's barely moved an inch. He looks so calm as he stares out the window. Altair. My Altair.

Despite his strength, I see through his mask of power. Inner pain shatters the calm in his eyes. Maybe I haven't seen him in ten years but I remember how to read him. A shadow of constant sorrow lingers in his presence.

I wonder what they did to him. Was he tortured? What did they do to make him qualify for the IA once more?

Whatever it was, they couldn't fully get rid of his former, rebellious self. He's still with me. He always has been.

He promised. His words from that day echo in my head. Does he remember that night? The night he saved me from having to sleep in that dark closet; the night he told me that I was akira; the brightness. He said he'd always be there. I remember the night I dismissed it as a lie–the night he was taken. Yet since he's returned, I've realized he hasn't broken his promise. Not yet.

His eyes shift from the window and catch my gaze for a split second before I break it. I pretend I wasn't staring and look out the window.

Why can't I talk to him? I was able to before I knew who he was. But now, it's not the same.

"You, too, huh?"

I turn to Luci, studying her face, and wait for her to explain.

"Anyone who looks at Dragon like that is bound to get a broken heart. Don't let him fool you." There's a sense of annoyance and anger in her voice that I can't quite place. She shifts her gaze back to the window.

"He was my friend. That's all," I tell her. But there's something about the way I say the words...something that makes it sound not entirely true. And I'm not sure why.

"I've known him for a long time, Jaina. He was my friend, too. I know him better than anyone." Her eyes are wide, and her eyebrows are raised high, as if it'll help her make her point.

I almost tell her to calm down, but decide that's probably not the best idea. I turn away, and she glances at me, then looks back to the window.

Did she know him better than I did? He never mentioned a Luci. Not that I can recall, anyway. When we were young, he and I didn't have many friends. Just Liam.

I'd ask Liam what he thinks about all this, but he'd probably work around it and make my life that much more difficult.

"I think we're going to take off soon," Avan says.

Xana laughs. "We're already moving."

"No, I mean in the *air*."

Her grey-green eyes widen. "Wait, we're going to be flying?"

"How else did you expect us to get there?" I ask.

She shakes her head. "I-I don't know. I guess I didn't think about it, but I'm afraid of heights!"

Liam snickers. "How the *shaav* are you afraid of heights? I thought all Trial contestants had to be tough."

"Like you?" I ask him, raising an eyebrow.

The speakers crackle to life. "This is your captain speaking." There's a short pause. "If you'd like to switch seats with someone, I suggest you do it now. We'll be taking off momentarily."

Except for Liam, I really don't have a reason to move, and he's already leaving his seat to sit next to Xana. Kavi takes the seat to my right, probably to get away from Seth.

I ignore Dragon's quick glance—or at least pretend to. Catching it out of the corner of my eye makes my stomach stir with excitement.

The captain's voice is more mechanical this time. "All right, everyone, buckle up, we're approaching the runway."

As the transport takes off, I close my eyes. I'm shaken right then left and back again. For five minutes, I'm afraid I'll be shaken to death.

Finally, there's silence. Out my window Virana grows smaller.

The tropical forest covers the entire island, and the early morning fog buries the undergrowth like a blanket. The sun glitters on the water, reflecting bits of light on the waves.

"Say goodbye, everyone," Kavi says.

Every lesson I've learned, I've learned there. But there comes a time when the child must leave the teacher and experience things on her own.

I let go of the beauty and harshness of the jungle and sea. Regret and sorrow, excitement and joy. It all flows down the waterfall of time. There's nothing there for me now. Looking forward to the stormy clouds on the horizon, I feel as if I could take on the universe.

Rain falls around us. Bolts of light flash across the sky, and unforgiving grey-blue clouds hide the sun from view. The pilot knows what he's doing, I reassure myself, but as the ship lurches to the right, the comforting thoughts disappear.

Kavi moans like she's in pain. When I turn to her, she's eyeing Seth who's in the seat beside her. He's in a deep conversation with Liam.

"Kav," I say, tapping her knee to get her attention.

She snaps her worried eyes onto me like I caught her stealing candy from Master Tomash's secret stash of sweets. "What?" she asks.

"Honestly," I whisper. "What's your deal with him?"

"I told you, already." Her voice is softer than the Virana wind on a calm day. "We were friends, and then we weren't. And when he suddenly decided that ditching me was the wrong decision, I told him to *shaav* off."

"I'm sorry," I pause, trying to find a nice way to put it, "but I really think you should forgive each other and be done with it."

"Forgive him?" she snaps. Luckily the conversation in the ship is loud enough to mask her outburst. "No way. He hasn't even apologized."

I shrug my shoulders. "It's silly."

"Easy for *you* to say," she huffs. Sighing, she shakes her head in disapproval, then focuses her attention to the window. She shoots a few glances toward Seth, and when he notices, the two strike up another heated conversation.

I inhale sharply. Things have to get better. We aren't exactly a team yet. The Trials aren't going to end well if the majority of us can't talk to each other.

But instead of talking to people, I gaze out at the clouds, deciding a little eavesdropping couldn't hurt. I'm pretty good at it. Better at that than talking, anyway.

"It was always about you, Kavi." Seth sneers.

Ugh, their conversation is the last thing I want to hear. Hopefully they're the only ones about to kill each other. They make me nervous.

"He gave us a mission: find her and bring her back." Dragon's voice is soft and secretive. "We don't have to tell her."

"That's a little harsh, don't you think?" Luci replies.

"I have my ways," he says. "When the time comes, I'll get it done."

"Do you think she's really the one?"

He hesitates. "I'm not allowed to talk about it. If she is, she isn't ready to find out yet. Either way, we've been sent for her."

"But–"

"Look, I can handle it, okay?" he replies. "I'll figure something out."

I pull myself out of their conversation. Who's not ready for what? Mission to bring someone back? The one?

By the stars, what am I doing spying on my own team? I bring my hand to my forehead and press on my eyelids.

"How long have we been in the air?" I ask, feeling the slightest bit nauseous.

"About an hour and a half," Liam replies. "Don't you know how to read the sun, darling?"

"Shut up. The sun isn't even out."

"*You* asked," he counters.

I grip my knees with my hands in anticipation. "We should be there by now."

"Have you ever heard of patience? It just takes a while to get to where we're going," he answers. His voice is so calm I want to pinch him.

"When did you get so smart? Did you read the Galactic Concordance or something?" I ask harshly.

The corners of his lips rise into a smile. "It wasn't to impress you; I can assure you of that."

My eyes narrow into a glare. Why did he have to be chosen for the Trials? Him of all people. Maybe the Imperials selected him to torture me.

Something tells me to turn around. Dragon's looking at me. No, he's *staring*. His eyes meet mine, and my pulse quickens. He turns away almost as fast as I do. I'm not sure why the short moments of eye contact weigh so heavily on my mind. It annoys me that I even care.

But Dragon was *staring* at me.

No boy stares at me. Except for Liam, of course, but for some reason, I don't count him.

I start to feel all jittery, and I have to do everything I can to keep it from showing. *Stop it, Jaina.* Just breathe and that too-happy-excited feeling will go away.

"I won, and you know it!" Kavi shouts.

"No, you didn't! You cheated!" Seth shoots back. "I'm not sure why the *shaav* you'd do it, but everyone knows you did. Right, guys?"

I massage my temples, and shut my eyes. Dealing with them is the last thing I want to do right now.

"What are you even *talking* about?" Liam asks them.

"Remember that tournament the Masters held three years ago? I beat Seth in it, and he thinks I cheated!" Kavi laments. "But I didn't!"

I glance over at Dragon and he rubs his tired eyes. He catches my gaze and I gesture to Kavi and Seth, silently asking him to please stop this.

"In the name of the stars!" Dragon cries.

For the first time, the room goes silent.

"That was three *shaavez* years ago! Just shut up and let it go, for galaxy's sake!" He looks back at me, as if to ask if that was good enough.

I can't help smiling. He smiles back with a sleepy, yet suspicious curl of his lips.

Light conversation strikes up in the ship again. The attention fades from Kavi and Seth's problems, and all goes back to normal. Or as close to normal as it can be.

"All right, Dragon," Kavi spits. "Since you're so insistent and I can't stand sitting next to Seth for one more second, why don't you take my seat?"

Uh oh. Not a good idea. That means he'll be sitting next to me. I'm not sure I'll be able to handle that.

Dragon shrugs casually. "Get up and I will."

She raises an eyebrow. "Fine then." With that, she stands, and saunters over to Dragon. "You just gonna sit there or get your *nav'ra* out of your chair?"

He gets up and glares at her, then takes the seat next to me. Oh, *shaav*. This is really awkward. Catching glances and all is one thing. Sitting next to him...well, that's another. I stare out the window, trying to keep to myself.

"Glad that's over with," he mutters.

I turn to him and laugh, struggling to sound normal. "You really think it's over?"

He smiles. "Not really, but it's good enough for now."

Tension fills the air and I don't know what else to say, so I pretend to be interested in the clouds out my window. Anything would be better than this rigid silence, but I can't bring myself to say a word. Since when am I so shy?

"Jaina," he says quietly. "Can I ask you something? Honestly?"

"Sure." My voice trembles as I meet his eyes.

He glances to the others in the ship, as if to make sure they're not listening then leans in toward me.

I have the sudden impulse to pull back, but I stop and scold myself for being so on edge. He's not even *that* close to me.

He studies my face, and his expression falters with concern. "Are you scared?"

I study his cloudy-sky eyes and lightly tanned skin. "No, not at all," I reply, quivering from the fact that I'm talking to him. "Are you?"

A sly grin grows on his lips. "If you're not scared, why should I be?"

"I guess you shouldn't." I let my smile fade after realizing I'd been smiling. "I missed you." The words slip out of my mouth before I can pull them back. It's not entirely appropriate for the situation, and more embarrassing since I said the exact same thing yesterday. But it's true. I missed him so much. I never thought I'd see him again.

"I missed you, too." His voice is deep and soft, like chocolate. Dangerous and seductive, but sweet at the same time.

"What was it like?" I whisper.

He bites his lip. "The final treatment wasn't bad, but before they knew what to do with me...it was hell."

"I thought you'd been–" My voice cracks, and I shut my mouth.

"I know," he cuts in. "Most people thought I was. The Masters considered it, too. They started to think maybe I wasn't worth the trouble."

"I'm glad you're all right."

"I'm glad you are, too." He studies me for a few seconds, even after I turn away. I feel the warmth radiating from his gaze. Only when he's engaged in a conversation with Xana do I let myself breathe.

Had he worried about me? *He* was the one taken away and hospitalized. He should have worried for his own life. I lived the high life, received training every day and was constantly protected.

There wasn't anything I had to worry about. Except for him. Now, he's sitting next to me again.

I stare out at the watery vista. Fatigue crawls through me, softly coaxing and urging my eyes to close. But I can't doze off now. Not with him beside me.

Doing everything I can to stay awake, I rest my head against the window and stare down at the sea.

The ocean is like a blanket beneath us. Deep blue stretches all the way to the horizon. On Virana, we learned much about the ocean. How it covers more than ninety percent of the planet, and how much of the sea life has been gone for centuries. They told us that the ocean was like a haunted house. The only signs of life remain at the bottom of the sea in bones or in the occasional ghostly soul of a fish that's managed to survive.

They never told us how beautiful it is, or the awe-struck feeling one gets when flying over it. Or how, even though we brought the ocean to its current state, we are always and forever at its mercy.

My thoughts become hazy, and I struggle to keep the voice in my head talking.

Dragon peacefully watches the waves below us, his blinking slows so each flutter of his eyes lasts just a moment longer. Maybe it's okay to fall asleep while he's resting, too.

My inner voice drifts off. I wake myself up, but the sleepiness stays with me. I look around. Kavi's in a daze, and Dragon has allowed exhaustion to overcome him. He's so still now, resting his head against the wall. Something stirs within me. I want to reach out and brush his face with my hand.

I'm definitely not thinking straight. I let myself drift...into...sleep...

———

"Good evening...–one captain speak–..."

I open my heavy eyelids. The words I'm hearing don't make sense. My mind isn't processing things fast enough. Outside the windows, all is dark.

"We've officially arrived in the Uncharted Lands. Please proceed to the door."

Awareness takes over me. My head's resting on something soft and warm. Gentle fingers are nestled into my hair. And for some reason, the fact that I'm leaning against him and he's touching my hair doesn't bother me.

Suddenly, I freeze. Every muscle in my body tenses.

I bolt upright with a gasp.

"I'm so sorry," I manage. A dizzy feeling rushes through me, and embarrassment consumes me like wildfire.

Dragon grins, sleepily. "It's all right. I didn't mind."

My hand still rests on his leg and I pull it away.

Wake up. Snap out of it! I can't believe I fell asleep on him. Moreover, that he actually tolerated it! The sleepiness remains heavy, like a 200 pound boulder on my shoulders.

We enter a building. The walls are glassy, and make me feel like I'm in a fish tank. My body mindlessly follows everyone else until we're lead to the bedrooms. Beyond that, everything fades to black.

chapter

SEVEN

I open my eyes. I'm in a comfortable bed with five layers of blankets on top of me, warming me down to the bones. Sitting up, I'm flooded with a sudden rush of memories.

We're in the Uncharted Lands.

I woke up on Dragon last night.

I cover my face with my hands in embarrassment, cringing at the thought. By the stars, I really hope I didn't drool on him or anything. As if I'm not ugly enough when I'm awake!

He had his fingers in my hair; my weird, too curly, too fluffy hair. It was all...too close. I let him see me completely exposed. Vulnerable.

I close my eyes ridding myself of the frustration, then take in my surroundings.

The walls, windows, ceiling, floor, even the door, seem to be made of glass. Luckily, the surface is wavy, so I can't see much except for colors on the other side. Through the wall to my left, a distorted silhouette climbs out of bed. I guess it's one of my teammates.

On my nightstand, I find a small sphere propped up by four tiny legs. I pick it up and twist the top half of it to the left. It peels open like an orange while the flaps spin, allowing it to hover. Lightly tossing the tiny ball into the air, it floats above my hand. The green translucent word *Identification* floats above it. I place my index finger on the bottom of the sphere and wait for it to read my fingerprint.

"Jaina Indera identified," a mechanical voice from the sphere says. "Message for Jaina Indera. Do you want to proceed?"

"Proceed."

The green letters disappear and are replaced with the holographic image of a man. He bows to me.

"Jaina Indera, my name is Shirez Melohem. I am the Prince of planet Earth and the owner of this castle. You and your teammates will be trained by me for three days, then you'll be transported to the first arena. Collect your team, head to the bottom of the stairs and into the training ring. I'm sure you can find it. I'll meet you there."

The recording fades. I stand up and dress as fast as I can and open the door.

Kavi steps from her room. "I saw you getting up in a hurry. What was the transmission about?"

"The Prince wants me to collect the team and head downstairs."

She laughs. "Prince? You don't mean the one you fell asleep on last night, do you?"

My cheeks burn. "Cut it out Kav. I was tired, okay?"

Her smile suggests she doesn't believe me. "All right, all right! Calm down. So, Prince Melohem is actually here?"

"I guess so."

Luci approaches us, and I start talking to her before Kavi can say anything else annoying. "Hey, Luci, you want to go wake up the boys? Tell them to meet at the stairway over there."

She nods but doesn't look too happy to see me. What is it with her? Is she still upset about the way I looked at Dragon?

"Kavi, can you go with Luci?" I ask, though it's more of an order than a question. She obeys. Maybe Kavi can help soften Luci up?

I get Xana, which takes a little longer than it should. Apparently she's a deep sleeper. I nearly have to push her off the bed just to get her to acknowledge I'm there!

Finally, the two of us hurry over to the rest of our team. I spot Dragon and avoid eye contact. It will all be okay, I reassure myself. *Just act normal.*

"Sorry about the wait," I tell them.

Liam answers for the rest of the group. "No problem."

I almost wait for him to add *sweetheart*, but it doesn't come, so I move on. "We've gotta get downstairs."

Seth raises an eyebrow. "What's the rush? Are we late?"

My eyes meet Dragon's and my chest tightens up. *Shaav.* So much for acting normal. "Nothing," I reply. "We've just gotta go."

We make our way down the long, glass staircase. The walls are carved with intricate designs. If I look closely enough, I make out little pictures between the lines. Some form birds, and trees, and others form mountains. I have to restrain myself from brushing my hand against the carvings.

The glass beneath us is thick; so thick I can't even make out shapes on the other side. The only colors in the glass palace are variations of icy blue.

I wonder what this Melohem guy is like. He's a prince, so he must be rich beyond belief. The question is, will he be the egotistical rich-prince, without a care in the galaxy? Will he even help us with the Trials?

I'd constantly heard of trainers who neglected their students. Trainers who honestly didn't care. But really. If you're rich as hell, why would you?

After we reach the end of the stairwell, we enter a large, glass room.

A man approaches us, seemingly out of nowhere. The Prince. He's tall with a strong, commanding presence. His strides are powerful and confident, yet there's an aura of gentleness about him. His dark hair is peppered with subtle shades of grey, and his kind eyes radiate a familiarity I can't begin to understand.

He glances over us and rests his bluish-grey eyes on me, the last person in line. "Good morning, everyone, I trust you've slept well?" His voice is accented, not fully pronouncing his R's. Commanding, yet not at all like Master Zoma's voice. It's gentle, and caring. The sort of caring I'd expect of a father.

"Yes sir, thank you very much," I answer.

He smiles kindly. "I am Prince Melohem, overseer of everything that happens on planet Earth and lead trainer for Trial contestants from Virana." He nods to Dragon. "Nice to have you back."

Dragon bows. "Thank you, sir."

I look at Dragon, too surprised to feel embarrassed about glancing at him. Dragon was here before? Confusion surges through me. But he was in a reeducation camp...wasn't he?

Shirez takes in our team as a whole, studying us with a critical eye. He brings his hand to his lips, then onto his strong chin. "So. You think Master Zoma taught you how to fight?" He pauses. "Well, I'm here to tell you she hardly scratched the surface. One against another in battle is only a small portion of what you'll experience out there. What she failed to teach you is how to work as a team. How to be many acting as a whole. Not the other way around. And that is what I'm going to teach you. Teamwork."

Xana shyly raises her hand.

Shirez acknowledges her with a nod.

"Excuse me for asking, but we're only here for three days. How are we going to learn this in such a short time?"

The Prince smiles suspiciously. "I have my ways. You'll see. Now, I'd like to present you with your..." He looks down at a silverscreen in his hand. "Ah, yes. Individual assignments. Form up."

We fall in line.

"Seth, Luci, Kavi, Liam, Avan, Xana, Altair, and Jaina. Correct?" He glances back at the silverscreen then looks up at us in turn. "I've studied your files. I know your personalities and your fighting styles. I know your strengths and your weaknesses. I know you better than you know yourselves."

This guy might not look the part, but he definitely knows what he's doing.

He approaches Liam. "I've designed your team in such a way that you'll gain power even from your weaknesses. Liam, right?"

"Yes, sir."

"I've taken note of your interest in being...disruptive in class. I've seen how you excelled in your navigation and engineering classes–"

"Liam excelled in something other than annoying people?" Xana blurts out.

I struggle to stifle a laugh.

Shirez glares at us, his kind eyes suddenly stern and stone cold. "Is there a problem, Xana?"

She glances at the ground, visibly doing her best to force the smile off her face. "No, sir."

"You mock your teammates like that again and I'll have you doing target practice all night," he threatens.

Her eyes widen. "You'd do that?"

"Ask Altair. He'll tell you."

Okay, I totally underestimated this guy.

Shirez turns back to Liam. "On the team, you'll be the navigator and mechanic."

"Thank you, sir."

"Xana, you're the battle tactician and weapons specialist." He pauses to look at the silverscreen. "Avan, you are to be a medical specialist. Luci, you're the language specialist and assistant to Avan in medical procedures.

"Seth and Kavi, you're spies. If your team needs information about the status of another team, you'll be the ones to carry it out." The prince takes a moment then turns to me.

"*Shaav*," Kavi mutters under her breath. Seth only smiles.

I look around and realize the only two people without a job yet are Dragon and me.

We're going to have the same job, aren't we? How can I focus on my duties while working with him?

"Altair and Jaina," he pauses, "you'll be the team leaders. Everyone else will follow your orders and your orders only. Understood?"

There's a reassuring silence from the team.

Shirez presses a button on his silverscreen, then motions to the rest of the room. "Now, go on! Head to your stations. I'll be around to check on all of you."

All around us, sections of the wall shrink into the ground to reveal new rooms.

There's a piloting station equipped with flight simulators. The weapons room is filled with countless swords and pistols, as well as plasma and electric guns. Others, like the language and the technical stations are pretty small and contain an android as well as a few different books.

Dragon gently taps me on the shoulder. "Jaina, this way."

I follow him.

"Dragon, how does the Prince know you?"

"They sent me here for specialized elite training after about a year in reeducation. The advanced teachers didn't know what to do with me there, so they asked Shir-um, Prince Melohem to train me. I spent six years here after the Masters gave up on me."

We reach our station and sit at a small table across from each other. I watch him as he switches on the computer. How his thick, sandy-brown hair falls around his forehead. How his lips press together as his blue-green eyes study the holographic screen before him.

What the *shaav* am I thinking? It takes tremendous effort to pry my eyes from him and focus, but somehow I manage.

I find a black touch screen embedded in the table and press my index finger onto it. Dragon does the same on an identical screen.

"Jaina Indera and Altair Kasev identified. Authorization from Prince Shirez Melohem is required," says the computer.

"*Aaliz li ahn,*" Dragon says.

The computer whirs to life. "Permission granted."

"How do you know the code?" I blurt out.

I wish I'd keep my thoughts to myself for once.

He looks down at the computer screen, pressing buttons on the control panel. "It's just something I picked up."

"It's not Cora...is it?"

He shakes his head gently. "It's Shaserin."

Shaserin? That must not be an Imperial language.

His eyes flicker to mine. "Okay, so in order to be granted the title Team Leader, we must first learn to make decisions together." He doesn't look up from the computer controls and continues pressing buttons. "It'll give us a problem, and five minutes to agree on an answer."

"And if we can't come to a decision?" I ask.

"If we can't come to a decision, or we make the wrong decision, we'll fail."

"Your first problem is," the computer pauses, searching for something to ask, I assume. We're left staring at the hologram, not wanting to look at each other.

"You have two teammates who aren't getting along, and it's disrupting team morale. How do you get them to work together?"

"Easy. Sit them down and make them talk it over." My voice is stronger and more confident than I expect, but I continue, "That's Conflict Resolution 101."

He meets my eyes with a mechanical intensity, like he's heard my argument a thousand times. "We don't exactly have time for that. In a classroom, I'm sure it's fine. But in the Trials?" Dragon replies. "I say send the two on a mission. That will force them to work together in a dangerous situation. They'll realize the importance of trusting each other."

I raise an eyebrow in protest. "If they don't work together, their loss of focus could endanger the entire team. They could be captured or—"

"Our job," he cuts me off, "is to keep the team working as a unit under every circumstance and complete our mission before anyone else."

"But if they get captured, we'd be stuck with a rescue mission on our hands!"

He nods as if actually contemplating my suggestion, but it's clear he's not changing his mind. "It would be worth the risk," he says finally.

"Your time is up. Have you reached an agreement?" the computer asks.

Dragon looks from me to the computer. "No."

"Please state your answers."

"Make them talk it over," I say.

Dragon shakes his head. "Send them on a mission together."

"Altair Kasev is correct."

Right. Of course. He was always right when I knew him before. What made me think he'd be different now? My face burns like I've spent an hour too long in the sun. I lower my eyes, hopefully hiding my cheeks under my long, brown hair. "This is going to be harder than I thought," I mutter.

He half-smiles as a glimmer of sadness surfaces in his eyes. "It always is, Kira. It always is."

What?

Did he just call me Kira? My entire body tenses. I can't believe he remembers. Akira means brightness in Cora. He used to say that I was the only one who could make him laugh. A warm, peaceful sensation envelopes me. What else does he remember?

He's still looking at me and only seems to realize that after I meet his gaze. He glances down at the computer, as if pretending he wasn't watching.

He clears his throat and says, "Proceed to next program."

"Program found. Beginning now."

The next round begins. We have no luck this time either. The sessions start to blur into one big disagreement. Pretty soon, the computer dismisses us for lunch. Maybe it's had enough of our unwillingness to compromise.

We stand and head to the center of the training room with the rest of our teammates.

"How'd it go, Jaina?" Kavi asks.

The memories of my quarrels with Dragon are replaced with the softness of his voice. *Kira.* He remembered.

"Terrible," I spit out the word like it tastes bad in my mouth. It's not quite a lie. "We can't agree on anything." Now change the subject before she asks me anything else. "What about you? How's your class?"

"Okay, if you ignore the fact that Seth and I *do not* get along. I don't know what the Prince was thinking, putting us two together," she complains.

I laugh. "Oh Kavi, deal with it. He isn't that bad, you know. Maybe things never happened the way you wanted them to, but you have to let it go."

"He's the one who needs to let it go," she murmurs.

We follow Shirez up one flight of stairs into a small cafeteria and sit down at a round table after getting our food. The dishes are simple, consisting of mostly vegetables with a side of white meat and rice. As my teammates sit down, I hear snippets of their conversations but their words don't fully reach the depths of my mind. Because one thought won't leave me alone.

He called me Kira. *He called me Kira.*

Dragon approaches the seat next to me, but the Prince steps in front of him and takes the seat for himself. I stare at the two, a little surprised. Dragon steps back, slight disappointment registers in the soft blue of his eyes. Shirez takes no note of it, as if he hadn't seen Dragon coming.

"Sorry, Altair. Would you mind taking this seat?" Shirez asks, gesturing to the seat next to him.

Dragon's jaw twitches and he bites his lip in annoyance. "Not at all," he answers under his breath.

Well, that was awkward.

The Prince smiles kindly at me. I try to smile back, but I don't think it's very convincing.

"So, Jaina and Altair. I didn't get to check on you. How was your class?" the Prince asks. My gaze rests on Dragon, but I avoid eye contact.

"We are in need of assistance," Dragon replies flatly.

Prince Melohem raises an eyebrow. "Is that so? I thought you two would be fine on your own. What are you struggling with?"

"We're like..." I hesitate, "opposites. We can't agree on anything."

"Figures," Dragon mutters.

Prince Melohem shoots Dragon a glare then turns to me. "All right, I'll try to get to you tomorrow. After lunch, we're going to have the whole team train together. This will be your schedule every day until the Trials begin."

"Yes, sir," I reply.

Dragon looks at the Prince and after an awkward pause, he quickly replies, "Yes, sir."

"Call me Shirez. Between the three of us," the Prince adds in a much softer tone, so only Dragon and I can hear.

I shrug. "All right, Shirez."

Despite my calm demeanor, I can't help feeling completely confused. What's going on between the two of them?

After a few hours back in the training room, Shirez hands me two small cylinders with an extended lip on the top.

"What are these?" I ask.

"You'll see, but don't play with it yet," he warns.

He hands out fourteen more, two to every person on the team and keeps two for himself. "All right, listen up!" Shirez shouts. "These little weapons will be very important to your success in the Trials. The Imperial Alliance wants to see your accuracy and strength. These are called MED's or ME Daggers." He flips it around twice in the air then activates it in his hand. A blade appears from the end. He inspects our line, making sure each and every one of us is paying close attention.

"Despite their size, they're lethal, as I will demonstrate." He spins around and throws the MED at a wall. Its point sinks into the bullet proof metal. Shirez nods in approval, then steps over to the wall and lightly tugs the blade out. The hole which the dagger created is lined with red hot metal, like it melted upon entry. He spins the dagger around in his hand, stops its rotation, then presses a button to deactivate it.

"Not only can this cut through almost any material, it electrocutes on contact. If you prefer, you can turn the electric current off, and it becomes a normal blade. This is only one of the many new weapons you'll use in the Galactic Imperial Trials," Shirez tells us.

"One question," Liam interjects.

"Go ahead, Liam."

He fumbles with the dagger in his hands, keeping his eyes on the floor. "Isn't killing someone in the Trials sort of...frowned upon? I know it's allowed but–"

"Yes, Liam, but other teams will be more violent and you will need to defend yourself. Who knows what sort of environment you'll be in? They've got wild animals from other systems and all kinds of ridiculous abominations to send after you."

"Right," Liam agrees. "But if someone on our team kills someone, would that reduce the chances of us going to the Crystal City?"

Shirez remains silent for a moment before replying. "No. It will not hurt your chances at all." He picks up a silverscreen from a desk near the wall and presses a few buttons. A target practice course appears out of the wall in front of us.

"Activate your MED's and get to a station. You're allowed to leave after an hour."

I quickly choose a station and find myself standing between Dragon and Luci. Doing my best to ignore the two of them, I throw my MED at the holographic target. The image blinks twice as the dagger flies through it. Master Zoma taught me well.

It feels so natural, training like this in silence. Training alone. Was it really only two days ago that we were put together on this team?

Throwing another dagger, the image falters again.

The target begins to move slowly. After I get used to hitting it at a slow speed, it moves faster.

A weird feeling tickles the back of my neck, like someone's watching me. I try to ignore it, and let it pass, but the urge to glance to my left is irresistible.

Luci stares at me. Her eyes are fixed in my direction. But as I take an uncomfortable step backward, her gaze doesn't follow me. I trace her line of sight to Dragon. She drinks him in. With a mixture of power and grace, he throws the dagger at the image.

Flawless.

He's got perfect form. The target blinks twice, confirming the hit.

I realize I'm staring at him, too.

Shaking my head disapprovingly at myself, I take a step between them, throwing my dagger again. I don't look back at Luci, but know she's gotten back to work.

You're not threatened, are you?

The question sounds ridiculous in my head, but I can't help the dull, aching bitterness bubbling in my gut every time I see her talk to him.

By the stars, am I really jealous of her closeness to him?

Oh, shut up! Of course I'm not threatened! I'm not jealous! What do I have to feel threatened about?

I cut my thoughts off and miss my target.

He called me Kira. He remembered. Shirez knows him and trusts him.

I throw again and miss. *Na'lav. Focus, Jaina, Focus.*

"You all right there, Jaina?"

I whip around so fast my braid hits my cheek. Shirez stands a meter behind me with that look of calm about him I've seen so many times on Dragon.

"I'm fine," I tell him.

"You sure?" he asks. "I didn't think you were going to miss that last shot."

"It's just...I was just...thinking too hard."

"Take a few more shots. Sometimes it helps."

My eyes lock onto my target with such intensity it feels like I'm glaring. I inhale deeply, then take the shot. I hit slightly off my mark, but the dagger flies right through the hologram. It blinks twice then fades.

"Very good. You're dismissed," he says.

"We're done already?"

"We've been done for an hour." He laughs. "I guess you didn't notice when the time was up. Though, you're not the only one still here." He gestures to Dragon. "You can go to bed now." No one but Dragon and I are still here. I hand him my two MED's.

"What about him?" I ask quietly.

"He'll probably stay up for a few more hours." Shirez doesn't take his eyes off me. "Off you go."

"Thank you, Shirez," I say.

He smiles. "Jaina, you are eternally welcome."

chapter

EIGHT

"Your time is up. Have you reached an agreement?" asks the computer in a clear, crisp tone.

"*Shaav*, no," I curse. I run my fingers through my hair, trying to think.

Dragon looks calm as ever, making it harder for me to hold back my frustration. He glances at me with a little sympathy, but says nothing.

"All right. What's the problem?" Shirez asks, looming over us.

"The problem is I'm right," Dragon answers. "She just doesn't want me to be."

Shirez's eyes narrow into a glare, and his brow wrinkles with disapproval. "Don't be overconfident, Altair. I'm sure you're just as much in the wrong as Jaina is."

Dragon sighs, shifting his gaze to the table. "She doesn't look at the bigger picture."

"And he can't see the smaller one!" I protest.

"That's not a problem at all. Don't you see?" the Prince says.

I shake my head.

"What you need is balance. Jaina, you seem to go by the book, whereas Altair, you like to bend the rules. Standard procedures are there for a reason, but sometimes it's beneficial to everyone when they're ignored." He pauses. "Remember, many people will try to over think the problem. And that's why they fail. If you remain calm, you'll see how, despite your opposing thoughts, you can work together. The answer will surrender itself to you."

The soft chattering of our teammates in the center of the room grabs my attention. Thank the stars. Lunch time. The three of us push away our chairs to stand and head to the dining room. Once again, Shirez sits between Dragon and me. It's almost like he's trying to keep us apart.

Between bites of the same vegetable dish with a side of meat and an added slice of bread, he asks, "So, Jaina, where do you come from?"

I shrug my shoulders then stuff a forkful into my mouth. Once I'm done chewing, I swallow and reply, "I don't know. The IA chose me early, so I don't really remember my parents or my home."

Shirez nods, but his expression is blank. Almost forcefully so, as if he's doing everything in his power to keep me from reading his face. "How old were you when you were brought to Virana?"

"They said I was one year and three months. I don't remember much from before, only a warm glow...from my mother, I think." I pause. There's an uncomfortable silence that I can tell he's trying to ignore as much as I am. When I can't stand it any longer, I say, "What about you? Where are you from?"

"I was born in the Polaris Isles, then moved here to be married."

"You're married?" Shirez doesn't seem like the kind of guy who'd want to be married.

"I was. She died not long after."

I hesitate. "I'm so sorry. I didn't–"

"No, it's all right," he cuts me off. "It was an arranged marriage. The two of us weren't meant to be. I became more involved in...other matters." He stares off into the distance. "I met someone else."

I wonder what those "other matters" were, but I'm pretty sure he isn't planning on telling me.

"So," I pause carefully, hoping this *someone else* isn't dead too. "Where is she now?"

"I don't know. Her name's Amara." He lingers on the word. "I made her a promise, you know."

"And what was that?" I ask, slowly lifting the fork to my mouth again.

He smiles. "That I would protect the one she loved most." He rests his gaze on me as I chew my food, as if he expects me to add something to it.

"Why are you telling me this?" I ask, startled by his sad story.

"To make conversation. It helps my students understand me better. Makes them realize that I'm human." He laughs, but it's not a happy one. More of a sad, constricted laugh. "Anyway, tell me something about you."

"There's nothing to tell. My story's nowhere near as interesting as yours, I'm sure."

"Oh I doubt that." He trails off and glances at Dragon. Dragon's jaw tightens ever so slightly, and I get the feeling there's more going on than either of them will admit.

Something on Shirez's wrist beeps, and he glares at it, annoyed.

"Back to training, everyone!" he announces, standing up with an empty plate.

We head to the training room and prepare for another vigorous session of throwing, target practice, and whatever else Shirez has in mind.

"I find it hard to believe that anyone is having a worse time than I am," Kavi complains.

All of the girls are in my room, probably because I'm the team leader. But if it were up to me, I would much rather collapse onto my mattress and fall asleep. Apparently I'm not in control of when or where the "meetings" are held.

"It's just awkward since Seth and I used to be friends," she continues. "We try to have a civilized conversation, but it never works."

"You used to be friends?" Luci asks.

Kavi nods. "Yeah. But the son of a *katiaj* ditched me until recently."

"Maybe if you didn't act so barbaric around him things would work out," I reply.

Xana laughs but Kavi doesn't find it as funny.

Kavi rolls her eyes, while twirling her long, dark hair. "Enough about me. What about you guys?"

"Weapons training is tough," Xana murmurs. "It's a *shaavez* nightmare."

"You think weapons training is hard?" Luci begins. "You should try the medical science class with me."

Xana shakes her head. "I've never been good around blood. I'd throw up on the patient," she says, mimicking a sickly tone. "How's your class going, Jaina?"

My neck tingles at the thought of Dragon. "Oh, you know. It's going pretty well," I start casually. "But we can't agree on anything."

"I thought you guys were good together," Xana bursts out brashly.

"What?" Luci cries.

"No, no, no. I think you've got this all wrong. I don't–" I pause, trying to find the words. My heart pounds in a nervous fury. "I don't *like* him."

Xana raises an eyebrow. "How could you *not* like him?" she cries. "Just look at his muscular arms, and those soft blue eyes...do you think he has abs?"

"Of course he does." Kavi replies as if the answer were obvious.

I run my fingers through my hair, my cheeks burning with embarrassment. "Guys! Stop it!"

"No really, Jaina!" Xana laughs. "When you fell asleep on him...that was adorable!"

"Okay, about that–"

"It's okay," she interrupts. "I know you used to be friends and all. Kavi told us. But he *is* pretty cute..."

"It's not like that," I insist. "I want to get to know him again, but it's not like I *like* him or anything."

"I agree with Jaina." Luci sneers. "They don't exactly 'go together,' if you know what I mean. And they can't agree, so leave the subject alone."

Without thinking, I shoot her a glare. It shouldn't bother me, but it does. Who is she to say who goes together and who doesn't?

"All right, all right," Kavi says. "Still, I'm going to keep an eye on you two."

"I think he likes you," Xana giggles.

"Stop!" I demand, trying to stay serious, yet unable to keep the smile off my face. What if he *does* like me? "Get to bed already, would you?" I laugh, pointing to my door.

Everyone files out of my room, and I climb into bed with a sigh. My body aches from training countless hours of the day. Even my jaw hurts from talking too much. I want to punch my pillow as hard as I can, thinking of Luci. Why would she say something like that? Okay, sure, she was agreeing with me, but she didn't have to be mean.

I close my eyes and fall asleep almost instantly.

———

"A teammate refuses orders. What do you do?" the computer asks us.

"Restrain them." I glance at Shirez immediately after I say it, hoping he'll nod or give some inclination that I'm right. But he doesn't. Instead, he remains still, and silent. "I'm not really sure what else we can do," I continue. "If they're not following orders, it would certainly encourage the others to do so as well. And we can't afford mutiny."

"But what if it's a bad order?" Dragon challenges. "We don't want mindless automatons as a team. They need to think for themselves as well. If they refuse orders, maybe they have a good reason for it. We should listen to what they have to say instead of condemning them."

"Okay, well shouldn't they at least try to express their concern discreetly?" I ask.

"The computer never said they didn't."

"But the Masters didn't teach us to question our orders. We carry them out because we know those above us are of higher knowledge–"

"Jaina, stop," Dragon cuts me off. "People can be wrong. No matter who they are. I don't care if it's the Emperor we're talking about. What if he ordered all Imperial Troops into battle and the soldiers knew they couldn't win no matter what they did? Would it be right to sacrifice their lives for nothing?"

How can he think like this? It's just not right. "That wouldn't happen, Dragon."

"But it *could*." His voice is stern, and he touches my hand.

I meet his gaze, and involuntarily pull away. The moment I do, I wish I hadn't.

His cheeks flush red and he looks away. "Sorry."

Warm electricity shoots through me along with a cool apprehension flowing into my veins.

"Your time is up. Have you reached an agreement?" the computer asks.

"Almost. Does that count?" I ask.

"No," he sighs.

"New program found. Do you want to proceed?" it asks.

"Affirmative," Shirez replies. He shoots me an odd look, and I hope it's not because of what just happened. Maybe he didn't even see. "Is this the closest you've gotten to, um..." He clears his throat. "Agreeing?"

"Pretty much," Dragon says.

"Try a few more. Once you do, we can get lunch, so I suggest you hurry. I'm starving."

I let out a breath of relief. My hunger is making me nauseous. "Thank you."

Shirez winks. We complete the next few tests and agree on a few, but it doesn't really feel like an improvement.

"Program found," says the computerized voice. "If another teammate betrays you yet stays with the team, what would you do?"

My stomach shifts. I'm startled by the question, and something about it makes me nervous.

"Could we do anything about it? I mean, once we know that someone has–" I pause, still trying to ignore the queasiness building in my stomach and throat. "That someone has betrayed us...we couldn't possibly trust them anymore. We would have to restrain them or..."

Dragon stares at me. "You all right?"

I nod, trying to ease the nausea that makes my hands quiver. "Well," I breathe. "What would you do?"

He shifts uncomfortably in his chair, and there's a moment of silence. "We'd have no other choice."

"Your time is up. Have you reached an agreement?"

I nod. "Yes."

"State your answer."

"Terminate them." He answers without hesitation.

The two of us sit there for a moment. Thoughts race through my mind. If a teammate did betray me, would I be able to give the ultimate punishment? What if it was Kavi? Or Liam? Or even Dragon?

We're hardly adults. It shouldn't be right for us to decide something like that. I glance at him and can tell he's thinking the same thing.

In the name of the Emperor, I hope we don't have to face something like that.

Dragon's eyes focus on me after he turns off the computer. "Would you really do it?"

The answer is no, but I can't bring myself to say it. Yet he sees the answer in my eyes and he nods.

"Would you?" I ask softly.

He shakes his head. "It's not the way I do things."

"But it's the way the way the Imperials do things." My voice is hardly a whisper.

A dark shadow appears in his crystal-blue eyes, yet he doesn't break his gaze. "Then I guess one of us has to change."

The food in the dining hall is the same. I'm getting used to it. On Virana, they had some vegetarian choices, but Kavi was the only one I knew who actually preferred fruits and veggies to meat.

If it came down to it, I could eat like this every day. Maybe it's the cool air or the extensive training Shirez is putting us through, but I think it's the food that's giving me such a clear mind.

Liam, who's sitting to my right, across from Kavi and Xana says something that makes the two of them burst into laughter.

"You'll be dead by the time the Trials begin," Xana tells him.

His mouth drops open, as if he's surprised by her insult. "You're gravely mistaken. If anyone's going to be dead it'll be *you!*" he cries. "And I can be smart when I want to be!"

Xana rolls her eyes. "You'll probably hit the ground and fall into a sinkhole."

"If that happened, you'd be very sorry you ever made fun of me," he teases. "Just wait and see."

"Stop with your insults," Shirez orders. "Liam is an integral part of the team and just as capable as the rest of you." His voice is calm and casual, almost amused. He clears his throat, and his voice echoes through the dining hall. "I know you're all excited to get to the Trials, but does anyone know the objective?"

Kavi and Xana's laughter slowly fades out along with Liam's constant joking and stupidity.

"I take that as a no," he says. "Every year the Trials are different. Each Trial takes place in a different setting. Can anyone tell me how many Trials there are?"

"Four," Kavi, Seth, and Luci say in synchrony.

"Correct." Shirez puts his elbows on the table and leans forward. "During each Trial, there will be many hardships. Wild animals will hunt you down. Other teams will threaten and maybe capture one of you. On top of that, you have an objective. This year, your objective is to find a crystal."

The room is still.

"A crystal?" I ask.

Shirez nods. "Seems simple enough, doesn't it?"

"Sounds easy," Liam mutters arrogantly.

Shirez glares at him. "It's not. There's one crystal per Trial. Each crystal is hidden somewhere in the arena. When you find it, you'll know what to do."

"Can't you tell us what to do?" Liam asks.

Shirez's eyes are full of a sorrowful blankness I can't describe. "Unfortunately, I don't know. But at least you have some idea as to what you must do once you get into the arena." Shirez picks up his empty tray. "Time for weapons training everyone. We've got a lot of work to do."

I hold the door for my team as they exit the dining hall.

Shirez puts a hand on my shoulder and smiles sadly. "It's almost time for the Trials to begin. I pray you understand your great responsibility to this galaxy."

With that, he continues forward.

Puzzled, I follow him. As team leader, I'm responsible for everything we do. But so is Dragon. I'm not sure my responsibility is to the entire *galaxy*. Maybe Shirez misspoke.

We head back to the training room to practice with new weapons. One of them looks similar to a crossbow but shoots a magnified beam of light at a helpless target. A shiver courses through me, realizing we could be using these against real people. Or someone could use them against us.

"I warn you to be extremely careful with these." Shirez hands each of us a silvery, smooth, cylindrical object. "Do not play with this until I say so."

I examine mine with extreme care, making sure I come nowhere near the activation button. Who knows what this thing can do?

"Now that we're all set, point the top of the object away from you," Shirez instructs.

We all do. Liam presses his finger against the activator and a long, silver blade springs from the handle. He jumps backward. "Whoa!"

"See what I mean?" Shirez grumbles. "Now, let me demonstrate." He activates his own blade. "Call it whatever you want. Scimitar, saber, sword, I couldn't care less." Shirez flips it around, as if he were playing with a toy. His blade glides gracefully through the air.

I glance at Dragon and I swear he rolls his eyes. He's already done this before? Maybe Shirez has taught him everything.

"Unlike the electropistols or lasers we've been working with," Shirez continues, "these require experience and training."

He has us practice with it for what feels like hours. We run through different styles of attack and defense that I didn't even know were possible!

Shirez looks at us and a silence fills the room. "Tomorrow you must be on your way to the first Trial, and a good night of sleep is important. Each of you can choose one scimitar to keep." He gestures to a large table, with around fifty scimitars laid out carefully for the occasion. "When choosing a blade, understand that you do not choose it. It chooses you."

I approach the table with my team and look at the beautiful, intricate designs carved into each hilt. I pick up a few and activate them, wondering what Shirez meant by *it chooses you*. So far, I haven't felt chosen by anything.

Some are heavier than others, and it doesn't take long to realize that each one is different from the next. Like snowflakes. No two are the same.

Among so many blades, a single one catches my eye.

The hilt is decorated with lines and curves like the rest, but they form the faint outline of something, maybe a bird. It's hard to tell since the lines are worn from years of use. I thought these were supposed to be new...

I touch it.

As the metal connects with my skin, I gasp. Energy flows through me like cool water and I never want to put the blade down. Slowly, I lift it from the table. A soft vibration rings within me. I activate the blade and glide it gently through the air. It's smooth and light.

The silvery metal of the blade sparkles in the overhead lights of the room and I'm hypnotized by its beauty. I back away from the table and search for the small compartment on the blade that electrifies it, but there's nothing there.

"Shirez?" I call, not taking my gaze off the blade.

"Yes, Jaina?" Shirez's footsteps become louder as he approaches me and I look at him.

"How does this work? How do I turn it on?"

He only stares at me, like I've uncovered some forbidden secret. Maybe I have.

"*That*, Jaina, is a very old weapon." His voice is soft and knowing, even a little sad. "Its power comes from the one wielding it. It's been passed down throughout the centuries to people like you."

"What do you mean?" I ask. "People like me?"

"That's not important at the moment," he retorts. "But know it's not the most high-tech blade of the lot. Are you sure you wouldn't like to choose another?"

I look at him with my brow furrowed in confusion. "No, it's...it's fine. Can I keep it?"

Shirez smiles, but something about it is sad. "If that is what you wish. It's all yours. Keep it with you at all times. No matter where you are. Now get some rest. You'll need it for tomorrow."

———

I know this place.

I know I'm dreaming, but no matter how hard I try to wake myself, consciousness won't return. I have to escape before it finds me. I'm not sure what it is but I know it's coming.

"Jaina," it calls.

I shiver and run, but the voice is close behind. The shadows fill every open space, until they're an ocean of black before me.

"Jaina," it calls again. "Justice prevails." The voice isn't a voice at all. It's a ghost, a shadow. "Destroy the Dark."

chapter

NINE

Today is the day. We're heading out of the Uncharted Lands to the first Trial.

I stand in front of the full length mirror in my room, pulling my hair back into a French braid. Kavi taught me how to do it a few years ago. I can't do it as well as she can, so a few strands of hair fall out when I finish, but it'll have to do.

There's a jitter in my hands, but I do my best to keep them steady. Excitement surges through me, running wild like waves in a hurricane. My stomach tingles with anticipation.

I finish quickly and walk out the door. Xana's already waiting for me, and Luci makes her way over to us.

"Did I miss anything?" she asks.

"No more than I did," I reply.

She glances at the approaching boys.

"Here comes the circus," Kavi moans. "Get ready for another long and tiring day."

I laugh. If it weren't for the boys, we wouldn't have half the problems we're having on this team.

"What's so funny?" Liam asks, arrogantly.

"None of your business," Xana shoots back.

"Come on, guys," Dragon says. "Enough of this. We've got to get down to the main training room in five minutes."

"He's right. Let's go," I order.

It's strange having people follow my orders. I'm not used to such authority and never fully expected it to be granted.

The last person in our line is Dragon, and I wait for him to pass me like the rest of the team did. Instead of heading out in front of me though, he waits. We lag behind the team in silence. My throat closes in as I rack my brain for something to say. My heart pounds in my ears, and I pretend to take sudden interest in the floor of the hall.

"Are you ready for this?" There's a slight tremor in his voice.

"I think so."

"It's going to be a lot harder than you think."

I raise an eyebrow. "And you know this from experience?"

"It's not only the Trials. If we win, we've still got the Crystal City to worry about."

"If we win, we won't have *anything* to worry about. The Imperial Alliance will take care of us," I whisper.

"Yes. *Very* good care of us." Dragon rolls his eyes then looks away.

"What are you trying to say?" The whole point of going into the Trials is to get to the Crystal City, but it's almost like he doesn't care. Why would he try out?

He glances at me, and our eyes meet. "Nothing. I don't know. Just enjoy this while you can. It might be the most we have."

"Dragon...are you all right?"

"Yeah. I'm fine," he murmurs. He averts his eyes to the ground, and his jaw tightens ever so slightly. "Sorry."

My heart aches, knowing his pain, and I so badly want to reach out and touch him on the arm. Something's bothering him, hurting him. I wish I could ask him what's wrong. I wish he'd tell me things like he did before. But I refrain. The strength doesn't exist within my shy soul to ask him. Sure, I can fight three warriors and still come out on top, but the battle of our friendship is one I'm afraid I can't win.

We reach the training room behind our team.

Shirez greets us then begins the lecture. "Now pay attention. The rules of the Trials are very strict and the punishment for violating these rules is severe. Rule number one: bring as many weapons into the arena as you can carry. Two: don't leave the marked boundaries of the Arena. They're almost impossible to escape anyway, but if you do leave the boundary, you will be disqualified and punished accordingly. Three: you may take prisoners. Four: fatalities will occur, but terminating another contestant isn't encouraged. Five: please don't die."

Despite the seriousness, we laugh.

Shirez isn't quite as giddy. He's frowning, and the worry in his bluish-grey eyes is so clear, I'd have to be blind to miss it. He continues. "The first Trial will take place in Kaskada, a province once known as Russia. Remember, no one is watching you. The IA can't see or hear you. You will be completely cut off from the outside world. The only way you'll get out of the arena is to follow the flashing light that signals a checkpoint. Once your fingerprint is scanned, you'll be confirmed as winners and you may leave. But before then, your team is all you have, so stick together.

"We'll transport weapons to the first of four Trials. You'll be able to choose the weapons you wish to carry into the arena from there. Is everyone ready?"

A sly grin grows on Liam's face. "If I said no, would it matter?"

Shirez rolls his eyes. "No, it wouldn't."

Shirez leads us to the cockpit then to the passenger hold. Here we can rest for a few hours before we arrive. I take a seat between Kavi and Seth and immediately regret the decision.

As if on cue, Shirez walks in and shakes his head. "What do you think you're doing? Sit in your groups."

"Shirez, please–" Kavi moans.

"No. You must sit in your groups. Dragon, Jaina, take the middle seats. The rest of you, form around them," he orders.

Once we're all situated in our "correct" seating order, he finally leaves and heads toward the cockpit of the ship.

The floor of the transport vibrates as we lift off. The surface of the Uncharted Lands grows farther away.

The sky is dark with storm clouds. The wind whips across the desolate landscape. As we rise higher into the atmosphere, the land disappears behind the clouds.

I'm about to look to my left until I remember Dragon is next to me. *Do not fall asleep this time!* As if the first time wasn't embarrassing enough...

Of course I have to sit with him. It shouldn't be a surprise. We were both the best in class but why can't I talk to him? It's not like I like him, yet it doesn't explain why my lungs contract and my throat wants to collapse in on itself whenever I speak to him.

He used to be my best friend. Nothing should feel wrong about talking to him. Is it because of his light, sun-warmed skin, steely blue eyes, and a body any girl would die for? I laugh at myself with the thought and try to forget it. It *might* have something to do with it.

Just looking at him makes me tingle with excitement.

Behind his façade of power, calm, and control, something is tearing him apart. I see it surface now and then in his eyes. A spark of pain shattering their clarity like shards of broken glass.

If only I knew what torments him. I wish I could say something to him. Ask him what's wrong. Comfort him. The moment seems right. Everyone else is busy in conversation, except for the two of us. Maybe he's waiting for me to say something. I face him and take a deep breath.

His hard cheekbones and dark hair look orange in the early morning sunlight. I wonder what it would feel like to run my fingers through his hair or to be held in his embrace.

Shaav, what's wrong with me? I should slap myself for thinking that.

"Jaina, do you think I'm cute?" Liam cuts in.

"What?" I squeak. My cheeks flush with warmth.

"Do you think I'm cute? As in good looking?" He's got that cocky smile on his face and it makes me want to smack him.

"Um..." I glance at Xana, who's sitting next to Liam. She shakes her head. Is he trying to impress her, or me? "No...?"

Xana smiles triumphantly, as Liam turns back to face her. "See? Told you."

"Okay wait." Liam pushes his hand out toward her, like he's telling her to put on the breaks. "What do you consider cute?"

She crosses her arms over her chest. "Funny, nice, tough, smart and let's add 'handsome' to that."

"Okay. Jaina," he turns to me. "Am I funny?"

I'm trying to keep the smile off my face but fail miserably. "Yes."

He nods appreciatively. "Good. Am I nice?"

This "game" he's set up is proving to be tiring. "Are you talking about now, or before? Because before you weren't–"

"I'm talking about now, of course," he replies through his teeth.

I shrug. If telling the truth about him would do me any good, I'd be more than happy to warn Xana about him. But maybe he'll be distracted by her for a while. "Yeah, you're sort of nice, now."

"Thank you! Am I tough?"

"I guess..." He couldn't have made it into the Trials if he wasn't the slightest bit tough. I'll give him credit for that.

He grins. "Am I handsome?"

Dragon turns to us, and I can feel him watching me. What's the safest response I can come up with?

I hesitate. "Depends on what you mean by that. I used to think so."

Liam nods. "All right, I can handle that. Am I smart?"

I sigh. What, exactly, does he want me to say? I could lie for him if it gets him and Xana together. That way he wouldn't bother me. But, should I lie about it? I clear my throat. "Um..."

Xana giggles.

"Jaina, am I smart? I need you to answer." Liam's trying to conceal his smile, but he's not doing a good job of it.

"Let's put it this way," I begin. "You're not the brightest bulb of the bunch."

Xana bursts out in laughter.

Liam smiles wryly. "See? I'm almost a perfect match!"

She continues laughing but manages to get out, "Yeah, everything but smart!"

He raises his hands, spreading his fingers like he's holding a nevya ball, about to shoot for the winning point. "Okay, that's *one* thing. And I won't deny that I'm not very sharp, but I might surprise you once in a while," he persists.

"Well, in my book, being smart is about the most important quality a man or woman could have," she says.

"Yeah but–"

"Listen." She cuts him off. "I'm not really interested in you at the moment."

He raises an eyebrow and shoots her a seductive smile. "Does that mean I have a chance in the future?"

"Oh, shut up!" Xana giggles and I join in the laughter.

"All right fine. But I'm not giving up on you yet," Liam says.

"And how many other girls have you said that to, recently?" Xana asks.

His face flushes a shade redder, but he laughs. I smile but don't look at him. The poor guy feels embarrassed enough already. I wonder if he's really into her, or if it's to make me jealous. Either way, it's not working. I glance out the window. Time passes as if it were all a dream.

The transport lands on the roof of a tall building in Kaskada's capital city. The sky is dark, but the city lights outshine the stars. I'm too tired to think, or notice my surroundings. Tomorrow is the first Trial but I hardly care at the moment.

Shirez leads us through the halls of the building and we stop at a large white door. "This is your room for tonight," he says.

"There's only one?" I ask.

He opens the door. "Go in and take a look."

We move into the large, circular room with a spectacular view of the city. There are ten doors, five on each side of the room. Two of the rooms are bathrooms and the rest are individual bedrooms for each team member. There's a kitchen here, too. In the center of the room there's a crystal coffee table and three white, plush couches.

"So, you're all set?" Shirez asks.

Dragon nods. "I think we'll be fine."

"All right. I'll pick you up here in the morning and take you to the arena. Rest well." Shirez leaves our room and closes the door softly behind him.

Despite Shirez's words, the night is long, and sleepless. The hours pass in a slow, rhythmic succession, slower than it would take a slug to move a mile. Yet when morning finally comes, it's as if I'd raced through the entire night, and all I want is for it to be dark again.

Shirez comes.

None of us speak.

We reach the drop ship and climb aboard. It doesn't feel much bigger than the last one, but it's mostly because of the rows and rows of weapons, held in place by the large racks.

"You made all of these?" I ask Shirez.

"No." Shirez laughs, crossing his arms over his chest. "But I designed quite a few with the help of some friends." He glances at Dragon, then looks back at me.

"Choose the ones you like," he orders, turning to face the whole team.

We move through the short aisles of guns, swords, daggers, snipers, throwing stars, spears, and crossbows in awe. I pick up five MED's, the electrified throwing knives we trained with last week, and attach them to my holster belt. A stun pistol finds its way into my hands as well as a large silver dagger I simply can't resist.

"Jaina," Shirez calls. "This is for you and your team. Each of you gets one. I made them especially for this year." He gently places a white gauntlet in my hand.

It fits snugly over my hand and forearm. It's thin and stretches to about my elbow. There are so many buttons and compartments on it I'm not sure I'll have time to figure them out.

Shirez approaches me after handing out seven more, one to each teammate. "Altair, show them."

Dragon steps forward. "You might want to watch out," he says to me. He aims his gauntlet at a target on the wall. I back away.

A bright burst of energy and blue light flashes across the room. The target is now a pile of ashes.

"Whoa, what was that?" I ask.

"It's a plasma bolt," Liam replies.

Shirez nods. "I don't have much more time to show you everything it can do. Just experiment with it, and I'm sure you'll figure it out. Now, strap on your armor. We're approaching the arena."

It's a hassle to choose a suit because there are so many and they're all similar in color. The one I finally settle on is black splattered with silver. I take off my holster belt, then pull the armor over my tight undergarments. A plate fits over my biceps and shoulders and another over my chest. The remaining few pieces I fit over my shins and thighs.

It's not as heavy as I expect and I can only hope it's thick enough to block a plasma bolt. The single area left unprotected is my stomach. Maybe that's for a reason. So an enemy has a definitive weak point.

We hardly have any time left with Shirez. And though he says this first Trial shouldn't be too challenging, every moment to come is a moment we could be killed.

"Remember," Shirez begins, "find the crystal, then get the *shaav* out."

I swallow hard.

Shirez turns to Dragon and looks at him intensely. The two seem to have a private conversation through their eyes. Finally, Shirez says, "Anything you want to say to your team?"

Dragon breaks Shirez's gaze and steps forward. "This is it, everyone, the moment we've been waiting for since our training began. No matter what happens down there, we'll stick together. We'll overcome every challenge these Trials have to offer. Understood?"

By the way he says it, I know it's not a question.

We nod.

The ship slows dramatically and though I can't see out the windows, I can tell we're descending. *Almost there*.

My ears start popping. I do my best to ignore the dropping sensation in my stomach. Every little bump sends my mind racing, praying to the stars we'll be okay.

We come to a stop. My heart nearly does the same. The sound of machinery whirrs in my ears. Light floods the cargo hold. Turning to face the landscape beneath us, all I see is white.

Frigid air fills my lungs, and I gasp as it freezes my lips. Soft, white specks float down from the grey clouds overhead. Snow?

I've never seen snow before, except at a distance in the Uncharted Lands. Here, it falls from the sky like rain.

Shirez's lips are tightly pressed together. His body looks as stiff and cold as the air feels on my skin. Does he think we'll be able to make it out of this?

I glance at Dragon.

He meets my gaze. "You ready for this?"

"What's the worst that could happen?"

Dragon only smiles.

The transport doesn't fully land but is suspended about a meter from the ground. Liam and Xana throw themselves off and fall lightly on the soft, sturdy ground. Seth, Kavi, and Luci all jump next, then Avan.

"After you, Jaina," Dragon urges.

Forcing myself off the ship, I land next to Xana who's holding a repeating plasma gun aimed at nonexistent targets in the forest, making sure the coast is clear. Dragon lands next to me.

I turn back and look up at Shirez. The drop ship rises meter by meter, and the noise of the engine makes everything inaudible. We watch as the transport ascends into the sky and is finally absorbed by the clouds.

It's all up to us now.

chapter

TEN

Dragon leads the way, and I stay close behind him. At least he acts like he knows where he's going, and for some reason that makes a difference. The wind is raw and severe, whipping across the frozen landscape. The icy air stabs at my lungs and tears at my throat. I want to stop already, but force myself to push on through the thin, dry air.

I can't stop shivering. My teeth hurt from chattering. I have no idea how long we've been walking, but it feels like hours.

Dead trees surround us. There's no steady rhythm to this world and it's unsettling.

It's been hard to keep my mouth shut. Hard not to complain. But as team leader, I have to set the example and accept the situation. I should be glad nothing has attacked us yet.

Dragon's a few steps ahead of me. His dark hair is dotted with white, sparkling snowflakes, and it's hard to deny how handsome he is.

"Dragon," I say, catching up to him.

He turns his head to me, yet his eyes are still distant.

"Do you think we should look for a place to stop? I'm not sure how much longer we can take this." A shiver shoots through me and I scrunch up my shoulders, bracing myself for another chilling onslaught of wind.

"Sounds like a plan," he replies. "I haven't seen a place we could stop though."

The land is flat. Now that I think about it, there hasn't been a single hill or cave in sight. There's not the slightest indication of a change in altitude around.

I'm so cold.

I swallow hard, trying to ignore the sudden desire to stand next to Dragon and feel his warmth.

"Do you have any idea where the other teams might be?" I ask, just trying to keep the conversation going.

"Not any more than you do." He keeps his eyes down as he trudges forward through the snow.

"*Na'lav*, it's cold," I mutter.

"No kidding."

He's shivering, too. A cloud of mist escapes his mouth and I wonder if I would melt in the heat of his lips if I could touch them.

In the name of the galaxy! What the *shaav* is wrong with me?

"Hey, guys," Dragon announces, pulling me out of my thoughts. "Keep an eye out for a place to stop. If you see something, let us know."

"Yes, sir," Seth responds mechanically.

"I don't know about you, but I'm dying for some action." I shift my attention forward, trying to end the awkward moment I've created in my head. I wonder what he'd say if he knew the things I thought about him. He'd be creeped out, I'm sure.

"Careful what you wish for," Dragon says. A smile brushes his lips. "But I feel the same way. Anything to take my mind off this cold."

I try to think of something else to say that wouldn't embarrass me, but Xana's voice cuts me off.

"I can't believe you, Liam."

"I'm not asking you to believe me," Liam argues, his voice sounding whinier than ever.

I take a deep breath, struggling to control my frustration. They've been bickering on and off for the past who knows how many hours.

"You want to go back there and make sure they don't kill each other, or should I?" Dragon asks.

"I'd be glad to lead for a while; maybe you can sort out their problems." I'm not in the mood for Liam right now.

Dragon takes in the forest around us, making sure the coast is clear then looks at me. "Sure, sounds good. Keep an eye out for predators."

I nod, and he falls to the back of the line with Xana and Liam.

The sound of footsteps breaking through the powdery snow fills my ears and Kavi moves to stand next to me. "Jaina," Kavi whispers. "Do you know where we're going?"

I shrug. "No idea. But then again, we're not really supposed to."

She shivers. "I'm freezing."

"I know, I'm dying up here," I say.

She laughs, but it comes out more choked and half-hearted. "I thought that they'd give us a climate we're used to."

I scoff. "Apparently not. Either that or we're just extremely unprepared."

"Shirez said this Trial shouldn't be too much of a problem."

I smirk. "Speaking of problems, how's it going with Seth?"

"Problems indeed," she mutters with a cringe. "We've had a *few* civil conversations."

"That's an improvement. Do you mind giving me details?" I ask, ignoring the frigid wind eating away at my neck and hair.

"That's none of your business!" she cries.

Coming from the person who'd tell me everything, I can't help but be surprised. "Anything that goes on in this team is my business. I'm the *leader*, remember?"

Kavi looks down at the white ground. "Yeah, I wonder how that happened."

I glare at her.

"Fine." She adjusts her holster belt, fitting it tighter around her waist. "We talked about Virana and school."

She's got that suspicious look on her face.

"Kavi?" I say expectantly. "Finish, please."

She furrows her brow. "Who said I wasn't finished?"

"Your tone of voice suggested it, and so did your expression. Now hurry up, get on with it. I'm still your best friend!"

She sneers. "I thought *Dragon* was your new best friend."

The words sting. I'm not used to her being so defensive. Why is she holding back so much? "Dragon isn't my *best friend.* He's...he's an old friend." It's not entirely true, but it's the best answer I can come up with.

She sighs in defeat. "Well, you act like it. But Seth..."

"He what? Did he try to kiss you or something?" What would a kiss feel like? I don't allow myself to continue the thought, too afraid of where it might lead.

"No, Jaina, it's not that. He just–" She runs her fingers through her straightened black hair. "What he said was complicated. So I told him that I don't want to talk to him. Although, I may have said it worse than that...a *lot* worse than that."

"What the hell did he do?" I struggle to keep my voice down. "Why would you say something like that?"

She narrows her eyes and scoffs. "It's not like I can help it!"

I bring my hands to my face and rub the exhaustion from my eyes. When I look up, her black, almond-shaped eyes are studying me.

Kavi sighs. "He got mad and hasn't talked to me since yesterday."

Shaav, this is bad. I brush the snow from my hair, trying to think of a solution. "Kavi, you're supposed to be getting along with him! How are we supposed to fight enemies outside of our team if you've got enemies inside? It can't work this way."

"I'm sorry but I can't get along with him! I can't stand working with him! He's so..."

"So *what*? He's only trying to get your attention. He's nice," I insist.

"I just don't know how–"

"Look. One of you has to change, and fast. If you're not willing to risk your life to save a teammate, and I mean *any* teammate, we might as well all give up now." My voice is cold and flat. I don't relent.

She stares back at me, her eyes serious as death. With a sly rise of her eyebrow, she asks, "Even Liam?"

I roll my eyes, but the smile I try to hide forces itself onto my lips. "Unfortunately."

"Fine. I'll see what I can do." She scrunches up her nose like there's a foul smell in the air and tilts her head as she studies the ground. "You know, don't take this the wrong way, but I've never seen you this strict."

Without thinking, I snap, "I picked it up from you."

"Me? I'm not strict." She acts oblivious to my annoyance.

"You might be surprised."

Her lips widen into a cunning grin. "I think you got it from Dragon. Are you trying to impress him?"

"Of-of course not!" I burst out. "I'm only doing my job. If you ask me, I'd rather *not* be like him." If only Kavi knew the things he's said...I'm surprised he hasn't been executed for being so rebellious. It's a wonder we used to be so close. Yeah. *Used to be.*

Kavi looks somewhere off in the distance, her expression blank, numb to emotion. "Well, I better get to *making up* with Seth."

"Good luck."

She nods and heads back to her position in line.

Used to be. The thought returns. What are we now? Are we still friends?

Our surroundings look exactly the same in every direction. It's *all* the same. The only thing separating this moment from the next is that I'm colder with each passing second in this forsaken landscape.

Something tingles at my back. I brush the snow off my neck, hoping the cool, anxious sensation fades. The stress from being in the arena must be getting to me.

Turning my head, I glance back at Dragon. He stands next to Liam, making quiet conversation in the mind numbing wind. Things are so different now. I'm surprised he remembers me at all.

My legs stop. *What's wrong with you, Jaina?* My eyes scan the area with such concentrated intensity that it makes me worry. The senses in my body begin to kick into gear, the way they do when I'm in trouble, or in a duel. The way they did when Roshiva Korr locked me in a dark closet.

There's nothing. *Nothing* in sight.

I keep moving, but that strange feeling doesn't go away. Like we're being watched.

All we have to do is find a crystal. How hard can that be? If we win all four Trials, everything will be taken care of. In the Crystal City, I won't have to worry about boys, or what job I'd qualify for. The IA determines it all, based on DNA, personality, qualities, and all. If only we could–

The back of my neck prickles with agitation. I whip around, frustrated. Once again, nothing. *Na'lav,* what's wrong with me? Luci gives me an annoyed glance so I face forward. I'm going crazy.

Something moves out of the corner of my eye. Without hesitation, I pull out my pistol and fire into the trees. I stop dead and only then feel the raw fear burning through me.

I face my team. "Did you see that?"

All fourteen of their wide eyes stare back at me with a mixture of fear and surprise like I'm wanted for murder.

Liam furrows his brow and touches the gun on his holster belt. "See what?"

I know I saw something. It couldn't have been my imagination. Snow flutters to the ground to the right. I lift my weapon ready to fire. There's movement to my left, but all is silent.

My eyes flick to Dragon. "Please tell me you saw that."

He swallows hard and pulls out his scimitar. "Yeah, I saw it."

Something jumps behind me and I turn, ready to shoot.

"What the *shaav* was that?" Xana asks.

None of us have an answer. The world is silent except for the occasional jump. A screech sounds to the right, and I do my best to aim at the source. There's nothing.

"Jaina, look out!" Dragon snatches my wrist, and yanks me backward, but he's too late.

Searing pain shoots up my my arm. There's another screech as Dragon's scimitar flashes in front of me.

I'm lying in the snow. Pain radiates from my arm which has become considerably heavy as I try to sit up. I can't move it.

My eyes glance down at my forearm. It's frozen. Frozen solid in a chunk of ice spanning from my fingertips to my elbow. Nausea claws its way up my stomach into my throat, so I look away.

Dragon kneels down next to me and puts a hand on my shoulder. "Jaina, you're going to be okay."

I grit my teeth. "I better be. Can someone please defrost me now? It's starting to go numb." Attempting to wiggle my fingers and melt some of the ice, an intense, claustrophobic sensation takes over. What if I can't get free?

Avan sits next to me and pulls out a small, pen-sized torch from a compartment in his gauntlet. "This is really the best I've got. Unless you want me to use the flame thrower."

"Let's go with the torch," I say quickly.

"That's what I thought." He turns it on and keeps the flame a few centimeters from the ice.

It melts away quickly, but my arm remains numb. All I feel is cold. When I try moving my fingers, no sensation or warmth pricks them to life.

"What was that thing?" I ask, massaging blood back into my fingers.

Avan shrugs. "I don't know, but it took off pretty fast."

"*Na'lav*," Dragon mutters. He looks around, his eyes surveying the area. "I think it's a dirin."

"And how the *shaav* would you know?" Liam snaps.

"I took a galactic biology class on Manincia," Dragon replies. "I went to school there for a while after I left Virana."

"What's a dirin?" Avan asks.

Dragon runs his fingers through his hair and shifts his gaze down onto the snow. "They're furry little guys who live under the snow or ice. They come up to the surface to hunt, and they kill their prey by freezing it to death with their...with their spit."

"This doesn't make sense," Luci mutters.

"I know," Dragon replies.

Liam moans in annoyance. "What now?"

"Dirin hunt in groups to take down larger prey such as humans," Dragon says. "So unless it was lost, its pack shouldn't be far away."

"How much damage can they do?" Avan asks.

"One shot could freeze up both of your legs. And if that's the case, it's over."

Luci helps me up. "We should get out of here before the rest of them arrive."

A piercing screech shatters the serene winter landscape.

"Let's move," Dragon orders.

Struggling to rub life into my arm, I stand next to him, keeping my pistol ready.

"How's your arm?" Dragon asks.

"Okay, I guess." I hold it up for him to see.

"Does it hurt?"

"Too cold to hurt. If I could feel it then I'm sure it would." I laugh.

He smiles, but his intense blue eyes recognize my discomfort. "I wish we had something to wrap it up with. No one thought to bring a bandage. I guess we'll have to grab some for the next Trial."

"If we make it to the next Trial," I point out.

"We will. Trust me."

I meet his unrelenting gaze with a casual smile, pretending to ignore that look on his face. He's tense, and yet partially relaxed. Like he knows every step we're going to take, and afraid of what's to come.

"Hey, hey, hey," Seth whispers urgently, tapping my shoulder. He puts his index finger to his lips and warns us with a glare.

Dragon and I look at him. Seth glances to the left. A two meter long ball of snow lies motionless among the trees. The longer I stare at it, the more I realize the white object is not in fact snow, but fur. It drowsily breathes in and out and I recognize the shape. Much like the small dirin we saw before, only two times larger.

I glance at Dragon as if to ask "now what."

"We have to keep moving," he mouths and jerks his head forward.

Slowly, I step into the soft, new fallen snow, hoping that I don't make enough sound to wake the beast. *In the name of the galaxy, let me get out of here alive.* Something snaps. I whip around so quickly it makes me dizzy. My eyes fix on Liam and I glare at him.

"Sorry." His voice is barely audible.

Shifting forward, I glance at the beast. Only, it's not there.

I tap Dragon hard on the shoulder to get his attention, but he doesn't budge. After following his gaze, I wish I hadn't.

No more than three meters away waits the adult dirin. Its golden eyes sink into me, and its silvery teeth beg for violence. A low-pitched growl sends a wave of tremors down my spine.

Another five linger behind it, and approach with patience.

A new type of ice freezes me solid, one colder than what the dirin can spit at me. It's the icy grip of fear.

"Don't make any sudden move," Dragon whispers.

A gunshot sounds. I recoil. Xana's bolt completely misses the dirin and falls into the snow at its feet. The dirin screeches and springs into the air at us. The other five burrow into the snow.

"Take out your scimitars!" Dragon calls. "If they fire at you, try to block the shot with your sword."

I keep my pistol ready as I extract my scimitar. Three of the dirin fly out of the snow with surprising speed. They shriek with blood-chilling hunger before disappearing once more.

All is quiet. This can't be a good sign. I try not to think. *Use what you've learned.* No fear. Just calm. I hardly have time to see the crest rising near my feet and hear the crackling of ice before I'm falling to the ground. An unbelievable pressure builds on my chest. Claws dig into my arms and draw blood. I realize I'm screaming, and calling for help. No one comes. The attack has begun. Dragon and the rest of my team have been engaged.

The dirin's toothy jaws snap directly above my face. Its dog-like body is surprisingly heavy for its size. Claws tug at my arms and I cry out with pain and fear. The dirin looks me in the eye, its icy breath falling across my face. I pull my arms free of its blood-coated claws. It opens its mouth and snarls, frantically aiming for my face. The moment it fires, I jerk to the right. The ball of icy saliva hits the ground beside me.

It screams in rage, yet doesn't make any move to get off me. The dirin shoots several times. One shot skims my cheek and freezes a bit of my hair. Unable to hold the dirin's hungry jaws and double rows of teeth away much longer, I search frantically with my free hand in the snow for the hilt of my scimitar. The dirin's jaws nip at the air and its scruffy whiskers scrape my cheek.

Come on, where is it!

My hand touches something hard and cold. The dirin's muscular body is too strong for me to push away any longer and the hand holding it back is cramping.

I clamp my fingers around the hilt of my scimitar and activate it, thrusting the blade into the dirin's throat. It writhes in pain and struggles to breathe through the bloody gash in its neck, the dirin finally falls still.

I sigh and push the dirin's lifeless body off me. The fight isn't over yet.

Deciding close combat isn't such a great idea with these things, I pull out my pistol and target the dirin tormenting Kavi and Liam. The plasma hits the dirin in the leg, but I can tell my gun isn't working right. The reaction time is slow.

Seth fires a shot near me and a dirin lies dead at my side. A searing piece of fur releases a small cloud of smoke as the plasma dissolves into its body.

Dragon fights furiously with one of the beasts nearby. Another lurks behind him, holding back. He slashes at the first one and skims the dirin's chest. It screeches in pain while the second readies itself to fire.

"Dragon, behind you!" But there's nothing he can do. I charge toward him as the icy bolt leaves the dirin's throat.

With a forceful blow, I ram myself into him, knocking the two of us into the powdery snow. The dirin in front of us is now a ball of solid ice and the other retreats into the forest with the rest of their remaining brethren.

Dragon's strong, muscular chest beneath me is smooth and warm as my body presses into his. His hand is clasped around my uninjured arm, like he'd never in a million years let me go. I shoot upward, finding my feet faster than I ever have and reach down to help him up. He takes my hand.

"Sorry," I say, my voice trembling.

His hand lingers an extra moment on my own before he lets go. "Don't apologize for saving my life." He laughs breathlessly, his eyes wide.

My team comes alive before me, stunned and still shaking from the battle.

"That was crazy," Avan pants.

I try to catch my breath, but there isn't enough air in the world to fulfill me.

"Come on man, that was nothing," Liam replies.

Seth rolls his eyes. "Yeah, because you stayed at the back of the group the entire time."

"Let's get out of here before they return," I say. "We'll find a place to camp for the night and then continue walking in the morning."

Everyone nods and starts walking. Luci takes the lead and Dragon and I hang back.

He glances at my arm and I suddenly remember. I try to stop myself from looking, knowing it'll make me feel queasy, but I look anyway. The gash on my forearm stings with heat as deep, red liquid oozes from the wound. My blood soaked sleeve makes it look a lot worse than it actually is, but my stomach knots, threatening to discard its contents.

His brows furrow in concern and he touches my arm. "You're hurt."

I wish my hands would stop trembling, and I'm no longer sure if it's because of the adrenaline, the cold, or him. "It's okay. I'm fine. Really."

"I can't tell how bad it is, but I think it should be bandaged. How do you feel?"

"All right, I guess. I don't like the way it looks, though." I feel the color drain from my face. If Dragon is worried about it...maybe I should be, too. "I thought you said we didn't have any bandages."

"Hold on." He stops me and closes his fingers around the bottom portion of his shirt and tears off a long strip of cloth with some effort.

My gaze falters to the ground as my neck burns hot with embarrassment. "You didn't have to do that."

He tilts his head to the side dismissively then returns his deep, blue eyes to me. His lips gently crease into a smile. "It's fine." He laughs. "I've got another shirt on under this. Now I'm not exactly a pro at this, but it should help."

My skin warms with his soft, soothing touch, and I wonder what he looks like under his second shirt. My thoughts dissolve as he pulls back my sleeve from the bloody gash.

"This might hurt a little." Carefully he wraps the bandage several times, then pulls the knot tight.

I grit my teeth as stinging pain shoots down to my fingertips, and I suck in a deep breath.

"Sorry." He pulls it a little tighter. "You okay?"

I nod, only because I don't have the strength to answer in words. He's close to me. Very close. His soft blue eyes stare into mine, unflinching.

My cheeks burn, despite the cold. "Thanks."

He turns away, blushing, too. "You're welcome."

chapter

ELEVEN

The cave Luci found is more like a small den in the cliff face. It keeps out the wind and snow, but the winter air remains crisp. Seth's fire keeps us from freezing to death, but it doesn't stop the cold from coming in. The smoke exits out a large hole in the ceiling, and we can only hope the other teams aren't close enough to spot us. It's crowded in the small space, but it'll have to do.

I'm still confused about what happened between Dragon and me earlier. He touched me. He cut off my circulation a little bit, but he *touched* me. I'm not hurt that badly; I could have gone without a bandage, and yet he wanted to help me. And he blushed!

I smile, stifling a giggle. Since when does Dragon blush?

"What's so funny?" Kavi asks. She's been sitting next to me on the cold stone floor for the past ten minutes. She pretends to be observing the entire team, but I know she's had her eye on Seth.

"Nothing," I say secretively.

"Liam, why do you care?" Xana exclaims.

I look up at the two of them, sitting across from each other near the fire. Liam holds his plasma rifle across his lap as he cleans it with a cloth. Xana leans forward aggressively, and Liam angrily scooches away from her.

"I can't concentrate when you're humming like that!" he snaps.

Xana moves closer to him. "I can sing whatever I want!"

"By the stars, you're so annoying! Get away from me!" he cries.

Kavi turns to me and raises her right eyebrow.

Rather than stop them myself, I'd like to see if they ever stop on their own. I don't get up.

"How do you like the cave?" Kavi asks sarcastically, rubbing her hands together to keep warm.

"It's better than nothing, but I might freeze to death, anyway."

Kavi glances at my injured arm. "Hey, who gave you the bandage?"

Shaav, I knew she was going to ask. It surprises me she didn't notice before, and I was hoping her interest in whatever Seth was doing would make her forget. Guess I was wrong.

"Dragon," I breathe.

A wry smile grows on her lips. "Oh really? How sweet of him." She nudges me in my injured shoulder.

"Ouch," I murmur, pretending not to be embarrassed.

"Oh, stop it." She rolls her eyes, grinning. "Maybe if you snuggle up to him by the fire you'll be nice and cozy."

"Kavi!" I cry, putting my hands on her shoulder and pushing her over. My eyes frantically scan the room to make sure no one was close enough to hear that.

Kavi shakes her head, laughing. "Sorry. Is Liam jealous yet?"

He's still arguing with Xana about her singing.

I sigh. "Not that I know of."

She waves her hand in annoyance. "You can never be sure with him."

Avan and Luci try desperately to end Liam and Xana's little fiasco, but the two are inseparable. Luci grabs Liam's shirt and pushes him backward to prevent him from throwing a punch at Xana, who's shouting so loud I'm afraid it might attract attention from another team.

Dragon sits placidly nearby, leaning against the cave wall, watching them, but not bothering to move. What the *shaav*?

I turn to Kavi. "Looks like I've got to intervene."

She smiles weakly. "Good luck."

"Shut your mouth," Liam barks. "Your whiny voice is giving me a headache!"

"Stop being a baby and toughen up," Xana hisses in reply as Avan holds her back.

"Stop it!" Luci cries.

There's a desperate look on Avan's face. "This is pointless!"

Running my fingers through my hair, I step between them and shout, "Would you two shut up!"

Xana and Liam both turn to me.

"Jaina," Liam begins, his voice kind and pleading. "Could you please tell her to stop bugging me?"

"Xana, stop bugging him," I grumble.

Her eyes widen in defense. "I didn't–"

I hold up my index finger in front of her, stopping her from continuing. "Now someone needs to get more firewood. And it's going to be one of you because you're the one's arguing."

"Kavi and Seth argue," Liam protests. "Why can't they go?"

"I don't argue with Seth!" Kavi retorts, flinging her arms to her sides in defiance.

Liam raises an eyebrow. "Um, yeah, you do."

I roll my eyes. "I don't care! Liam and Avan, go."

"What! Why us?" Liam asks. "Is it because of me?"

"It's because you need to be taught a lesson!" I say. "I'm sorry, Avan, but I don't trust him going by himself and I can't afford sending Xana with him or she might drag him back, *dead*."

Avan complies. "I can handle it. As long as they stop, I don't really care."

"Thank you."

Avan grabs Liam's arm. "Come on, man, let's go."

"*Shaav* you, Xana," Liam curses, resisting Avan's guidance. "You'll pay for this."

Avan takes Liam outside. Finally, they're gone.

"Thanks, Jaina," Xana says.

I turn to her. "Nice try. Check the perimeter. We can't have any teams following us."

"Yes, ma'am," Xana mutters. "You can be a real *katiaj* sometimes."

My mouth drops open. "I'm *sorry*? What did you call me?"

"I said you can be a real *katiaj*. I don't take it back, either. You think just because you're team leader you're more important than everyone else."

I stare back at her, trying to contain my anger. "You think it's easy being team leader? You think it's easy trying to keep everyone together? You want to take responsibility for every little mistake the team makes? Because if our team fails the Trials, it won't be you or Liam or Kavi or Seth who will be most severely punished for it. Dragon and I will take responsibility for your mistakes. You think you can handle that?"

Xana puts her hands on her hips. "You're damn right I could handle it. You're just lucky I don't want to switch teams."

Rage surges through my veins, and I lunge toward her.

A hand grabs my arm, stopping me in my tracks.

"Don't." Dragon's voice is soft and stern at the same time. "It won't solve any problems." He glances at Xana then says, "Go. I believe you have an order to carry out."

She takes a moment, contemplating his order, then obediently climbs out of the cavern. Why do people listen to him more than they listen to me? Don't I have enough authority? Maybe I've got to step it up.

He sighs, loosening his grip on me. "I have to admire your way of keeping the troops in check, but I'm not sure that was all true."

"Sorry. I just couldn't let her go on like that," I moan.

"Usually it's the team leaders who are most rewarded if their team wins," he says.

"If we lose, they won't execute us...right?"

"Nah. Not unless you personally commit treason or something," he says. "Reconstruction Camps are about the worst they can do."

Avan charges back into the cave, his breath quick and despite the cold, his brow is wet with perspiration. He smiles through his panting and chokes out a breathy laugh.

I lean in toward Avan as he puts his hands on his knees, which are considerably scrawny even under his armor. "What?" I ask.

"Liam's..." he gasps. "He's...a little tied up."

Dragon studies Avan with questioning eyes. "What do you mean?"

"You've just gotta come with me," Avan replies.

Avan, Dragon and I walk outside a little ways from the cave. Someone calls for help not too far away, and I start to worry.

"Is that...Liam?" I ask.

Avan smirks wryly, but says nothing.

Pretty soon we reach a clearing.

"Jaina!" Liam calls.

Following the sound, my eyes shoot a meter upward and find him hanging in a net above me. I jump back.

"Liam, what the *shaav* are you doing?" I ask, holding back a laugh.

His arms are stuck behind his back, probably trapped in one of the ropes of the net. He sighs in distress. "Can you get me out first? It's not exactly comfortable up here."

"I kind of want to know what happened," I say, hoping he'll recognize this as punishment for tormenting Xana, and me, during the short period of time I actually liked him.

"I can explain," Avan interjects.

"No it's all right, I'd rather say so myself once I get down," Liam snaps at him.

"No, it's okay. I think my version will be better anyway," Avan says then turns to me. "Dragon, Seth and I were out checking the perimeter a few hours ago, when we found this old tattered net. So we decided to set a trap."

Liam rolls his eyes. "Wrap it up, Avan, I'm dying here. I'm still confused as to why you didn't tell me the net was here before I stepped into it!"

"Dude, I thought you saw it!" Avan says, unable to keep from laughing.

"If I had seen it, wouldn't I have tried to *avoid* it?" Liam retorts. "Now can someone be a decent human being and get me outta here?"

"Do we have to let him out?" Dragon complains.

"Unfortunately," I mutter. "Liam, this should teach you not to bother your teammates so much."

"All right, okay, just get me down!" Liam begs like a whiny kid in a holo-game store.

"Will you go apologize to everyone after we get you out?" Dragon asks.

"That's a little embarrassing, don't you think?" I whisper to him.

Dragon shrugs. "That's why he's gotta do it. Unless you think otherwise."

I study his pretty blue eyes a moment, then nod. "No, I like you're idea."

Liam grimaces as if in agony. "Really? You'd make me do that?"

"Yeah. But you've got to agree before we let you down," Dragon replies.

The net sways to the side a little and makes a creaking sound like it's going to fall if straining to hold his weight.

"I'll *shaavez* apologize," he murmurs. "Just get me out of here. I swear this thing is getting smaller."

"I think you're getting fatter," Avan shoots back with a laugh.

"*Shaav* you, Avan," Liam spits.

"Okay, so who's going to get him down?" I ask.

Avan's thin lips break into a huge grin. "Well, I'm headed back to the cave. Have fun!" With that, he takes off into the snow.

I'm not exactly sure what to do. I don't want to be the one bringing Liam back, but I can't just leave the job to Dragon, especially after he bandaged my arm.

"For the galaxy's sake, could you just make up your mind?" Liam asks. "Jaina, come help me out, please."

Turning to Dragon, I nod my head in the direction of the cave. "I've got this."

"You sure?" From the reluctance in his voice, I know he doesn't *really* want to help Liam.

"Oh, yeah," I insist, giving him the most convincing smile I can muster. "I've had to deal with far worse. Trust me."

Dragon nods politely. "All right. If you need me, I'll be back at the cave."

"Thanks."

My eyes follow him as he leaves.

Liam clears his throat. "You gonna help me or continue taking in the view?"

I whip around sharply, and lock my gaze with Liam's. He stares back at me bravely, despite his awkward position in the air.

"It's not what you think," I finally say, walking up to him.

"What is it, then?" He raises an eyebrow and behind his grey-blue eyes, I only see anger. "Because something is going on between you two. I've seen it since the day we became a team. No, wait. It was before that."

"It's nothing," I assert, keeping my eyes on the ground.

I pull out my MED and start sawing away at the rope. It's tough and rubbery, like someone covered it invisible tar.

"It's not *nothing*," he hisses. "Do you think I'm blind?"

Biting my tongue to prevent myself from cursing, I take a deep breath. "It's complicated, that's all. I told you I was done with that sort of thing until we get to the Crystal City, when my match will be chosen."

"But you're not denying it then?" he presses on.

I could ask him to shut up, but I decide not to. "Denying what?"

Stupid question.

"You know."

Of course I know. I don't *like* Dragon. At least not in the way Liam is suggesting. Just because Dragon is unbelievably handsome, smart, brave and overall amazing, doesn't mean I like him in that sort of way. Does it?

Liam's gaze is locked on my eyes, and I wish I could courageously stare him down. But I can't. Not when Liam is asking questions I dare not ask myself. My face is warm and I'm not sure if it's from my sudden anger or embarrassment. I turn the electric current in my MED on and touch the blade to his leg.

He shrieks as the shock travels through him. "*Na'lav*, Jaina!"

"Could you be any more annoying?"

"Yes." He sneers. "I could."

I sever a few more ropes and he falls into the powdery snow with a thud. He groans in pain and I'm a little more satisfied.

"It's a long story." I start to move away. I'm not having this conversation.

He stands up, and jumps in front of me, placing his hands on my shoulders. "We've got time."

"I don't want to talk about it." I try to walk around him, but he doesn't let me go.

"*I do.* And though you outrank me, I feel I have the right to know. What's going on?" His mouth twitches like he wants to say more.

My throat has become dry, like it's filled with sand. I push his hands off my shoulders. When I look into his eyes, I furrow my brow. "Why do you pretend like you don't know him?"

His eyes narrow and his lips press together in perplexity. "W-what?" His voice is a few pitches higher than his natural tone, like my question stunned his vocal cords. "How would I know him?"

"416 years After the Stellar Wars. It was the sixth standard month of that year. Do you remember what happened?" I ask.

Something about the way he stands makes me nervous. It's not right being here alone with him. I used to see his soft blue eyes as irresistible and captivating. How his voice made me tingle with excitement. It's strange how he's hardly changed, and yet I feel completely different.

"A lot can happen in a month, Jaina. And I was only six years old, same as you." His gaze falters to the ground. In that simple look, that accidental gesture, I know he's hiding it all.

Anger rushes through my veins. "You know what I'm talking about." My voice is low, and dark. "Why do you pretend you've forgotten?"

Liam clenches his jaw and takes a deep breath. "I haven't forgotten. But Altair is dead."

"What are you talking about?" I scoff, fighting the urge to push him backward.

Liam cranes his neck slightly to lock his eyes with mine and grabs my shoulders again. "You heard me. The

Altair we knew is dead. He's different now." His lips are so close to me, I'm afraid he'll lean forward and kiss me.

I pull myself out of his tight grip, but hold my ground "He's still with us," I say through my teeth.

"He's *not*. Don't deny it, Jaina," Liam breathes, coming closer. "You know that look in his eyes. Like he's seen all the horrors of the world. The boy we knew wasn't like that. Altair was innocent, and even though everyone hated him for his honesty, you couldn't help but love him. That Altair is dead. He's Dragon, now."

"You didn't know him like I did!" I cry, stepping back from him. "How dare you talk about him like that! He promised he'd always be there for me, and when they took him away I lost everything! Don't you dare tell me he's dead!"

He looks back at me. "Why are you defending him?" His his lips falter in tormented rejection. "You're falling for him, aren't you? You said you were done with *that sort of thing*."

I close my eyes. How can I make him understand? "I am. I might as well spare myself the heartbreak. Why should I waste time with someone I know I can't–"

"Then why him?" he blurts out, his voice rising in anger. The optimism in his eyes has been shattered like a window. They plead me to piece them back together because I'm the only one who can. "Why?" he whispers, brushing a strand of my hair behind my shoulder.

"Liam, please–"

"I've done everything, Jaina. I was nice to you–"

"You were? Because I didn't really notice," I shoot back.

"I was nice to you for a while. I tried to help you. I switched to trying to making you jealous." Liam bites his lip. "Why is it the only time you ever loved me was when I didn't feel the same?"

His words force the air from my lungs. My chest tightens. Snowflakes cascade to the ground in slow motion, hushing the galaxy to listen to me.

"You-you love me?"

His breath is unsteady, his eyes full of a sad and painful longing I've never noticed before. Yet now that I see it, I realize it's been there this whole time.

"Liam, do you love me?"

He spins around and kicks at the snow. "I...I'm... I don't know." He runs his fingers through his dark, almost black hair. "I don't understand you, Jaina. You told me that until you met *mister perfect-genetic-match*, you wouldn't put yourself through this. And then *he* comes along. Why is he so different?"

I'm not sure I can answer that, yet.

"Jaina, you know what they'll do to you if you fall for him," he says softly.

I glare at him. "And why do you care all of a sudden? You're not one for following rules."

"Things are different now. If we make it to the Crystal City, they'll execute you if you refuse to accept your genetic match."

I try to push past him but he doesn't let me. "Liam, I order you to stop and let me go," I try to say sternly, yet my voice trembles. Tears well in my eyes, and I bite my cheek to prevent them from showing. He's right. The situation is utterly hopeless.

"Why do you feel like I'm cornering you?"

I avoid eye contact. "Because you are."

He's about to say something but nods and backs down. "Thanks for getting me out."

"I'm regretting it already."

Liam and I enter the cave, finally able to shelter ourselves from the icy wind.

"I heard Liam was having some trouble collecting firewood, so I took it upon myself to get the job done correctly." Xana's lush, pink lips form a wry smile as she tosses the firewood into a heap near the cave wall. Her long, blond hair slips delicately over her shoulders. She pulls it back, then shoots Liam a terrifying glare.

"Thank you, Xana," I reply, hoping to ease the pure emotions in her eyes.

Liam purses his lips and furrows his brow, but to my relief, says nothing.

Dragon touches my shoulder and pulls me aside. "How'd it go?"

"Not bad." I avert my eyes to the ground before I can say more. I'm afraid just looking at him might tear me to pieces. Liam's right about what they'll do if I fall for him. But that's not what's happening. There's no law against taking note of someone's extremely good looks.

"Is that all? Anything you wanna tell me?" His armored chest makes him look even more muscular than he is.

"Yep. I mean no! I don't have anything to tell you..."

He raises an eyebrow. "You okay?"

My eyes focus on the ground and my stomach shifts in place. "Yeah, yes. I'm fine.

His gentle fingers touch my chin, lifting my gaze back to him. "Are you sure?" His voice is soft and persuasive. Sweet, like honey.

I'm unable to resist, and my lips find words I didn't think I had. "We had an intense conversation. He really knows how to get to me. That's all."

"You want to talk about it?"

"No." I shake my head. "Not really."

"Okay...Did you learn anything from your *intense conversation*? Because something is obviously on your mind." He glances at Liam, who's glaring at me from the other side of the room.

"Liam's so annoying." I sigh, then take a seat on a large bolder behind me and glare back at him.

Dragon smiles and sits beside me. "We already knew that."

I manage a laugh. "I really missed you."

"Yeah." He nods and leans forward, resting his elbows on his knees. "Me too."

"Hey guys," Liam announces. "I'd just like to say that I've been ordered to apologize. So, I'm sorry."

"It's okay, Liam. Just try not to do it again," Luci says. "Now, would you like to share with us what happened while Xana was collecting the firewood for you?"

Dragon and I look at them with interest, but I'm not planning to intervene anytime soon.

"Not in particular, no," Liam replies. Everyone is silent and stares at him. He stands up and dusts himself off like he's about to make a long speech, then says, "I got trapped."

"Really?" Kavi asks.

"Yes, in fact, I did."

"By what?" Avan asks, trying hard to hold in his laughter.

"A net." There's a quiver of embarrassment in Liam's voice.

Xana bursts into uncontrollable laughter, and Luci smiles with delight.

"Come on, it was hidden pretty well and I didn't see it coming. End of story," Liam says, obviously not amused.

"Avan," Seth calls. "Was it the one we set up?"

Avan raises his eyebrows and nods enthusiastically.

I look at Dragon, wondering whether to smile or try to keep a neutral expression. Dragon has a mischievous smirk on his face, so I choose to smile.

"That net was completely fool proof," Seth cries.

Luci shoots him an evil grin. "Apparently not."

"Shut up, Seth," Kavi chimes in. "You can be so mean sometimes." At that, she begins to pace back and forth near the wall of the cave.

"Wait," Dragon whispers to me, "I thought Kavi liked Seth."

"I think she secretly does," I reply. "This is probably just to get a reaction out of him."

"Thank you!" Liam smiles through his teeth and shoots me a glare. "At least *she* is a decent human being."

"Kav," Seth calls, "you've got to be kidding me."

Kavi faces him angrily. "No, I'm not, Seth. Because I'm not like you."

"The other day you said you hated–"

"Don't listen to him, Liam. I think we both agree," she gestures to Liam and herself, "that you're not as great as you think you are, Seth."

Liam smiles. "Thanks, Kav."

Dragon turns back to me, his gaze darts over my face as if hoping to find an answer. "Okay, we've got to do something."

"Like what? They're out of control. They aren't appreciative of each other or our leadership. What could we possibly do?" I ask.

"I have no idea. This isn't good for the team. Everyone is all..."

"Split up," I finish.

"Right. For this team to work, everyone's gotta be close."

I wonder if that means us, too. My mind tingles with excited apprehension, and I feel uncomfortable sitting this close to him.

"So, h-how are we going to do that?" I ask, blinking away my feelings.

Dragon stares forward, concentrating on the stony floor beneath us. "Remember the class we took in the Uncharted Lands?"

"Of course," I reply wanting to scoot away from him and move closer at the same time. Would I feel like this if he was only a friend?

He studies me momentarily with an unreadable expression, as if sensing my scattered mind. "There was that question...Something like if two teammates aren't getting along, what do you do?"

"Yes! Wasn't your answer to send them on a mission together?"

He raises an eyebrow, and the corners of his mouth lift into a questioning smile. "What do you think?"

"I don't know. Did you get the question right?"

He smiles slyly. "Of course I did."

"Of course," I echo, rolling my eyes. "I guess that's what we've gotta do, then."

Dragon nods. "Do you think she actually likes him?"

I hesitate then look at the two of them. "I think so. I'm not sure why she acts so mean."

"The IA doesn't recognize unapproved relationships, remember." A dazed expression lingers in his eyes as he stares into the dazzling, golden flames. "Still, I don't think that's a good reason to be mean to someone."

"You think it's okay to..." I pause seeing Liam glaring at us out of the corner of my eye. Liam sighs and turns away, yet a shadow of disgusted frustration remains with

him. I glance back at Dragon. "To send them off alone?"
I finish.

He takes a deep breath, the kind I take when I'm
trying desperately hard to control myself. His eyes are
still trained on the fire. "Yeah, I think they'll be okay.
We'll tell them later, though."

"They're not the only people who aren't getting
along," I say. "Liam and I aren't doing so well. Xana, Luci
and Liam seem to have issues with one another. I think
Luci might hate me, which is weird because I swear I'd
never spoken a word to her before the try-outs–"

"I know, I just kind of need you right now," he
glances at me, meeting my gaze for an instant. "I mean,
we're both team leaders, and we've got to plan things and,
you know, that sort of thing," he mumbles nervously,
looking down at the ground.

A smile lifts the corners of my lips.

Dragon sighs. "Unless you'd *like* to go on a mission
with all of them. Which in that case–"

"Oh no, I'd much rather stay here with you." *Na'lav*,
that was an awkward statement. I rush to add, "We're
team leaders and we've got stuff to get done."

"R-right." He bites his lip and glances away from
me. "So we'll figure out a plan. If you come up with any
ideas, tell me."

"Okay, sure. Sounds good." I start to move away.

"Oh, Jaina, wait."

Immediately I turn around. "Yeah?"

He approaches me and glances around the cave like
he's afraid someone's watching. "I..." He stares at me. His
arms rest uncomfortably at his sides, like he's not entirely
sure how to move. "I just, um..."

I've never seen him this way before. He looks
apprehensive. Hesitant. *Nervous*, even.

"You okay?" I laugh awkwardly as I realize I feel the same way.

He smiles gently then relaxes a little. "I wanted to... thank you."

"For what?"

"The dirin behind me, I wouldn't have seen it in time to get out of the way. You saved my life."

That's right. I saved his life today. But then, we all saved each other. "It was nothing, really."

"No, you saved my *life*, Jaina. And not just once. You were the only one who kept me moving forward after they took me. If it weren't for you..." He courageously meets my eyes. "I don't think I'd be here. I just wish I had some way of returning the favor."

Return the favor? If that means risking his life for me, then I'd rather keep him in debt. "Dragon, having you around is enough of a reward."

His cheeks flush red and I try not to laugh. "Thanks."

I walk back over to the rest of the team and pretend to listen to the conversation. In reality, I feel distant. He really believes I kept him moving forward? If it weren't for me, maybe he wouldn't have gotten taken away in the first place. I could have rushed over to help him, but I just stood there, watching them take him from me.

I could have saved him before, but I didn't.

I saved him today.

And for the first time in my life, I said something fairly romantic without making a fool of myself. That's progress, right?

A chill sweeps through the cavern. The night is dark, and there's not a single star in the sky. Dragon and I have come up with a plan, but I'm not quite sure how it's going to work. Still, Kavi and Seth need to spend some time together alone so they can work out their problems.

Kavi hasn't left Liam's side since she started defending him, obviously trying to get a reaction out of Seth. Seth, on the other hand, continuously bombards Liam with insults, attempting to prove to Kavi that she's defending a weakling. And Liam. Oh, what I would do to forget his words from hours ago. Could he actually love me? I don't hate him, but I could never love him again. Especially now that Dragon's around.

I can't stop thinking of him. There's no possible way he could like me. Which is okay, since I don't like him. Still...the way he thanked me...and the way he acted...that adorable, nervous stammer as he spoke...the way his eyes flickered back and forth from mine to the ground then back again...how he blushed when I told him that having him around was 'enough of a reward'...I find myself sighing but cut myself short as Dragon approaches.

"Think we should tell them now?" he asks.

I shrug. "Might as well get it over with."

I glance at the team. Everyone's involved in a discussion about the Imperial Alliance Army. Luckily, Kavi and Seth aren't playing a big part in it. I tap her gently on the shoulder. "Um, Dragon and I need to speak with you."

I watch Seth get up reluctantly on the other side of the fire pit. Kavi on the other hand, doesn't budge.

"If this is about Seth, then I'd rather not get up," she snorts.

"Come on, Kav. Orders are orders." I wonder if this counts as insubordination...

Finally, she stands and marches past me.

"Well, some one's mad," Seth remarks.

"No comments, Seth," I shoot back, though I'm thinking the same thing. "Come on, let's go."

The four of us move back to the empty portion of the cave. It's farther from everyone else, so it's much quieter.

"What's this about?" Kavi asks.

Dragon raises an eyebrow. "I think you know."

Kavi crosses her arms and rolls her eyes. "Look. I've told Jaina many times that Seth and I can't get along."

"I disagree," Seth says. "The whole reason we can't get along is because she doesn't do anything about it!"

"Well, that just shows how well we work together. We can't even agree about getting along!" Kavi puts her hands on her hips and sighs.

"Which is why we're sending you two on a mission," Dragon says.

Kavi's expression turns from one of annoyance to horror. "Wait," she glances from Dragon to me, "you're joking."

"Does it sound like we're joking?" I ask.

Her jaw drops so low I'm afraid it'll come unhinged. Her dark brown eyes glint with the reddish flames of anger.

Seth doesn't look too surprised. He stands with his arms are crossed over his muscular chest. "What's the mission?"

Dragon looks to me. "You want to explain?"

Thanks a lot. I glare at him and he smiles.

"According to Liam's calculations, we should be getting close to the crystal," I begin.

"How can we know that? We don't know where the crystal is," Kavi says.

Dragon's jaw twitches in irritation. "The arena is a circle. We all know that. Based on the curvature of the arena, Liam calculated that it has an area of about twenty kilometers. So we're assuming that the crystal is at or near the center of the circle."

Kavi leans forward aggressively. "But we don't *know*?"

"No, Kavi, we don't know, but it's our best shot. Unless you have a better idea," Dragon replies.

She turns away from us and kicks a pebble into the wall.

"So what's the mission?" Seth asks again.

"You're our scouts. Our spies," I reply. "We need you to walk toward the center of the arena, which is to the north. If you find anything that could lead us to the crystal, including another team, let us know."

Dragon nods. "We apologize for not warning you earlier, but this needs to be done. It's essential if we are to win this round."

"Understood," Seth says.

Kavi grits her teeth like she's in pain, but ultimately gives in. Her eyes bore into my skull, promising me she'll get me back for this.

Seth glances at Kavi and grins. "So when do we leave?"

"As soon as everyone falls asleep," Dragon replies.

"Fine. Let's get this over with as fast as possible, shall we?" Kavi raises her arms in defeat.

Seth takes a deep, frustrated breath. "We'll be ready."

———

The universe has been hushed to sleep. Besides the low, caressing purr of the wind, there's only silence. It's quiet enough that I start to wonder if time has stopped altogether.

"Do you think we should wake them now?" I ask quietly.

"It's about time," Dragon replies.

I tiptoe around the burning coals of the fire to Kavi and gently shake her awake. "Kav. Kavi, time to get up."

She yawns and dreamily rubs her eyes. "Yeah, sorry. I'm getting up."

"Get moving, you two. You've got a lot of work to do," Dragon says once both of them are awake enough to understand. They're obviously tired and I feel bad sending them away this late. What if they get captured? The thought hadn't occurred to me until now. What if I never see them again?

"All right, see ya, Jay," Kavi whispers to me on her way out.

"We'll be back before you know it," Seth says. They rush outside and disappear into the darkness.

"I've got a bad feeling about this. Do you think they'll be okay?" I ask. There's a hollow, churning in my stomach. Something isn't right.

"You used to say, 'sometimes a sacrifice is needed to make things better. The overall victory is worth it.' Do you still believe that?" He spits mockingly.

A chill runs through me. I remember as clearly as if it were yesterday. But to sacrifice Kavi and Seth so that we may win...

"Is that an insult?" I retort.

He shrugs, and his voice remains soft. "Depends on how you take it."

"Dragon, don't talk like that." I should just tell him that it's what I believe, but something keeps me from doing so.

How dare he. He has the nerve to question what the masters taught us without a single appreciation for what they've done. The IA brought the galaxy to peace. They trained us to be leaders. Made us strong. And he's *questioning* them?

"It's a simple question, Jaina," he persists. "Do you believe it or not?"

I stare off into the darkness but can tell Dragon is looking at me. Anger floods my veins at Dragon's rebelliousness. After all his time in reeducation and training, he's still the same.

I turn away from him. "It's the way of the Imperial Alliance."

chapter

TWELVE

"Jaina," the waves whisper, "Jaina."
They crash around me, and I want to fall into their soft
blue medium.
"Jaina," they call again, but their voices are different.
Harsher.

"*Jaina!*" Kavi calls. "Jaina, wake up! Jay, please wake
up!"

There's a moment of falling and air rushing through
me. My eyes shoot open with an electric intensity, and I
automatically sit up. I want to ask what's wrong, but the
look on her face scares me so much I can hardly speak.
My limbs are numb from the cold, and my blood flows
lazily through my veins.

Perhaps no, wait.

"Seth is gone!"

I blink twice. "*What?*"

"Seth is *gone*," she cries, breathlessly.

I stand up, trying hard not to believe her. "What happened?"

"We found a place not too far from here. We think the crystal is inside. We were on our way back and..." She stops, gasping for air. "We were ambushed and I started running. When I realized Seth wasn't with me, I turned and they had him. He yelled at me to keep running."

"But he's okay?" I ask.

"For now!"

"What's all the fuss about?" Liam asks, waking from his beauty sleep.

"Seth was taken captive," I say.

"Hurry, wake the rest of the team, we've got to go!" Kavi says.

"In the name of the Emperor," Liam mutters, rubbing the sleepiness out of his eyes.

Kavi briefs them quickly and we're up and ready to go within minutes. We gather our supplies and leave no trace we were ever here.

"Dragon, do you think we should split up?" I ask as Kavi leads our team through the frozen landscape. *Keep your distance, Jaina.* He insulted me for trusting the IA. I'm still shocked he could even think that way.

"Why?" he asks.

"I don't know...Seth's been captured, there aren't many places to hide...Shouldn't we have some sort of plan?" I ask.

"We don't need a plan."

"Well, I'd kind of like one. I'm not so good thinking on my feet," I reply.

He groans with impatience. "All right, fine. Tell me your plan."

"We'll split up. You take half the team and go whatever way we don't. We'll send two people to retrieve Seth, while the rest of us remain hidden. The moment our enemies make a move, we spring the trap and take out as many of them as we can. Then we find the crystal."

He laughs. "So much for not being able to think on your feet. Good plan."

A line of evergreen trees separate us from the next clearing, but Kavi tells us to stop and we duck behind the needle-like leaves.

"This is where he is," she whispers. "Past these trees, there's a clearing, and a little past that is the camp-site of the Rylos team."

"Do you know where he is?" Liam asks.

"This way," Kavi breathes. "But I suggest you crouch. I'm not sure where their teammates are."

"Hold on," Dragon says quietly. "Avan, Xana and Luci, come with me."

The three of them follow Dragon.

Kavi looks at me. "What's going on?"

"Ambush," I say.

She nods, then leads us forward. Something catches my eye. A large wheel around two meters in diameter is tipped on its side as if the captain of an enormous ship drove his vessel straight into the earth.

At the base, Seth kneels, his hands tied to one of the large spokes.

There's a red gash across his left cheek, and his right eye is badly bruised, but other than that he seems okay. The Rylins must be nearby.

"They're planning a trap," I remark.

"No kidding," Liam says.

"Liam, I need you to take your MED and cut Seth free."

Liam's eyes widen and his eyebrows climb higher on his forehead in surprise. "Jaina, I don't know how qualified I am for this–"

"Why are you here, then? Do you think you would've made it into the Trials if you weren't qualified?" I ask sternly.

"You seem to think so," he spits back.

"Do you want to save Seth or not?" I snap. "Dragon's sending out someone else to help you. Liam, you have to do this. Once Seth is free, send him over to Kavi who will help him gear up."

"What do we do once the Rylins open fire?" Kavi asks.

I hesitate. "I haven't thought that far."

"So, just 'wing it'?" Liam asks.

"Yeah, pretty much."

Liam nods and slinks from one tree to another until he reaches Seth.

My hands start to shake. *Take deep breaths.* I have to act strong in front of the team.

From across the clearing, Dragon nods. Avan rushes in, pistol in hand to cover Liam and Seth.

I can hardly breathe. Making a single sound could get someone killed. I close my eyes, trying to calm down.

Seth whispers something to Liam as he begins to cut him loose, but I'm too far away to hear. He's nearly finished cutting through the thick rope.

Come on, Liam, hurry up.

The moment Seth is free, an electrically charged arrow hits the ground, skimming Seth's knee. There's a moment of stillness as the imminent attack processes in my mind. Dragon takes his electrified crossbow and fires into the trees above me. A moan fills my ears and the cracking of branches from above makes it all the more terrible. A thud to my left startles me and I jump back in fear. My mouth is dry and my throat constricts.

An unfamiliar man lies in the snow beside me. Plasma bolts rip through the air, but the man, who looks no more than seventeen years of age, intrigues me. That could have been me.

He grips the arrow lodged deep in his shoulder. He's going unconscious. The battle rages before me, but I can't bring myself to move.

"Jaina, we need your help!" Dragon runs over to me. "What are you doing?"

"I-I don't know."

"Come on, now's not the time to choke," he says. "We're under attack."

"I'm sorry." I swallow a large gulp of icy air.

Seth runs toward Kavi and Luci to grab weapons for the battle.

My body moves on its own. I take my stun rifle and manage to find cover behind a large, fallen tree. Taking aim is hard, mostly because the Rylins are all wearing shades of brown. I can hardly tell them apart from the trees.

I lock onto a girl with a rifle aimed at me. My heart skips, and I pull the trigger. An instant later, she falls, her weapon tumbling to the ground. I hear my breathing, strong and steady; like a soft undertone in my chest.

Someone fires a shot. The bolt plummets toward me, and I jerk myself backward as it melts through the snow, centimeters from my boots. I scan the trees for my attacker but find nothing.

I look through my scope. Another shot blazes past me. Pulling out my stun pistol, I search for new cover.

Hanging around in the same place too long will get me killed.

A wave of plasma bolts stream by me as I dodge behind a tree. I peer around the tree trunk and fire. My target clutches his leg in pain, but he's not knocked out. Guess I didn't hit him in the right place.

Aiming at him again, I pull the trigger. Nothing happens. I pull my pistol back and check the charge. *Shaav.* Looks like I'll have to wait for it to reboot.

I've trained for situations like this. I should be running up to the enemy instead of cowering behind a tree. I still have my rifle with me; I've got knives, my scimitar and one of the old-fashioned guns that shoots actual metal bullets. But I don't *want* to kill. For now, stunning is enough.

"Hello, there."

I jump at the sound of Liam's voice. "Since when did you get here?"

Liam hugs his rifle to his chest as he lies awkwardly in the snow. "Like five seconds ago. Is the plan working?"

"It better be," I mutter. "Use your stun pistols. It's pretty effective."

"Doesn't look like yours is working so well," Liam replies skeptically.

"Shut up, and take orders!" I shout over the wave of adrenaline coursing through me.

"All right, fine! Do you want me to tell the rest of the team?"

"Yes. We'll finish this battle much faster if we use these." I hold up my pistol.

"See you 'round, then." He fires at another Rylin and takes off.

I glance back at my pistol. Almost charged. Come on.

Merciless wind bites at every inch of me. In spite of the cold, sweat streams down my back and through my hair. An electronic beep sounds from my pistol and I fire without hesitation.

I take out another two of the Rylos team and search for more, but only silence follows. I wait a little longer, wondering if they're trying to ambush us, but no one comes. I step out from behind the tree and take a look around.

"Is everyone still alive?" Avan calls.

"Yeah," I answer. "It's safe. I think."

The rest of my team files into the clearing.

"Did we get everyone?" Kavi asks.

"Either that, or they ran away," Dragon replies.

Kavi rushes up to Seth and lets herself fall beside him in the snow. "Seth! In the name of the galaxy, never do that again!"

He laughs and pushes a strand of her black hair out of her eyes.

I avert my gaze from them, sensing that this isn't a moment I should be watching.

Dragon approaches me.

"Was anyone..."

"Killed?" he finishes. "I don't know. I tried to get everyone to use their stun rifles, but I'm told a few weren't charging. Why do you care?"

I choke out a breath of disgust, my face heating up with anger. "What do you mean? You think because I'm willing to make sacrifices that I wanna go around killing people?"

"That's a little un-Imperial for you to say, don't you think?" he fires back.

"Stop." My heart cracks at his words. "Don't say things like that."

"Would you rather have me lie?" His eyes are cold and emotionless. And it hurts me so much more than it should.

"No. Just...keep it to yourself."

"And how will that solve any of our problems?" he seethes.

"As if complaining about it will?" I shoot back.

Dragon looks down at the powdery, white ground. I'm right and he knows it, but why would he bring it up at all? I thought he'd learned this lesson when they took him. I thought the Masters cured him. Purged him of such treasonous thoughts. If he gets taken again, they'll kill him. The thought of losing him again hurts more than his insults.

Seth slowly drifts toward us through the snow, then pats Dragon on the shoulder. "Hey, I just want to say thanks."

"Thank *Kavi*. If it weren't for her, you might be dead," Dragon replies, his voice still devoid of emotion. His gaze lingers on me.

Liam nods toward the large black wheel. "So, what do we do with this?"

"Turn it?" Luci asks.

There are eight spokes. *Eight people on each team.* Looks like we're on the right track. We each grab onto one and turn it to the left. The cold wood is rough and rubs my skin raw. The grinding of stone fills my ears. Metal screeches, and the ground trembles beneath us. What if it's another trap?

The adrenaline from the previous battle hasn't fully worn off. What if we unleash something terrible, like another pack of dirin? Or something worse?

Finally, our labor pays off. A large metal plate moves to reveal an opening in the ground, wide enough for a small starship to enter.

We let go of the wheel and stare down into the dark depths of the cave.

"Come on," I say before taking the first few steps onto the stone stairwell.

"Are you sure?" Liam asks. "It doesn't look safe."

"Of course it's not safe," Dragon replies in an edgy tone. "These are the Trials, remember?"

Liam's eyes lock onto Dragon with such intensity I'm afraid he'll lunge at him any second. "Yeah, I *shaavez* remember."

"What makes you think this is the way to go?" Xana asks.

I stop, turn around, and shrug. "It's our only lead. Besides, the Rylins were here. Maybe they thought there was something significant here."

Dragon's jaw twitches, one of the things I notice he does when he's holding something back. Instead of speaking, he moves obediently into the stairwell, and takes the lead.

The rest of us trail behind him.

I take a deep breath, and the dark musty air fills my lungs. In some weird way, it tastes like spring. Everything smells like dirt and moss. When I cough, the sound echoes off the rock.

Dragon is only a few paces ahead of me, and I study him in the dimming light from outside. I wish he wouldn't talk that way. It's the sort of thing that got him taken away. I can't handle losing him again.

The grating of rock sends shivers down my spine and I turn around, just in time to see the door to the cave close us in. Darkness envelops us, and none of us move. Standing for a moment in complete silence, I don't dare to breathe. What if coming down here was a terrible mistake?

A bluish light glows on the wall, and Luci approaches us with a glowsaber. Relief washes over me but I keep a straight face. I can't let Luci know I was scared. In the strangest of ways, she threatens me.

"Activate your glowsabers," she orders.

The tunnel comes alive with light. Before us is a fairly straight but downhill path.

"Are you still glad we went this way?" Liam whispers to me.

"Face your fears, Liam. It'll make you braver," I reply monotonously.

He's standing behind me so I can't see him, but I imagine he's rolling his eyes right about now.

I quicken my pace, trying to get ahead of everyone. I'm not exactly in the mood to talk. Fifteen minutes into our descent, I begin to wonder if the path will ever come to an end. A shimmering object up ahead catches the light of my glowsaber.

"Hey, I think I found something," I say, approaching a pedestal at the center of a small cavern. "It's the crystal!"

"Nice one, Jaina." Avan nods, clearly impressed.

Kavi shrugs and reaches for the crystal. "So, that's that."

"Don't!" Avan shouts.

Kavi jerks her hand back before she can touch it, and I jump. Avan's so quiet, I never expected him to yell in a millennia!

"What the *shaav* is wrong?" Kavi asks.

"It's not that easy," he says. "Shirez said it wasn't supposed to be easy. This first Trial might be easier than what's to come, but that's all."

She crosses her arms. "Can't we just grab it and go?"

Liam walks up to the pedestal. "No, Avan's right. The Trials aren't just a bunch of physical activities. There are mental tests as well. There should be some sort of trick to this. This crystal is here to deceive us. Make us think it's easy to get. Look around for something that might hint at what we need to do," he says.

I search the bare walls, not expecting to find anything, but I want to be sure.

"What's this triangle thing?" Xana asks, gesturing to a triangular prism on the side of the pedestal.

"Don't worry about it," Luci murmurs. "Looks like a piece of glass."

"Found it." Seth gestures to the pedestal. "Of course. Back of the pedestal."

He waits for the rest of us to come around before he shines light on the silver words engraved in the pedestal. I read them aloud carefully:

> "By itself, it's just one color,
> Yet when broken, it is many.
> You can't get much in the dark,
> But in the day there's plenty.
>
> It grows more in the summer,
> And shrinks throughout the fall.
> There hardly is a place,
> That has none of it at all.
>
> When in colors, it is separate,
> When white, it's become one.
> Through the darkness of the universe,
> It gives hope to those with none."

"Well, that was helpful," Liam groans sarcastically.

"Take it in pieces," Seth advises. "By itself, it's only one color. That could be a lot of things. *Yet when broken it is many*. That makes no sense at all."

"You don't get much in the dark but in the day there is a lot. Could it be energy?" Dragon asks. "Energy doesn't have color, though."

Luci touches her chin and her eyes are dazed, like she'd rather be anywhere but here. "Growing in the summer, and shrinking in the fall. Plants? I don't know if they shrink in the fall but they change color."

"But it gives hope to those with none," I reply.

"A tree growing can symbolize hope, can't it?" she asks.

"But it doesn't shrink," Dragon differs.

Seth doesn't look satisfied. "The sun?"

"Guys," Avan cuts in.

Liam stops him. "Shh, I'm still thinking."

"Guys," Avan persists, his voice is louder this time. "I think I figured it out."

"Okay, what is it?" I ask.

He hesitates, as if pausing for dramatic effect. "Light. The answer is light."

There's a long silence as his words sink in.

Avan clears his throat. "When it's broken by a prism, you see all the visible wavelengths of light! Of course, there's none in the dark, and there's a lot in the day. Growing in the summer when the days become longer, and shrinking when the days become shorter."

"When light is white, or pure," Liam adds excitedly, "all the colors are united. Through the darkness of the universe, there are the stars."

"And it gives hope to those with none." Dragon's tone is solemn, like he knows some forbidden secret. His eyes fix severely on mine as if trying to tell me something. They no longer contain the cold contempt they held before. I can only look back at him, wishing I could understand.

"Dragon," Luci says to get his attention.

He hesitates, then looks at her.

"Do you think my glowsaber will work?" she asks.

"I think it needs to be real light. Like the light of the sun," Avan says.

I happen to glance at Liam. His eyebrows are raised so high they might float off his head. He looks completely ridiculous, and it's all I can do to keep from laughing.

"Um," he starts. "I don't think you're seeing what I'm seeing, Avan."

"What?"

"We're underground. It's pitch black down here, and I don't see any windows. I can hardly see my own hands!"

"Maybe you need glasses," Xana replies.

"Very funny."

"I agree. We need real light," I say. "But how?"

"Mirrors," Kavi says. "We could use mirrors."

"Where're we going to get–" Luci stops as Seth raises a few mirrors from a sideboard in the wall.

Kavi smiles. "Problem solved."

"There's a window a few meters in that direction. It's in the ceiling," Xana interjects. "I was just checking the area out."

"Good, that should work," Liam says. "Seth, hand me the mirrors. Dragon, I'm sure Shirez didn't forget to teach you this, right?"

Dragon nods. "I'm a step ahead of you, Liam. How many mirrors do we have?"

"Seven," Seth replies.

Liam takes a deep breath and runs his fingers through his hair. "All right, we can make it work. We're going to need everyone's help. We've got to position the mirrors at an angle where they can reflect the light onto that prism." He points to the clear, triangular prism next to the crystal. "I'm assuming that the light should fall on the glass for it to work."

"So what do we do? Just hold them in position?" Kavi asks.

Liam hands Kavi the first mirror and pushes her into position. "Yup. Stand here, Kavi. Hold the mirror right there. Now, don't move once I give it to you."

"What happens if we fail?" Avan asks.

"I'd rather not find out," I murmur.

Kavi holds the mirror still, and the beam of light remains steady. Dragon takes Seth and has him hold the next mirror, catching Kavi's beam and reflecting it further ahead. Xana's handed the next one, then Luci. The beam shines from one mirror to the next.

"Avan, I need you to grab the crystal after we reflect the light, okay?" Dragon asks.

Avan salutes him limply. "Yes, sir."

"Stand over there so you won't interrupt the beam." Dragon gestures to the front of the pedestal, on the opposite side of us.

Liam takes up position with his own mirror.

"All right, Jaina, I'm taking this spot, and you aim for the crystal," Dragon says.

"Wait, Dragon," I start. "What if I miss?"

He smiles encouragingly. "Come on, you're great with that sniper of yours."

I shake my head. "That comes with a scope."

"How much different can it be?" he asks.

"Very. I really don't trust myself with this," I whisper.

"But I trust you." He touches my shoulder gently then shoves the mirror in my hands. He moves over to his place and the beam is reflected perfectly in my direction.

Did he say he *trusts* me?

I glance at the beam of light then down at the mirror in my hands. Here I go. I step into the beam and catch light reflected from Dragon's mirror. Slowly, I turn in the direction of the prism. The beam starts to shift on its own.

"Stop moving back there!" I shout.

I adjust the mirror a final time. Light engulfs the prism. An array of colors slowly forms on the glass.

chapter

THIRTEEN

I stare in awe at the rainbow of colors perfectly reflected onto the glass. The crystal rises into the air. *It worked.*

"You think it's okay now?" Avan asks.

"Yeah, go ahead," I reply.

Avan gently lifts the crystal off the pedestal, and we lower the mirrors. He hands me the crystal and I stuff it into a pocket in my holster belt. The ground rumbles beneath our feet for about five seconds then stops.

"What was that?" Xana asks.

Liam glances around skeptically, then shrugs. "Doesn't matter. It's gone now."

The ground trembles again, longer this time. It knocks me off my feet, pushing me into Dragon, who's next to me. He grabs my arm and helps balance me as he presses his hand to the wall to keep from falling over.

Finally, it stops.

Loose chunks of dirt and rocks fall from the ceiling and land with a dusty splash on the ground.

Luci coughs, covering her mouth and nose with her arm. "Is anyone allergic to dust?"

Avan sneezes then plugs his nose and nods. "Yeah, I am."

The dust clogs my lungs, and I taste the bitter dirt on my tongue. "This is bad."

Dragon tugs on my arm. "Come on, we have to get out."

"How?" Kavi asks. "We can't go back the way we came! The Rylins are probably waiting for us!"

Seth runs his fingers through his blond hair, frustration flickering in his eyes. "No wonder the fight was so easy."

"You call that *easy*?" Liam cries. "I almost got killed fifty times!"

"I should have figured it out," Seth continues. "Everything was too set up. Their plan was to drive us into the cave so we'd bring the crystal right to them."

"So, what choice does that leave us?" I ask.

Luci shrugs. "The window?"

Liam furrows his brow. "No, the window is too small to fit through."

"Too small for *you* to fit through," Xana mutters. "I'm sure *I* could."

"Really, Xana? Was that necessary?" I ask.

"Would you shut up and focus on the task at hand?" Luci shouts. "How about there?" She points to a dusty, frayed rope ladder stationed halfway between us and the end of another tunnel.

"Oh of course," Liam snorts. "And why hadn't we seen that before?"

"Because you need glasses," Xana reminds him.

"Shut up." He pokes Xana in the arm, and she shoves him back.

"Jaina, she punched me," Liam cries.

"She did not, now stop being a baby, so we can get out of here!" I say.

We rush to the ladder. The Rylins won't be long in realizing that we're not coming back.

The ladder leads to another long, dark pathway. The ground quivers beneath our feet, the intervals between each shake grows shorter.

The path is steep but we break into a run. The soft dirt beneath my boots flicks backward with each agonizing stride. Sunlight streams into the cave only meters away. My legs feel close to giving out, straining against the added weight of my armor, but I continue running. My body craves food, leaving me dizzy and nauseous. We hadn't had time to eat before rescuing Seth.

I'm so close. We've almost won. With a final few steps, we break through the darkness of the cave into the powdery snow and the blinding light of day.

———

"Do you know where we're going?" I ask Dragon. My fingers feel numb from the cold and I can hardly move them. It's only been a few minutes since we escaped the darkness of the cave, but all I can think of is how much warmer it was down there.

"The checkpoint should be somewhere over there." He points to the area of forest ahead of us.

A bluish light flashes in the distance. I turn to Dragon and cock my head. "How could you have possibly known that?"

"Shirez likes to, um, bend the rules," he replies, keeping his eyes down on the snow. "Told me things I probably shouldn't know."

I take a cautious step away from him and raise an eyebrow. "Are you saying we have an unfair advantage over the other teams?"

He narrows his eyes, but doesn't look up at me. "Being from *Virana* gives us an advantage. The whole point of the Trials is to defeat everyone else by any means necessary. The IA doesn't care how it's done. That's why they don't monitor us."

"No, the point is to keep life pure. It separates the weak from the strong," I shoot back. I try to keep my voice down so our teammates don't overhear us, but it's harder than I thought.

"Would you rather have me keep these things to myself?" he snaps. "Because I can if you want me to. Maybe I'll just let the rest of you figure it out."

Steam slides from my lips as I struggle to stop myself from moaning in annoyance. "Of course not, it's just—"

"What's wrong?" Dragon interrupts. "You've been acting weird since last night, and I can't figure out what's gotten into you."

"*Me*? What about *you*? You've been snappy all morning!"

His lips twitch, like he's about to reply, but he says nothing. His tense expression sinks, and his gaze falls to the ground.

"What you said," I start, my voice softening, "about me not caring for the lives of others. And about sacrificing people. It makes me feel..."

"Terrible?" His blue eyes stare deep into my soul.

I nod. "But it shouldn't. Because that's what the IA has taught us."

He leans closer to me, and in a whispered voice says, "Do you believe it's right?"

I hesitate. "Dragon, the IA knows what's best for us. Maybe you don't like the things they say or put us through, but we can't change that. They must have reasons for what they do, reasons we can't understand."

Dragon clenches his jaw. "Please don't say that."

"I'm just trying to help you."

He inhales deeply then looks me in the eyes. "Why do you want to help me? Do you honestly believe it will do any good? Aren't I Inferior in your eyes, because of my weakness?" His voice cracks with pain.

My throat constricts at his words and my heart hurts. "You're not Inferior, Dragon."

Unable to resist the temptation, I reach out to him and lightly brush the snow off his shoulder. I'm afraid he'll pull away, but he relaxes with my touch.

"I want to help because you're my friend," I say.

He attempts a smile then turns away. His pace quickens and he leaves me behind. Why does he shut me out like this? What isn't telling me?

"Jaina," Kavi whispers.

"What?" My voice is harsher than I intend, but I pretend not to notice.

She grabs me by the elbow and pulls me aside. "This is kind of important."

"What's going on?" I ask.

"Someone's following us. When Liam first reported it, I thought he was joking. I haven't seen anyone, but I think he's right. I've got a feeling that we're being watched." Her eyes flutter to the trees around us, as if expecting someone to jump out at us any moment.

The trees are dense, too thick to see long distance, but as far as I can tell, we're alone. "Are you sure?"

"Sure enough to be worried about it," she replies.

"I'll tell Dragon. Put everyone on alert."

She nods, then retreats, falling back with the rest of the team.

I walk behind him reluctantly, not exactly wanting to talk at the moment. But this is important. People could get hurt. *My* people.

I clear my throat. "Dragon."

"Yeah?" He doesn't turn to face me.

I hesitate. "There have been reports of another team following us."

"I'm glad they finally noticed."

"You knew?" I nearly stop in my tracks, seething with aggravation.

"I had a feeling," he says. "No proof but my feelings tend to be on target."

"You could have told me!" I cry.

He raises his palms in defense. "You were already upset I insulted you. I didn't want to worry you."

Burning resentment charges through me like electricity. I have the irresistible urge to swear. To slap him, to scream at him. Convince him I'm not who he thinks I am. That I'm not heartless and cold, and I don't want to be a killer, even if it's what the IA wants me to be. But I hold my temper.

"Excuse me for being worried about you," I reply sarcastically. "I just don't want you to get hurt."

He glowers at me. "As if my situation could get any worse?"

That makes me stop.

What does *that* mean?

Before I can ask, he raises his hand, cutting me off. "You know what? It doesn't matter. At the first sign of attack, split the team. Take four people with you and the crystal. The rest of us will take a different route. Once you get to the checkpoint, activate the homing beacon as quickly as possible."

"How long have you been thinking about this?"

"A while," he says.

So...after all that arguing, he's not mad at me? Or is he just putting it out of his mind so he can get the job done? I guess the latter would make more sense, so I decide to do the same.

"The transport wouldn't leave without you, would it?" I ask.

"I don't think so," he replies. But seeing the worry in my eyes, he changes his mind. "No, they won't leave without us."

"Are you *sure*?"

"We'll be fine," he assures me.

Snap.

The sound echoes through the serene forest. I scan the area, searching for something, *anything* that might give our attacker's position away, but I find nothing.

Dragon puts his arm out in front of me, forcing me to stop. With his other hand, he pulls out his scimitar.

The blood rushes to my legs, preparing me to run.

The snow sizzles and melts next to Dragon's feet. Only a second later do I process the high-pitched screech of a plasma bolt crackling through the air. Dragon yanks me forward.

"Go, Jaina, run!" he cries.

I don't have time to feel the shakiness in my joints or to be afraid. I just run. I put a hand over the pocket on my holster belt, making sure I still have the crystal Avan handed me.

There's a group of Rylins on our tail.

Keep running west.

We split when our path is blocked by a large rock wall. I take Avan, Kavi, and Liam with me and can only hope that the Rylins chose to follow Dragon.

Keep running west.

"Kavi," I say, gulping in the frigid air.

She catches up to me. "Yes?"

"Are they gone?" I ask.

"For now," she replies.

A blue beam of light flashes not too far ahead of me. It sits atop a four-foot-tall pedestal containing a scanner.

I stop so abruptly, I almost trip into the snow.

"We made it," I gasp, trying to keep my lungs from collapsing.

"Hurry, press your finger to the scanner. Once it reads your fingerprint, our team will be confirmed as winners," Avan says.

Frantically, I activate the scanner. It comes to life and prepares to read my fingerprint. We've won. We've almost won.

Silence envelops us, and at the moment, it's reassuring. As long as there's silence, it means no one's found us.

The screen on the pedestal says *Loading 54%*. I scan for other teams. If only the *shaavez* thing would–

"Hold it right there," orders a deep, masculine voice.

The cocking of weapons fills my ears, freezing me to the bone. I tilt my head upward to take in the situation.

We're surrounded.

This can't be happening! Not this close to victory!

"Drop your weapons, Virana. Hands up," says the boy.

Avan, the only teammate in my field of vision, slowly sets his scimitar in the snow, then raises his hands above his head in surrender.

I flash my gaze back toward the scanner. Of course, it's ready *now*! Talk about terrible timing. I could easily reach out, press my thumb to it and be done! There's no way I'd get away with it, though.

There's a gun to my head. The cold metal touches the hair at the nape of my neck and sends shivers down my spine.

"Did you not hear me, girl?" He presses the gun harder into me. "I said *drop your weapon.*"

I'm not the only one being held at gunpoint. A sudden move could get Avan killed, and I'm not going to risk that.

I drop my scimitar into the snow.

The boy with the gun at my neck shifts attention to another one of his teammates.

Now's my chance.

I reach out toward the scanner and press my finger down, hoping by the time they notice, the scan will be complete. A green light flashes, and despite the current situation, I smile. We've officially won.

"Hey, you," says the boy. "Hands up!"

At this point, it feels like a game. The thought that they could kill me at any moment doesn't seem real. It's only a matter of time before the helitransport comes to retrieve us. We just have to hold out long enough.

"Who's your team leader?" asks the boy.

No one says a word.

"Are you?" His voice is directed toward Avan, but he has no defense. When Avan doesn't answer, the boy nods. "Shoot him," he says to the girl holding a gun to Avan's head.

"Stop!" I hear myself cry.

The boy grabs my shoulder and twists me toward him. He's got me at arm's length, one hand clamped around my shoulder, the gun pressed against my forehead. He raises his eyebrows.

"You know..." His voice is calm and controlled, but I feel his nervousness in his tense grip. "I'm impressed with your bravery, but you can't win. You're the team leader?"

I've already won.

"You're not very threatening." He laughs, softening his hold on me. He can't imagine I'd try anything stupid at this point. Not with a gun at my head.

He's wrong.

I smile darkly. "Things aren't always as they seem."

Without a moment of delay, I clamp my hand around his wrist, forcing the gun away from my head, then bring my right hand around, flexing my wrist. The small dagger is ejected from its resting position, and I thrust it into the soft underside of his forearm.

A screech of agony registers in my mind, but I'm not entirely sure if it's from him, or one of his teammates.

I twist his hand in a direction I'm positive it shouldn't go, and the gun falls to the ground. Before he has time to react, I pull my right arm away, along with the dagger and land a left hook in his jaw.

He stumbles to the ground, cradling his blood-drenched forearm.

"How's that for threatening?" I ask through my teeth.

He doesn't reply.

The five Rylins now lie in the snow, dead, unconscious or severely wounded.

Out of the forest, Dragon appears with the rest of our team. He rushes toward us. "You still have the crystal?"

"Of course," I reply.

A shadow forms over our heads, and a ladder falls from the helitransport. I let out a sigh of relief. My team climbs it, leaving only Dragon and me in the snow.

"We've won," he says.

"Yeah." I smile. "Yes, we did."

"After you, Jaina."

I climb the ladder, and Dragon follows close behind. The moment I reach the top, I'm filled with such a sense of joy I can hardly contain myself. I whirl around, bending down to help Dragon, but freeze. Just over Dragon's shoulder, the boy who was holding me raises his rifle.

"Dragon, hurry up!" I shout. "Watch out!"

He glances down and jerks to the right as a bolt of plasma comes crackling through the air.

The transport sways left then right. I help Dragon up, hoping the *katiaj* won't fire again. I lift the ladder and close the hatch. Rushing to his side I try to speak, but my voice catches in my throat.

We sit on the floor next to the hatch. He clutches his shoulder and moans.

"Dragon, are you all right?" I ask desperately. "Were you shot? Are you hurt?"

He pulls his hand from his shoulder and glances tentatively at the wound. The dark grey material of his shirt has been burned away, melting it into his skin.

"I'm okay." His voice falters as he says it, and he winces.

I wonder if he feels the way I did after the dirin made an ice cube out of my arm.

"Are you sure?" I ask, attempting to keep myself under control. I feel so stupid, acting more worried than he is, but I can't help it. "Do you need me to get a doctor?"

"They won't have any aboard this transport. It'll have to wait," he says through his teeth. "It's just a burn."

I sigh in relief. "I thought you weren't going to make it." The urge to embrace him is suddenly unbearable. I do everything I can to hold it back.

"It's okay, Jaina, I'm all right."

"If that ever happens again—"

"I'm fine, I promise." He puts a gentle hand on my shoulder, and I relax a little. His blue eyes meet mine. He pulls away without warning and appears to find interest in a dent on the floor, like I do when I'm pretending to be occupied. "Come on, let's go sit down."

He reaches for my hand, I give it to him and he pulls me up. My arm tingles with an electric sensation as his touch registers like a fire through me. I'm not sure whether to feel excited or terrified. A red warning light seems to be flashing off and on in my mind.

"Are you okay?" he asks.

"Yeah, I'm fine." I stand up with some difficulty. My legs won't stop quivering. We sit with the rest of our team on a bench at the back of the transport. Dragon still holds onto his shoulder, but he seems to be okay. When the adrenalin wears off, he'll probably be in more pain. But by then we should be at the hospital.

"Well, my finely trained students," Shirez's voice makes me jump. "You did it."

After stopping back at HQ, we collect our belongings, get something to eat and are examined by the doctors of Kaskada. My hunger is satisfied, and my wounds are merely bad memories.

We head to the ship that will transport us to our next destination, Amarija, for the Worlds competition. It's a continent far to the west. In ancient times, it was a free nation called the United States of America.

The walkway to the ship is long. The silvery path shines in the sunlight as Shirez leads the way.

Suddenly remembering something, I run up to him. "Shirez," I begin, "I had a question."

He nods, encouraging me to continue. "What is it?"

I remove the clear crystal from my pocket. It glitters in the sunlight. "This is the crystal we found in the Trial. I didn't know what to do with it so–"

"Keep it."

"But, sir, I have no need for material things like–"

"Just keep it. It might be important," he insists.

Could this be part of the Trials? Maybe he's trying to hint at something. "All right. I just wanted to make sure I wasn't stealing or anything."

"Bring the matter up with your teammates," he says, reaching out to the transport and entering a code on the hull to open the ramp. "It may be important."

"Of course." I smile, then climb aboard.

The transport is slightly larger than the last ship. The inside is white; walls, furniture, carpet and floors, a complete opposite of the black, reflective surface of the ship.

I take a seat on one of the chairs scattered around the room. It's harder than I expect, so I hit the cushion with a little more force than I'd hoped. Dragon sits next to me while everyone else explores the interior.

"How's your shoulder?" I ask.

He grins. "A little sore, but nothing I can't handle."

I laugh, but it's really just to postpone the awkward silence that's already beginning to fill the air. I swallow hard, trying not to be overcome with emotion. Which emotion, I'm not sure and don't care to examine.

"So, you have something important?" Dragon asks.

I feel the transport lifting off the ground and my stomach drops slightly with the pressure. "Yeah. How'd you guess?"

"I can tell." He pauses. "And Shirez told me to ask you about it. So what is it?"

If I'm wrong, I'm going to sound terribly stupid..." I think there may be a message concealed in the crystal. I have a feeling it might have something to do with the next Trial. Shirez told me to keep it and bring it up with the team. So I think it must have some significance to the Trials."

Dragon sighs and leans back in his chair. "That's our cue. We'll tell them but I think we should wait until we arrive at our destination to open it."

"Okay, sounds good."

He smiles slightly, but it fades. His gaze shifts to the ground, and his hands clench into fists. "Jaina, I'm- I'm sorry."

I blink twice, not sure I heard him right. "For what?"

He shakes his head. "I insulted you and made you feel bad. I was frustrated at the time and I said things I shouldn't have."

At first I'm stunned, but suspicion begins to overcome me. Guys don't apologize unless they think they can get something out of it. It happens all the time. Take Liam for example.

"It's...it's okay," I manage.

"What can I do to make it up to you?"

My lips move, but no sound comes out. What in the galaxy would I want him to do? Does he really trust me like this? I could ask him to do something really embarrassing. I could ask him to challenge Liam to a duel then lose miserably in front of the whole team. It's all I can to hold back a laugh. But I couldn't make him do something like that. It'd be too sad, seeing he worked up the nerve to actually *apologize*.

"You don't have to do anything," I reply. "Just stay out of trouble for me."

He laughs. "Of all the things you could ask of me, I should have known you were going to say that. It'll be difficult...but I guess I'll have to now. For you."

There's a long silence, but this time, it's not really awkward. I feel like I'm melting into the universe. It's as if I no longer exist; the only thing I'm conscious of is him. Those eyes, his lips, that face and strong, defined chest...

"We should, um..." He clears his throat. "We should get to work, I guess."

"Right. Yeah, okay, I'll go talk to the team." I stand up and start to leave the room. "Bye."

"Bye," he says softly.

Shaav, he's making me crazy. I can't have feelings for him, though. To love someone the IA hasn't chosen for you is an act of treason. We'd both be executed for it, even if he doesn't feel the same for me. As long as I keep myself at a distance, neither of us will be hurt.

I take in a deep gulp of air as I force myself to continue forward. He's my *friend*. Just a friend.

We arrive at our hotel in Amarija nearly seven hours after takeoff. Shirez takes us to our room which has the same layout as the last. It's weird being in a completely different place but having almost the exact same room. Shirez leaves us and goes wherever he goes after dropping us off.

Nine doors lie along the walls of the circular room, and a tenth room to the left is a small kitchen.

"So, now what?" Kavi asks, sitting herself down on one of the soft white couches before a large glass window.

"Just as we did before," I reply. "Wait, and hope our nerves don't bother us until tomorrow."

"So we're in Amarija, right?" Liam asks.

Dragon nods. "Yes. Once known as America."

"Why'd they have to go changing all the names?" Liam asks. "I mean, it's just confusing because on Virana we had to memorize the new world maps, but then they started teaching us the old ones!"

I take a seat on the couch next to Kavi, while Dragon and Luci sit adjacent to my left.

Luci rolls her eyes. "That's because they split the old countries into districts, and the continents became like provinces. It just makes things easier for the emperor."

"Wasn't the United States the place the first republic was born?" Seth asks after inspecting a holographic bookshelf on the wall.

"Not the first ever but the only one that survived the Great Flood," Luci says.

"I don't remember learning about the Great Flood," Avan cuts in. His hands rest on the back of the couch to my right for support.

"We learned about it last year," I protest.

Luci nods. "Avan's fifteen, remember. He's a year behind us, so he missed out on that class."

"Okay, we should get to work," Liam says, which is weird, because at Virana, he was the one always goofing off. "You guys mentioned something about the crystal? Something about a code or message?"

I interlock my fingers nervously. "Yes. We think there's a message concealed inside."

Liam lets himself fall into the soft cushions of the couch Avan's leaning against. "And why would you think that?"

"It's just a guess," Dragon replies. "But if we're right, there will be a code to access the message."

"You need someone to decipher it?" Liam asks.

"Yes."

"No problem." He bounces right back up from the couch, and approaches me, then shoves his hand at me. "I've got it covered."

After handing him the crystal, he backs down.

"Seth, you want to help me?" Liam asks.

"You think I'd let you have all the fun?" Seth replies.

They head off into the kitchen and begin their decoding without another word.

With nothing else to do, I stand and approach the bookcase. I swipe my finger across the digital screen. Book covers zoom past me, some filled with color while others are simple and black with a single line of small text for the title. There are quite a few books on the IA, and how the first Emperor brought the galaxy out of the Great Stellar Wars. Nothing I haven't read before.

Kavi materializes to my right. "Since when do you like to read?"

"I've always liked to read," I say. "Just never really had time for it."

"Read anything interesting, lately?"

"Not really. You?"

"Depends," she replies. "I like reading ancient history. Stuff about the Earth before we came in contact with ET's."

"Yeah, I know." I stare at the shelf, not really looking at anything in particular. "Kavi, do you think there could be a..."

She rolls her wrist, signaling me to continue. "A... what?"

I lower my voice. "Could there be a Republic again?" The words sound so rebellious, like something Dragon would say. But I have to get her opinion on it.

Kavi's smile fades, but she doesn't act like what I've said is wrong. So I assume everything will be all right.

"That's not something I can answer. You know me. I'm extremely biased and opinionated," she replies.

There's a breath of silence. The air is crisp and tense around me, like I'm back in the snowy arena. I can tell she's uncomfortable.

Kavi sighs and takes a step away from me. "I will say this. History tends to repeat itself, for better and for worse." She shakes her head, sadly. "Most of the time, for worse."

"Hey guys, I think we've got something," Seth calls.

The sun has abandoned the sky, plunging the world into darkness. The city bustles below us. Yet the sleepy energy in the room instantly transforms into an excited rush of questions. I dash over to Liam and Seth as the rest of my team follows behind me.

"What'd you find?" Kavi asks over Seth's shoulder.

Seth sneers at her. "Like I'd actually tell *you*?"

Liam nudges him. "There were codes surrounding the outer edges of the crystal, each hinting at the answer to the next. Once I got those sorted out, I was able to figure out a code to unlock the first few layers of the crystal using the other answers. If I can open this last shell..." He presses a few buttons on it.

On the table lie the three, outermost shells of the crystal. In his hands, Liam holds the final shell. I hadn't realized it was layered. He uses a microscope Luci happened to find in the closet about an hour ago, though I'm pretty sure the creators of the Trials put it there specifically for this.

There's a click.

"Got it!"

Dragon jumps forward. "Read it," he urges.

Everyone huddles in to see. Dragon's chest brushes against my back as he squeezes in closer and I catch my breath, feeling his warm body so close to mine.

Kavi who's standing next to me notices. She raises an eyebrow as her lips break into an amused smirk.

"Stop," I mouth to her.

She giggles.

"Seth, go ahead." Liam hands a tiny paper scroll to Seth.

> "Only in the moonlight,
> Can you find me placed sky high,
> On a lake of fire water,
> Where most would pass on by."

Seth looks up after reading. "A lake of fire water?"

"It's probably figurative," Avan says.

"By the stars, I hope so."

"Is that all?" I ask.

"No, there's more," Seth replies then continues.

"Stop the time to rescue me,
You must not be too late,
Every prize has a price to pay,
If you fail, you've sealed your fate.

That's all."

"This is obviously important. Maybe it's both figurative *and* literal," Dragon ponders, taking a step back.

"The trouble is figuring out which is which," I murmur in reply.

"In the moonlight. Either way, we'll find the next crystal at night," Liam says.

"Probably on a mountain or something," Luci adds. "I can't imagine we need to literally travel sky high."

I put the pieces together. "Agreed. So at night, on a mountain."

"And the lake of fire water?" Xana asks.

Liam laughs. "I'm sure we'll recognize that when we see it."

Xana nods. "Fair enough. What about the 'where most would pass by'?"

"Sounds more like they just added that for the rhyme scheme," Luci says. "A place sky high shouldn't be invisible, or too well hidden."

"Stop the time to rescue me, you must not be too late, every prize has a price to pay, if you fail, you've sealed your fate," Seth reads again.

"Stop the time?" Dragon asks.

Kavi shakes her head, crossing her arms over her chest. "That part has to be figurative. There's no way any of us can stop time."

"Right. So maybe stop...a timer?" I ask.

"That's possible," Seth replies.

"All right, so there are just the last three lines," Dragon continues. "The second and last lines of the stanza are pretty clear. If we don't get the *shaav* out of there, we're dead."

"Is there something that must be sacrificed? The third line. 'Every prize has a price to pay,'" Xana points out.

We all fall silent. A price to pay?

Liam swallows hard. I can read the worry in his eyes. "We'll sleep on it."

"Come on," Dragon orders. "Everyone pick a room and get to bed."

Dazed, I find a room for myself.

Would the IA call for a human sacrifice for the sake of the Trials? None of us can overrule what they've ordered, but if the IA asked me to give my life for them... I'm not sure I'd be able to do it.

chapter

FOURTEEN

Everything glows orange and red. The walls are made of rock. Not crumbling stones, but large boulders over seven meters tall. There's a pedestal, like the one we retrieved the crystal from, but instead of a crystal, there's a skull.

My team and I rush toward the pedestal. I'm not sure why, but it's important that we hurry. I whirl around finding a man standing in the only exit. Something about him makes me want to choke. He's a nightmare. So dark that I want recede into the ground.

He flicks his wrist. A silver object spins from his gauntlet. Luci topples over in a pool of blood. Pain shoots through me and I feel like I'm falling. I can't tell if I've been hit, or Luci.

Everything goes dark and a shadow whispers in my ear, "Justice prevails...Beware the Dark."

I sit up with a start. The sun is just rising, though the sky is still a deep, dark blue. A hint of pain flairs behind my eyes, and I press on my forehead, remembering what happened. *Luci.* The dream flashes before my eyes. It didn't feel like a dream at all. It was much more real than that.

I stand up to dress. Sifting through a drawer of clothes, I find a dark green and black camouflage top in the dresser. The shoulders are open, and two pieces of stretchy fabric wrap around each of my arms forming a sleeve, spiraling down to my wrists. It's only a few inches in thickness, but it will keep me warmer. My dark brown pants have slight variation in color, and I assume it's supposed to resemble the ground or tree bark.

Opening my door a crack, I peer out at my teammates. Dragon, Seth, Luci and Kavi are the only ones I can see. I try to eavesdrop, but they speak too quietly for me to hear.

I close the door, and try to clear my mind, but I hear; *"He can't save you...Beware the Dark."*

I shake it off. It's only a dream. No matter how real it was. It was only a dream.

———

At around 7:00 a.m. The sun peaks over the horizon, casting an orange and pink glow into the center room. Everyone else is awake now, but I don't think any of us have gotten enough sleep. Avan yawns then pinches his arm as if struggling to stay awake.

Seth rubs his eyes dreamily. "Are you guys ready?"

"Of course," Xana snorts. "We won the first Trial, and I have a feeling we're unstoppable."

"Don't be overconfident," I remind her.

"You know what time we've gotta be in the arena?" Avan asks, lying down on the couch.

"No idea. Hopefully soon. I hate waiting around," I reply. "Is anyone hungry?"

"It's too early to be hungry." Seth ruffles his blond hair then turns to Dragon and continues the philosophical discussion they've been in all morning.

Some of the girls are listening to them, while others are talking amongst themselves. No one's listening to me, and for the time being, I'm okay with that.

"I'll go with you," Liam says, standing up. "I'm bored, anyway."

I didn't mean *him*. We head over to a small table in the kitchen, which is tucked away from the rest of the room. Windows line the wall to my right, and we find a stash of food in the cupboards to the left.

I grab a circular jar out of the refrigerator, a white goo is in it. "What is this?"

Liam examines it a minute. "I don't know what it's called, but people used to eat it a lot. It's something like yergot...yargat? I don't know. Something like that."

"What's it taste like?"

"I don't know. I've never tried it. It's supposed to be good." By the way his voice catches, I can tell he's not sure. "Have some."

I spoon some in a bowl then try it. The creamy, silky texture is soothing and a sweet tanginess lingers on my taste buds.

"How is it?"

"Pretty good, actually." I hand him a bowl and pour him some.

He takes a reluctant spoonful, and shuts his eyes. Finally, he swallows and relaxes. "That wasn't so bad."

"I wouldn't feed you something gross," I reply, though he wouldn't have hesitated to give me something awful last year. Despite how my feelings for him have washed away, I can't bring myself to get back at him.

"How are things with Dragon?" he asks, a little too nicely. "You still *just friends*?"

My cheeks flush with warmth and I avert my eyes to the granite table. "Liam, please."

"I'm sorry, Jaina. I've been sorry for so long. I feel like I can never apologize enough to you." He runs his fingers through his hair and focuses on his bowl.

"Liam, I'm not the type to hold grudges. Even though it was mean, I accepted it. You wanted to stay the way you were, and that meant not talking to people like me. But I've moved on," I say. "And I didn't move on because of what you did or said. I just...changed."

Liam bites his lip and glances out the large window, gazing across the morning vista. He turns to face me. "How do you feel about him, Jaina?" There's a desperation in his eyes. Before I can answer, he adds, "Honestly, Jaina. It kills me, not knowing. Is Dragon my friend or nemesis?"

My voice hardens. "He shouldn't be your enemy, no matter what I answer."

"Just answer me, Jaina. Please?" He insists. "Put me out of my misery and just tell me the truth."

I sigh. "He's...He's um, very good looking, I'll admit. Besides, if we get to the Crystal City, they'll choose someone for you, too."

He grits his teeth and lowers his voice to a growl. "I don't care. Now answer the question."

"Honestly, he's just my friend. That's all I want him to be."

"But could that change?" he asks.

"I-I don't know." I try to swallow my food, but my throat tightens at his words. I don't want to be having this conversation.

"I'm completely okay with you two being friends. But if he tries to make a move, he is going to have the fight of his life."

"Liam stop. Don't take this out on him. I'm not yours to fight for. I don't know what I feel but–" I suddenly get the sensation that someone is behind us. I turn to see Dragon leaning against the doorway.

"Hey," Dragon says, staring at me dreamily. "Is everything all right?"

Shaav, I hope he didn't hear any of that. "When did you get here?" I ask, doing my best to mask the nervousness in my voice.

"Don't worry, I wasn't eavesdropping. I wasn't really paying attention. Was there something I should have heard? Or maybe *shouldn't* have heard?" He glares at Liam.

"Let's just say it's a private matter and leave it at that," I cut in before Liam can come back with a stinging retort.

Dragon shifts his gaze back to me. "I'm going to go get ready. I'll see you in a little bit."

My whole body feels tense as I study him. His mysterious eyes and brown hair look lighter in the early morning sun. "Sounds good," I manage.

He smiles gently then leaves.

Liam rolls his eyes. "*Shaav*, I hate him."

"I thought you said as long as he doesn't make a move you'd be fine," I reply.

He stares at me blankly as if I had just fallen for the stupidest prank in the galaxy. "Are you *blind*? Do you see the way he looks at you, Jaina? He stares at you like he's gazing at an angel."

I'm speechless. That can't be right. "Liam, he doesn't like me. He couldn't."

"I hope you're right, but I'm watching him like an eagle, okay?" He leans forward placing his elbows on the table threateningly.

"What's that supposed to mean?"

His eyes circle around the room as if he's trying to figure it out, himself. "I'll be watching him very closely. And if he makes a mistake...he's a goner."

"Liam, you don't have to–"

"I know you don't take this seriously, but I do, okay?"

"Okay," I reply, calmly, yet deep down, he's scaring me. What would he do if I were to fall for Dragon or, impossible as it may seem, what if he fell for me?

Back in my room, I put on my gauntlet and check the settings. I skim through the basics and find color. After I press a few buttons, I change the color template to black for this mission. On my command, the gauntlet ripples before slowly changing to black.

Finally I strap on my holster belt and carefully place my scimitar in the magnetized compartment on my hip. I stroll out of my room and find the rest of my teammates, ready to go.

Shirez knocks. This time I'm not quite as jittery. Liam opens the door.

"This one won't be so easy," Shirez says.

Liam cocks his head, irritated. "Nice to see you, too."

"Not nearly as easy. The second trial is harder. Very much so. You're battling to represent the world now. The competition is tough. You're going against the best of six territories. From this moment on, it gets much, much harder." He almost sounds sad. "Time to go."

Shirez leads us through the halls of the hotel then takes us onto the roof. There's a ship waiting for us packed with weapons and supplies. This time I know what I have to bring.

I grab a stale pack of rations and stuff them into a pocket on my holster belt. The throwing knives I had in the previous Trial didn't do me much good, so I only take one. I use the extra space in my belt for a long dagger, a stun pistol, and a gun that can be set to shoot either plasma or bullets.

Avan snatches up a stun pistol, some medical supplies and bandages. They don't all fit in his holster belt, so I help him find a plasma proof backpack.

"Strap on your armor," Shirez orders.

We obey. This time, my armor is green and silvery, similar to my clothes.

The transport hovers a meter above ground, and we jump into our new landscape. I view the new world with relief. Though it's not a jungle like Virana, at least it's warmer than the last Trial. The crisp northern air brings my senses alive with new smells and sights. A minty freshness fills the air, yet it's not overpowering. It's like medicine for my lungs.

Tall green trees surround us. Their leaves high above shade us from the sun, but not in a messy way. The jungle trees on Virana seemed to merge with one another, closing us in and shielding us from the world. Here, the trees aren't so close together. They're spaced out, distanced from one another, as if they're all neighbors, not family.

The transport recedes into the sky.

The moment my feet touch the ground, an odd, tingly sensation slithers through my body. I can't shake the twinge of fear that looms over me. Something is wrong.

It will all be all right. It will all be okay. And slowly, I begin to think, what could possibly go wrong?

Birds chirp like wind chimes in the canopy. I thought I could get used to it. After all, I lived in the jungle of Virana my entire life. But these birds are different. There's no backdrop of the ocean waves, or the smell of the sea breeze lingering faintly on everything.

And after nearly three hours of listening to the same birds chirp in slight variations of their own songs, I want to plug my ears and scream.

Avan, who's ahead of me, stops dead like he's hit an invisible wall. "Did you hear that?"

"If it's another one of those ice spitting things, I'm running for my life," Liam mutters.

"What's wrong?" Dragon asks.

"I think we're being tailed." Avan looks up at Dragon nervously, as if he's not entirely sure of himself.

Dragon nods. "Kavi, Seth, check the perimeter. If anyone's around, circle back, and ambush them."

"Yes, sir." Seth salutes, and the two of them take off into the trees.

"Liam, Xana, position yourselves in those trees. We'll have an advantage over them." Dragon gestures to the trees to our right.

They leave as Luci and Avan form up around us, waiting for something to happen, waiting for a reason to attack.

I look up and find Xana high in a leafy tree. Her green camouflage helps her blend in, and if I didn't know she was up there, I wouldn't be able to see her. She raises her sniper and signals to the east.

A hissing echoes through the air. My eyes hone in on a tiny glowing object spinning towards me.

"Look out!"

I'm not sure who calls the warning, but it doesn't matter. Pain burns in my thigh, and I fall to my knees in agony. A throwing star is lodged deep in my right leg. Dragon pulls me to my feet, but my legs tremble with adrenaline.

Another team approaches. They're from Vishtu, the continent once known as Africa. They all share the same midnight-sky dark skin. We had many classmates on Virana from Vishtu.

I pull my hand away from my leg. It's dripping with blood. *Shaav*, this isn't good, but the need to fight burns through my veins. The pain dulls to a mere pinprick in the back of my mind.

Four of them charge us. The fifth falls to the ground as an MED strikes her in the back.

Another throwing star hurtles toward me, but this time I'm ready for it. Just as it should slice through my neck, I duck and roll to the left. The four Vishti have drawn their swords and begin their assault.

A boy about my age approaches me, swishing his black shimmering blade in the air before me. I swing my scimitar in an arc toward him, but his sword bends and twists around mine. The snake-like movement scares me out of my wits and I jerk backward, bewildered.

He keeps at me and skims my jaw with his serpentine blade. I yank my scimitar free from its coils and slice it into pieces. It drops from the boy's hand as he pulls out a long dagger.

He lunges at me, and his blade skims my torso. The warm red liquid oozes down my waist. I ignore the pain and continue slashing furiously at him. I'm breathing heavily and need to end this soon. I swing at his throat, but he ducks just in time. He stands and kicks me in the stomach.

I gasp and stagger backward, unable to breath. I back into a tree with such force I drop my scimitar. He charges forward with the rage of a wild animal, his sword raised high. *I'm about to die. By the stars, I'm going to die.*

My hand tangles itself around the hilt of an MED in my holster belt. I wait until the last possible moment, then duck with my dagger held out. My eyes shut.

He rams into me.

Warm, gooey liquid splatters my face.

I pull my MED from his chest.

Short, panicky breaths overwhelm my lungs. They're the only relief from the shock knifing its way into me.

His lifeless body topples to the ground, blood drips down his stomach and discolors his clothes. My legs won't move. I want to turn away from the horrible sight, but I'm frozen. My eyes are locked on the gruesome wound, still gushing as death turns his body cold.

Dragon rushes up to me, coming between me and my victim.

"Jaina," he says sternly. "Jaina, are you all right?"

I find no reason to answer. A girl lies dead on the ground, only a meter away. The other Vishti take off into the woods, dragging the wounded behind.

Dragon's gaze rests on my leg, and his face drains of color as my thigh drains of blood.

"Oh," is the first sound that escapes his throat. He looks frantically at the team. "Luci! Avan! Get over here!"

I try to tell him I'm fine, but the words don't come. My dagger slides out of my fingers and hits the ground with an echo.

I killed him.

What have I done?

Dragon's hands clasp around my arms, and he helps me sit down. "Jaina, you'll be okay. Just breathe. You'll be fine. I promise." His voice reverberates through my skull, but I can't grasp the meaning of his words.

The world spins, and my vision blurs. Nausea overcomes me, and all I see is the fading outline of Dragon's face. A dark tunnel forms around me. Dragon's lips move, but I can't hear a word he's saying. Finally, the lights go out and consciousness is lost in the dark.

We're taught to show no mercy. The weak should die. But they never told us how wrong it would feel.

This is the way of the Imperial Alliance. This is how it must be done. To think otherwise would be treason. But by the stars, it's wrong.

The hushed undertone of rain is present in my mind.

Rain.

I've missed it. I welcome the damp feel in the air, and the cool taste of earth on my tongue.

If the color silver had a sound, it would be that of the rain. Comforting, like a lullaby. Reminding me of home.

I open my eyes to find a rocky ceiling above my head. We must have found a cave. *No. Not we.* My team must have found it. How long have I been out?

Dull pain radiates in my leg, and I wince as something shifts unnaturally in the wound on my thigh.

Luci's face appears in my vision. She's holding down my arms with both of her hands. Another pair of hands hold down my ankles. I lift my head as far as I can and find Xana at my feet. Avan's fingers clutch my thigh, cutting off circulation to my entire right leg. In his other hand is a metal tool, shaped like a pencil with a fishhook on the end.

I swallow hard. "What's going on?"

Avan looks up at me with a gasp. "Oh no. Luci, you've got to knock her out for this."

Luci scoffs. "What do you want me to do, Avan? Punch her?"

"Figure something out!" he cries.

"No way!" she snaps back. "Xana, just help me hold her down."

My gaze shifts from face to face. "What's going on?" I repeat, straining against Xana and Luci's grasp. "What are you doing?"

The pain grows in my leg. Burning. Throbbing with heated agony. I gasp for air and pull away from them.

"Keep her still, will you?" Avan orders. "This is the last part."

Luci presses my head back to the ground. "Jaina," she says. "I need you to listen to me. We're not trying to hurt you. Okay?"

I swallow hard as another wave of pain shoots up my leg and into my spine. "Okay," I breathe.

"In the fight back there you were injured. Remember?" she asks.

I grit my teeth and nod.

"Good. Avan has to get the blade out. If it stays in, you'll get infected, and you will die. He's a trained doctor," she continues in an even tone, "but he can't do this if you struggle. I need you to cooperate. Stay as still as you can and relax. Understood?"

"Okay," I murmur.

"Avan, are you ready?" she asks.

"Yeah, I'm ready."

Luci looks back down at me. "He's going to take it out now." She takes a steady breath. "On three. Just breathe, and don't struggle. Keep your body loose. Okay?"

"All right." I gulp in the air, anticipating the pain. Maybe it won't hurt so much. Maybe it'll be numb.

"One," Luci begins.

I can be tough. I can handle this.

"Two."

Another gulp of air. I seal my eyes shut.

"Three."

First, there's nothing.

Then, I scream.

Wave after wave passes over me. Pure, raging pain. Fire in my blood. In every cell, in every vein. Every beat of my heart brings more. Luci covers my mouth to drown the uncontrollable shriek escaping my lips. I clench my teeth together and moan through my tightened jaws.

Slowly, but surely, the sensations retreat to a heated numbness around the gash. Luci lets go of my hands, but for the moment, I lie still. I can't bring myself to move yet.

My breaths are short and choppy. I have no control over them and can only listen to myself moan.

"There," Avan says. "All done."

Finally, my muscles relax, and I'm able to sit up. I inspect my wound, but there isn't much to see. My pant leg is caked with drying blood, but the cut has been sealed over with a white medpatch.

Luci nods toward Avan. "I can handle the rest."

"You sure?"

"Yeah, I got it."

Avan gets up, his hands stained with the deep redness of my blood. He holds up the throwing star and hands it to me. Without a word, he goes his way.

"How're you doing?" Luci asks.

I sigh unsteadily and place the bloody throwing star on the ground next to me. "You tell *me*. You're the doctor."

"Don't go giving me much credit. I just held you down. Avan's the one who saved your life."

"How long until I'm back to normal?"

She smiles. "You won't be back to normal until you receive full medical attention. But this medpatch is lined with a powerful painkiller so you shouldn't feel much."

I glance up at her nervously.

"Don't worry. They won't affect your ability to think or fight. As long as the patch stays on, you can do almost everything you could do before," she answers.

I raise an eyebrow. "So I could stand up and walk around?"

She nods. "Yeah, pretty much."

I tense the muscles in my leg with caution, afraid to bring another onslaught of anguish, but none comes.

"Where's everyone else?" I ask.

"Seth and Kavi went for a walk to who knows where. Probably to sort out their miserable problems. Liam and Xana went to get firewood just now. I don't know where Dragon is, but he'll be back."

I sigh and survey the cave. It's not very big, but I can't tell how far back it goes. Grey light spills in through the mouth of the cave as the rain falls in sheets outside.

I stand, putting most of my weight on my left leg, then tentatively shift over to my right. My thigh tingles, and without the painkillers, I'm sure it would be screaming with pain.

Seth and Kavi stumble inside, soaking wet and disheveled. Her hair is frazzled and she picks frantically at her fingernails.

"What happened to you?" I ask.

"Well, we were um, running, and I thought we were going to get caught so we kept running. I think we outran them," she mumbles.

I've got the feeling she isn't quite telling the truth. "Seth, is that what happened?"

He hesitates. "Uh, yeah..." he pauses. "That's exactly what happened."

"Should we check the perimeter?" I ask. "They might still be around."

"No!" Kavi shouts. "I mean, I don't think that's necessary. We, um, we outran them by quite a lot. I'm sure they aren't around anymore."

"I agree," he adds. "I fully agree with Kavi. Good thinking, Kav. We would never have outrun them if it weren't for you."

There's something in their tone of voice that makes their lie obvious. I laugh, then let it go. The question is... where were they? And what was going on?

Over time, they all return. Dragon, Liam, Xana... all of them. Things move along much smoother than they did in the last Trial. Every one's getting along so far, but the serenity of the atmosphere is infuriating. We're on a time sensitive mission, and everyone's just standing around. How can they be so relaxed?

Dragon moves past me, but I grab his arm.

"What the *shaav* are we doing?" I demand.

"I'm glad you're okay," he replies. "And what are we doing? I've got no *shaavez* clue. That battle scared the hell out of them." His voice is harsher now.

"How long have I been out?"

"Too long, if you ask me. Four hours." He glances down at my leg and relaxes a little. "How are you feeling?"

"I'm okay. No pain, really. It's just numb. Luci and Avan did a good job."

He attempts a smile, but it's not convincing. "So, what's your plan?"

I raise my brow. "What makes you think I have a plan?"

Dragon crosses his arms and studies me. "You've got that look on your face. Like you've got an idea."

"I do."

The light of the fire dances on our faces. Luci passes out our meager rations; just a few small pieces of some plant and dried food cubes from my holster belt. We aren't lucky enough to have meat tonight.

The food is dry and about as flavorful as sand, but at least it's something.

Dragon looks deep in thought and peacefully sad as he stares into the fire. I can't explain him. Conflicted, at peace, ignorant, and understanding, all at once. The fire flickers across his face, mimicking his expression. One minute it's light, and the next it's as deep and bottomless as his eyes.

I clear my throat. "We should start figuring out where this next crystal is."

Everyone goes silent, and the pressure shifts to me. Even Dragon stares at me, like I'd just dropped a bomb in the room.

"If we want to win, we have to hurry. We've wasted enough time." I know they have to give in. And finally, they do.

Seth sighs. "Hand me the crystal."
I do, and he opens and reads it.

> "Only in the moonlight,
> Can you find me placed sky high,
> On a lake of fire water,
> Where most would pass on by."

"We've already agreed that the place is something like a mountain," I point out, hoping others join the discussion.

"Good, we have that covered. Did we discuss the 'lake of fire water'?" Seth asks.

"We couldn't figure out what that was," Xana says.

"What about 'only in the moonlight'?" Liam asks. "Does that mean we can only truly find it in the moonlight?"

There's a slight pause while we think about that one. The only sound is the crackling and popping of the fire.

Avan shrugs. "That would probably make the most sense."

"I think the moon is supposed to be out tonight anyway," Kavi says.

"How do you know that?" Liam asks.

She grins, revealing every one of her shiny white teeth. "Found a weather app on my gauntlet."

Dragon laughs. "That's Shirez, looking for every possible problem we could come up against."

Liam shakes his head, smiling. "At least the guy knows what he's doing."

Kavi continues studying the hologram hovering over her gauntlet. "Anyway, unless it's cloudy, most of the moon should be visible. Tomorrow night it's supposed to be full."

"Even if it's cloudy, I don't see any danger in searching tonight," I say.

Dragon nods in agreement. "All right, we should get some rest. We'll wake up early, a few hours before sunrise and search until the sun's up."

There are quiet murmurs and nods of approval.

Now all we must do is wait for darkness to engulf the world.

I'm deep in sleep and not ready to wake. Someone touches my arm, but I remain still. It's probably Kavi wanting to bother me with her problems. Something cold brushes my shoulder, and I flinch. Sensation returns to my hands. The tension in my arms hurts with an achy pain that won't subside.

"Stop," I try to say, but it comes out as a muffled "sopff". My lips are sealed shut. My eyes fling open.

The starry sky is my only roof. What's happening? My back is being dragged over the leafy ground. I'm not with my team.

"Sir, I think she's awake," says a girl.

"Let her go," a boy replies casually. "I'll get her to talk." His voice is similar to Shirez's. They share the same accent.

Despite the fog in my mind, I know I've got to get out of here. I want to stand up and run away, but my joints aren't working the way they should be. My movement is slow and uncontrolled. What's *wrong* with me?

"Tie her up," he orders.

"Sir, she's so weak," says another.

"She *seems* weak, Desan. Remember, she's from Virana," the boy fires back.

You got that right.

Someone approaches with a long, black rope and binds my wrists behind my back. They hold my arms and pull me to my feet as my strength lazily comes back to me.

I have to get away.

In a burst of sudden motion, I duck and ram the girl on my left in the stomach with my shoulder. Gasping in pain, she clutches her belly. I kick the boy on my left in the shin.

The clicking of weapons fills my ears, and I stop. All seven of their guns are aimed at me. The boy who acts like he's in charge raises his hand at his teammates.

"Put your weapons down," he says. "I'll handle this."

He lunges toward me and shoves me into a tree. My shoulder scrapes against the bark, and I let out a soft moan as droplets of blood are purged from my skin.

He twists his fingers around the top of my shirt and holds it in a fist. He presses me into the tree, his face only centimeters from my own.

"Struggling won't help you, Jaina," he says, stroking my cheek. "You're terribly outnumbered."

I pull away from him. Revulsion claws its way into my stomach.

He digs his fingers under the tape on my mouth and tears it from my lips. The bottom half of my face feels like a hundred tiny needles pricked into it, and I yelp.

"Answer my questions and I'll let you live."

My body shakes with fear, yet I struggle with all my might to stay strong.

"I am Azad Viraak. Leader of the Manincia team."

If I could break free, I'd punch this guy's face in. I grit my teeth, wiggling my wrists to loosen the rope around them. But it does no good. "How do you know me?" I ask.

Azad smiles. "I have good sources."

I let my eyes meet his. He's not someone I want to upset. It's too dark to see much, but I can make out a pale scar under his left eye. He's large and muscular, his hair is darker than coal. His emerald green eyes are piercing, and despite the difference in color, they remind me of Dragon's. Because deep within them, behind his anger lies a deep pitted sorrow. That sliver burrowing into him, like the one I've seen while looking at Dragon.

Everything about him makes me want to shiver. He pulls me closer but I lurch backward in resistance.

"What do you want with me?" I spit through clenched teeth.

Azad's grip loosens slightly. "I'll cut to the chase. There's a traitor to the IA on your team."

My eyes widen in disbelief and my breath catches behind my lips. "How dare you." How *shaavez* dare he.

"Oh yes," he insists. "And I have evidence of it."

"You're my enemy," I hiss. "You expect me to believe you?" None of my teammates could be a traitor. Heated anger surges behind my fearful eyes.

"I'm your competitor, yes. Your enemy, maybe. A liar...no." A dark, half-crazed grin plays at his lips and a smoky smell lingers on his breath.

I study him a moment longer. "H-how do you know?" My voice falters as I speak, making me sound weak.

Azad takes a step back and laughs. "I *know*."

A cold tingling drips down my spine and around my waist. My lungs contract with fear, but I grit my teeth. "You're wrong."

"Just because you wish it so, doesn't mean it is," Azad mumbles. "And unfortunately for you, I'm not lying. I have a proposition for you."

Proposition? He wants to make a deal with me? I'm not that desperate.

He slowly raises a knife to my throat and drags it lightly across my skin.

"Wh-what is it?" I stammer.

"Having a traitor on your team would get you disqualified. I could easily tell the authorities. But, if you help us, I won't say a word. If your work satisfies me, I'll tell the Imperials how you helped us and that you're worthy of entering the Crystal City."

"I'm not working for you," I snap. How could he think I'd do such a thing?

Azad takes a deep, frustrated breath. "Are you not scared enough? Do you know what happens to a disqualified team?"

I hesitate, then reply, "No. I don't."

"The traitor will be executed. And it's not a painless death for a traitor. In whatever manner the Imperials decide, he will be tortured to the point that he'll be begging for death. The traitor's team shall be interrogated and forced to work in a Recon Camp." He touches my chin and lifts my gaze to his. He's so eerily gentle, and my fear is too great, so my body complies. "There's a boy on your team who might share the fate of all traitors. Would you want this for him, even if he has betrayed the IA?"

I think of Liam and Seth, Dragon and Avan. What if I knew one of them would have to suffer because of me? What if he was tortured and executed because I failed to do anything about it? We shouldn't have sympathy for traitors, but if it was a friend of mine...

"What sort of thing would I have to do?" I ask, defeated.

"You'll give me information. Simple things like where the crystal is, if you know, or the answer to a riddle.

Where your team is heading and keeping us hidden from them. But," he pauses, "if you give us false information or personally diminish my chances of victory, I'll kill your partner. Do I make myself clear?"

Dragon.

"What if I say no?" I only breathe the words.

Azad brings his hand to my jaw and forces me to meet his eyes again. I try to jerk away, but he's too strong. He raises his knee to my thigh and presses hard into my injury. The pain flairs, and my body tenses. Fiery streams of heat shoot through my leg and up my back. A moan escapes my throat, yet I clench my teeth together in defiance. Tears rush to my eyes, yet I hold them in. I can't let him think I'm weak.

"You can't. Now, I'm going to let you go. We'll return for you, and you'll tell me *everything* I want to know. You will not tell anyone about this conversation," he says coldly. "Understood?"

I bite down on my lip, trying to ease the sensations in the rest of my body.

"Do you understand?" he repeats, pressing harder.

I gasp with the pain and nod, violently. "Yes. Yes, I understand," I manage.

He lets go of me and takes out the small, silver stun pistol.

"We'll be watching you." He brings the weapon to my shoulder and fires.

chapter

FIFTEEN

My eyes open with a start. A dim light flickers across the cavern walls and I lift my head from the rolled up cloth I was using as a pillow. Crickets chirp outside, along with the rustling of the wind in the trees.

"Jaina," a voice whispers.

My eyes scan the room as agitation tingles at my fingertips.

"Jaina," he whispers again.

I contemplate asking who's there, but my voice catches in my throat. A horrible nausea settles in my stomach as I realize I'm alone. My team is gone, yet blood stains the floor.

"Dragon!" I clutch the hilt of my scimitar. "Dragon!"

A hand closes around my throat, and I reach up to push him away. Struggling to breathe, I look into Azad's eyes. I claw at his hand, attempting to tear it from my throat, yet he doesn't let go.

He pulls me to my feet and presses me into the wall. His eyes burn red with hatred, but his voice is calm and pleading as he whispers into my ear, "Do not fail me."

The sensation of dropping fills my body and I scream. I lash out at him, but my hands find nothing to hit or scratch.

My palms smash into the floor, and I open my eyes, tearing at my throat. The room is completely dark.

"Jaina." He touches my hand.

Gasping for air, I pull away from him, yank an MED from my holster belt, push him to the ground, and press it to his throat. He grabs my wrist sternly, but with a gentle force that makes me stop. My eyes meet his.

"What the *shaav*?" Dragon cries, holding the dagger away from him. "Are you okay?"

I don't move, continuing to resist his strength and pressing the dagger closer. He squeezes my wrist so the MED falls to the ground, and I let out a breath of relief.

What just happened?

Where's Azad? Was it all just a dream?

"Everything okay back there?" Liam calls.

My eyes shoot toward him, and my breath is choked from my lungs when I realize Dragon's holding me by the wrists while I'm awkwardly on top of him. If Liam saw me press the dagger to his throat, he might understand a little better, but it's clear this is all he's seen.

I pull back quickly and take a seat on the ground, trying not to sound embarrassed. "Everything's fine, Liam."

He nods, unconvinced, but he goes back to whatever he was doing.

I rub the graininess from my eyes. "What time is it?"

Dragon shoots me a glare, asking for an explanation. "What was all that about?"

The muscles in my throat contract. I can't tell him. I can't let him know. Azad said he'd kill him and I'm going to take his word for it.

"Nothing." Only after I say it do I realize how ridiculous it sounds.

Dragon raises an eyebrow. "So then it's just every day you'd hold a knife to my throat?"

"No, that's not it at all!" I retort. "I just…"

I let the silence take its hold and rake my fingers through my hair. How am I going to do this?

Dragon leans in a little closer to me and I resist the sudden urge to press myself into his arms.

"Was it a dream?" he asks softly.

He doesn't avert his gaze, confidently meeting my own. He'd know what it's like to be affected by dreams. He'd understand.

"How long are we going to explore this morning?" I ask instead.

Dragon's lips press together, obviously hesitant to leave the previous conversation. His eyes are partially squinted despite the dark, and his jaw is set slightly to one side. "Until the sun rises. I know we're tired, but we've got the rest of the day to sleep."

I wonder where Azad went with his team.

A chill runs through me just thinking of him.

Dragon guides me outside after we scatter the ashes of last night's campfire. We can't let anyone know we were here. Little does my team know, we're already being followed.

My eyes flicker to the trees around us, but there's no sign of them. If they're watching, they're doing a good job of remaining hidden.

Dragon puts a hand on my shoulder, and I jump with his touch. I turn to him, then glance at our team standing nearby. It's clear they're not enthusiastic about this mission.

"Are we ready to go?" I ask.

Dragon nods. "Yeah, we're all set." He lowers his voice and squeezes my shoulder a little tighter. "Don't think you've gotten out of telling me."

With that, we begin our journey into the night.

———————

The sky is as dark as the bottom of the sea, and the moon remains the jewel of the heavens. No other team should be awake unless they've discovered what we have.

A darker thought comes to me, and I can't push it away. I have to know who the traitor is if I am to protect my team.

To my left, Liam laughs while in a conversation with Avan. A traitor wouldn't be so carefree, would he? Only if that was part of his cover. But Liam's too cocky to be a traitor. Avan's too nice. The Imperials say traitors are heartless souls that believe the weak should rule. Seth just doesn't seem like he would be the one. And Dragon... he's...he's not a traitor. He just isn't. If he were, the Imperials would have killed him long ago.

Azad must have been lying. There's no traitor on my team. But maybe that was his plan. Maybe he's just blackmailing me into giving him what he wants. Would I be able to get out of this if I told him I knew the truth? Or would he kill me for wasting his time?

I don't *want* to know who the traitor is. If I know, I'll have to turn him in. That's the law.

My leg flairs with pain. The painkillers are wearing off. Needing to stop, but too proud to say anything, I spot a tall tree to my right and get an idea.

"Kavi," I say, "climb that tree and see if there's anything that could be considered sky high."

She places her hands on her hips and scoffs. "Why *me*?"

Ugh. Why does she have to resist every order I give her? I rub the sleepiness out of my right eye. "You're small and you were a good climber on Virana."

Kavi scans the tree up and down, a fearful reluctance in her eyes. "What if there's something in there?"

"Just follow orders, Kavi. You'll be fine." I take my gun out of my holster belt. "If anything happens, I'll cover you."

Kavi sighs nervously then begins climbing.

"Careful, Kav," Seth shouts to her.

"Yeah, yeah, I'm trying!" She finally reaches the top.

I turn to Dragon. "What do you think we'll find?"

"Sky high?" he asks. "A mountain, a really tall tree, or..."

Kavi jumps from her perch after climbing most of the way down. "There's forest in all directions and nothing obviously tall except to the south," she reports.

"And...?" I ask.

"There's a volcano," she says. "Or a big mountainy thing."

Dragon smiles at me. "That works, too."

"It's about seven klicks in that direction." She points a few degrees to the left of the direction we've been walking.

I nod. "Let's move out."

The team follows closely behind, not saying much. They're all so tired. If someone or something were to jump out and attack us, would we be able to defend ourselves?

I let Dragon take the lead, too lost in thought to keep track of which direction we're walking. Even though I'd hate to know, I have to find out who the traitor is. If there's one at all. Maybe if I just go talk to some of them...

"Where are *you* going?" Dragon asks me.

"Just in the back," I reply quickly. "I'll probably end up next to Liam because Xana hates him."

He stands up straighter at the sound of Liam's name. "Why don't you just stay up here? They've got to learn to sort out their own problems."

I laugh casually but can't ignore the sudden, pounding in my chest. Does he *want me* to stay with him? No, he probably just wants to ask me what all the fuss was about earlier. Embarrassed, I glance down at the ground. "Okay, sure."

It's uncomfortable, being in the front with only him. When I'm fighting, I'm in control. I know the possible outcomes, and I'm willing to accept that. But when I'm talking to Dragon, I'm not in control, and I have no idea what the outcomes could be. It's this constant state of not knowing that drives me insane.

Unable to stand the silence any longer, I decide to take over. "I guess that makes 'the lake of fire water' more plausible."

"Having it be lava, you mean?" He keeps his eyes forward and doesn't look at me.

"Yeah. It makes sense now that the volcano part is clarified. I'm pretty sure most of the teams won't go searching in a volcano for the crystal."

"I'm still not so sure what the second half of it means. It makes me worry," he ponders. "'Every prize has a price to pay...'"

"What do you think it means?"

His left arm hangs beside his holster belt, and his hand rests on the hilt of his scimitar. Like he suspects he'll need it any moment. "I don't know. I tend to think about the worst that could happen and hope it's better than that. But in this case, the worst is pretty bad...I honestly don't know what it means, Jaina. And until we have to face it, I'd rather not know."

I stare up into his shimmering, crystal blue eyes. The stars shine perfectly in his dark hair, and the moon casts a pale glow upon his face, making him even more irresistible.

I have to tell him.

No, I can't. He could get hurt.

But if I said something, maybe he could help me.

Either way, I can't hold it in any longer. Azad scares me too much to face him alone. "Dragon," I say. "I have something I need to tell you."

He smiles. "I knew you'd come around eventually. You mind talking about it when we're more...alone?"

"No, that would be better."

Dragon nods. "Don't bail on me, though. For this team to function there can't be anything that keeps us apart. No secrets."

No secrets. Right. Okay.

I begin to have second thoughts. Part of me wants him to know, but I'm afraid of putting his life at risk. I want to be honest with him, but I know he's not entirely honest with me. Maybe I *shouldn't* tell him.

We walk nearly two more hours but at least the birds aren't chirping this early. But we've got about two klicks left. As the sky transforms from black to a deep ocean blue, we find a dense cluster of trees hiding almost everything inside. The trunks are thicker than four normal trees put together. Some of the branches merge, creating platforms above our heads, big enough to sleep on. I'm not sure we could have found anything better. If we walk a little longer there might be another cave, but we can't be searching in the daylight. The riddle said we need to search at night. Reaching our destination in the light might mean we'd have to defend the crystal until dark.

Kavi steps in front of us. "There aren't enough trees for everyone to get their own. Besides, it might be dangerous to sleep alone. So I say we put two people to every tree."

"Kavi and I can take the last one," Seth says slyly.

"Very funny, Seth but that won't be happening. I'm bunking with Xana, but Jaina, since you're the leader maybe you should go with Dragon." She raises her eyebrows suggestively.

My cheeks flush with heat and I almost protest, but Luci cuts me off. "I can go with Dragon."

"It's okay, Luci, I can go," I say, annoyed at the thought of *her* going with him.

She shoots me a glare. "Are you sure you want to do that?"

"Luce, it's okay," Dragon says. "Jaina and I are the leaders. We'll take this opportunity to talk strategy. Okay?"

My body tingles with the idea of sleeping near him, and only him. I can't quite tell if it's out of excitement or anticipation of how awkward this will be. It's probably a little bit of both.

Liam's eyes cloud with darkness. "I *really* don't like this idea."

"What's your problem, Liam?" Dragon asks.

Liam stares back at us. "You know what? That can wait until another time. I'll just *mindlessly* follow your orders until then."

He and the rest of the team go to the trees and take up position high in the flat branches.

"What's up with him? Why the *shaav* does he care?" Dragon spits. "Every time I try to say a word to him, he comes back with some rude remark."

"It's a long story, Dragon." Kavi's the only one I've told. The whole story, anyway.

"We've got a while."

Dragon and I approach one of the empty trees. I'm not really sure how this is going to work. The leaves are dense, but can they shield us from view?

I press through the poky, needle-like leaves, and climb to a platform of branches nearly half-way up the tree. Dragon follows closely behind. The thick branches and sharp, pointy leaves should keep anyone or anything from finding us. From the inside, I can hardly see out. Would Azad be able to find us here? He seemed to have an easy time kidnapping me from our camp.

"So you wanna tell me?" he asks, taking a seat next to me. His arm brushes my shoulder.

I can't tell him, but as I peer into his cool, oceanic eyes, everything I know wants to fly from my lips. I hesitate. "After you left..."

"That's what the others called it? It's when I *left*?"

"Yeah. It's an understatement, I know. But not many people were there to see it," I say.

He shakes his head. "Go on."

"After you left, Liam and I became good friends. I met Kavi at around the same time, but that's kind of beside the point. It was only last year that I..."

Dragon smiles, amused. "Go ahead, Jaina. You can say it."

My face goes warm. Thank the Emperor the sun hasn't risen yet, and my face is still hidden in the shadows.

"Last year, I really started to like him. Of course, that's the year he became too good for me, so he kept his distance. I got over him and don't like him anymore," I say, then reconsider. "At least not in *that* way."

"But he likes you now?"

I shrug, remembering how Liam spoke to me in the last Trial. "Maybe."

Dragon studies me, intensely. "So what does this have to do with me?"

Oh no. How am I supposed to answer this? My fingers rest on the large, flattened branch beneath us and I pick at the bark, breaking off little pieces into my hand. "Um, I-I think he's...jealous," I stammer.

"What does he have to be jealous of?"

"I don't know," I reply softly. "He doesn't like that you get to be with me all the time."

He brushes a strand of hair from my shoulders and smiles. "I love spending time with you."

Just his words, 'I,' 'love,' and 'you,' process in my head, and I feel compelled to kiss him or *something*. I have to change the subject before I go crazy.

"Jaina," he whispers. "What's wrong?"

I take a deep, painful breath as I tear my gaze from him. "Dragon, can I talk to you about that boy..."

"The boy you killed?" he finishes.

"I feel terrible, Dragon. I know it's a weakness, but it's hurting me. What should I do?"

"As long as it's out of self-defense it's okay," he says. "It's hard, Jaina. I know."

"You've killed people before?"

Dragon shifts uncomfortably. "Yes. It's nothing to take lightly. But you can't let it get to you or you'll go crazy."

"I could've just as easily been killed," I murmur. "He was strong. What gave me the right to kill him?"

"Sometimes," he says painfully, "it's unavoidable."

He speaks with such a tone of sorrow and remembrance it becomes clear he's killed many more than I have. And he's hurting with their memories.

The thought of him doing such things sends cold shivers down my spine. There's still so much I don't know about him.

I yawn and rub my palms over my eyes. Trying to change the subject, I say, "Should we get some sleep?"

He moves closer, not once shifting his gaze. His gentle hand strokes my hair, and his eyes peer deeply into my own. "What happened earlier, Jaina? You said you had something to tell me."

The words stick in my throat, and I can't answer. I try to speak, but words won't come.

"Why do you have a stun mark on your arm?" He traces the outline of the mark near my shoulder. I hadn't even noticed it was there.

Warmth spreads through me. His touch is so soothing, so seductive, and it makes my body tingle with anticipation.

"People don't just get these, you know," he says, keeping his hand on my arm. His posture becomes questioning, even predatory, yet his voice remains soft. "What are you hiding from me?"

I can't tell him. Can't let him get hurt again. Last time, it was my fault. I could have done something. Instead I let them take him. Let them tear him from my life. I will not let that happen again.

"It's nothing." I stand up and move away from him. I can't bear to look in those eyes and lie.

Dragon stands and rests his hands on my shoulders, turning me back to face him. My heart jumps into a nervous frenzy. He holds me sternly, but I'm not scared, not by him.

"Jaina I'm–" His brow is knit with worry. "I'm sorry, but I have to know. Who did you talk to last night?"

I stare back at him, wondering how he knew I talked to *anyone*. "Nothing happened, Dragon." I try to sound convincing, but it sounds lame, even to me. "Besides you don't tell *me* everything. Why should I tell you?"

"I'll admit I keep things from you. I keep things from everyone," he says. "But I don't *lie*."

"What have you kept from me?" I pull away from him.

He acts as if that's the last thing he expected me to ask. "I'll tell you. Just not now. It's not important at the moment. But I get the sense whatever you're keeping from me *is*."

There's a long pause, and our breathing is the only sound that fills the silence.

"I can't. I don't want you to get hurt," I confess.

"I won't get hurt, Jaina. Who did you talk to?" He takes my hand softly in his own.

"Dragon, please." My voice is hardly a whisper, and despite myself, my eyes begin to well with tears. I can't think of losing him. Not again. "He said he'd hurt you."

"He can't hurt me, Jaina," he whispers.

He takes a step closer and pulls me into his arms. I close my eyes, holding back tears as I rest my chin on his shoulder. He runs his fingers through my hair and I shiver with his touch. I feel his lips near my cheek.

Memories from that night resurface with his touch. His heart-shattering cries for help as the guards took him away. How I stood and watched.

"It wasn't your fault," he breathes. "You couldn't have stopped them."

I pull away, only slightly this time. His lips are only a breath away.

"But I can stop this."

He shakes his head. "Not without my help."

Azad isn't going to let me get away with this. I know that. But in Dragon's arms, I have the strength to reply. "Viraak. Azad Viraak of Manincia."

Fear flashes through his eyes, and the color drains from his face. He blinks a few times like he's been stunned. "*Who*?"

"Azad Viraak," I whisper.

"*Shaav*, I should have known," he mutters, stepping back and glancing at the thick tree branch under our feet. "What did he want from you?"

"You-you know him?"

His expression grows dark. "Much too well."

"He wanted me to help them. Give them information about where the crystal was."

"And you *agreed*?" he asks.

"He didn't give me a choice," I reply, harsher than I should. "He said he'd kill you or..."

"Or what?" He squeezes my hand.

"He said there's a-a...a *shariin* on our team." I can't bear the word *traitor*, so I say it in Cora instead.

His eyes narrow and his expression hardens.

"Dragon, please, you can't tell anyone. Azad said he'd tell the Imperial Alliance and get our team disqualified—"

"Azad knows who he is? The...*shariin*?"

"Yes..." Only now do I realize Dragon said *he*. Azad knows who *he* is. I stare at Dragon, wanting to keep the thought away. Trying to deny it in my head. "Dragon." My heart sinks as I speak. "Who is the traitor?"

He nervously glances away from me. "It's not something you should know right now."

Slivers of ice seem to pierce my body and melt beneath my skin, freezing me with fear. Dragon knows. He knows who the traitor is. There's really a traitor on our team.

"Tell me! You said there should be no secrets between us!"

Taking a step back, Dragon holds my gaze with an intense sense of longing in his eyes. Finally, he shakes his head. "No."

"Why can't you tell me?"

"I can't risk splitting the team. Once you know who it is, you'll do your best to distance yourself from him. And that can't happen if we are to make it out of this alive."

"Dragon, please–"

"I said *no*. I'm sure you'll find out soon enough, anyway," he shoots back. "I can't imagine the Imperials being oblivious to it for long. Especially if *shaavez* Viraak knows about it."

I swallow hard. "Dragon, if he finds out I told you..." My voice quivers. "What should I do?"

He runs his fingers through his fine hair and leans back against the trunk of the tree. "Just do what you said you would. If he asks where the crystal is, tell him. We can't risk the lives of our teammates because we want to be stubborn. Give him what he wants, and we'll have to prove we can still win."

I feel my expression go blank with shock. "You want me to give away where the crystal is?"

"We're forced to choose between the success of our mission and the lives of our teammates. Under no circumstance will I risk that." He raises an eyebrow. "Would you?"

He's questioning my faith in them. The Imperial Alliance versus my team. And in my heart, I know the mission isn't more important their lives.

"They'll come for me again. I shouldn't be long unless..." I can't finish.

"If you're gone too long, I'll come for you. He won't kill you. Believe me on that," he reassures me.

"How do you know?"

"I *know*," he insists, a twinge of anger hardening his voice. He sighs, shaking his head in painful remembrance, and sits back. "It's a long story. You should get some rest."

"What about you?"

"I need some time to think," he replies. "Be careful, Jaina. I can't win this without you."

Lying down on the smooth tree branch, the cool air washes over me. I can't win without him, either.

chapter

SIXTEEN

It's nearly five in the evening by the positioning of the sun. It wasn't so hard to sleep in the daylight. The inside of the tree is so dark I hardly knew the sun was up.

As awareness slowly surrenders itself, an unnatural warmth envelopes me. I look down to find Dragon's cozy, muscular arm around my waist. His body is positioned protectively beside me, and even in his sleep, he looks ready for action. I wonder if he'd wake up if I brushed a few loose strands of hair from his forehead.

A twig snaps outside, and I lift my head. Cool apprehension floods my veins like a minty breath freshener. I don't welcome the feeling.

I shift my body to peer out from behind the thick leaves, but not enough to leave Dragon's embrace. A boy stands nearby. His weapon is raised, and his eyes rest on me. My body tenses. It's Desan. The boy with Azad.

Were they following us? Maybe they overheard our conversation last night.

My eyes rest on Dragon, and the breath is squeezed from my lungs. I won't let them take him from me.

The soft undertone of his breath is so soothing; it momentarily puts my fears to rest. He's so peaceful in sleep. The subtle hints of inner anguish that plague his handsome face in the day have faded. If it weren't for reality coming back to me, waking him should be considered a sin. I gently touch his shoulder.

"Dragon," I whisper. "Dragon, wake up."

His eyes flutter open. With a sharp intake of air, he jerks his arm from around my waist.

"Sorry," he murmurs.

I smile, remembering how embarrassing it felt when I fell asleep on him.

He glances down through the trees and spots Desan. Anger and rage splash his face, and he grits his teeth.

"I have to go," I say, forcing the fear from my voice.

"No." He grabs my hand as I move toward the edge of the thick tree branch. "I could kill him. Let me go for you."

I shake my head. "Our team isn't awake yet. If you tried to face them alone, they'd overpower you. I have to do this."

"You don't."

More than anything, I want to stay. It would be so easy to let him shoot Desan and get this over with. But that would only put more lives at risk. A leader must be willing to give their life for the people.

"Dragon, I must."

He bites his lip, realizing no matter what he says or does, he can't stop me. "You're going to come back, Jaina."

I gulp down the nausea climbing in my throat.

"Say it," he demands. "Promise me you're going to come back."

"I'm going to come back," I whisper.

He nods, his jaw is clenched in nervousness and his grip remains tight around my hand. "If you're not back in fifteen minutes, I'm coming for you. And if he hurts you...I'm going to kill him."

He pulls me to his chest and holds me in his embrace. My breath is as unsteady as his. I can feel the raw worry raging in his heart.

After a moment, I gently pull away and make my way to the bottom of the tree. Even after I reach the ground and push past the thick leaves into the open, his words linger in my mind. *'Promise me you're going to come back.'* I wonder if he was speaking to me as a friend, a teammate, or...something more.

I approach Desan, turning my face into an indifferent façade not even Dragon could read.

Desan grabs my arm and presses his thumb into the mark left from the stun pistol. I let out a hard breath and grit my teeth.

We move through the forest a little ways without a word. When I risk a glance back, I'm no longer able to see the trees we slept in. If things go wrong, I can only hope Dragon will be here to help.

Azad stands at the center of a small clearing as he talks to a girl. Her hair falls in beautiful, thick, black waves over her shoulders and her looks remind me of Kavi.

"Watch the perimeter," he says to her. "Take the rest of the team with you. As always, if you come across anyone, kill them."

She nods, then disappears with the rest of their team into the forest. Only Desan remains behind me, his rifle pointed squarely at my back. Cold sweat prickles at my neck.

"Get on your knees and put your hands behind your head," Azad orders.

I do as he says. My hands are shaking. Whatever's going on, it's not right.

He laughs, then approaches me. "You're such a bad liar, Jaina. Unlike your precious *Altair*."

My stomach wrenches and my hands tighten into fists at his words.

"I haven't lied to you," I reply through my chattering teeth.

"You broke your promise, love." His eyes burn through me. "And you thought you could just get away with it."

"I don't know what you're talking about."

"I know you're not stupid, so don't pretend to be. I said if you told *anyone*, you would pay dearly for it. Did that mean nothing to you?"

He retrieves a curved dagger and swiftly swings it at me. Pain registers on my cheek and I moan. I start to lose balance on my knees and I bring my hand to my cheek. Yet Azad catches my wrist and holds me still.

"Embrace the pain," he hisses. "You better get used to it around me." He raises his dagger to my throat. The cold, merciless blade presses into my neck. I try to keep my breathing slow, hoping that if he decides to kill me it'll be quick. I stare into his envious jade eyes, and my stomach knots as he glares back.

"You should be begging for your life," he says. "You're braver than I thought. I'm impressed."

"Are you going to kill me?" I manage to ask.

He sighs and puts his dagger away. "No. Only because Altair was smart enough to let you give us the information." He pauses. "So where is it?"

"The volcano," I reply shakily. "That's all I know."

He raises an eyebrow. "That's *all*?"

I nod. "Yes."

"We'll be there," he says. "You're lucky, darling. Much too lucky. Tell Altair I look forward to seeing him again." Azad glances to Desan. "Take her back. And hurry. Her team will be waking soon."

———

Desan pushes me through the trees and dense foliage then he leaves me on my own. I stand up and race through the trees in the direction I hope our camp is. My foot catches on a root and I trip into the dirt. My hands burrow into the ground, skimming them raw. I roll on my back as tears rush to my eyes.

The sky is a deep, dreamy blue. The pre-evening kind of blue that grows a little darker with each passing moment.

I'm not sure whether to cry or laugh because I'm still alive.

Slowly, I turn on my stomach and stand.

"Jaina, are you all right?" Dragon runs up to me and helps me out of the dirt.

I look around. I'm back in the clearing we slept in. By the look of things, no one else is awake yet.

"By the stars, I was..." He pulls me to his chest and holds me in his arms. "I was so worried about you."

"Dragon, he knew." I frantically wrap my arms around his neck and squeeze him tightly to me. "Somehow he knew. This morning, when I told you what happened. He would have killed me if I hadn't told him where it was."

"Is that what this is all about?" He touches my bloody cheek. A seething fire coruscates in his eyes, and his eyebrows knit with worry. His lips curl up in anguish, like a wolf barring its teeth in warning.

"It's not that deep," I say.

He shakes his head and grips me sternly. "Did he hurt you more than this?"

"No." I stare up at him, suddenly feeling the impulse to move closer. My eyes want to close as he gently brushes the hair out of my face.

"What did he say?"

I'm disappointed. *What did you expect? You thought he'd kiss you?* No. The only reason he's doing this is because he's my friend. Why do I always want to assume it's otherwise?

"He asked me where the crystal was. And I told him. He said he looks forward to meeting you again."

"We have to get to the crystal before he does." He walks over to the other trees. "Help me wake the team, okay? We've got to go."

―――――――

We begin climbing the volcano at around six in the evening. The walk drags on forever. When Liam asks why I have a gash on my cheek, I tell him I fell out of the tree while sleeping. He seems to believe me, and doesn't bother me about it afterward.

The sun hasn't even begun to set, and I'm already worn out. The slope isn't really so bad, but the short hours of sleep have made it hard on us all. Dragon doesn't show it, but I can tell he's having trouble staying awake. I feel just about dead by seven.

"Dragon, what are we going to do when we get there?" I ask.

"If we're lucky enough to get there before they do, we'll figure out the riddle and try to get out before they even arrive. If not, we'll have to fight them off," he says.

My stomach churns, thinking about having to fight Azad. Having to kill someone else. Having more blood on my hands.

Dragon seems to sense my discomfort. "Jaina, I know you're still upset about what you did, but these Trials were made to separate the weak from the strong," he says. "I never thought I'd have to tell you that. You were the one always reminding *me*."

"I never thought...I didn't think it would feel so wrong," I remark. "They tell us the weak are meant to die. But that boy was strong. If I had made one simple mistake, it would have been me."

"Which is why I'm glad you didn't make that mistake," he replies.

"How do you walk away not feeling guilty?"

Dragon's eyes falter to the ground and a painful breath escapes his lips. "I don't. I just hide it and pretend like it's nothing. With every life you take, a part of you dies. It hurts, living with what you've done. But if you defend yourself in every way possible and wait for them to make a mistake, it seems less terrible."

"Do you think it's that way for everyone?" I ask.

"Not for Azad. Not anymore, anyway. If you put lives at his disposal, he'll use them to his advantage."

"You talk about him like you know him well."

"When Shirez took me in," he begins, "we traveled a lot. Of course, we had to come back to the Uncharted Lands every summer to train the next round of Trial contestants, but Shirez had a lot of business elsewhere. We traveled to Manincia many times and I got to train at the school in Dovol. That's where the two of us met."

"Were you friends?" I ask.

"Yes." He stares off into the distance, like the trees and volcanic slope before us don't exist. "We were the best friends we could be. We fought on the same teams, we won and lost battles together. We shared everything. Our sorrows, our joys..." He laughs. "Even the girls we crushed on. We had the same tastes."

I raise an eyebrow, yet a smile tugs on my lips. "You were a real bad-boy, then."

His eyes meet mine and he grins, a seductive glimmer in his eyes. "We were trouble makers. Everything was a game to us. We were equals."

"What drove you apart?" I ask.

His smile fades and he takes a sharp breath of air. "He was...jealous. I was well liked, and he wasn't." He shakes his head, his face tight with sadness. "And suddenly, he hated me. We fought like animals, Jaina."

"Who won?"

"Depends on what you mean by that. I beat him up pretty badly, but Azad got me expelled."

"How long ago was this?"

"About three months ago," he says.

"That recently?" I ask, wondering how violent Dragon really is.

"Look, it was sudden war. He was set on getting revenge, and I did what I could to defend myself." His posture becomes defensive, like he's expecting me to doubt his reply.

I study him a moment, then say, "But you beat him once. You can do it again, right?"

"Fights aren't only physical. And even when you're not around each other, the fight can go on."

"What makes him think he can win?" I ask.

"I don't know. But I'm sure he's got a plan."

"That makes me feel so much better," I mutter. "What'd you do to make him hate you so much?"

Dragon's aqua blue eyes cloud like the sky on a stormy day. He shrugs sadly then rests his eyes on the ground. "I don't know," his voice lowers to a dark whisper.

"Whoa," Avan cries. "Check this out."

Dragon and I turn around to look at him.

"What is it?" I ask staring at a chain attached to the ground.

"Bad news," Liam says. "It's a tripwire. If you'd stepped in the wrong place, you coulda been blown to pieces!" His voice is harsh, as if he's cursing.

Dragon shoots him a glare. "How the hell were we supposed to know?"

"Maybe if you'd been *looking* for it and not so lost in thought," Liam snaps, "you might have seen it coming."

"What's the big deal?" Xana asks. "Can't we just walk around the tripwire and be on our way?"

"Are you serious?" Liam cries. "Look at the ground in front of us. See how the leaves are all messed up, not all matted down? That's because someone was tampering with it. This whole area is a trap."

"Let's just go around it," Luci suggests.

Dragon shakes his head. "No, that would take too long. The entire base of the volcano could be rigged. We don't have time to search for someplace else."

"Okay, so who's going to lead?" Kavi asks.

"I will," Dragon and I say simultaneously.

Liam's eyebrows rise, and a pleased grin splashes his lips. "I don't know if it matters much, but I vote for Dragon."

"That's not fair. I'll lead," I say.

Dragon's stares at me. "No, I'll lead. You've already put your life in danger."

"Haven't we all?" Luci shoots back.

"It's not quite the same, Luci," he replies.

Liam scrunches his shoulders casually as if the decision is his to make. "Take the lead, Dragon."

Dragon glances at me before taking a cautious step forward. "Try to step in the same place I do," Dragon warns as I follow close behind.

With each of his steps, my heart quickens. My breathing echoes through me, as if the rest of the world has suddenly fallen silent.

Without warning, a twinge of pain shoots up my right leg. *Shaav*, the painkillers are really wearing off. I lose my footing, and before I have time to be scared, a hand catches me from behind.

"Careful, Jaina," Avan says.

I regain my step. "Thanks, Avan."

"Is everyone okay?" Dragon asks.

"Yeah, we're fine," Kavi answers. "How are you?"

"Um..."

I peer around Dragon. Something is obviously wrong.

"There's a little furry thing coming this way," he finishes.

"It's a squirrel," Liam says.

"Well, I'm sorry, but it's about to walk over the tripwire!" Dragon shouts.

"What's going on up there?" Luci asks from behind us all.

"Dragon, you have to keep moving," I urge.

He sighs. "Okay, I'm moving."

He takes a few more tentative steps forward. Something snaps. The whirring of machinery comes to life.

"Run!" Dragon shouts.

Too late. The ground beneath us begins to collapse. I realize I'm screaming as I fall through the ground. I hit the bottom with a thud and roll to the side. My hands grind across the rocky floor, burning through my skin. My shoulder hits a wall and I cough, feeling like my lungs are collapsing.

"Guys, are you still there?" I ask.

"Yeah, we're here." Seth groans, obviously in pain.

I stand and look at my hands. A small trickle of blood runs down them, but there's no serious damage. "Dragon, are you okay?" I ask.

"Yeah, I'm fine." He gets up and looks at the sky above us. "*Shaav*," he curses. "Maybe we should have gone another way."

"Now what?" Xana asks.

There's a long, dark silence. I glance around the rectangular cave. No other entries. No other exits. "There has to be a way out," I say.

As the words come out, the ceiling begins to close us in, leaving us in darkness. Only a few beams of light shine through.

"No, Jaina, there doesn't have to be a way out. This could be a dead end. Literally," Liam retorts. He steps threateningly in front of Dragon and glares into his eyes. "Thanks to *you*."

An animal-like cough escapes my throat at his remark. I move closer to the two of them and step between them. "Don't blame him. I could have easily made the same mistake."

"Yeah, we know." Luci places her hands on her hips. "You couldn't have gotten us across half of what Dragon did."

"Don't start, Luci," Dragon warns.

"I'm just saying I think the leadership on this team could have been chosen differently." Her eyes are fixed with anger on me. "Maybe that would make things better."

"Are you suggesting I shouldn't be the leader?" I ask, raising my voice. My face flushes with anger, and I struggle to keep it down.

Kavi puts a hand on Luci's shoulder. "Calm down."

"That's *exactly* what I'm suggesting, Jaina," Luci shoots back.

My retort catches in my throat at her bluntness, but the words quickly return with my fury. "Did you ever consider that I'm in this position because I'm at the top? I worked harder than *anyone* to get here."

Dragon steps between us and moves closer to Luci. "Don't make things worse."

"I've had enough of your ignorance, Jaina," Luci continues.

"I've had enough of your complaining!" I fire back.

Xana raises her voice. "Guys, stop fighting!"

But Luci doesn't stop. "The only reason you got your position was–"

"Shut up, Luci!" Dragon's voice reverberates off the walls of the cavern, and his sudden outburst makes me jump. I've never seen him lose his patience like that. The room falls silent. "Save it for another time," he continues. His face is twisted into a mixture of anger and awe, like he isn't entirely sure how it could come to this.

The ground rumbles.

"Powerful words, Dragon," Liam remarks. "But it's not really helping the situation. I'm just as mad as I was before we fell into this *shaavez* pit."

"Cut it out, Liam," I snap.

The ground shakes again. An earsplitting screech echoes nearby.

"What was that?" Xana asks.

"We're going to die," Avan says, his voice quavers.

"We are not going to die!" Dragon insists. "Whatever it is could lead us out of here. Activate your scimitars."

I pull mine out before he finishes speaking. The ground rumbles again, this time harder than the last two. I hold on to the nearest person to keep myself from falling, which happens to be Liam. The wall to our left starts to retract into the ground.

"What's going on?" Xana asks.

The screeching returns along with a low pitch growl, hardly distinguishable from the rumbling of the ground.

Unable to help myself, I squeeze his shoulder in fear. "Liam, what sort of thing makes a sound like that?"

"I have no idea," he whispers.

The wall stops moving as it settles in the ground, creating a huge, dark, open doorway. Everything is silent for a moment, and I find myself hoping there's nothing coming for us, that everything for the next few minutes will be all right.

Of course, I'm wrong. Into the light, only three meters away, steps a lion-like beast. Its large, feline face and long, golden mane are three times as big as my head. It's crouched on all six of its long, bulky legs, ready to spring.

The hairs on the back of my neck stand on end as it swings its spiny tail in anticipation. Two more beasts approach from the darkness. They're only a little shorter than I am.

I glance over at Dragon and keep my voice soft so as not to startle the new creatures before us. "Any advice?"

"Not really," he replies nervously. "Maybe go for its underbelly, but that's just a guess."

"How about trying to surround them?" Liam asks.

"Okay good call, let's try that," Dragon replies.

The first creature cries a warning, hitting both a low growl and screech at once. It's so close now I could reach out and touch its face. I breathe steadily.

"Hold your ground, Jaina. Maybe it'll back off," Dragon replies.

Maybe isn't very reassuring.

I take a hesitant step closer, hoping it doesn't decide to pounce and tear me to pieces. I point my scimitar squarely at its nose, ready to strike if it makes a move. *In the name of the Emperor, let me get out of this place alive.*

The creature pulls the front half of its body up off of the ground. It towers over me, approaching nearly two and a half meters high.

"Now what?" I ask.

"Uh..." Dragon hesitates as the creature raises a paw. Its claws slowly extend from it. "Defend yourself!"

Its claws swing down at my face, and I skim its paw with my scimitar. It screams in anger.

The beast snarls and claws at me, but I jump back before it can hurt me. Xana and Liam close in to help, and we form a circle around it. The other two beasts attempt to take down the rest of our team. Liam tries to poke it with his scimitar. The creature's response is instantaneous.

"Liam, watch out!" I shout.

The beast swings its deadly tail, skimming Liam's side. Blood oozes from his waist, and he cries out, bringing his hand up to stop the bleeding and backs away.

The creature advances toward him. I pull out an MED and plunge it into the top of its leg. Now it doesn't only scream, it roars, twitching uncontrollably as the strong electric current flows through it. Its tail flails about. Blood rushes through my ears, pounding through my head. I'm breathing so heavily I worry my lungs will explode.

Xana makes the final move as she plunges her scimitar into its lower chest. Its wails soften, and it staggers backward. Finally, it topples over itself and hits the ground.

The rumbling of the ground resumes. The wall that opened to bring the creatures to us begins to close us in.

"We have to hurry!" My voice echoes over the sounds of battle. The other two creatures advance from the back of the room. One is mortally wounded, but it refuses to back down. Its eyes rest on Liam, leaning against the wall, his hand still clutching his bloody shirt.

"Jaina, come on!" Xana calls.

"Make sure everyone gets through," I reply. "I have to get Liam!"

Dragon and the rest of our team retreat from the remaining beasts and climb over the rising wall. When I reach Liam, I try not to vomit at the sight of all the blood. One of the spikes from the creature's tail broke off in his side and is lodged deep in his flesh. His wound is much worse than I thought.

"Liam," I say as calmly as the situation allows, "come on, you have to get up."

Now that no one's fighting the two creatures, their attention turns to us. The uninjured one snarls and crouches low to the ground, slowly stalking nearer.

"Just leave me," he moans. His face is going pale from loss of blood or fear, I can't tell which.

"Don't talk that way," I order. "Now get up."

He pushes my hand away with such determined force I nearly feel rejected. "Save yourself and get out of here!"

"I'm not leaving you!"

Liam slams his fist into the ground angrily. "*Shaav*, Jaina, just go!"

The beast licks its lips and raises its tail in anticipation.

Grabbing Liam's hand, I pull him to his feet. He almost resists, but he gives in as I pull his arm around my shoulder. I help him limp toward the wall that's now a meter high and rising. Dragon pulls out his crossbow and fires at the creatures. Finally we reach the wall, and Liam's legs give out.

Glancing behind us, I watch them charge. All that keeps them from reaching us is Dragon's relentless rain of electrified arrows, striking them with deadly accuracy.

"Come on, pick yourself up," I say, pulling Liam to his feet.

He tries to climb but is too weak to pull himself over. The creatures are only meters away. I push Liam onto the thick wall. Dragon grabs him and pulls him over the side, as I scramble up the rising wall. I push myself over the edge and fall to the ground. The creatures jump up, trying to reach us, but Dragon fires an arrow into the largest beast's eye and it falls back to the other side. The wall finally closes us in a large, dark hallway, illuminated only by a few lights near the top.

I fall to my knees next to Liam. His eyes are clenched as he moans deliriously. The thick, needle-like spine stuck in his side makes me feel sick, but I can't tear my eyes from him.

"Avan, you have to help him," I pant.

Avan sits down next to me. "Can I get a glowsaber, Luci?"

Luci lights hers and stands over Liam, illuminating his wound.

"How bad is it?" I ask. "Will he be all right?"

"Oh *shaav*," Liam moans through his teeth, holding his hands over his wound. "Oh, *shaav*."

"I don't know," Avan murmurs. "It shouldn't have pierced any organs, but I can't say for sure yet."

My breath catches. "What can I do to help?"

"Keep him still, Jaina," he replies. "That's all you can do."

I pull his hands away from his side, and he squeezes mine tightly. Leaning over him, I touch his face. His breaths are short and choppy.

"Liam," I say, brushing the hair from his soaked forehead. "Liam, listen to me."

He swallows hard and then looks up at me.

"You're going to be okay."

Liam shakes his head. "I'm going to die."

"You aren't going to die," I insist. "Look at me, Liam. *Look at me*."

"Ahh!" he screams, then grits his teeth as Avan removes the spine. Avan brings a cloth to the wound to suppress the flow of blood.

"Liam." I tilt his head away from the sight. "You're going to be okay. I promise. All right?"

Liam nods and takes a deep, strained breath. His hands quiver, and he shuts his eyes. His body tenses, and his jaw tightens as he suppresses another moan.

"How bad is it?" he asks. "Avan, tell me honestly."

Avan looks up, his hands and the cloth drenched with blood. "You'll be okay. But I'm not saying this won't hurt." He pulls out a needle and a clear plastic thread.

Liam squeezes my hand tighter. "Why? What the *shaav* are you doing?"

"Mind your own business," Avan snaps.

"This is my *shaavez*–"

Before he can finish, his own cries of agony cut him off. They're so loud I can't help hurting for him. When his cries cease, each pant is followed with a groan. If only there was something I could do to make him more comfortable. I hate seeing him in so much pain.

"Avan, is he okay?" I ask.

He nods. "I'll give him a medpatch, and he should be fine."

I glance back to Liam and touch his forehead as his breathing slows. He's burning with sweat. "Hang tight, Liam," I whisper to him.

He laughs through his teeth. "You don't have to stay by me, Jaina."

Caressing his cheek I whisper, "I just want to make sure you're okay."

He takes my hand and squeezes it. "I'll be fine, now. Thanks."

I nod, then head back over to where everyone else is. The ceiling is high, yet completely made out of dirt, not stone. A suffocating feeling rushes through me.

"Is he going to be all right?" Luci asks.

"Avan says he thinks so." My voice is shaking. Dragon faces the darkness before us. He looks dazed as I approach him. "What are you doing?" I ask softly.

A shaky breath is released from his chest. "I'm not good with blood."

I raise an eyebrow, and my lips twitch into as much of a smile as I can muster. Dragon afraid of blood? I never would have guessed.

Liam moans again, and I glance toward him. My stomach knots at the sound of his pain.

"Will he be okay?" he asks.

"Yeah." My voice sounds unsure, even to me. By the stars, I hope he'll be okay. I decide to change the subject. "You think this is the way into the volcano?"

He stares forward, his arms crossed over his strong, sturdy chest. "As sure as I can be."

"What if it's another trap?" I ask.

Dragon turns to face me. "Do you think it's worth the risk?"

I bite my lip and let my eyes fall to the ground. "If it could mean someone else getting hurt...I don't know."

He bends down a little so his eyes are realigned with mine. "Where would you have us go?"

I shake my head. "*Shaav*, I guess you're right. We don't really have another option."

"Jaina," he says, touching my arm. "We've come this far. We'll make it."

"All done!" Avan cries.

Liam sits up, glancing down at the medpatch on his waist. "I thought you said it wasn't supposed to hurt anymore."

"Don't be a *katiaj*," Avan replies. "It shouldn't hurt that bad."

Liam wrinkles his nose. "Oh, right. Like *you* know how it feels to have a spine stuck through you?" He touches the white medpatch and winces. "Isn't this supposed to have painkillers in it?"

Avan shrugs.

I rush to his side and take his hand. "How are you feeling?"

"Seeing that I almost *died*," he says, "I'm feeling okay."

"In the name of the galaxy," Avan murmurs. "You weren't going to die."

Luci takes a seat on the other side of Liam. "I might not like you very much, but I don't want you going off and getting yourself killed!"

Liam laughs then turns to Avan. "Is it okay if I get up now?"

"It will hurt for a little while, but yeah."

Liam nods. "Thanks. And Jaina..."

"Yeah?"

He looks deep into my eyes as Avan stands to leave. "You didn't have to save me." His voice is a deep whisper.

"Yes, I did."

He furrows his brow. "Why?"

"I can't afford to lose you."

Dragon awkwardly clears his throat.

Liam glances up at him, then averts his gaze. "Are we moving onward, or what?"

"You ready?" Dragon asks.

"I've been ready!" he cries. "Just give the order, and I'm with you."

"Good, then let's move."

We begin our walk through the long, dark tunnel, braving every corner, following the slope uphill. I pretend to be unafraid, but at every turn, I find myself wanting to hold Dragon's hand or stand behind him. Through my mask of courage, I can't help feeling that from this point on, things could go very, *very* wrong.

———

There's only one thing worse than feeling trapped. That's feeling trapped in the dark. And right now, that's exactly how I feel.

I'm not afraid of the calm, peaceful darkness of the night. But *this* is the darkness I can't stand–the darkness that can cut you like a knife and stab at your soul.

It's as if we've fallen into hell. The intense heat from the magma buried deep in the volcano radiates through the rock. We must be on the right path.

"Now what?" Liam asks.

I follow his gaze to two paths in front of us.

Dragon shifts attention to me. "What should we do?"

"We've only got one shot at this," I reply. "I've got a good feeling about going right."

"Wait," Dragon puts his hand in front of me as if to stop me from moving forward. "I think we should go left."

"Why is it any different from right?" Liam interjects. "It's just as dark and we know just as little about both of them."

"Are you sure, Jaina?" Dragon asks turning to me.

I study the path again, beginning to question myself. "Fine, let's take a vote."

Liam raises an eyebrow. "A vote?"

I nod. "Yes. A vote. What do you guys think?"

"I vote right," Kavi says. "I'm with you, Jay."

"Yeah, I say right," Seth adds.

Luci rolls her eyes. "Dragon, I'm with you."

"Left," Xana says, along with Avan.

Liam shrugs. "Right."

Dragon rubs his eyes and groans. "Well, that didn't help. Just take the lead, Jaina. We'll go right."

I walk forward confidently, taking us through the twists and turns of the cavern. It isn't long before I realize how wrong my judgment was. Here before us is the deadest end I've ever seen.

"Dragon, you were right," I moan.

"It's okay. We'll find our way back. At least this passage isn't long enough to get lost in," he replies.

Keeping my eyes low to the ground I say, "I should have listened to you."

"It's okay. You've got to make your own mistakes. It's the only way to learn."

"Nice job, Jaina," Luci says, sarcastically.

We turn around and begin our short walk back. I stand next to Dragon as we lead together. I'm not proud, that's for sure, but I need to learn to trust myself. If I can't trust myself, how can I ever fully trust anyone else?

"Whoa. This wasn't here before," Avan says suddenly.

Sure enough, there's another dead end.

"Did we take a wrong turn?" Xana asks.

"I didn't think so," Seth replies with a puzzled look on his face.

"We must have," I insist. "We would have remembered–"

"The volcano must change," Liam cuts in. His eyes are full of fear and remorse. "The chambers shift and connect new paths to older ones. It's the only thing that makes sense. It's only been five minutes when the walk to reach this point should have been ten. We're in a moving maze."

"How are we going to find the crystal?" Kavi asks.

"We know we fell in at the bottom of the volcano," Liam replies. "The crystal should be at the center, meaning we have to continue uphill. That's the only way we can find it."

Kavi sighs. "Let's hurry. I don't know how long we've been in here but I'm exhausted."

Seth kneels down by the rocky wall blocking our path and grabs some of the sandy material making up the ground. "The path leading through this door is the only path that has these silver grains of sand. All the rest are darker. I think if we wait for this door to open we'll find our way."

"Good observation," Dragon says, patting Seth on the shoulder. "We'll stop here and rest for a while until the passage opens."

We take a seat around the door as we wait for it to open. The silent stillness begins to worry me. It's like time has stopped. *Stop the time to rescue me.* Could this have anything to do with it? My thoughts become blurry and muddled.

I realize the sudden darkness around me. I open my eyes and look at the others. Their eyes are mostly closed. I do my best to fight the strong fingers of sleep, but they tug at me, pulling me down farther and farther until everything I've known to be true slowly, but surely, ceases to exist.

chapter

SEVENTEEN

Sleep is easy with the warm air around me. Yet things gradually change. Slowly at first. Almost unnoticeable.

The air in my lungs becomes hot and dry. So hot in fact, that it takes increasingly more energy to suck it in. Even through my closed eyelids, the outside world seems to glow. The heat is unbearable. I fling my eyes open.

"Everyone wake up! Hurry!" I shout. A few of my teammates open their eyes and I move over to wake the rest.

Liam moans as I shake him. "What's the matter?"

He follows my gaze down the tunnel in the direction we came from. A river of lava crawls slowly toward us.

"Hurry, we've got to get out of here," Kavi says.

The passage we've been waiting for is open now. It's the only path we can take.

We rush down the path. There are a few forks in the road, but we continue on the path that's black with silver specks in it.

The molten rock trails close behind. The heat nips at my back like wolves.

A reddish glow appears at the end of the dark hallway, and all I can think is *this is it*. We're all going to die. Lava in front of us, and behind us. We grow closer and closer to the end, and I take a deep breath, preparing myself for the pain.

Yet the moment we leap into the glowing room, I realize it's not lava in *front* of us. It's merely in pools surrounding the path.

"There's the crystal!" Luci shouts.

We're in the crater of the volcano. The moon shines down on us through the tube-like opening at the top. There are seven other paths, each equidistant from one another, leading to a large circle in the center of the cavern. Between each path are large, luminous pools of lava. The entire room glows red and orange.

We reach the pedestal. The bright, blood-red crystal sparkles in the moonlight overhead, clashing with the red-orange colors of the chamber.

Kavi kneels down and reads the riddle:

"When light and dark collide,
When you can't see what's ahead,
When life and death are just the same,
What once was blue turns red.

What boils when it's raging,
What's drowned out by the beats,

When hungry beasts are raving,
It spills freely in the streets.

When the balance has been broken,
Where there's nothing false or true,
When we become our demons,
What now is red was blue?"

Kavi looks up in confusion.

"Goes from blue to red..." Liam murmurs.

"Fire!" Xana cries. "The bottom of it is blue, and the top is reddish-yellow."

"Fire can't spill," I say.

"Water can spill!" Seth cuts in. "Wait, that was stupid. Water isn't red."

"What about stopping time in the previous poem? I'm a little concerned about *that*," Avan interjects.

"I figure the sacrifice comes first," Liam replies. "We don't have time to worry about the other riddle yet. We'll get to that."

"Lava!" Kavi suggests.

"Yes that makes sense! Maybe going from blue to red symbolizes going from cold to hot," Seth agrees.

"What about an emotion? Like anger or sadness?" Liam says.

"I like how you're thinking, but how are we going to get lava or an emotion on the sacrificial pedestal?" Dragon asks.

Liam curses. "Didn't think of that."

Dragon's face pales. "Guys..." His voice is soft, yet I hear the cold fear in his tone, like he expects the galaxy to collapse in on itself any moment now.

"Hold on, we're still thinking," Liam replies.

Dragon taps him, forcing him to stop. "We've got company."

"Well, well, well. We meet again," Azad hisses. "I didn't think you'd have the guts to join us, Altair."

Dragon straightens up confidently. "You can't win, Azad."

"It's unfortunate I won't have the pleasure of killing you myself. There's someone else I'd like to deal with." Azad sneers.

He scans me up and down, drinking me in. I feel his cold gaze engulf me and I wish he'd look away. Anger rises up in me like a bubble of molten rock, rising to the surface of the earth.

"Leave her out of this," Dragon urges. "This is our fight, not hers." His body is positioned for defense. His hand rests on the hilt of his scimitar, and his eyes are narrowed in fury and desperation.

Azad turns back to him and raises an eyebrow. "Are you *defending* her?" He laughs. "You've made this her fight just as much as it is ours. She just doesn't know it yet."

Confused, I glance at Dragon.

"I'll have my revenge, Altair."

"Don't do this!" he warns. "Let it go!"

"Let it go?" Azad nearly screams. "I will *never* let it go! What are you afraid of? You coward!"

"This won't end well."

Azad grins. "Not for you it won't." He activates his weapon then reaches for something in his belt. Time slows down. He flicks his wrist.

Images flash through my mind like lightning. *The red glowing room. The knife. Luci. Blood. Pain.* The pictures fade, and I snap back to reality. The knife comes at me with such incredible speed I hardly have time to react.

I jump to the side to prevent it from stabbing me in the stomach, but the sound of the blade piercing flesh freezes my blood. I stand up quickly, ready for the oncoming attack, yet glance to my right in time to see Luci collapse in a pool of blood. The knife is stuck in her shoulder.

The words from my dream echo in my head. *"He can't save you...Beware the Dark."*

I'm frozen.

Dead frozen.

The beating of my heart echoes through my mind.

It all comes back.

Something inside me shuts down. My morality, my rationality, the side of me that's sane...all of it falters and turns off. I know what I must do.

The hot tendrils of rage trickle up my fingertips and through my arms. The heat grows and ignites, and what I desire most is to kill him. To watch him die and smile at his pain.

My body moves on its own. I watch my hands pull out my dagger and force it into a girl's stomach. My legs push me forward, making me to forget what I've done.

Just as Azad is about to strike me down, I activate my scimitar.

Our blades clash and part. I glare into his eyes, filled with the same burning hatred as mine.

"You have no hope of defeating me," I hiss at him.

"We'll see about that."

I lunge at him, but he backs out of the way. The thought hits me that if I keep it up I could back him into the lava, but that would be too good for him. He'll die by my hand, and my hand only.

He jerks to the left. I'm prepared to block, but he attacks to the right. Blood drips from a fresh cut on my arm. His lips twist into a deadly smile. The pain only makes me stronger.

I swing at his neck, and he ducks. I jab at him but miss. We both know how this is going to end. One of us will be dead.

And it's not going to be me.

He lunges at me, then swings at my legs. I jump to avoid his blow. Our swords clash again and again. I kick him in the stomach, and he falls back a little. *Not far enough.* I run at him, hoping to knock him off guard, yet he blocks in time. My joints are quivering from the adrenaline and rage circulating through me.

"Just answer me this, Jaina," he says through strained breaths. "Are you the Light?"

I pull away and bring my sword down on him from above. Once again he blocks then strikes at me. I avert his attack, and our swords hold together. His face is glossy with sweat, and his eyes are full of rage. Pure, undying hatred.

"Don't tell me he hasn't told you, yet," he continues.

Our blades part as we stand facing each other. A cold sense of recognition tugs at my mind. My dream about the Dark and the Light...how would he know? "What are you talking about?"

Azad only laughs. "By the stars, you really don't know, do you?"

Shaav, he's not making sense! My fury grows greater than I thought possible, and I lunge at him. Again, our blades lock. His eyes burn red from the surrounding glow of lava.

"He'll betray you, you know," he whispers. "He's not who you think he is."

I hear Dragon's voice from years ago resurface. *"I'll always be there for you."*

"And when he does, the entire galaxy will fall." His voice is gruff and lathered with resentment.

A dark, coldness runs through me with his words. "Liar! You're nothing but a liar!"

He pulls away and swings at me. I try to block, but the split-second thought of Dragon slows my reaction. His blade slices my ribs, and the stinging pain makes containing my rage even harder.

He hits my blade so hard it drops from my hand and falls to the ground. I pull out my MED. I shall not give in to this.

"I don't want to hurt you, Jaina," he says softly. "Listen to me."

"No, you're lying!" I shout through my teeth.

I touch my ribs. They're coated in blood. Somehow it doesn't worry me. At the moment, I only live to see him die. This can't kill me.

"They say you're the Light," he says.

"*Who* says I am?" I ask through my teeth.

He smiles. "The people he's working for."

He moves in to strike, but I turn, aiming my blade at his throat. And his is at mine.

"Are you going to kill me? Or should I go first?" His smile is as bloodthirsty as my knife.

I glare at him.

Though my blade is a centimeter from his throat, he moves closer to me. He holds his dagger back. He moves so close I can feel his wretched breath on me. His neck is pressed so tightly against my dagger I'm afraid it will draw blood.

"Who is he working for?" I growl.

He shakes his head, sadly. "He will betray you."

"Why should I trust you?" I shoot back. "Give me one reason why I shouldn't slit your throat!"

"Because I know things. I know things he won't tell you. I know things you wouldn't *dare* say aloud."

"I know all I need to know! Anything he hasn't told me is for my own good."

"He isn't who you think he is. He's lying to your face, Jaina, why the *shaav* can't you see that?"

"Shut up!"

"Listen to me, Jaina. Don't you wonder why he's here? Why he's *really* here?" he asks. "You think they just *happened* to bring him back the same year you entered the Trials?"

I press my teeth together, holding back every ounce of resentment I have for him. "I should kill you."

"Then do it," he whispers. "*Do it.*"

I swallow hard, but I can't force myself press the dagger into his throat.

He smiles again, but the fire flickers back to his eyes. His smile transforms into a hateful cry of rage, and his blade moves so fast across my arm I have no time to react. Warm blood drips down my skin and into my palm.

He clasps his fingers around my wrist, squeezing the dagger from my hand and pushing me to the ground. I hold tight to him and pull him down with me, then twist in the air, positioning him beneath me to soften my fall. His back hits the ground with a thud and my chin slams into his chest, making me dizzy. He snarls with rage. I push myself up and bring my fist down, but he grabs my wrist again before I can touch him. His grip is so tight I almost cry out. The bones in my wrist feel like they're being melded together, and tears well up in my eyes.

Spying my dagger just out of reach, I pull away from him and roll over the ground to it.

As my hand brushes the hilt, he clasps my arm and brings himself on top of me. His fist makes contact with my cheek. My eyes sting with tears of fury.

His fingers close around my throat, pressing harder with every second.

I struggle to breathe, but it's no use. He's too strong to push away. Black dots cloud my vision. Sensation begins to fade. The world darkens, and my body begins to go cold. The difference between imagination and reality blurs.

"The Dark has found you," he whispers in my ear.

His hands are no longer around my throat and I gasp. Lips are pressed to mine and I lash out at him. I take him by the shoulders and dig my fingernails into his flesh. He jerks backward.

"Jaina, it's okay!" he cries. "It's me, Avan! I'm not trying to hurt you."

I open my eyes and sit up. Avan is next to me, panting nervously and rubbing his shoulders. There's a gash on his cheek, and blood dots the top of his arms. I glance down at my fingers. They're tinted with red.

"I'm so sorry, Jaina, I was just trying to bring you back," he says breathlessly, then gently touches my arm. "Are you all right?"

My lungs expand and shrink so quickly it hurts. I nod, then rub my throat. "What happened?"

Dragon rushes up to me, falling to his knees in the dirt beside me, and meets Avan's gaze. "So...it worked?"

"Yeah, it worked. She tried to *kill* me, but yeah, she's fine," he replies.

My head spins, and my eyes take a moment to focus. I bring my hand to my forehead and run it through my hair. "Sorry, Avan. I thought you were...I thought..."

He smiles. "It's okay."

I turn to Dragon, and he helps me stand. "What happened?"

He grits his teeth, and his expression hardens. "He got away. Like he always does. That *shaavez*–"

"Avan, I need you over here!" Xana screams. "Avan! Hurry!"

Avan runs toward her and the rest of the team. Dragon and I follow close behind.

Luci lies near the pedestal, her scimitar in hand and a dagger lodged deep in her shoulder. Blood spills from her wound and into the gravel beneath us.

"Luci..." My voice trails off.

"I'll live," she breathes. Her face contorts in pain as she takes hold of the dagger still lodged in her shoulder.

"Luce, let me get that," Avan insists.

"No, I can do it." She takes both of her hands on the hilt of the blade and takes a deep breath.

Not wanting to see the bloody gash I know will be there I move toward Liam and Kavi, trying to solve the riddle. Something stirs in my mind. "Kavi, reread the poem," I say.

She does, and it all hits me.

"It's...it's blood," I murmur.

Kavi and Liam look at me dumbfounded.

I move closer. "When you don't care if you live or die, your morals fall away. When enraged, your blood boils. When people..." I stop, thinking how I felt only moments ago, so intent on killing Azad. "When people become demons, they are bloodthirsty. And blood goes from blue to red when it is spilled."

"All right. So someone spill their blood," Liam says.

"Why can't it be blood that someone has already shed?" I ask.

"Because. The riddle speaks in future and present tense. Not in past. I take it to mean the sacrifice must be made for *this specific purpose*. Not already made," Liam replies.

"How is anyone going to know?" I ask.

"We better not risk it," Seth says.

We all exchange glances. Even Dragon doesn't speak up.

"I can do it," Luci calls softly. "I'm already bleeding all over the place."

"You need to save as much blood as you can," I reply. "I'll do it." I'm the leader, I should be the one.

I approach the pedestal and take out my MED. Holding the blade in my hand, I try hard not to think about the pain or the blood. *It's not going to hurt.* I drag the blade over my open palm.

The pain is bearable. Nothing like Luci's injury. I twitch when the blood starts oozing. I close my eyes and clench my fist over the sacrificial bowl. The blood drips into it, slowly and painfully. When it's identified, the crystal rises, and Liam grabs it.

"Jaina, give me your hand," Liam says.

Dragon steps in. "It's okay, I've got it."

He positions himself in front of Liam and takes a cloth from his holster belt. He gently wraps my hand in the cloth, keeping it tight, but not too tight. The memory of him holding me in his arms is overwhelming. I fight the urge to fall into his chest and press myself close.

Liam clears his throat, a jealous fire in his eyes. "Now all we've got to do is stop time."

"How do we do that exactly?" Dragon asks as he finishes up the bandage.

The lava begins to bubble.

"What was that?" Avan points to one of the bubbles.

"It's exactly what we'll look like if we don't get time to stop!" Liam yells. The noise around us has become considerably louder.

"I think the lava's rising," Kavi breathes.

"No *shaav*," Seth murmurs. "It wasn't even half-way up the paths when we first got here. The paths are shrinking!"

"Found it!" Liam shouts, jumping up from his kneeling position in front of the pedestal. Yet he quickly brings his hand to his side where the spine was stuck into him and curses to himself.

There's a little deformation in the perfect black of the marble pedestal. Liam gives it a tug, and the front panel opens.

"Here we go," he mutters.

What I see is unmistakable. A mess of wires and bright red numbers glowing on a little screen that reads *49*. The number changes to *48*, then *47*. It's the time. Each second that ticks away, the lava bubbles become considerably more violent. I hear the poem echoing in my head. *Stop the time to rescue me, You must not be too late, Every prize has a price to pay, If you fail, you've sealed your fate.*

An even worse thought knifes its way into my mind.

"It's a bomb!" I scream.

"You don't think I can *see* that, Jaina?" Liam shoots back at me.

I stare at Liam, watching the time slip away as he runs his fingers over the wires. My heart beats in time with the seconds. I'm always up for a fight, but this is a fight I couldn't win if I tried. I can only hope Liam knows what he's doing. He's on his own battleground, and if he fails, the stakes are high. I resist the urge to help him; I'd only be a distraction.

"I've almost got it." Sweat drips down his forehead as he speaks and cuts a few wires.

I glance at the timer.

Twelve seconds.

Come on, Liam. You can do this.

He glances up at me with panic in his eyes. "I don't remember the last wire to cut."

The clock only has seven seconds left. Before I can stop myself, I fall to my knees by his side. I squeeze his shoulder. "Liam, just choose one," I urge.

His eyes are vacant. Completely blank. "I don't know which one. I don't remember."

By the stars, Liam. Don't do this. Don't fail us. "You have to!" I order.

Liam's voice quivers. "What if I'm wrong?"

"If you don't try, we're all going to die. Do you understand? You need to *try*."

His eyes fall back to the mess of wires.

Four seconds.

"Please," I whisper.

Three seconds.

He takes his MED and holds up a blue and red wire. His hands shake. His breath is deep and steady, yet it's obvious he's so completely afraid.

Two.

I close my eyes.

One.

A tiny *snap* fills my ears. My eyes are still clenched tight, and half expecting to be dead, I finally open them. A cold void doesn't engulf me. The world remains as it was. Glowing red lava, and my team standing around me.

We remain like statues, and I wonder how we could possibly still be alive, wondering if the timer will suddenly continue. When it doesn't, I collapse into Liam's arms and hold him in relief.

He sighs, returning my embrace. "By the stars, we're still alive."

"I knew you could do it!" I cheer, pulling away slightly.

Luci grins at him. "An admirable achievement, Liam."

He laughs. "I thought you were going to thank me for saving your ungrateful *nav'ra*."

"I'm not *that* nice," she snaps back, her eyebrow raised.

"Hey, I don't mean to interrupt the celebration, but we should really get moving," Dragon says.

"What path did we come from?" Seth asks. "Because I think there were a few more choices when we got here."

Though the lava has stopped rising, only three remain of the original seven paths. The other four have disappeared. I glance up through the volcanic crater and see not the moon, but a pink and purple sky. The sun is rising.

"There!" Xana points to one of the three paths.

I don't have time to question her judgment. Any reason at all is sufficient.

We make our way down the path. Finally, we reach the exit of the large lava chamber. Dragon and I are in the lead, side by side as everyone breaks into a run.

"Dragon, do you think the other teams know where we are?" I ask.

"It's likely. I'm sure they've set up an ambush outside," he replies.

"So what are we going to do?"

He grins. "I'm open to ideas."

I shoot him a glare.

"What?" he asks, breathing heavily now.

"You're not being very helpful," I reply.

"What do you expect? I don't know everything!"

I know he doesn't, but he acts like he does. He sees so much I can't.

I look back and am glad to see that everyone is keeping pretty good time. Even Luci's moving quickly with Liam and Avan's help. Her good arm is slung over Liam's shoulder and around his neck, as he keeps her steady with his hand around her waist. He pulls her up with every stride, hopefully easing the pain she must be in.

"Dragon, do you know the way out?" I ask.

"Just as well as you do," he replies.

For a moment, I think he's just trying to shut me up, until I glance down and see the black and silver sand beneath me.

"I've been following you the whole time," Dragon says.

"I don't know where I'm going!" I cry. This whole time *I've* been the one leading?

"Why didn't you say so before?"

"I assumed you'd take the lead!"

"I can't lead the entire time, Jaina! I hardly ever know where I'm going. I just happen to end up in the right place!"

This better be the way out or this is going to be over very soon. Though this *is* the third time I've expected to die today, and miraculously I've lived. Could we all be saved one more time? We'll need a lot of luck, but we might be able to pull this one off.

I see the light ahead. Not the deep, blood red light of the lava. This is the golden, soothing light of the sun. And with a few final strides, we escape the cruel darkness and flames of hell.

My eyes take a moment to adjust to the brightening world around me. Cool, fresh air fills my lungs, and relieves me of the dangers of the volcano, setting me free. I don't think I've ever been so thankful to be outside. We come to a stop.

Kavi gasps. "We did it!"

"Not quite, hang in there," Dragon pants. "We've still got to make it to the checkpoint."

A few specks form in the distance. At first I dismiss them as large boulders, but they progressively become more shapely and human.

"Dragon?" I say.

"What?"

"I think we're being followed again." I point to the ridge of the volcano at the approaching specks.

"Can we make it to the checkpoint before they reach us?" he asks. "It's right up ahead. About twenty meters downhill."

"We'll try for it, but be prepared for anything," I reply.

A terrible hissing splits the air. The smell of scorched sand is overpowering. I find myself dodging dirt that springs from the ground. Bolts of plasma rush past us in a flurry of light.

I can't tell who they are, but their firing accuracy isn't so great, especially at their current distance. I duck behind a wall of boulders with the rest of our team, waiting for them to move into range.

I yank out my pistol, yet I hesitate in using it. Killing is the last thing I want to do, especially after what happened in the volcano. I watched myself become something I'm not. Let myself become a demon. Breathing deeply, I prepare to fire.

Dragon grabs my arm. His fingers are clamped around me so tightly all thought of the battle fades from my mind.

"Do not freeze up," he tells me sternly, pulling me close.

My gaze shifts to the ground, afraid he'll see right through me and read my thoughts.

He bends down slightly, forcing me to look at him again. "Do you understand?"

I stare back at him, unmoving. I don't want to do this.

"Jaina, do not hesitate to kill." When I don't respond, his face hardens and he furrows his brow. He grips tighter, and I wince. I can tell it's unintentional because his eyes, though stern, hold only worry for me. "Answer me, damn it! I need to know you won't do that again!"

I clench my jaw. "Who gives us the right to end their lives?"

"The Imperials."

"So you're just going to go along with it?" I retort. "You're just going to kill like Azad does?"

He bites his lip, his face tight with anguish. "You will kill to save your life, or I'll kill them for you. That's an order." The darkness in his voice makes me shiver. "Either way, Jaina, they'll die. By my hand or yours, it doesn't matter."

"I don't take orders from you," I hiss.

He pulls me closer. "You'll do exactly as I say. Your life is one I cannot afford to lose, no matter the costs."

I study his face, wondering what in the galaxy he means. "Why are you protecting me?" I ask, pushing myself out of his grasp.

A sad smile flickers across his lips. "Because if you die, I will have failed."

The firing stops, and I peer over the boulder. They're close. Only three meters away. One of them spots me and fires. I duck, and the bolt of plasma hits the rock instead.

Dragon gently touches my shoulder. "I need you to tell me that you won't–"

"All right," I cut him off. "I won't."

He stares at me for a moment, then nods.

Footsteps crunch in the gravel near us, and I load my pistol. Defending myself isn't murder. I close my eyes and wait for the moment.

It comes too soon, as it always does.

The gunfire.

I scan the area and lock onto another stack of boulders nearby, but to reach it, I'd have to cross an area open to their line of fire.

Liam peers over the rocks and returns fire, hitting one of them in the leg. The girl falls to the ground, moaning and screaming. I wince, watching her writhe in pain as another of Liam's shots plummets into her shoulder.

"Jaina, come on," Dragon says. "We need to get over there."

I follow his gaze to the stack of boulders I've been considering.

"You first," he urges. "I'll cover you."

Deep breath.

I can do it.

Dragon nods to me, and I charge toward the boulders. My lungs jump into my throat as a bolt of plasma rockets toward me. It whizzes past my head, and I almost have to stop in the middle of the clearing. I make it to the boulders, and relief floods my veins. Dragon nods to me again, and it's my turn to cover him.

He makes it without much difficulty and is at my side before anyone has time to shoot at him. "You okay?" he asks.

"I've had better days."

I peer over the rocky ridge, and another shot plummets toward my face. Dragon jerks me back out of the way.

A boy steps out from around the corner, and his angry eyes lock onto Dragon. I wonder if he's someone else Dragon's upset in his past.

I ram myself into the guy. He stumbles backward and throws me to the side, luckily not out into the open where I could be shot. His eyes lock onto me with a powerful, blood-chilling glare. I try to stand, but he lunges at me and knocks me back down. My back hits the ground with an agonizing thud.

He reaches for my ankle as I kick at him, and he jerks me to the side. He raises his gun and aims for my chest.

Suddenly, his body freezes and blood oozes from his lips. A silvery form of a dagger is lodged in the side of his throat.

Dragon pushes his lifeless body to the side, and the boy collapses to the rocky ground. The bloodstained dagger retreats back into Dragon's gauntlet as he flips his wrist. There's a demonic fire in his eyes. Frantic, worried, and enraged, all at once. He bends down to help me up, examining me as he pulls me to my feet.

"What do we do now?" I ask. Our team is still engaged with the others, serving as a perfect distraction for Dragon and I to reach the checkpoint.

He studies me a moment, then looks around. "Someone's got to sprint to the checkpoint. Once the helitransport arrives, we'll be all right, but we need the helitransport first."

"I'll do it."

"No," he insists. "You won't."

"You're not going to let me?" I cry. "The checkpoint is four meters away. I'm a fast runner, and I'm smaller than you. Swifter. If anyone has a chance at this, it's *me*."

"You don't understand!" He presses his hand to my cheek. "I. Can't. Lose. You."

I stare into his deep, endless eyes. My gaze travels from his wrist, to his arm, to his eyes, and finally to his lips. My heart tenses in my chest. I want him to pull my body to him and feel his lips touch mine. All he'd have to do is tell me to kiss him and I'd be his.

I'd be helpless.

A slave to my feelings.

And still, I'd do it.

This isn't the time for that sort of thinking. Pursing my lips, I shake it off and say, "Distract them for me, Dragon."

With that, I pull away from him and sprint toward the checkpoint.

Half a meter to go.

Dragon has done as I asked. There's hardly a shot fired at me. The sounds of gunfire remain behind me. I reach the checkpoint and activate the scanner. It asks for my fingerprint. Bullets and bolts of plasma split the air, and a few explode into the rocks around me.

I press my finger to the scanner then send the transmission. Officially, we've won. Now all we've got to do is hold out long enough for the helitransport to arrive.

Twinges of regret poke and jab at my ribs. I should have kissed him.

Only when I glance down at my waist, do I realize it's probably not regret that's hurting me. The gash Azad's blade made is now a darkening pool of red on the fabric of my shirt. His sword grazed my skin where my armor couldn't have protected me. After wondering why I hadn't felt it before, I realize it was probably from the adrenaline rush. The more I look at it, the more it stings, but it's not fatal.

Another shot is fired. A silvery flash pierces the air in front of me, then disappears. The breath is knocked from my lungs, and I find myself sprawled upon the ground, gasping for air.

At first I feel nothing.

Shaav.

I'm dying. By the stars, I'm dying. I stare up at the bluish-purple sky, paralyzed with shock. There's still so much I have to live for! I don't want to die!

When I can breathe again, the moment passes, and the full force of the blow shoots through me. There's a burning pain in my shoulder, and despite my agony, I welcome it. I'm not dying.

The whirring of engines snaps me back to reality. The helitransport looms above like a paradise just out of reach. I try to make my muscles move, but my efforts are in vain. Each attempt brings on another wave of agony. I moan, bringing my hand to my shoulder.

Looking down to examine my wound, I realize it's not a plasma burn like I expected. It's a bullet. An old fashioned bullet is lodged beneath my skin. Silvery liquid taints my flesh. Shimmery lights flicker in my eyes.

Panic sets in. I touch the silvery liquid emanating from my flesh. It's stickier than blood and makes my fingers go numb.

My body is searing, and lament wells up within me. I curl up like a child, groaning at the horrible sensation.

"Jaina!" Dragon's voice sounds distant and echoes in my mind.

The next thing I know, he's at my side.

"I warned you!" he shouts over the screeching whine of the engines and my cries. "Listen to me. This is going to hurt, but you have to hang onto me."

"What–" I manage through my panting. My body tenses with another onslaught of fire. When I finally catch my breath, I continue, "What's happening?"

"Just hang on," he replies. His voice echoes, as if he's somewhere far away, down a long, empty corridor.

He walks past me and suddenly it's fear that hurts more than my wounds. He wouldn't leave me, would he?

Hands pull me up into a sitting position. I try to keep myself upright, but my strength is fading. Every strain of my muscles brings on a radiant heat in the rest of my body, pulsing through every nerve ending.

His arms encircle my waist and I moan as he drags me backward. My side stings from the slash Azad gave me, and it hurts more as Dragon presses into it.

The helitransport lands, and a ramp extends from the back of the ship. Dragon pulls me inside. Blurry figures follow, fading in and out of my vision. They climb aboard the transport, still parrying gunfire with the opposing team.

The ramp closes, and the ship lifts off the ground, safely carrying our team out of the arena and into the air. The cool air in the transport overwhelms me, and its lack of natural light makes it hard to see.

"Avan," Dragon says, leaning over me as I lay on the floor. "Help me."

Avan falls to his knees by my side and exchanges worried glances with Dragon. "Help me clear the wound," he finally replies. "Remove her armor gently, and sterilize it with this." He hands Dragon a bluish bottle and a white cloth.

"Dragon, what's..." I grit my teeth as my body burns with pain. "What happened?"

"You'll be fine, okay? I promise, Jaina. I promise." It sounds like he says it more to convince himself.

His hands tremble as he gently removes the armor from my shoulder. He grimaces, turning away and takes a few deep breaths.

I almost sit up to look, but Avan stops me. "Don't look, Jaina," he says in a calm, orderly tone of voice. "You don't want to see. You've been hit with a highly toxic bullet. The poison causes severe, burning pain, but you'll be okay."

Dragon takes a dagger to the fabric of my shoulder. He cuts a gash in the cloth, then carefully pulls it over my shoulder, exposing a good portion of my flesh around the wound. I wince as the bloodstained fabric is pulled from my skin.

"Luci," I manage. "What about Luci?"

"She's stable," Avan reassures me. "She's in need of serious medical attention, but there's nothing more I can do for her. I'm a doctor, but I'm not *that* good."

Shaav, Avan. That's really supposed to make me feel better?

Avan nods to Dragon, who pours the blue liquid onto the cloth in his hand.

"This might hurt," Avan says, "but it will be much more painful if we leave it alone. I might have to hold you down."

"Just do what you have to do and be done with it," I return through my teeth. "As long as it stops the pain."

"Dragon, go ahead," he orders.

Dragon breathes deeply as he stares at my bare shoulder with a mixture of horror and worry. He tenderly lowers the cloth onto my wound and presses it into my shoulder.

Pain rages through my body without restraint, and I clench my teeth together. A muffled scream is purged from my lips. Tears of agony well in my eyes, and my body convulses uncontrollably. Dragon quickly pulls away.

"Dragon, keep the pressure on!" Avan shouts.

I feel my head roll back with another wave of burning, raging anguish. Finally, the pain subsides, my body goes limp, and I'm left in peaceful unconsciousness.

chapter

EIGHTEEN

I wake to a strange sense of calm and peace. I move around and surprisingly feel no pain. Glancing down at my shoulder, I expect to see a terrible sight. A bloody gash. Stitches. *Something.* Instead, there's only a scar. A small, barely visible scar. I know these doctors are more experienced than the ones I'm used to, but this is just... unbelievable.

Moving my arm sends twinges of dull pain through my body, but it's nothing I can't handle. My head feels cloudy, and as I sit up, dizziness overcomes me. Immediately, I know it's the aftermath of painkillers.

The room is dark. Not completely black, but the light doesn't sting my eyes like it normally would after waking. A curtain is drawn to my right, splitting up the room. Someone might be behind it. Nervousness tickles the pit of my stomach.

"H-hello? Is anyone here?" I ask.

"Jaina, is that you?" The voice belongs to Kavi.

"Yeah, it's me. Do you think we're allowed to get up yet?"

"I wouldn't know..." she says thoughtfully.

There's some shuffling, then she walks into view. She presses a few buttons on the side of the door, commanding it to open, but it doesn't budge.

"Locked. I guess they don't want us escaping." She laughs.

I sit up, and she strides over, taking a seat on my bed.

Kavi studies my face. "You don't even have any scars."

"I have a few," I reply. "But I'm hardly in pain. I still can't believe we've gotten this far."

"Really? I guess I was thinking we'd at *least* win Worlds."

"Why would you think that?" I ask.

"Last year Virana's team made it to the final round and we've got a great team this year," she says. "Great team leaders, great minds and physical strength...so much variety."

I nod. "We really lucked out, didn't we?"

She smiles, yet her eyes falter to the marble floor. In them, I read her emotions. She's been my friend for so long, it would be hard to miss that look. A kind of cloudiness, apologizing for keeping something from me.

"Maybe it wasn't luck," she murmurs, then turns back to me. "Either way, we have a good team."

I consider asking her what this is about. Maybe if I made a big deal about it, she'd tell me. But the camera in the top left corner of the room convinces me otherwise.

"Yes, we do. Even *you* have to admit Seth isn't so bad."

She's silent for a moment, as if deciding what to say. "Can I...Can I tell you something?" She pauses. "But since you're my best friend, I expect you won't tell *anyone else*."

"I promise. Now tell me," I reply.

"Do you remember the night Seth and I went out to collect firewood?"

"Is that the night you two were acting really weird? And your hair was all crazy; you made up that ridiculous story about someone chasing you?"

"Probably." She touches her hair. "Wait, my hair was crazy?"

I laugh. "Yeah...no offense, but it was awful."

"*Thanks*," she mutters rolling her eyes. Then, she opens her mouth, and closes it again. She has so much trouble working up the courage to speak I wonder if she'll ever say it. Finally, she grins, and her cheeks flush a bright, pink. She brings her hands to her cheeks, like she's embarrassed to be blushing, and laughs. "He kissed me."

The words take a moment to process. "He-he *what*?"

"Seth *kissed* me." She giggles.

My eyes widen in amazement. "Wow...what does that mean?"

"It doesn't *mean* anything. If we end up going to the Crystal City, it won't really matter. But still..."

"Do you think you guys are good then? Like previous wrongs are forgotten?" I ask.

"I can't say that. I still hate him for all he's done. And I'm sure something like that won't happen again. It was just...an accident."

I laugh. "Well, congratulations."

She laughs too and fakes a bow. "Why thank you."

"Can I ask you something?" I lower my voice, afraid the camera will pick it up.

"Sure."

"Now I'm embarrassed, but...what was it like?"

She raises an eyebrow. "What was what like?"

"You know. Kissing him."

"You've never kissed a boy?" she cries in disbelief.

"Shh!" I snap, squeezing her wrist as if hoping that will make her be quiet.

"Sorry," she whispers. "But you've never...?"

I shrug, feeling uncomfortable. "Should I have?"

Her jaw drops. When she sees my annoyance, she shuts her mouth, but can't keep the astonishment out of her eyes.

I roll my eyes. Last time I checked, there wasn't a *law* saying you had to have kissed someone by the age of sixteen. Unlike her, I was busy working on developing my skills to survive the Trials. Not flirting with boys.

She sighs dreamily. "It wasn't quick, like some are. He held me close and kissed me gently, and touched my hair and my cheek. It sorta just...happened. You know? It was right before we reentered the cave. I guess that's why we were a little frazzled." Her distant eyes suddenly become focused, and she glances at me. "But it was so perfect, Jaina. You can't imagine what it's like."

My lips twist uncontrollably into a smile. "Are you *sure* you don't like him?"

Her face contorts into one of frustration and rejection. "*Shaav*, Jaina, of course not! Besides, even if I did, it wouldn't matter in the Crystal City." She does well to hide it, but the remorse in her voice is distinguishable. She likes him. Maybe even loves him.

I find myself grinning with the thought of Kavi head-over-heels for Seth. They just go together.

The lights suddenly become so bright it hurts to make eye contact with Kavi.

"I think that's supposed to wake us up," she says.

The door clicks open, and a small woman in a complete surgeon's uniform tiptoes in. Her hair is blue, tainted with flecks of silver. I wonder if she colored it or if that's how it naturally looks. Her small, piercing eyes are a little too close to the bridge of her nose. Her skin is a light golden color. Clearly, she's not human.

"Oh, good, you're already up," she says in a strong, Huarainian accent. She raises a thin, blue eyebrow. "Prince Melohem is awaiting you're presence."

I stand up feeling, rejuvenated and wide awake. I still can't help marveling at how quickly these doctors work. I've made a full recovery in a few hours.

The small lady leads Kavi and me through five corridors and into a large room. The walls are red, and the furniture varies from purple and pink to white. Pictures of previous Emperors hang on the walls and a small desk rests on the other side of the room.

Shirez and the rest of our team, minus Luci, are waiting for us.

"Where is she?" I ask Liam quietly.

"We've all been wondering the same thing, but Shirez wanted all of us to be present," he says.

"Shirez, the only person absent is Luci. Can you please tell us the news?" Avan asks.

"All right." He pauses and lets out a breath. "First of all, the next Trial will be held on the planet Kovra Ryn–"

"Wait, we're competing on another planet?" Avan asks.

Liam rolls his eyes. "That's why they call it the 'Systems Competition,' you *nav'ra*. Because the 'systems' in our sector of the galaxy are competing against each other."

"Right. That makes sense."

Shirez sighs. "Are you done now?"

"Yes, sir. Sorry," Avan replies.

"You'll be competing on the jungle world of Kovra Ryn where the gravity is slightly lower. Now, about Luci. Her injuries are much worse than the doctors originally thought."

There's a long, cold silence, and Shirez stares at Dragon.

Dragon's gaze falters to the floor, and his body noticeably tenses at Shirez's words. The silence in the room suffocates me. The tendrils of glassy stillness are held in my throat, and I feel like the slightest sound could shatter it to pieces.

"She's not..." Dragon chokes before he can finish.

"She will be fine," Shirez replies, "but she needs more time to recover. She *will* be competing in the next Trial with you."

There's an audible sigh of relief throughout the room.

"Why couldn't you have told us before they got here?" Xana says.

"It's more efficient this way," Shirez replies. "I'm not blind to the fact that all of you are merely children. And children tend to exaggerate. *Tremendously.* I don't want any of you thinking this is a life and death matter for Luci. We'll have to wait in the transport until she's recovered."

"So...now what?" Liam asks.

Shirez nods. "You're dismissed."

The shuttle door opens with a whine. The ramp thuds to the ground. Before I get caught up in a conversation with Liam I don't want to be a part of, I decide to explore the ship. I'm going to be sitting down the whole day, anyway. Might as well stand while I can.

"It's already been an hour. Shouldn't she be ready by now?" I hear Shirez's voice as I pass one of the rooms. The door is closed, but it's definitely not soundproof.

"I'm sorry, sir, her condition is not yet stable. She must remain here a while longer," an unfamiliar voice answers.

"You said she would be ready by 12:00 a.m. We need to be leaving *very* soon if we want to be on time!"

"I'm sorry, sir, but–"

"Is she in a fatal situation?" Shirez asks.

"It depends on what you mean by fatal, sir. She cannot be moved in her present state. She would not survive. Under our care for a while longer, she will be fine."

Shirez sighs. "Then we'll have to leave."

"Thank you, sir. We'll do our best to speed up the process, but not *too* quickly of course. We cannot afford to damage a Superior." The man exits, nodding courteously to me as he passes by.

I inch forward through the doorway. The room is mostly white with a shiny, black tiled floor. Shirez is seated on a bench, made from a hollowed out portion of the wall.

"Shirez?" I barely whisper.

He jumps, but relaxes when he sees me. "I didn't know you were there."

My eyes flick to the floor, then back to Shirez. "Is Luci all right?"

He nods sadly. "She should be fine."

I take a seat next to him. "So what's the plan? Do we sit here and wait?"

"We have to leave without her."

"Excuse me?" I ask, hoping I heard him incorrectly.

He runs his fingers through his black hair, peppered with grey and silver. "She'll still be competing with you. They'll ship her out when she's ready, but if we don't get there on time, we could be disqualified."

"Will she really be okay so soon?" I ask.

"They do a great job," he murmurs. "You want to tell the team?"

"Shouldn't you or Dragon–"

"No, Jaina, it should be you. You and Dragon have the same amount of responsibility, and you've been letting him make a lot of the decisions," he says.

"How do you know?" I retort. I feel the back of my neck warm with embarrassment. My jacket suddenly seems too tight around my wrists, and I have the urge to shift around in my seat.

"He told me." Shirez smirks. "Only because I asked him, of course. Jaina, you're so used to taking orders. You have to learn to make your own choices."

I bite the inside of my cheek, but force myself to nod. "Okay, I'll tell them."

———

"You're joking, right?" Liam cries.

His voice echoes through the large room painted a royal red. Empty tables are scattered here and there.

Avan's jaw drops. "How can we leave without her?"

"I know we're a team," I say, "but it's better than not competing with her at all."

Dragon drops his forehead into his hands and he stares down at the table he's sitting at.

"She'll still be competing with us, right?" Kavi asks.

"Right. She'll be shipped out tonight and should arrive a few hours after us. It'll be like she was never gone."

There's a long silence, and I start to feel uncomfortable with everyone staring at me. Liam finally nods and says, "Well, I'm not sure there's anything else we can do. If it's the only way she'll get better, we don't really have another choice."

"*Shaav*, it's weird being all split up," Seth mutters.

Kavi glares at him, but he doesn't seem to notice.

Liam shakes his head, stands up and leaves the room. The eyes of our team follow him as he leaves, and gradually, everyone else follows behind him, leaving me and Dragon alone.

"The ship should be taking off any minute," I say, taking a seat across from him at a small, round table.

He nods, staring blankly at the floor.

"Dragon, are you okay?"

He looks up and studies my face. His expression is soft and conflicted at the same time. "Yeah. Yeah, I'm all right." He turns away again.

Taking a deep breath, I say carefully, "Dragon, I know you're strong, and you can defend yourself. But there are things you can't deal with alone," I pause. "Will you please tell me what's wrong?"

His jaw tightens and at first, I'm afraid he'll reject me. Tell me it's none of my business and ask me why I care. Then he sighs and says, "Luci and I have always been friends." His voice is calm, but I hear the tremble in his breath. "There's a lot of history I can't tell you, but we were really close." His eyes meet mine, and all I see is confusion. His brow is knit with frustration and misunderstanding. "She thought we were more than that. I feel so terrible that I hurt her."

I place a hand on his wrist. "It wasn't because of you."

"It *was*, Jaina," he insists. "I've done things...such terrible things."

"We all make mistakes–"

"But my mistakes can kill people." He nearly spits the words at me, but it's not in an angry way. More like he's afraid. "Azad knows how to hurt me."

"I thought you said he can't hurt you."

He bites his lip and leans forward pulling his wrist from my light grasp. He drops his head in his hands. "I wasn't exactly telling the truth," he admits. "He doesn't want me dead. He wants to break me. And to do that, he'll hurt the ones I love."

My chest tightens uncomfortably, and a lump rises in my throat. "Do you love her?"

He sits up and smiles sadly. "Not like that. But she was the second best friend I ever had..." His eyes meet mine and he smiles.

I laugh, and feel my face turn warm as I smile. "Thanks."

"You don't know how much I thought of you when I was away," he whispers, and carefully touches my hair. His fingers brush my cheek, and warm shivers travel through me with his touch. He studies my face, as if he's seeing me for the first time. He pulls his hand away from my face and rests it on my own. "I only had good memories with you. When...when they hurt me...I'd think of you. You gave me strength. A reason to go on."

I watch as he gently moves his thumb across my palm. Afraid to meet his gaze, I keep my eyes down. "The Masters told me you wouldn't return. I almost gave up on you, but I couldn't. I always wondered when you would be back. It gave me something to look forward to."

"So what are you looking forward to now that I'm here?"

A smile forms on my lips. "I'm living in the moment."

———

His face haunts me. His dark skin, and dark eyes. The twisted look of agony on his face as he falls to the ground. Blood pooling from the hole in his chest and overflowing into the dirt.

In an empty room of the shuttle, I stare out the window at the stars shooting by. I think back to the moment I killed that boy. I killed a girl, too, come to think of it. According to the IA, I should be proud. There are now two fewer Inferiors in the galaxy. By killing them, I've taken a big step forward to becoming a loyal Imperial.

Does it really have to be this way?

Yes. The IA must remain strong. There must be no weak link in the chain of power or the entire system could collapse.

No. The IA is stronger than that. If only one could bring down the entire IA, then what could fifty do? A hundred?

Stop. Don't think, just do.

But what if the IA really isn't as strong as we think?

The door to my right slides open with a hiss and Kavi strolls in.

"Hey," she says with a smile. "What are you up to?"

I shrug. "Just thinking. You?"

She takes a seat next to me and takes a deep, nervous breath. Her smile is pleading, like she's already begging for an answer.

I roll my eyes, tired of waiting. "What do you want to ask me?"

She laughs casually, but her face quickly turns solemn. "I was just thinking that maybe you wanted to tell me something...since I'm your best friend, and all."

"And what might I want to tell you?" I ask.

She shrugs. "I dunno. Maybe about someone you've taken an interest in?"

"What are you talking about?"

Kavi nudges me in the shoulder. "Oh, come on! I told you about what happened with Seth, now admit it. You like him, don't you?"

I furrow my brow, and feel like I've been struck with a hammer. How could she think that? "I don't like Seth! I mean he's handsome and all, but not my ty–"

"Not Seth!" She laughs. "*Dragon.*"

Oh.

Right.

Of course.

"No," I say quickly. "I don't like him."

Her eyelids hang low over her eyes. She can see straight through me. Her lips transform into a sly smile. "Liar."

"It's true!" I insist.

Kavi crosses her arms. "Yeah, sure. That's what you told me before I figured out how much you liked Liam."

"Kavi–"

She shakes her head. "Admit it. I'm not taking no for an answer. I know you like him."

I glare at her. "If I were to admit it, would you admit something to me?"

"I've said enough to you!"

"I'm not going to say it if you don't."

"Damn, you're so stubborn!" Kavi moans. "Fine. I admit it. I like him. Okay? Is that too terrible?"

"If we're going to the Crystal City, then yes, it's pretty bad."

"*Shaav* it, Jaina. You're always ruining it," she murmurs, then looks up at me. "Now it's your turn. Say it to my face and don't lie."

I groan in reluctance. "This is...it's a big decision to make."

"It's not a *choice*, Jay. It's not like you can help it. Now, do you, or do you not like him?"

"I..." I haven't even admitted it to *myself* yet. I meet her gaze. "Yeah. Fine. I like him."

She giggles and claps her hands in mock applause. "There you go! I *knew* it! I just knew it!"

"You have to swear you won't tell anyone, though."

"Who the *shaav* would I tell?" she asks, as if revealing my secret never actually occurred to her. "It's not like I'd just go tell the entire galaxy about it. Except for Dragon of course."

I grab her arm. "You wouldn't..."

"I'm just kidding!" She pauses. "Well, sorta."

I tighten my grip, and she half-laughs, half-cries out in pain.

"Okay, okay, stop!" Kavi screeches. "Fine, I won't tell him."

"You better not tell him!" I shoot back, still not letting go of her arm. "If you do, I'm going to tell Seth you like him."

"I swear in the name of the Emperor!" she pants. "I won't tell, I won't tell!"

I let her go, and the two of us sit facing each other. After an awkward moment of silence, we burst out into laughter.

"I miss laughing with you," I tell her.

Her lips straighten out into a sad, regretful expression. "I miss *talking* to you."

I glance down at the table. "We'll still be friends in the Crystal City, right?"

"I'll be your friend as long as you want me to be."

I shake my head. "And why would I ever not want you to be my friend?"

She attempts to smile, but her eyes tell me there might be something she's hiding, something that, if I were to find out, would make me reconsider our friendship.

"What is it, Kavi? Don't think I can't read you like a book. What's been bothering you?"

She stares out the window at the passing stars and takes a steady breath. "I'm sorry. I'm not...I can't tell you."

"We tell each other everything. Can't you tell me this?"

She glances up at me. "Not this," she corrects, painfully. "I've been...*instructed* not to tell. You can't know. Not yet."

I shake my head in disbelief. "What do you mean? Why do I feel like I'm the last to know everything?"

The metal door slides open with a quiet swish, and Shirez walks in. Kavi turns to face him, then shoots me an apologetic look.

"I'm not interrupting anything, am I?" Shirez asks.

She shakes her head. "No, not at all."

His gaze meets mine, then moves back to Kavi. "Kavi, dear, would you mind leaving Jaina and I alone for a while?"

"Of course not, sir." She stands and leaves the room, abandoning me with Shirez.

He approaches me, but I don't bother looking up at him. He sighs. "Well, don't *you* look troubled." When I say nothing, he nods, then continues, "How do you think you did in the last Trial?"

I scoff. "Besides almost getting Luci killed? We barely made it out of there."

"What about the first boy you killed?"

My first reaction is to ask him why he'd want me to answer that, but I keep my mouth shut. I lower my gaze, hoping he sees my discomfort and lets me off the hook.

"You can tell me," he persists. "Dragon told me how you reacted."

Why the *shaav* does Dragon tell him everything? I raise a hand in defeat and let the words fly from my mouth. "I feel...horrible. I regret it. I didn't want to *kill* him. I thought he would back away when he saw the dagger. Shirez, I really didn't mean it. I know I was only protecting myself, but to think that I've killed someone—"

"What did you first feel when you realized what happened?"

"I..." I hold back a sudden urge to cry. "I felt like I lost something in me. I don't know what it was, but now it's gone."

"Jaina," Shirez begins sternly, "you must promise to never tell anyone what you just told me. Not Kavi, or Dragon, or an official. *Especially* an official. Openly admitting remorse for killing an Inferior is a capital offense and could get you executed."

"I know."

He puts a soothing hand on my shoulder, but there's a sense of urgency in his grasp. "Don't talk about not wanting to kill an Inferior. Jaina, I know this is hard, but you need to trust me."

"I swear something happened to me and ever since...I feel horrible for what I've done."

"I know."

My breath falters as I suck in the air. It tastes stale in my mouth. "Why don't you turn me in?"

"That's not the way I do things," he replies. "I have faith in you, Jaina. We all do."

Smiling, he stands and leaves the room before I can protest.

Why should I trust myself when I feel this way? Is there something wrong with me? Dragon obviously doesn't feel so terrible about taking someone's life.

I shudder as I remember the glimmer of anger in his eyes as he plunged his dagger into that boy's throat.

Shirez could have turned me in. And he didn't. If I do anything worse than what I've done, I won't be able to live with myself. But if I hesitate before killing another or feel remorse for the deed afterward, then I am a traitor. An Inferior.

That is the way of the Imperials.

We reach the planet Kovra Ryn of the Madriza system. From space, the place looks mostly blue, mixed with greens and purples. The shuttle lands and we're escorted to our hotel.

The room Shirez leads us to is larger than the last two we've stayed in with an even more spectacular view of the city glittering with lights far below us. The dark of the night accentuates Kovra Ryn's three giant moons, hanging low in the sky. With nothing better to do, six of us sit on the couches near the large window while Xana goes into the kitchen.

She brings out a bag of sourdough bread. It's sorta tough, but it tastes all right. Everyone tears off pieces of it, but none of them speak. The routine of tearing off bread and stuffing it into my mouth becomes mechanical, and I begin to forget I'm eating.

Xana stands up suddenly and puts her hands on her hips. "You know what? This is ridiculous. Just because Luci's not here yet doesn't mean anything's wrong. We don't have to act all depressed about it."

Liam scoffs. "Oh? And what the *shaav* do you expect us to do?"

"Why don't we make something?" she asks.

Liam furrows his brow. "Like what?"

Xana smiles and raises a finger. "I know just the thing. Jaina, come help me."

"Why me?" I protest.

Xana's eyes grow dull. "Just because. I need some help and I don't think anyone else will volunteer."

I sigh, and stand up.

Her glittery white teeth flash in the overhead lights as she smiles and leads me into the kitchen. When we get inside, she closes the door behind us. "Okay," she begins.

"We can't let them know what it is. Trust me, they'll be really surprised."

"What exactly are we making?" I ask, a little amazed. I thought she only knew how to fight.

She begins taking ingredients from the cupboards, studying them and tasting a few. "They're called cookies."

The word "cookies" doesn't mean anything to me, so I can only stare at her curiously. "What *are* they, though?" I ask.

Xana takes a jar of white powdery stuff and sets it on the counter, along with some of the other ingredients. There's a carton of eggs, a glass container of sugar, a box of cubed chocolate, and other things I can't exactly name. "Um..." She presses on her eyelids as if struggling to remember something. When she opens her eyes, she reaches into the cupboard and grabs something else. "They're these round things, with pieces of chocolate in them. Sort of like a really sweet bread. Here, I'll show you how to make them."

Xana gestures for me to come closer. She takes out a big, empty glass bowl and pours in the white powdery stuff she says is flour. A big puff of it fills the air and dusts my hands white. We pour in the sugar, and a deceptively delicious smelling liquid called vanilla.

"You wanna crack the eggs?" she asks, holding one up to me.

I grimace, and hold up my hands, taking a step back. "No, you go ahead."

She raises an eyebrow. "Come on, you afraid to get your hands dirty? *You're* supposed to be the brave one." She shoves an egg into my hand. "Now look, you go like this."

Taking another egg in her hand, she holds it up for me to see, then lightly taps it against the side of the glass bowl. Clear goo oozes from the cracks, and I swallow hard, wondering if it could *possibly* taste good with that in it. Xana pries open the shell and lets the contents fall into the mixture.

She nods, then drops the shell in the sink and washes her hands. "There. Now you try."

"Um...okay..." I hold the egg like she told me to, and tap it lightly against the bowl. But it doesn't crack. I furrow my brow.

"Maybe a little harder," Xana suggests, putting her hands on her hips.

I bite my lip, and bring it down with a little more force. *Too* much force. The egg completely splits in half, the yellow yolk slides into the bowl with some of the clear goo, but the rest slides down the outside and onto the counter. It gets all over my hand, and the slimy slipperiness feels gross on my fingers.

Xana bursts into laughter, and I can't help doing the same. The counter is a huge mess.

"Okay," she giggles. "I didn't say *smash* it!"

"Sorry," I reply, still unable to keep a straight face. "You sure it's going to taste good with all this gross stuff in it?"

Xana raises an eyebrow. "Eggs or vanilla?"

"Both."

"They'll be great." She pours in the chunks of chocolate, until it takes up nearly half of the batter. She pulls two big pieces out of the box and pops one in her mouth, then hands the other to me.

The moment I place it in my mouth, I feel like I'm in heaven. The Masters only had chocolate on special occasions, but they hardly ever gave any to us. They usually kept it in a jar on their desk to tempt us, but they usually ate most of it. The only way *we'd* ever get any is if the Master walked out and we stole a handful. Which was quite common.

After reaching back into the box for another handful, Xana takes out a silver baking sheet. I throw a few more pieces of chocolate in my mouth.

"Okay," Xana says through her mouthful of chocolate. "Now take the dough and roll it up into a little ball like this."

Digging her fingers into the sticky dough, she grabs a handful of it and rolls it in her palms. When it's pretty spherical, she places it on the sheet.

"Don't make them too big, though," she says.

"Why not?" I ask, tentatively digging my hand into the gooey mess.

She shrugs. "They grow."

My eyes widen in amazement. "They *what*?"

Xana beams. "Once we put them in the oven, they'll get bigger and flatten."

I laugh quietly, and shake my head. "This is so cool." I place a sphere of dough on the baking sheet. "Where'd you learn to make them, anyway?"

"When I was eight, I said something to Master Dryyn and he took it as an insult. So he said my punishment was to go help the cooks for a week," she says, placing a few more spheres of dough on the sheet. "There was this one really nice lady, and we kinda became friends. One time, I got sick and was in the hospital for two days, and she brought me cookies. She said that warriors weren't supposed to have them, but she made an exception. I begged her to teach me how to make them and...yeah, that's sorta how it happened. She was kind of like a mom to me."

I look down at the bowl of dough. There's only a tiny bit left, but the baking sheet is completely full.

Xana's grin returns. "Now, we have to go put them in the oven." She takes the sheet and slides it into the circular oven in the wall.

We take a seat at the table facing the large window, taking up the entire wall. We wait for exactly three minutes. I suddenly begin to feel nervous. It's as if everything that's happened in the galaxy has come down to this singular moment when we taste these cookies.

The door opens just a crack and Liam pokes his head through the doorway. "What smells so good?"

"Get out!" Xana shouts, standing up and pushing him back. "Get your *shaavez* little nosy face out of here and be patient!"

Liam fights her for a few short moments, but she closes the door and squishes his face.

"Ow!" he cries, but laughs at the same time. "Okay, okay! I'm going!" He wiggles his face from between the door and the wall and leaves.

I realize I'm smiling, as she rests her back against the door to prevent him from coming back in. The door knob twists on its own. Xana slams her fist against the door, and Liam curses.

"*Shaav* you, Xana!" he laughs. "I'm leaving now!"

She waits another few seconds. When he doesn't try to break in again, she comes and takes a seat back at the table next to me.

"By the stars," she sighs. "He's annoying."

"It takes awhile to get used to him," I reply. "I've known him for a long time and I'm *still* not used to him."

Xana shakes her head and smiles. "He can be nice. And ridiculously funny. But annoying."

The timer rings and we move to see what we've created.

I can hardly believe my eyes. The spheres of dough are no longer spheres, but flattened circles. The fragrance is overpowering, and it makes my stomach grumble with hunger. The smell is so sweet, I can almost taste it.

The chocolate weaved into each cookie is glossy, and absolutely beautiful.

I fight the urge to pick one up and stuff it into my mouth.

"Jaina, go get a plate," she orders.

Sifting through the cupboards, I find a big one and bring it over to her. She takes all the cookies–definitely more than eight–and places them on the plate.

"Check it out!" she cries. "Let's go show everyone!"

I hand Xana the plate then open the door for her. The whole team looks at us, and Xana steps into the room like a princess. Everyone stares at her as she approaches the first of the three couches, and lowers the plate for Seth.

Seth looks at the cookies in confusion, like he's not sure what to think of them. "What are they?" he asks, picking one up.

Xana moves the plate in front of Kavi. "They're called cookies. And I *guarantee* you'll like them."

Kavi grabs one and Seth takes a bite. His eyes widen, he looks at Kavi as Xana moves the plate near Dragon.

"Is it good?" Kavi asks.

Seth can only nod as he takes another bite. Kavi tries it and it has the same immediate effect. I wonder if there'll be any left by the time Xana and I can have one!

"In the name of the galaxy!" Kavi shouts, her mouth half full. "These are amazing!"

Xana makes her way to everyone, but skips Liam who's sitting at the end of the third couch. She takes a cookie and hands it to me, then grabs one for herself.

Liam glares at her expectantly.

"I got everyone, right?" Xana asks.

"What the *shaav*?" Liam cries. "That's not fair!"

Dragon laughs as he takes a bite, but says nothing in his defense. Rolling my eyes, I sigh and give my cookie to Liam.

"Jaina!" Xana says. "Why'd you do that?"

"Because!" I laugh. "He deserves one, don't you think?"

Xana sneers, then shoots a seductive look toward Liam. "Fine. Maybe he does." She turns to me and hands me another cookie. "Now eat!"

The sweet aroma of chocolate and vanilla mix into a symphony of colors in my mind. The flavors burst into a grenade-like explosion on my tongue. The sweet, crunchy dough mixes with the flavor of the few pieces of chocolate we added.

I nearly gasp. "This is probably the most delicious thing I've ever tasted!"

Xana gestures to me, like I've said exactly what's on her mind. "I know! See, I told you guys!"

Dragon makes space between him and the end of the couch. "Here, Jaina, you can sit," he says.

I take the seat next to him, and I can't help realizing how right Xana was. The moment I began cooking with her, I started feeling better. I wonder if everyone else feels the same.

Luci returns to us after a few hours. Xana offers her a cookie and Luci's face brightens when she tries it.

"Luci, how are you feeling?" Kavi asks.

She laughs. "Pretty good, actually."

"We really missed you, Luce." Dragon affectionately pulls her into his arms.

Luci smiles as if she's in heaven, and rests her head on his shoulder for a long moment. She sinks into his embrace.

My stomach wrenches uncomfortably. Forcing myself to turn away, I suck in a deep breath to clear my mind. He said he didn't love her.

I bite down hard on my cheek. Who the *shaav* made Dragon's business my business? Maybe I admitted to Kavi I like him, but it's not like it will make a difference.

When I glance back at them, she's finally removed herself from his arms and stands at a comfortable distance.

Luci flashes a smile in my direction, and I'm tempted to glare back at her. Instead, I smile, like nothing's bothering me. Because nothing *should* be bothering me.

"Where's Liam?" she asks. "He's the only one I haven't seen yet."

Dragon clears his throat awkwardly as if to ask why she'd possibly want to go see Liam.

Luci furrows her brow. "He helped carry me to the helitransport. I should thank him."

"I think he's working on the hint to the next crystal," Kavi answers.

"Yeah," Seth agrees, "but he says he doesn't want to be bothered."

"Oh, all right. I'll thank him later," Luci says as she presses her back to Dragon's chest.

Unable to stand her closeness to him any longer I ask, "You think it would be okay if I went to check on him?"

Seth shrugs. "He gets distracted so easily. Meaning he'll be angry if you interrupt him. But go ahead. He's annoying anyway."

I advance toward Liam's room door and knock. When there's no response, I open it slightly. "Hey, can I come in?"

He's sitting at a desk with another microscope and a small needle. He still doesn't answer, so I close the door behind me, pull up a chair and take a seat next to him.

"How's it going?" I ask.

"Good until the moment you barged in." He holds the crystal in one hand, twisting it and examining it from all angles. Tiny symbols line the edges of the crystal. Some are swirly, reminding me of the way Kavi and I used to draw snails when we were kids. Others are more square-like with lines inside. It's the written language for Cora.

I lean over on his desk, resting my head in my hand, and look up at him. "What's wrong?"

"This thing..." He presses a series of tiny buttons on the crystal with the needle point. "It's ridiculous. I mean, I've already solved the first three codes. But this fourth one...It doesn't make any sense."

"Maybe I can help."

"Doubt it."

"Try me," I challenge.

He lets out a breath of defeat. "Fine. The clue goes like this:

> The answer to this riddle,
> will make the crystal yours.
> The square that looms above you
> is not of two but four."

I look around the room.

"Already tried that," Liam says, "but there are no squares in this room. They are all rectangles or circles. I checked."

I think harder. A square is the answer to the problem. That doesn't make much sense.

Liam stares into my eyes. When I meet his gaze, he turns away. He chuckles shyly to himself.

"What?" I ask.

He glances at me, but it's not with the same intensity as it was a moment ago. A sad smile flickers on his lips. "Nothing."

My stomach knots. What changed in me? Why, when I actually have the chance, do I not see him the way I used to? Why does he suddenly feel this way for me?

I shake the thoughts from my mind and sigh. "It's sixteen."

"What is?"

I laugh. "Four squared is sixteen."

He looks from me to the crystal a few times, then back into the microscope. "Didn't try that yet." He presses a few buttons, and I hear a click.

"Did it work?"

He rolls his eyes. "Yeah, it did."

I rush to his room door and peer out into the open. "Guys, we figured it out," I call to the others.

"Tell us!" Xana cries, bounding into the room and nearly tripping over the leg of the couch as she passes it. The rest of them follow with a little more caution.

"Okay, here it is," Liam begins.

"Walk mindlessly through the forest,
The light will lead the way,
To the north you'll find your prize.
Do not be lead astray.
Upon reaching what is needed,
The crystal you shall find,
But your tears shall be shed,
For the sacrifice, this time."

"That's pretty deep," Avan says.

"Is it just me or is the sacrifice for each Trial becoming harder to give up?" Liam ponders.

"He's right," Luci says. "The first wasn't much of a sacrifice. The answer was light. The second one..."

"It wasn't so bad," Dragon says, "but it takes more courage to give up blood than light."

"With each Trial, the stakes become higher and higher. Whatever we've got ahead of us will be worse than losing a handful of blood," Kavi murmurs.

"She's got a point," Seth says. Kavi shoots him an emotionless glance.

"So I guess we just have to be prepared," I say.

Dragon nods. "We've got a long Trial ahead of us, and tonight might be the last night of good sleep we ever have. Might as well enjoy it."

chapter

NINETEEN

I stare up at my room ceiling. The fan blows cold air down on me. A chill runs through my body. From the fan or from the memories of my dream last night, I'm not sure.

In my dream, we were in the Amarija arena. I'd killed Azad, but his voice continued to haunt me. *"He will betray you Jaina."*

Dragon and Liam were there, their eyes were red from the angry glare of lava. Remembering it sends tingles of fear down my spine.

"Liar!" I shouted back at him.

Dragon approached me, and it occurred to me that *he* would betray me.

"He's lying to you," Azad's voice echoed in my head.

Dragon's eyes locked onto mine, pleading with me. *"You have to trust me."*

Yet Azad's voice didn't stop. *"The Dark will destroy you."*

I can't dismiss this as I have many of my dreams. It almost got Luci killed. If Dragon knew I could have stopped it, what would he say? He wouldn't be happy, I'm sure.

But what happened in my dream already took place. I didn't *really* kill Azad. My mind flashes back to the vague scenes that played out so clearly in my head. Dragon's eyes. Liam's eyes. Azad's voice. I shudder again.

I stand up and dress. I grab a pair of black, tight pants and a sleeveless, purple and green top that matches the climate. The pale morning light shines through the window. The foreign star shines bright and giant in the sky. Though the planet is about the size of Earth, the gravity is supposedly slightly weaker. I can't feel much difference though.

Azad could have been trying to throw me off my game. But what if it was the future? If one of my dreams foreshadows what's to come, couldn't this one, too? Will the traitor betray me? I wish Dragon would just tell me who it is, but I see his point. We can't afford to split up the team. I wonder how he can keep it to himself. If Dragon can keep that to himself, what else could he be hiding?

The only people in the dream were Azad, Dragon and Liam. Could one of them betray me?

No.

No one will betray me.

Shirez arrives at our room a little later than he should have and we have hurry to our transport. This one has open sides with no protection on the long ride to the arena.

The transport takes off, and warm air rushes through the ship. The wind brushes my hair behind my armor. We pass over small villages and see long legged aliens hard at work. Their houses are simple, made of wood and mud bricks. After so many technological advancements, how could there still be places as backward as this?

It isn't long before we come to a place where civilization has totally halted. There are no houses or any indication of intelligent design. There's only forest for miles around. Most of the trees are a dark green color; a few are blue or purple. Their leaves glisten in the early morning light, as if it had just rained.

"All right, here are your gauntlets. Make sure you use a camouflage setting for this world," Shirez says. "Choose from these weapons. I suggest taking less than you have before. In the last Trial, only one weapon is allowed, and you should take your scimitar. Might as well prepare for it now. I think you're skilled enough. You can keep your gauntlet, which has quite a few weapons of its own. That should cover you."

Though we've already won two Trials, the chances of survival are severely plummeting. If we don't make it to the end, we'll be sent into Reconstruction. A silver marker in the forest catches my eye. We've officially entered the arena.

"Strap on your armor if you've not done so. The entire arena is a jungle and there's a lot of life down there. You'll need as much protection as you can get. All right, here we are!" Shirez says.

I look down at the rapidly approaching ground. The helitransport hovers a meter above the wet muddy surface of the planet. We jump off. My waterproof boots land in the mud with a splash. The color of the ground isn't brown like it is on the Earth. It's black.

"Good luck!" Shirez shouts over the whining of the transport engines.

We nod, and the transport vanishes in the distance.

The entire world is a death trap. We don't know anything about this place. The only thing that makes every team even is the fact that no one can guess what's right around the corner. I've heard of planets where flowers can swallow a human in a few seconds. I've heard of forests where the trees and plants can communicate with each other and throw things at an unfortunate passerby. I've heard of places where the life forms can fade in and out of visibility and kill their prey without ever showing their face. Could this forest be anything like those?

The bark of the trees is rubbery and bendable when the wind is light. When the wind is rough, the rubbery material contracts, making the tree shorter and sturdier.

The only sound that brings me comfort is Dragon's soft and steady breath as he wanders through the arena beside me. Even the sound of my boots in the mud is different. Instead of the squeaking, squelching I'm used to, there's only a soft, grinding noise, like tiny grains of sand were mixed into the soil. It's hard, like the mud has already begun to dry.

The air is humid. I thought I'd be used to it, because the air on Virana was always humid. But here the air is thick, I feel like I'm trying to breathe through a straw.

I'm just glad it's not some substance other than water, like vaporized cyanide. That would really suck.

I can't say I'm excited about this mission. I just want this to be over, now. My body has been weakened from the lack of sleep the past week. The few extra hours I had in the hospital yesterday don't really count as resting.

"Do you know which direction we should be heading?" I ask Dragon.

"The poem said north. Other than that, I have no idea," he says. "Why don't you take the lead for a while? I have to go talk to Seth for a minute."

I nod, and he moves to the back of the line.

Without Dragon in the lead, the illusion of safety dissipates into thin air. I keep my right hand near the hilt of my scimitar hanging from my holster belt. I want to be prepared for anything that comes my way.

Up ahead, the forest becomes dense. The trees are spaced only a meter apart in any direction. It looks so uniform, too perfect to be natural. Could the trees have moved on their own to create a sort of defense?

The ground is covered with thick underbrush of dark green and blue moss and grasses. In some of the clearer areas, flowers grow.

A patch of the silvery-blue flowers lie before us. Their stalks are thick, measuring nearly the width of my waist, yet they're short, only half my height. I pass by one cautiously, wondering if these could possibly be the man eating sorts of flowers I've heard of in horror stories.

These don't have any petals. Only a satellite-like head sits atop the stem, and if I'm not mistaken, they move according to our position. I take a step to the right, and the one before me shifts slightly in my direction.

I turn around, to get a sense of what our team thinks of this. They look on in wonder at the fascinating creatures before us. Xana reaches out to touch one. I almost cry out to stop her, but her hand is already on the flower. She turns to me and smiles calmly.

The flower begins to glow with her touch. Its form seems to relax and shudder with delight as the glowing grows brighter, spreading to every part of its bowl-shaped head.

Liam gasps in awe. He steps forward and touches another one. It begins to glow, as well.

"What are they?" I ask, placing my own hand on one.

"They're called vicera flores," Xana replies in an even, peaceful tone. "Thought flowers. They reflect your feelings, and your inner self. If you are calm, they will glow."

Mine glows softly, and begins to grow with my touch.

"What does it mean if it grows?" I ask.

"They don't grow." Xana laughs, but when she looks at me, her smile fades. "Wow, never knew they could do that."

The vicera grows slightly taller, and I watch in wonder, unable to pull myself away.

Dragon grabs my wrist and pushes my hand away from the flower. His lips are pressed tightly together, and his eyes narrowed in worry.

"What was that for?"

"You could have killed it," he replies.

"Killed it? Xana's seems fine."

Dragon closes his eyes, and gently presses his hand to the head of the flower. The glowing fades completely with his touch, and it shrinks back down. Its color becomes dull and dark as it contracts from its previous form. Finally, he pulls his hand away.

"How did you do that?" Xana asks.

"Don't worry about it, Xana," Luci interjects. "He just does things like that."

Xana shrugs it off, like what he did was nothing, but I'm not convinced.

Luci turns to Dragon, a fearful expression etched into her eyes, as if asking him why he'd do something like that. He stares back blankly at her, and I can't read his reply.

He moves closer to me, and I can feel his warm breath on my cheek. "We should move out–"

"What was that?" I cut him off. "What did you do?"

He stares deeply into my eyes as if he hadn't expected my question, but his confidence quickly returns. "I did the same thing you did."

"Quite the opposite," I retort. "Why'd you think I was going to kill it?"

"I didn't think, Jaina, I *knew*."

"But–"

"I shouldn't have countered what you'd done, but it's over now," he insists sternly. "Forget it."

Liam clears his throat. He places a hand on Dragon's shoulder and gently pushes him a step away from me. "First of all, give the girl some space, would you? She can't breathe with you so close."

Dragon's jaw tightens, and a fire of frustration flickers in his eyes, but he doesn't fight back.

"And excuse me for interrupting your very private conversation, but what are those?"

I follow Liam's gaze and see five identical spheres. The smooth metal surface is obviously man-made. We move toward them.

"What do you think they are?" Avan asks.

Liam touches one. The moment he does, it transforms into a half spherical transport with a control panel. It hovers a meter off the ground.

Liam grins hysterically. "Hoverbikes. These things are fast."

"You've used them before?" Xana asks.

"Duh," Liam says. "It's one of the best transports around. They're fairly simple to use, but terribly expensive."

"Should we use them?" I ask.

"Damn right we should use them!" Liam cries. "Unless they've been sabotaged."

"Maybe we should check them first," I reply.

"It'll take a while to check them all," Liam replies. "But if you guys could find a cave or some shelter, I can get these babies up and running. It'll definitely be worth it."

Luci nods. "I've seen a lot of potential places to stop for the night already, so it shouldn't be hard finding someplace else."

"Can we bring them to the shelter and have you fix them there?" I ask.

"Yeah, don't worry, they aren't that heavy. That's why people like them," Liam replies.

"Good, it's settled then," Xana says, picking up one of the spheres.

Dragon gently takes my arm and pulls me close to him. I feel his lips near my cheek. "Keep your eyes open for anything suspicious."

"What is it now?" I ask, remembering my annoyance with him and push away from him. "Something else you should have told me?"

"This is serious, Jaina," he shoots back. "I think we're being followed."

"Again?"

"Yes, again."

"*Shaav*..." I curse.

He nods. "*Shaav* is right. Be wary." With that, he moves away and addresses the team. "Everyone, lend a hand. We're moving out."

———

It isn't long before we find a suitable resting place. It's only an outcropping in a rocky wall, protecting us from whatever substances might bombard this planet at night. Maybe acid rain, or some sort of poison we don't have on Earth.

It's too dangerous to send anyone out hunting tonight, but it's not like we haven't gone nights without food before. Back on Virana, if we missed training or were being punished, the Masters would deny us food. One time, the entire class went a week without food because Mira Nordan insulted our teacher.

The world has become grey, and a thick blanket of fog covers the ground. Visibility is low, and I can only see clearly ten meters in any direction. And after Dragon warned me about someone watching us, it's not comforting. Darkness is closing in.

Luci leans back on a large boulder and stares out into the fog. Her face looks pale and her eyes are locked on a distant object I can't pinpoint.

"You all right, Luci?" I ask, approaching her.

She continues staring into the mist. "Yeah, I'm fine...I think I might have seen something."

The moment the words process, my blood pressure rises. I follow her line of sight to the grey haziness before us. "Where was it?"

"I saw it right about there." She points out into the gloom. "Then it moved, and I don't see it anymore. At first I just thought it was the wind blowing a tree back and forth, and maybe that's all it was. But the more I think about it, the more I doubt that."

I look again.

"There it is."

Sure enough, the fog swirls, revealing a dark object. It stays there for a fraction of a second before the cloud swallows it up again.

"What do you think it is?" she asks.

"I don't know. But I'm going to find out."

She stands up and takes her place beside me. "I'm coming with you."

"It's okay, I'll take Kavi–"

"I found it," she interrupts. "And I want to know what it is."

Oh. I wasn't expecting that. Out of everyone, she's the one who volunteers to come with me?

"Okay," I choke out reluctantly. "Sure, I'll just go tell Dragon, and we'll be on our way."

"No," she says quickly. "If you tell him, he'll want to come along. Let's just get this over with."

"What if something goes wrong?"

"If something goes wrong, he'll find us," she replies. "Now come on. Let's get out of here."

She's right. Besides, why should I tell him everything when he tells me absolutely *nothing*? I take a deep breath and give in. With that, we head out into the fog.

———

"Are you sure this is where you saw it?" I ask, after about ten minutes of trekking through the creepy, humid atmosphere.

"No," she replies. "But approaching it head on probably isn't a good idea."

I kick at a small, colorful stone. It squeals as it rolls across the ground and flies somewhere into the bushes. It was actually *alive*? Even the stones could be dangerous.

Pretending it was nothing, I look up at Luci.

The question I've wanted to ask looms in my mind, but I refuse to acknowledge it. I'm not entirely sure I want to know. Yet remembering that look on Dragon's face as he brushed my hand away from the flower...remembering how Luci glared at him after that...the need for knowledge is too strong for me to pass it up.

"Luci," I begin. "What happened earlier?"

She smiles. "When?"

"When Dragon did that...thing..."

Her face darkens. "Why would you think I know what happened back there?"

I shrug, trying to look casual, but I can't help feeling nervous at her response. "He said you were good friends. And the way you looked at him after he did it...it seemed like you knew something."

Luci nods then fixes her gaze back on me. "You wouldn't believe me if I told you."

"Maybe I won't," I reply. "But I want to know."

She raises an eyebrow. "It's not something I can explain in a few minutes, Jaina. If I told you everything I knew about the Prophecy–"

"Prophecy?" I cut her off.

Her eyes widen, and she covers her mouth with her hand.

"What Prophecy?"

Luci's breathing is fast and worrisome, like she feels sick to her stomach. "I'm sorry. I...I misspoke..."

Does she honestly expect me to believe that? She's lying to me. Could she be the traitor? Dragon and Azad said it was a boy, but maybe Dragon was trying to defend her.

"What are you hiding from me?"

Her jaw tightens with anger. "If you want to know so badly, why don't you go ask Dragon?"

I stamp my foot on the ground, feeling so childish, but I'm unable to hold it in. "Why the *shaav* does everyone know these things but me!"

A tremor in the ground stops my ranting. At first, I think I'm the only one who feels it, but when Luci looks back at me, her eyes filled with distress, I know she felt it too. I touch the hilt of my scimitar, ready to spring into action.

Luci glances at me, and I press my index finger to my lips.

She nods then takes a few steps forward. "Check this out," she whispers.

It's a hole in the ground, about half a meter in diameter and who knows how deep. A shiver travels down my neck and into my spine. Surrounding the hole are a series of markings, like an extremely large worm would create while exploring the surface.

"Whatever it was it left in a hurry," she says. "And recently."

The sudden sound of plasma bursting and crackling through the air gives me a jolt. Our team.

"They need our help!" Luci cries.

We break into a run. The shouts of our teammates and their gunshots echo through the forest, but still we can't see them. Blood pulses through my body as my heart strains to keep up with the pace of my footsteps.

I keep my eyes on the ground to prevent myself from tripping, but in another instant, I'm falling anyway. I'm sprawled on the black soil next to Luci. The sound of gunshots continue. Luci moans, and I curl up, trying to breathe.

"You okay?" I force each word from my mouth.

She grits her teeth and stands. "As good as I can be, given the circumstances," she spits back. "What the hell did we trip over?"

I push myself up and scan the ground. "I've got no–" I'm cut off as my feet are swept out from under me once more. I hit the ground. Mud splashes up my arms and frustration surges through me. Luci's next to me on the ground again.

"*Shaav*! I *hate* this place!" she shouts.

I stand up again and study the ground with critical eyes. I ready my stun rifle for whatever it is. There's a quick movement. I squeeze the trigger, and a flash of electricity pulses out of my weapon and onto a rope-sized plant root.

"Luci, it's the *trees*!"

She shoots me a quizzical glare. "What?"

I look forward, and the mist has cleared up ahead.

A flower, standing about one and a half times taller than me, is closed. It looks like a large version of a hibiscus flower. One native to Earth. The petals are closed. It doesn't look frightening, but looks can be deceiving.

"What is it?" Luci asks, her voice quivering as she speaks.

"It's a Minithious Flower," I whisper. "I've read about things like it back on Virana. A sudden movement or loud sound could wake it out of its sleep."

"What's the worst that can happen in this situation?" she whispers back.

"It will squirt paralyzing nectar at us and will slowly digest us throughout the night," I hiss. *Na'lav*, we've got to find a way out of this.

"That doesn't sound pleasant," she says. "But at least it won't be painful–"

"Shut up. We're getting out of this alive," I cut her off.

"We only have one choice. We have to kill it." With that, she presses a few buttons on her gauntlet. In the split second it takes me to realize what she's doing, I lunge at her and pin her to the ground. A gunshot rings through the air, and I turn around to glance at the flower.

The sound wakes the carnivorous plant, and the bolt of plasma harmlessly bounces off the stalk of the flower. The creature slowly unfolds its black petals, transforming into the shape of a satellite. Veins of red color the center of the petals. It's as beautiful as it is deadly. Though it has no eyes, its sense of the world is enough to find us quickly.

I take cover behind a tree as the center shoots out a paralytic spray. Only a few of the droplets dot my hand, making it tingly, but Luci isn't so lucky. Her entire arm gets hit head on with the sticky fluid, and she falls backward with a thud. She scrambles to find shelter behind another tree. A vine from the deadly black flower creeps up behind her, and I fire at it before it can wrap itself around her ankle.

I jump out from behind the tree and flip my wrist, firing a round of energy toward it. As the plasma hits the petals, the dark colors of the flower absorb the bolts and radiate the energy as heat.

It shoots its paralytic acid at me, and I barely dodge its attack.

Luci sits behind a tree. "I found the electronet," she calls to me. "Distract it, and I'll take care of the rest."

I fire a few more bolts at it. The Minithious shrieks in pain, sending vibrations through the trees around us. Luci is about ready.

Just a few more seconds.

I toss an MED at it, and the blade rips right through the delicate petal. I pull out my scimitar as a vine rockets toward me. I easily slice it in half. The dark flower shoots a vine toward my midsection, and I only have time to duck before it hits me. I'm too late, and the vine twists itself around my arms and neck.

I drop my scimitar, struggling to breathe. Its grip tightens around me. *Luci, throw the net!* I want to shout, but I can hardly get air to my lungs. She stands only a few meters from me but makes no move to throw it. If she does, I'll be electrocuted, too. At least that way is quicker than suffocating. Black spots start to appear in my vision. I try to struggle free, yet the coil only winds tighter. Cold darkness starts to close in on me as the flower drags me through the mud, closer to its satellite-like head. Once again I try to breath, but nothing happens. I close my eyes.

A terrible, screaming pain surges through my body. The heat is like fire, spreading through my veins. My eyes fly open, but I can't see a thing. My body moves without control. My stomach knots and untangles violently. I try to scream, but nothing escapes my throat. The light falls out of my world, and I plummet into darkness.

chapter

TWENTY

"Jaina!" cries a voice from far away. "Jaina, you have to wake up!"

Someone jerks my shoulder back and forth. My eyes open with a start, and I see Dragon standing over me. I haven't taken a breath since the darkness closed in. I try to breathe, but it's useless. As my surroundings begin to make sense again, I feel something warm curled tightly around my arms and my throat. Much too tightly.

The flower. The pain. The Trials. It all comes back in a flash.

Xana shakes me again, trying to keep me awake. She pulls at the coils around my neck and holds the vine open for a few seconds, allowing room for me to suck in a few breaths of precious air. The flower tightens its grip around my throat, stopping my breath once more. Blood pulses through me so hard I think I might explode.

"Hold on, Jaina," Dragon pleads. "You have to hold on." He climbs over me and pulls his MED free from his holster belt.

We've won the past two Trials. We're so close to victory. I can't die now!

I'm suffocating. Consciousness starts to evade me again. This time I might not wake from it.

At least *he* is with me. That seems to make everything right. It's how everything started and how it shall be finished.

I remember his young, beautiful face as it was all those years ago. He was handsome, even then. I look at him again. Not too similar. But not so different from who he was.

I'm about to die, and all I can think of is him.

Dark spots cloud my vision again.

Things start to blur.

It becomes harder to think.

I feel cold. I try to free my hands and grab at my throat, but Xana and Dragon can hardly do the job themselves. The flower continues to fight back.

This is really it. I try to breathe a few more times before giving up. Nothing happens. My lungs constrict, and my head is pounding.

Just say it.

You've known the truth all along, says a voice in my head.

I close my eyes in defeat. Consciousness is fading fast. This is my last chance. And before I can let go of life, I have to say it. So I do.

I love you, Dragon.

I am, in every way, in love with him. I wish I could have told him. Now, I'll die and he'll never know.

There will be no escape from my imminent fate, and an eternity of cold.

Just as my eyes flutter closed, Dragon takes one swift motion with his dagger across my throat. The blade cuts so close to my skin I'm almost sure it'll draw blood. I pull away with my last reserve of strength. The tension around me is released.

An animal-like gasp escapes me as I take a hard breath of the sweet jungle air. I'm still alive. I can breathe, I can see.

My arms are still tied up tightly. Xana and Dragon work on freeing me. The cool, rough vines pull on my skin as they fall away. Its tight grip is suddenly gone. I bring my hands to my throat and take as many breaths as I possibly can. I never realized how thankful I should be for the ever present air around me. I'm light headed from the total lack of air and the sudden return of it.

Dragon kneels down beside me. I hold out one hand and watch it shake a little. He looks at it, then takes it in his own.

"Jaina, are-are you all right?" he stammers, frantically touching my arms, rubbing warmth back into them.

I continue taking in slow, deep breaths, but his voice calms me down. "Dragon," I pant. "Dragon...I'm... I'm sorry for not trusting you."

He touches my cheek and brushes a strand of hair from my face. "Jaina," he says softly. "You don't have to be sorry. I'm so glad you're okay."

"I'm fine," I say, touching his shoulder.

He pulls me to him, pressing my chest to his and wrapping his arms around me. I let my chin rest on his shoulder and struggle to fight back tears. I'm alive. I love him. His warm embrace is so sudden but fulfilling that I can hardly contain my feelings.

"I swear, I thought I'd lost you." His voice quivers with the words and I can feel his heart pounding in his chest.

I don't let him go until he pulls away. I laugh. "I bet you wouldn't know what to do with the team without me."

He smiles, though his eyes are narrowed with fear. "You're probably right."

I cough then take another set of long breaths.

"Where's everyone else?" I ask.

"Luci got hurt pretty badly," Dragon replies. "The plant flung her backward, and she was hit with a dose of paralytic fluid. Seth and I did our best to fight the thing off, but we needed the help of the entire team to do so. She'll be fine, according to Avan."

"What happened?" I ask. "Luci and I heard gunfire."

He nods. "The polyps of the Minithious flower invaded the camp. We fought them off within a few minutes, and then came to find the two of you."

Liam runs up to us and falls to his knees. "Jaina, are you okay?"

"I think so."

He takes an unsteady breath. "Jaina, you can't die on us like that. We need you a lot more than you think we do."

"Thanks, Liam." A stinging pain starts in my throat again, and I bring my hand back to my neck. "That thing had a tight grip."

"So I heard," Liam replies. "But the electric shock might have done more damage than you think."

"Can you stand?" Dragon asks.

"I think so."

"Here, I'll help you up." Xana reaches out for my hand. I take it, but my legs scream with pain and buckle beneath me.

"I can carry you," Dragon suggests.

"It's okay, Dragon. I got her," Liam interjects. The threatening edge in his voice scares me.

Before anyone starts making a scene, I interject. "If you could both just help me up, and walk me back to the hideout that would be great."

They grab hold of my hands and wrap my arms around their shoulders. Dragon is taller than Liam, making my steps uneven. I try my best not to look at Dragon. But how can I possibly ignore him? Now that I've admitted my love for him? I notice his strong arms and his soothing touch. The way he holds me up and holds my hand in his as we move across the ground.

Once we're back at our hideout, the two of them set me down on the soft black soil.

"Thanks," I tell them.

Dragon squeezes my hand. "We're a family, remember? I wouldn't let you go without a fight. You're too important to us."

I smile. "Of course I am."

He grins, then gets up to talk with the rest of the team. Liam remains beside me but doesn't say a word. He just sits there, staring.

"Liam, are you okay?"

His face contorts into an angry, tormented expression. "Of course I'm not okay," he shoots back, keeping his voice down. "I should have been there to help you, and I wasn't. You could have been killed, and I wouldn't have had time to say goodbye. Why am I always late?"

He looks me directly in the eyes. The words "Liam" and "intimidating" should never be heard in the same sentence, unless the sentence is "Liam is anything but intimidating." The words contradict each other. Yet in this instance, I can't help feeling intimidated by his intense stare.

"What changed between us, Jaina?" His jaw tightens. "Because even though it didn't seem like it, my feelings for you were always the same. I might have pretended, Jaina. But it wasn't real."

"Stop. Don't talk like that."

He touches my wrist. "You have a choice."

"No," I breathe. "I don't. If we win, we won't have a choice."

"Then let's lose."

I feel the blood draining from my face at the horror of his words. He wants us to lose? Because he wants to be with me?

"Liam, you know they wouldn't let us be together," I say carefully. "Even if we lost. There is no way we'd be able to choose."

"So why do you choose him?" he asks. "You're not even sure he feels the same for you. You hardly know him!"

"Don't tell me what I know or don't know about him!"

"He'll hurt you."

I clench my teeth in anger. "How could you say something like that? He just saved me. Without him, I'd be dead. You should be thanking him."

"He's toying with you."

"Shut up!" I cry. "Don't talk about him like that. He wouldn't do that to me."

Liam bites his lip and nods but looks nauseous. "It makes me sick, seeing how easily you're falling for him.

Just know I hurt every moment I see you like this." He stands to leave, then turns one last time to me and says softly, "I'll be there for you when he lets you go."

———

"I already told you I'm okay," I tell Luci, who's studying my throat to make sure I'm all right. "You don't have to do this."

"How are you feeling?" is her only reply.

"I'm fine. I'm a little sore, but considering I was electrocuted *and* almost suffocated, I'm actually feeling pretty good. How are *you* feeling?"

"I'm fine. The effects wore off quickly," she says mechanically. "If you feel any severe pain or headaches, please notify me."

"Nothing I can't handle."

"Some patients don't know what they're talking about," she replies.

"And would that be me?"

"Most of the time."

"Well, *that* makes me feel better." I roll my eyes. "Why do you care? You don't even *like* me."

She sighs and throws down her equipment. "Look, Jaina. I don't know why the *shaav* you were chosen as team leader. I'll admit, I think I was more qualified for the position. Unfortunately, you're doing a good job."

Embarrassed, I look away from her. "I really don't know what to say."

"There's nothing you can say, Jaina, so don't even try."

"Is there anything I can do for us to be friends?"

She smiles sadly. "I don't think so. Don't think it's your fault either. I don't blame you. Now get out of here and get some rest before you have to go on guard duty," she says, gesturing to the rest of the team, getting ready to sleep.

"I think I'm guarding first tonight, anyway," I murmur. "Get off to bed, Luci. You're going to need your rest for tomorrow."

The fog has cleared up a little but has been replaced by darkness, fingering its way into every open space it finds. It crawls like a predator across the ground. It's become a three dimensional being that could suffocate my soul if I let it in.

Everyone succumbs to sleep quickly, and I'm left with only the light of the three moons, the stars, and the glow of blood red coals to keep me company. Tonight, the darkness is soothing. I let it creep up my face and crawl around me. Its usual harshness has become soft and silky.

But darkness can quickly overpower. I cannot let it into my mind. The light can be harsh, too. It can be sharp, like a knife with rigid edges that slashes through the shadows. It cuts away the lies and exposes what is hidden. Its warmth isn't gentle and comforting, but intense. Light has a dark side of its own.

Tonight, there's not too much light or too much dark. It's balanced, as it should be. I stare at the burning embers of the fire.

I think back to my conversation with Liam. He's got such a fragile heart. If anything goes well for me, he'll break. I could never love him again. At least, I'm quite sure I couldn't. Ever since Dragon came along, Liam has changed. But it's not like we have a choice. If we win, I wonder who the Imperials will choose for me to marry...Out of everyone in the Crystal City, I'm sure they wouldn't choose someone I know. Just because I love Dragon doesn't mean they would choose him.

Then a horrible thought hits me. Even though his team lost, if Azad has strong DNA, he could be sent to the Crystal City. What if I see him there? What if the Imperials choose *him*?

My body tingles with cold. And if I had to marry him, surrender myself to him, I can't bear the thought. I'd rather die than ever have to be with him again. Maybe I *don't* want to go to the Crystal City.

Ever since the battle in the volcano, I can't get him out of my head. He's always in my mind, in some form or another. Taunting me, telling me to give up.

"They say you're the Light." His voice echoes in my mind. *"He's lying to your face, Jaina, why the shaav can't you see it? He will betray you."*

I wake to the sound of birds chirping far in the distance. As I come closer to the surface of consciousness, things begin to make sense. Dragon and Seth whisper quietly somewhere to my left.

"I wonder why," Seth says.

"Do you think it worked out for the best?" Dragon asks.

"I don't know. If not, we don't have another choice. That could have been our last chance to help her decide. If she remains undecided, there's nothing we can do."

"If worse comes to worst, I'm sure I can come up with some way of convincing her," Dragon says.

"I'll keep an eye out for opportunities, and you just do what you have to do. This has to work."

"All right, I think we should wake the team now."

"Agreed."

What are they talking about? Convince *who*? I open my eyes and sit up. Hunger grows within me. A dizzy, sick feeling overcomes me and I'm afraid I'll throw up the nothingness in my stomach. I can't be complaining. I'm lucky I'm still alive.

"Ahem," Liam announces. "Last night, I checked the transports. Only one of the five was sabotaged, and I, being the genius I am, was able to fix it."

There's a short round of applause, and Liam takes a bow.

"Oh, one last thing. You might want to get some practice on those things before you fly away. We can't afford one of us ramming into a tree and exploding, or anything."

Xana crosses her arms in annoyance. "That's a comforting thought. Thanks, Liam."

"I'm just telling the truth," Liam says. "Find a partner. That should leave two people to ride solo."

Dragon approaches me. "Jaina, I think one of us should go alone. It's not a great idea having both team leaders in the same place. It makes for an easy target. Do you think you can take the extra one?"

My heart sinks a little, and sad, unromantic thoughts shoot through my head. Does he not want to be around me?

"Yeah, sure, I can take it," I reply. "Who's going to be on the second one?"

"I'm thinking it should be Liam, since he's the only one who *knows* how to fly it. All he has to do is take us north until the fuel runs out, which shouldn't be too long," he says. "But I need you to be the overall leader, okay?"

I hesitate. "That's a lot of responsibility you're giving to the girl that almost got killed yesterday. Are you sure this is a good idea?"

He puts his hands on my shoulders, and I feel the ghostly presence of his warm embrace. "I trust you, Jaina. You should, too."

I nod, and he lets me go. We approach the shiny, metal spheres. Liam demonstrates how to touch the soft, smooth surfaces to transform it into a transport. I climb into the hovering object.

Liam instructs us how to use them, showing us how to steer and maneuver them through the trees. He flies over to me after everyone's sort of figured it out.

"How're you doing?" he asks.

"Fine."

I press a few buttons on the touch screen, turning on the engines. I carefully press my finger to the lever that controls speed. I'm jerked backward and release the lever. I stop abruptly and jerk forward.

He raises an eyebrow. "I wouldn't call that *fine*."

"I'm okay," I snap. Attempting to push away the memory of our conversation last night doesn't help calm me down. What he said, I can't forget.

"Liam and Jaina, I need you two to lead the way," Dragon calls from his transport. Kavi's arms are wrapped tightly around him from behind. She catches my gaze. Her eyes dart to Dragon, then back to me.

I have to look away from her to keep myself from laughing. It's not hard to tell what she's trying to say. He's a lot better than she originally thought.

Catching Liam's gaze he nods and ignites the engines. The rest of us do the same. When Liam begins to accelerate, I follow close behind.

The uniformity of the trees makes them easier to navigate, despite the dense foliage we encounter now and then. After about an hour, the fear of crashing into something drifts out of my mind, and I begin to enjoy watching the surroundings pass us by.

The hot jungle air rushes past me in a wave of cool escape. It's as if everything else has ceased to exist. I keep my eyes on Liam, just ahead of me, and glance at the touch screen on the dashboard to make sure we're still alone.

Why did I have to admit it yesterday? Now I have to live with the fact that I love him. But I have every right to love him, don't I? He saved my life.

The IA does not give me that right.

But we *should* have that right, shouldn't we? We should be able to choose who we spend the rest of our lives with. What if we got to the Crystal City and they chose someone like Azad?

A red light flashing across the touch screen catches my eye.

ENGINE FAILURE. SETTING TO SELF DESTRUCT.

I glance backward. My teammates don't look worried about anything. Maybe they don't notice the message, or maybe I'm the only one who's got it. I have to figure out something fast. I keep my breathing steady. *Focus, Jaina.* I let go of the lever controlling my speed, but the transport doesn't stop. I glance back at the screen.

OPERATION NOT POSSIBLE. SELF DESTRUCT IN 30 SECONDS.

I turn around. Seth and Luci seem perfectly unaware of whatever danger I'm in. *Think, Jaina. What are you going to do?* I don't know much about controlling a transport through the internal system, but I've done it before. "Should'a paid more attention in engineering class," I curse to myself.

I open the control panel and stare in dismay at the mess of wires before me. I look back at the screen.

SELF DESTRUCT IN 19 SECONDS.

I take a deep breath and pull out my MED. Think back to the class. The teacher explained to cut the wires attached to only one of the power cells, then to the main computer. Or was it the other way around? My brain hurts from the adrenaline rushing through me and the sudden stress of the situation. I can't save myself!

"Liam!" I shout over the whining engines.

He glances back at me and slows down to my speed. "What's wrong?"

"Tell me how to stop this from self-destructing!"

He glances at my touch screen.

SELF DESTRUCT IN 15 SECONDS.

"Did you try to stop it?" he asks, frantically.

"Yes! It didn't–"

"Just get close to me, and jump! We don't have time to fix it!"

I steer my transport closer to his, then pull away before I hit him.

"Liam, I can't make it." My voice is shaking and my body begins to give into my fear.

"You have to jump! I don't care if I'm not the team leader; I'm ordering you to jump!"

I start to stand up, but the transport rocks to one side. I look at the touch screen. *Ten seconds.* I grab Liam's hand, hoping I won't pull him off his transport when I land. I clear my mind and jump. Liam directs my landing and helps me into the seat behind him.

"Kick your transport away. When it blows, we don't want to go with it."

SELF DESTRUCT IN FIVE SECONDS.

I kick it to the side, and it flies off course. The transport ignites into a ball of fire, then explodes into ashes and spare parts.

"You okay?" Liam asks.

I breathe a sigh of relief. "I'm better now."

"We're running low on fuel. We'll have to stop in about an hour."

"Why would it just explode?" I ask.

"The Imperials must have programmed it that way so we'd have more to worry about," he says. "That's why they gave us five instead of four."

I wrap my arms around his waist to keep myself from falling off. It's uncomfortable being so close to him, especially after the things he's said to me. His body relaxes with my touch, and I can tell he's savoring this.

"How is everyone else doing?" Liam asks.

I turn around to check on the rest of the team. "They're okay."

"Good. Keep an eye out for...scary things."

I laugh. "That's the best you could come up with?"

"I don't know what the creatures here are called. How should I know?"

"All right, I'll keep an eye out for *scary things*."

The whirring of the engines fills the silence. I let my chin rest on his shoulder, and he breathes in deeply, like he's trying hard to ignore me. Like he's trying to keep me out of his head. Poor Liam. I hold him tighter, over-whelmed with the pity I feel for him. Maybe he'll take it as me being affectionate toward him, but I can't help myself. I can tell he wants to say something. And there are things I'd like to tell him, too. Yet neither of us say a word. We remain quiet, letting the silence speak for us.

———

The fuel eventually runs out. It's only been around forty-five minutes since my ship blew up, but we've covered a fairly good distance. We should be getting close to the crystal.

The transports slowly, but surely die. Liam and I climb off. The rest of our team forms around us, and Dragon rushes over.

"I know this is kind of delayed, but what the hell happened back there? All of a sudden I see Jaina jumping onto your transport and then hers explodes!"

"The Imperials programmed a self-destruct sequence into it, just to give us some other awful thing to overcome," Liam hisses.

"And how did you miss that when you were inspecting them?" Dragon shouts. "Why would you let her use that one?"

Liam steps back, opening his arms as if inviting Dragon to hit him. "I didn't know! It could have been any of us! It's not my fault it happened!"

Dragon doesn't relent. "You could have gotten her killed. If she'd been hurt, I'd–"

"Dragon," I interrupt, touching his arm. "It's okay."

He gazes down at me, and all signs of anger fade from him. Dragon glances back to Liam and backs down.

"You okay, Jaina?" Kavi asks, approaching us.

"I think I'm getting paranoid," I murmur. "I don't like the fact that I've come so close to dying two days in a row. I hate to put anyone else in my situation, but why me?"

"I guess you're just unlucky," Xana mutters.

"Yeah. Sure."

A quiet whirring cuts through the air. I only have time to process a small helicopter-like object flying at me before Dragon activates his scimitar. He effortlessly slices the object in half. In another instant, his scimitar is deactivated and back in his belt.

My heart quickens, knowing if the object had hit me, I could be dead. *Again*. The object on the ground, oozes a greenish substance into the dirt.

"Maybe you're right, Xana. The universe is trying to kill me." I bite my lip nervously. I'm not one to believe in fate, but this is scary.

"It'll do that to us, Jaina," Dragon mutters.

I'm about to ask what he means, but Liam interrupts. "Dude, how'd you do that?"

Dragon turns to him, his eyes dull like he's been studying Cora all day long. "Do what?"

"How the *shaav* did you see that thing coming?" Liam's brow is knit with confusion, the left half of his mouth is lifted in wild befuddlement.

Dragon shrugs, like it was nothing. "Practice."

"What was it?" I ask.

"The Minithious flowers aren't just deadly as adults," Dragon says. "That was one of its seeds. It's a good sign."

Luci grabs Dragon's arm. Kavi's next to her, her arms crossed and her face tightened with concern.

"Whoa, whoa, wait," Luci begins. "*How* is that a good sign?"

Dragon rolls his eyes. "The more danger we encounter, the closer we presumably are to getting there. Trust me, okay? I know what I'm doing. I'm sure the crystal has many more terrible traps around it."

When Luci doesn't reply, Dragon turns forward again. "Jaina, stick close to me."

"Why?" I ask. As if I need a reason to be near him, other than the fact that I love him.

"Call it what you will, but I don't want anything else awful happening to you," he reassures me. "I'm just worried about you."

Liam groans, indignation nearly dripping from his clenched teeth as he stalks to the back of the group.

I turn back to Dragon. "Yeah, okay, I'll stick to you. I mean, I'll stay close to you," I stammer. My eyes lock onto the ground as I'm unable to prevent my face from burning completely red.

Dragon laughs and shakes his head.

We continue north. I want to say something to Dragon now that we're alone at the front of our teammates. No one else would hear us if I thought of something to say.

My mind wanders, and the simple truth reveals itself to me. I realize I'm not, in any way, a leader. Everyone knows who's *really* in charge on this team. Despite Liam's harsh feelings toward Dragon, it's clear he trusts him to get us out of here alive. If he didn't, Liam would've stopped following Dragon's orders long ago.

It stings, realizing this illusion. Like rubbing salt into a wound.

"I'm not a leader, am I?" I ask.

Dragon glances at me. "Of course, you are. You're as much a leader as I am."

"In *theory*. But I don't act like a leader. What kind of leader has to get saved every five seconds?"

"You don't have to get saved *every* five seconds." He pauses. "More like every few hours."

"See?" I moan.

"Hey, I'm just joking." He laughs. "If I remember correctly, *you* were the one who dodged to the checkpoint against my orders in the previous Trial. We only got out of there because of you."

I shake my head. "That's different."

"No, it's not. But even if you're not a leader *yet*, you will be."

I look up at him. "Will you teach me?"

"Sure." Suddenly, he grabs my arm and stops me. "Hold on."

The omnipresent sense of danger clings to me with a dullness I can't quite describe. I want to roll my eyes at it. Enough danger, already! It's getting boring, having to fight every twenty seconds. "What's wrong, now?" I whisper.

Without warning, he takes his stun rifle out of his holster belt and fires at something to the right. There's a groan and a thud. He was right, again. His super fine senses are starting to creep me out.

I take out my scimitar and prepare my gauntlet to fire.

"Put your weapons away," Dragon orders to everyone.

"Are you crazy?" Xana asks.

"No, as a matter of fact, I'm not. Now follow orders," he shoots back, then turns to the trees around us. "Come out of hiding! We know you're there!"

There's no response.

"Show yourself!" he cries.

I'm so confused. Is he going crazy?

"Please don't hurt me!" a voice calls.

Dragon takes a step closer to the source of the voice. "Step out of hiding. Drop all of your weapons and keep your hands above your head where we can see them. We won't hurt you."

There's movement up ahead, and I keep my gauntlet ready to fire despite Dragon's orders. If they try to attack us, I'll be prepared.

From behind the dense trees, a girl with red hair steps into the light. Her skin is a bit redder than a normal human but other than that, she looks enough like a person. Her eyes are gold, and her high cheekbones are beautifully defined. Her hands are raised high above her head in surrender. She's a Martian.

"What do you want?" she asks. Her golden eyes dart from me to Dragon. Her voice shakes as she speaks. "Say anything, and I'll do my best to give it to you. Just please don't hurt us."

Dragon studies her a moment. "Where's your team? Is this a trap?"

"We're spies from the..." She swallows hard. "The Xiborex team...We're from Mars." She looks from me to Dragon.

"Did your team ask you to spy on us?" Dragon asks.

"Yes, they wanted us to find you and pretend to surrender. As we are doing now." She's shaking. Her hands are still behind her head.

Dragon keeps his eyes intensely trained on her. "Why'd you leave your team?"

"There's a traitor on our team. He-he tried to make us lose," she manages.

Cold shivers travel through me. A traitor on her team wanted them to lose. Hadn't Liam said something about that? Anxiety claws its way into my stomach and halfway up my throat.

"Did you tell your teammates about this?" Dragon asks, concerned.

"Only my friend. We don't want to be associated with them, and more than anything, we don't want them to win. Will you please let us be your hostages?" she asks. "Or prisoners or informants or whatever."

Dragon looks at me, asking for approval. She wants to be our captive? She must be mad! Either that or this is part of their plan. Maybe the Xiborex team is trying to ambush us right now.

"You keep saying *we*." Dragon notes. "Is that the person I stunned?"

She nods.

"Kavi, Seth, could you bring her partner over here?" I ask them.

Kavi and Seth drag the boy over. He's still knocked out and probably won't wake for another hour or so.

"Is this him?" Dragon asks.

"Yes."

I take a step closer to her. "What's your name?"

"Veronika Souav. And this is Orion Rajan." She gestures to her teammate.

Dragon looks at me, then back to Veronika.

I nod. "You can come with us. But at the first sign of betrayal–"

"I swear we won't betray you. We will follow as if we've been a part of your team," she interrupts.

"There are a few things we need to know before we continue on," Dragon says. "Did your team say anything about the location of the next crystal before you left?"

"Oh yes! We know very much about that! We can show you the way!" she cries. "Orion and I passed it when we were coming to find you. There are many dangers on that route."

"You saw the crystal?" I ask.

"Yes, but getting it will be hard. Many creatures guard it. It's a wonder we got out of there alive."

"Which way?" Dragon asks.

"Follow me!"

———

Veronika leads us in a curved direction for quite some time. Whether it's to keep out of harm's way or to keep us away from the crystal, I'm not sure. I don't know how much I trust her. She seems like she's telling the truth, and that's what scares me most. Dragon gave in to her request pretty quickly. A little *too* quickly.

I don't like this. Not at all. Veronika stays in the lead but keeps Dragon and I close behind. After a few hours trudging through the jungle, night starts to close in. We find a suitable place to rest, and I'm glad there's no killer plant near us. My only worry is of Veronika and her teammate, Orion.

They could so easily betray us. They could kill half of us with a few shots from a rifle.

"Dragon, how are we going to sleep with them around?" I ask quietly as we sit around our camp fire.

"Don't worry about it. That's really not what's bothering me," he replies.

"So what *is* bothering you?"

He takes a breath. "Let's talk about this outside, okay?"

I wish we wouldn't have to talk in secret like this all the time. It makes everything more...awkward, especially if we don't agree. And I'm officially in love with him, now, so that makes things even weirder.

We exit the hideout and move far enough from everyone so we won't be overheard.

His back is to a large tree that stretches so high, I can't quite make out where the top is. "They left their own team because there was a traitor," he breathes. "And I'm not even going to pretend you've forgotten about our own."

"I've tried not to think about it," I reply numbly.

"I'm glad, but we've got a problem."

"Which is...?"

"I'm not sure how to put this..." He awkwardly shifts his weight and keeps his eyes on the ground. "But both traitors are kind of...connected."

"What do you mean by that exactly?" I ask, my voice unintentionally rising. "Are they both part of the same cause or something? Are they mercenaries or pirates, or worse?"

"Jaina, I'm not allowed to–"

"Not *allowed*? Who's keeping you from telling me?" I take a step closer to him, my jaw tight with anger. "Are *you* the traitor?"

"No!" he cries. "No, Jaina, please, just listen to me."

"How do you know who both of them are?"

He doesn't reply.

I clench my fists, unable to help myself. My face feels tense and with every breath my hostility grows. "I don't understand why you can't just tell me."

He sighs. "Calm down, Jaina. Please."

"Dragon, this is dangerous. You're dealing with traitors!" I cry.

"It doesn't mean they're bad people," he replies.

"I know..." My tone lowers to nearly a whisper. "But I'm worried about you. I have no idea what happened to you that night, but it gave the Masters a good reason to take you away. And I won't let that happen again." I realize I've moved much closer to him, but I don't care.

His eyes are solemn, and he shakes his head sadly, taking my hands in his. "I don't want you to worry about me."

"But I do. I worried about you every day since you left. I wondered if you were still alive or if you'd ever come back. And when you finally did return...maybe I didn't act all that excited, but it was one of the best things that's ever happened." I take a deep breath. "But when you tell me you know things that could get you taken away again, or even killed–"

"I know how to handle these things," he cuts me off. "Listen to me, Jaina."

He puts his hands on my shoulders and pulls me closer. So close that I'm almost pressed against him. His touch is warm against the cool, evening air.

"From now on, a lot of things won't make sense. But I need you to trust me."

My eyes narrow until I realize I'm glaring at him. "I've blindly trusted them to know what's right. I trusted them when they told me I must kill the weak. And now... Now, I'm not so sure."

"I know how you feel," he whispers, and gently touches my cheek. "I remember thinking those thoughts before I was taken. It's what got me suspended in the first place."

"That's what they told you?" I choke out in disgust. "That you had to serve a ten-year suspension?"

He nods. "And it was because they couldn't 'cure' me of those thoughts." He brushes a strand of hair from my face. "To the Imperials, the ability to think and question is a disease that makes people impure. Some can be cured of it. And others, people like me, cannot."

His hand trails to my shoulder and to my arm. Warm shivers travel through me with his touch. Thoughts are blurred in my mind, and all that's clear is the longing to know if he loves me, too.

"I'm glad you weren't," I breathe. "I'm glad they didn't change you."

"I know it doesn't seem right for me to ask you to blindly trust me, just because I'm your...your friend. So I'm going to ask you something else."

"Okay."

In hardly a whisper, he purrs, "What do you want?"

My heart flutters with his words. What do I want? I want him to hold me. I want to feel his fingers in my hair and on my waist. I want the right to choose him in the Crystal City. I swallow hard, knowing that's probably not what he means. "W-what do you mean?"

"What do you want, Jaina? What does your heart desire?"

My voice comes quick and monotonically. "To go to the Crystal City."

"I'm not asking what the IA wants you to want." His hand finds the small of my back, and he pulls me closer. The air leaves my lungs and my hands move to touch his strong, sturdy shoulders as he leans in and whispers, "What do *you* want?"

I gaze intently at his lips. I want to feel them pressed to mine. I want him to love me. I want us to be together. *Stop it, Jaina. This is wrong.* "I want you to be safe."

He runs his fingers through my hair, and I feel his breath on my lips.

My stomach churns, but I force myself to continue, "I don't want to have to worry about you being taken away again. I don't want to fear for your life."

His full, perfect lips break into a grin, and his eyes gently close. He presses his lips gently to my cheek. My body shudders at the sensation, and I let my hands rise up over his shoulders and hold him to me. His lips trail across my cheek and arrive near my ear.

"If that's what you want," he breathes, "then trust me."

"If you get hurt–"

He pulls away, but keeps his hands on my shoulders. "I won't, Jaina. I told you I'd always be there for you, and I've already broken that promise. I don't intend on breaking it again."

"All right," I breathe. "I trust you."

chapter

TWENTY-ONE

I let the morning air seep over me, as thoughts swirl in my mind. I'm not really sure what all of that meant last night, but I savor every word he spoke to me.

And he kissed me.

My stomach tingles, remembering how his lips gently brushed my cheek. I trust him. More than I trust the Imperials. I can only be thankful that the Trials are the single time we're unsupervised by the IA.

Someone touches my arm and I sit up with a start.

"Get up," Liam says. "Come on, it's time to go."

We pack up our stuff as quickly as we can and scatter the ashes of the fire. Orion and Veronika wait at the entrance of the hideout and help prepare us to leave.

Avan takes a MED in his left hand and approaches me. It's deactivated, but it's unnerving to see him with one in a non-threatening situation. "You don't think she's setting us up, do you?"

"I'm not sure," I reply. "Keep an eye on the two of them. I don't trust them."

He acknowledges the order then joins the team near Veronika and Orion. I follow close behind him, and approach the Martians.

"How close are we to the crystal?" I ask.

Her teeth are smooth and flat, yet look menacing as she smiles. "We've only got a little ways to go."

"Take the lead," I order.

We all fall in line, and I take my place next to Dragon as we begin the walk through the jungle.

"You don't think this is a trap, do you?" I ask, thinking back to Avan's question.

"It's highly possible," he replies. "But I doubt they'd actually risk fighting us."

"What if their team leaders are like Azad?" I ask. "They didn't want an easy win. They wanted to fight us."

"Remember what I told you last night?"

Every word of it. "About them having someone on their team connected with someone on ours?"

"Yeah. If their team leader is who I think it is, we'll be fine. They'll have to fake the fight for the people who aren't involved."

"Like me and you?"

The trees grow menacingly dark around us, letting only a few tiny splotches of light to find the dirt. Dragon nods halfheartedly. "In a way."

"What if we have to fight them?" I ask.

"What do you mean? Of course we'll have to fight them."

I don't want to kill anyone else. "What if that *someone* on the other team gets killed?"

Dragon sighs. "Jaina, I hate to ask this, but...do you want that someone to live? I mean, they're an enemy to the IA."

That stops me in my mental tracks. "I—"

"There's the crystal!" Liam shouts.

Its shiny surface is as blue and captivating as Dragon's eyes: soft, clear, and aquamarine.

"This has got to be a trap," Luci mutters.

"Why?" Kavi asks.

"You really think they'd just leave the crystal in the middle of the jungle unprotected?"

"Read the riddle!" Kavi says to Liam. Liam kneels down and reads.

> "After light and dark collide,
> And after blue turns red,
> After what you should have loved,
> Is something you now dread.
>
> Through painful cries of sorrow,
> Through darkness and distress,
> How can you describe the pain,
> When you've lost what you possessed?
>
> When the rain falls in sheets,
> It can quell the passionate flames.

What will fall from you,
When what's lost you can't reclaim?

That doesn't make any sense!" Liam shouts. His eyes are wide with panic.

On the back of the pedestal rests a silvery box-like thing, with an imprint of a hand on it.

Suddenly, Dragon cries out in pain and clutches his left arm. His breath is short and choppy. When he pulls his hand away, his fingers are tinted with blood. Horror surges through me as I move closer to him. He leans against me, unable to stand on his own.

"Dragon, what's happening?" I ask.

He falls to his knees and then to the ground.

"Dragon!" I fall to his side and touch his arm. Lodged in his bicep is a small arrow. How could such a small arrow cause him so much pain? "What's happening?" I cry.

"Jaina," he moans.

Avan rushes over to us. "What happened?"

"I-I don't know! He was hit with this...this...."

"His breathing's slowing. And so is his heart," Avan murmurs. "It must be poison."

Luci glances at his wound, then exchanges looks with Seth and Kavi. "Jaina," she says soothingly. "He'll be fine. But we're going to have friends to entertain."

"What do you mean, he'll be fine? He's been hit with a poison dart!" I shout.

"Trust me," Luci pleads. "He'll be okay."

How would she know! Did she do something to him? He's obviously not okay! "Tell me what happened!" I order.

"It's none of your business!" she shoots back.

"It is my *shaavez* business!" I scream.

I can't lose him again. Not now. Especially now.

"You're sure Dragon will be okay?" Avan asks her.

"Yes, I'm positive. I've seen these before. They're used to stun, not to kill. Wouldn't I be more worried if I thought my best friend was dying?" she snaps. "Just try to wake him up. Jaina, start solving the riddle."

I'm too scared to disobey. "'After light and dark collide, and after blue turns red.' Does that refer to the two past riddles?" I ask. I can hardly think, seeing Dragon lying in pain on the ground.

"Let's just assume so!" Liam says. "The answers to those riddles were 'light' and 'blood.' So after light and dark collide, meaning when two separate forces go to war and after the blood is spilled, something that should have been good is now something bad."

Xana says, "When you're put through tremendous pain and have to deal with regret, in what way can you express your pain when you've lost what you possessed? Sadness?"

"How the *shaav* can you sacrifice sadness?" Kavi yells in frustration.

"If it isn't the mighty team of Virana!" an unfamiliar voice calls out.

Standing a few meters away is the Xiborex team. Orion and Veronika stand alongside them.

I knew it! They betrayed us!

A lump wells up in my throat, and I wish I could shoot Dragon a glare saying *I told you.*

"Last year your team destroyed us!" Orion shouts.

"You killed our friends," says a boy next to him. "And now, you'll pay!"

"We don't have to hurt them, Jeton," Veronika says to him.

"Wait!" Luci cries, her hands high above her head, asking for a few more seconds of peace. "Please, that wasn't us!"

"They must be avenged!" screams a girl.

Jeton sneers, then charges at us. The battle has begun. I watch him pull out his sword. I keep mine ready. He comes at me with a furious attack, so surprising and strong that I'm not sure my defenses can hold him off.

The power in each strike of his blade threatens to overwhelm me. He sweeps his sword up and down, left and right with such speed that I only have time to jump backwards instead of block.

"So you're the one we've been waiting for?" he asks, just loud enough to be heard over the sounds of clashing swords.

I say nothing.

"Just tell me, Jaina, is it true?"

"I don't know what you're talking about. How do you know me?" I ask, concentrating on blocking his next attack. When it comes, he almost slices my hand, but I jerk backward and avoid it.

"I think you know exactly what I'm talking about. Now answer the question every one's asking. Are you the Light?"

My blood runs cold. Azad's words echo in my mind. *"They say you're the Light."* By the look on Jeton's face, I can tell he got an unexpected reaction out of me. He keeps his sword locked with mine.

"I know nothing about it!"

He studies me, as if to make sure I'm not lying. "Oh, hell. You mean they haven't told you yet?"

He takes another swing at me and I bat it away, fiercely.

This time it's my turn to attack. I can't listen to him anymore or I might as well go crazy. I don't want to succumb to the same animalistic rage that I felt while dueling Azad. Had I gotten the chance, I would have killed him without a second thought. But it's not what I want. I want Jeton gone, not dead.

He smiles, but doesn't attack me. We've wandered a little ways from the main battlefield. The rest of my team fights the Xiborex furiously, not too far away. Luci defends Dragon with a fiery passion, and I know he'll be all right.

"I'm not the enemy here. I don't want to hurt you," he says. "In fact, my job is to make sure you get out of here alive."

There's a sudden crackling in the ground. At first I think it's because of him, but when I see the look of fear on his face, I know that it's something much, *much* worse.

The dark green vines shoot out of the earth, splitting the ground with so much force, small cracks appear beneath me. A ring of dark flowers open up around us. Our only escape is to fight.

"*Shaav*, not again!" I curse.

"Come on, we'll be safer this way," Jeton tells me.

Without question I follow him to the rest of our teams. Is he really trying to help me? He said he wanted to get me out of this alive...what the *shaav* did he mean by that?

All is silent as the Minithious flowers process where we are. If we stay perfectly still, they might not notice us. The idea is too good to be true.

All at once, the ten monster plants surrounding us lash out with vines, polyps and paralytic fluid. One of the vines wraps itself around a Martian's waist and throws her into its satellite-like mouth. She screams as the plant swallows her whole. It begins to grow taller, and the veins in its deadly petals flush deep red–her blood.

"Hurry! Cut the plants off before they've fully come out of the ground!" I shout. "They're still growing and if we let them continue to their full size there will be no hope for us."

Everyone, including Jeton and his Xiborex team, follow my instructions.

I approach a polyp that has begun to sprout from the plant that devoured the Martian girl and slash it in half with my scimitar. It squeals, then withers away. The plant it came from begins to grow a few centimeters per second.

Shaav, this is bad.

It rises above our heads, faster than I've seen anything grow.

Staring up at the giant plant, I grab the person nearest me, who happens to be Jeton. "Come on," I tell him. "We need to cut the head off before it can grow any more."

"All right, let's get this over with," Jeton replies.

I roll my eyes angrily. "How can you be this quick to team up with us?"

He smiles slyly. "Don't worry, I'll be this quick to betray you when we're through killing these plants."

I clench my teeth. "I should kill you right now."

"I'm kidding."

The thought suddenly occurs to me, and I can't help but ask. "Are you the–"

"Yes, I am, Jaina," he cuts me off. "Why else would I be helping you? Why else would I be trying to protect you? I don't like you very much. If I had a choice, I'd have killed you twenty minutes ago."

I shake my head. "Come on."

We rush over to the rapidly growing flower. It throws a set of vines at us. I cut through the powerful green ropes that try to snatch us into the air, then begin climbing the thick stalk of the plant, knowing the top will be thinner and more sensitive tissue.

"Hurry, we need to get to the top!" I call to Jeton.

His jaw drops. "That won't be as easy as you think."

"Just shut up and follow–" I'm cut off as something flies at us.

The plant begins spitting fluid from its satellite-head and a few of the drops fall on me. My pants and boots keep most of it out, but my arms start to tingle. *Shaav.*

The plant spits another dose at us. Jeton and I climb higher up the stalk where it can no longer target us.

I can't stand the annoying, arrogant look on his face. We reach the top despite the flower's violent writhing, attempting to keep us away from its new, sensitive shoots.

"Now what? Do we just saw through it?" Jeton asks.

"Yeah, and while we're at it can I saw off your head, too?" I hiss.

He smiles seductively. "We'll have plenty of time to play around later, my dear."

I do my best to keep from kicking him in the groin. "Some traitor," I mutter.

"What the *shaav* did you just call me?"

"Shut up."

I take my scimitar, and he takes his sword. We take turns cutting through the thickening stalk. The plant shakes viciously, much more than before; I'm not sure if it's because of an electronet or some other contraption from our team. Maybe it can tell we're doing our best to end its life. I look down, terrified, realizing how much taller this plant has grown. I'm at least ten meters off the ground.

"You afraid of heights?" I ask.

"Yeah, but I'm more afraid of you."

I can hardly hold on while I try to cut through the material. I need to use both hands now. "Jeton, help me!" I call to him.

"Here, I'll hold on to you while you cut it!"

"No way!" I shout. "I'll hold on to *you*!"

He shakes his head. "You're not strong enough. Come on, I'm not going to let anything happen!"

I gulp down my fear and move closer to him. Reluctantly, I let him grab hold of me while I continue sawing through the plant stalk. Finally, the Minithious flower's head becomes unstable. I haven't cut all the way through, but it's enough to finish the job. The stalk quivers uncontrollably. It's about to collapse under its weight.

"We've got to get out of here!" Jeton cries.

Uncomfortable, but seeing no other alternative, I wrap my arms around him. He doesn't seem to mind. We've only got a few more seconds before the plant will topple to the ground.

"Hold on tight!" he orders.

My stomach rises into my chest as we slide down the stalk. I hold back a scream and close my eyes, wishing it was Dragon I was holding on to. *You're pathetic, Jaina.*

We land safely on the ground as the plant falls away from us. I pull away from him so he has no easy way to turn on me. The rest of my team is occupied with the plants, though they aren't in enough danger to need my help.

The plants have been destroyed, and a few of the Martians lie motionless on the ground. By the look on

Jeton's face, he's only slightly surprised at the failure of his team.

"You play a bigger part in this than you think. If you are the Light," he breathes quietly.

"What do you mean? What's the Light?"

He only smiles and replies, "May the stars favor you."

With that, he backs away from me and pulls a capsule from his belt. He pulls off the cap and drinks the clear fluid within. He drops to the ground and loses consciousness.

Is he dead?

I crouch down beside him and touch his wrist. He's still breathing, and his pulse is normal. Why would he do that?

I leave Jeton where he is and find my team has been successful. I rush over to them, all standing around Dragon. I'm not sure what to say when I reach them, mostly because Dragon's only partially awake. His eyes are only slightly open, and flutter back now and then.

"Is he all right?" Xana asks, stooping over Dragon.

"He's okay," Avan replies.

Dragon takes a deep breath, opens his eyes and tries to stand with such urgency it freaks me out. He stares right at me with disbelieving fear like I've threatened to kill him or something.

"Whoa, slow down," Avan says, forcing Dragon to lie back down. "How are you feeling?"

Dragon's face is ghostly white and he studies our surroundings like he's not sure where we are. He touches his chest then examines his fingers like he's looking for wounds. His breathing slows and he looks at me again. "Are-are we back yet?"

"Are you okay?" I ask, sitting on my knees next to him.

"I think so...where are we?"

Liam groans in frustration. "We're in the arena, you *nav'ra.*"

"Shut up, Liam," I fire.

"We're *still* in the arena?" Dragon asks.

"Yeah, you missed out on all the fun," Liam returns.

He sighs and touches his shoulder and finds it slowly oozing blood from where the arrow was. "What happened?"

"You were hit with a poison dart," Luci cuts in. "My guess is it was the Martians before they attacked us. You should be okay, though."

"All right, we've got to get out of here."

"Dragon, wait," I start. "Shouldn't you let Avan bandage your arm?"

"No, it'll take too much time. We're almost done."

I take his hand and pull him to his feet. It was a small arrow, but it had plunged deep into his muscle tissue. How can he keep moving like that?

We approach the pedestal and read the riddle again.

"I know it," Liam says.

I turn to him and raise an eyebrow. "What is it?"

"What will fall from you, when what's lost you can't reclaim? Tears."

"Real tears? Like genuine tears of pain?" Xana asks. "Sorry, I'm not volunteering for this one."

Liam shrugs. "I don't know. Do we have to make someone feel terrible?"

Dragon gestures to the small box at the back of the pedestal, engraved with the imprint of a hand. "I don't think we'll have to make someone feel terrible. That should do the job."

My eyes lock onto Dragon. "What is it?"

"It's a..." He hesitates. "It's a torture mechanism. The machine sends electrical signals into your mind, stringing horrible memories and fears together. I'd never wish that kind of pain on anyone."

I'm about to ask how he knows when I realize they must have used it to "cure" him.

"Is it physical pain?" Kavi asks.

Dragon shakes his head. "No. It's much worse than that."

"Well, someone has to do it," Liam interjects.

"Liam figured it out," Xana suggests. "He should be the one to do it."

"Me? Maybe next time, I'll wait for someone else to figure it out!" He backs away from us.

"Stop it," Dragon says. "I'll go. I've been through it already and know how to handle it."

"You can't, you're injured!" I couldn't bear seeing him hurt so badly. "I'll do it."

"Don't be ridiculous, Jaina," he shoots back. "I'm going."

"All of you shut up!"

I jump at the harshness in Luci's voice.

"I'll do it," she breathes.

"Luci, you can't do this to yourself," Dragon says.

"Yes, I can. And I will." She spits the words at him, her eyes narrowed with rage. "It's not like this will kill me." With that, she strides confidently up to the pedestal.

"Luci, please. Don't do this."

She grits her teeth, her face constricted with anger. "Try and stop me."

"You'll want to pull away," Dragon says.

"Then force me to stay there," she hisses. "Jaina, help me. When I put my hand down, make sure I keep it there until the crystal has risen."

"Are you sure about this?" I reluctantly move toward her.

"Yes!" Luci takes a deep quivering breath, closes her eyes, then places her hand on the machine. Her face is neutral at first until her eyes start to twitch behind her lids. She tries to pull away, but I keep her hand in place.

"Dragon, help me," I say.

"I can't, Jaina. Liam, you go instead." Dragon turns away, running his fingers through his hair.

Liam helps me hold her wrist tightly to the machine. "How much is enough?" he asks.

Luci breathes, "Until the crystal his risen."

Her voice is distant, yet pained. She tries to clench her hand into a fist, but Liam and I hold her tight. My hand brushes the machine, and a picture of blood shoots through my mind. I shake it off.

"No," she cries. "Stop! Let me go!"

"Is she talking to us?" I ask.

"No," Dragon says. "It's the visions."

"Help me!" Luci calls. "Please, I'll do anything!"

Her small frame is wracked with sobs, and she tries to lash out at us. Slowly, the crystal begins to rise. Liam and I let Luci go. She blinks and wipes her eyes. Only now does Dragon rush over to us.

"Liam, grab the crystal," I say.

He does and hands it to me. I carefully place it in my holster belt.

Dragon touches Luci's face and places another hand on her shoulder. "Are you all right?"

Tears stream down her face, and her body quivers. "How the *shaav* did you bear that?" Her voice shakes.

"I convinced myself it was fake. It's the only way." He wipes her tears away.

I swallow hard at his actions and remind myself that they're only friends. At least in his opinion.

"Hurry, we've got to find the checkpoint," Xana says.

A blue light flashes up ahead.

"There it is!" Dragon says.

We charge toward it, and though no one is chasing us this time, I want to get out of here. Dragon activates it, sending a signal. The helitransport appears. We climb out of the arena and into safety.

After a few hours in the hospital being examined by alien doctors, we finally can get moving.

The ship taking us to Neraka, the planet of the final Trial, is beautiful. It's smaller than the others, but it's a much higher class vessel. The inside is just as impressive.

"Children," Shirez says.

"He calls us children when he's annoyed," Dragon whispers.

"This flight will be longer than the last two, which is why I upgraded our transport. I suggest you all get something to eat and some sleep, because the final Trial may be short but it's ruthless," he says, then leaves.

"Why is he annoyed?" I ask Dragon.

Dragon shrugs. "Who knows. He lets his thoughts bother him more than he should."

"So that's where you learned it?"

He laughs. "I wouldn't be surprised."

The two of us sit and wait for the ship to break the gravitational pull of the world. My body senses the vibration as the atmosphere tries to keep us in. When it finally subsides, I stand up and head to the dining hall.

"Hey, Jaina," Liam calls from behind me.

I take out the crystal from my holster belt. "Hey do you think you could get to work on this?"

"Sure." Liam's eyes shift about like he wants to say something else. He grabs my elbow and pulls me toward him. "Sorry for what I said about Dragon, I just can't bear seeing you hurt."

"Liam, please. It's not going to matter."

"The more I think about it, the less I want to go the Crystal City," he mumbles.

"We aren't in the last Trial yet. Please be careful what you say."

"Yeah, okay. See you around, Jaina."

———

I'm alone sitting at small table, and can finally think. My mind goes blank. What am I supposed to think about? I can't possibly start thinking about the IA. I'm afraid what I might convince myself of.

Dragon strides into the room. He approaches the cafe counter, says something to the android, then returns with a hot bowl of shanar.

"Do you mind?" he asks.

I smile. "No, go ahead."

"How are you doing?"

"As good as everyone else I guess."

He raises an eyebrow. "If that's as good as everyone else, I don't think there's much hope for the next Trial. You look...conflicted. What's wrong?"

I hesitate. There's still so much I'm not clear on. I said I trust him, and I do. But he's got more to do with this than I know. Should I really tell him? "It's Azad," I finally admit. "And now Jeton, too. Was Jeton really the traitor?"

He looks at the ground then nods. "Yeah, he was. And what about Azad?"

"He asked me..." *This can't be the right thing, can it?* I force myself to continue. "He asked me if I was the Light."

Everything about him changes. His eyes become clouded, betraying no emotion. "He asked you...*what?*"

Does he not believe me? "I know it sounds crazy. I'm not even sure what–"

"What did he ask you?" Harshness colors his voice.

"He-he said I was the Light. The Dark will destroy me."

The blood drains from his face.

"What's wrong?"

"D-don't tell *anyone* what you told me. Not Shirez, not Kavi, not anyone. Please? Promise me that, okay?" he asks urgently, as he stands.

"Where are you going?"

"Nowhere. Just promise okay?"

"Fine, I swear I won't say a word, but what does this have to do with anything?"

"Nothing just–" He almost trips over a chair and stumbles out of the room.

Okay, that was strange.

A sweet breeze sweeps across the island. Darkness has surrounded the world. Not the icy, cold darkness you curl away from in the middle of the night. This is a soft darkness that's knowing and protective. In the sky, stars shine like tiny islands of hope throughout the universe, as if to remind those people left behind that the light will return.

Everything disappears. All but two figures in the distance, coming closer. At first, their presence is welcoming. But as time passes, all hopes and dreams fade. The darkness becomes cold and harsh, no longer soothing.

"Beware the Dark."

The words come as dark and frozen as the night.

The two figures approach, and an unnatural redness lights their faces with a sickening glow. As they grow nearer, I realize their eyes are glowing red. Red as the lava in Amarija. Red as blood.

"Betrayal!" they scream simultaneously.

The sound is horrid and inhuman, like the screeching of demons. They are the ghosts of the words, the shadows of the truth. The screams stab at me like knives trying to break my soul into shards of glass.

"Betrayal!"

"They say you're the Light."

"Beware the Dark, Jaina."

"I'm bearing it for you."

I hold my hands to my ears, trying to keep the sounds away, but they come through as strong and repulsive as a river of blood.

"You mean they never told you? What are they trying to do with you?"

"Ignore my warnings."

"Beware the Dark."

"He will betray you."

I sit up with sudden understanding. I *know* what they're talking about. Just as quickly, the moment fades. The sensation of knowing vanishes, and everything I was about to understand, everything I was about to figure out slips from my grasp.

An annoying beeping prevents me from continuing my thoughts. I get up and leave the dark room. Even in the halls, the beeping continues. A ship-wide alarm?

I find my way to the cockpit to see what all the fuss is about. Shirez is spitting out orders at the pilots. The ship takes an unexpected lurch to the right. My shoulder crashes into the wall as I struggle to hold onto something to keep me standing.

"What's going on?" I ask frantically.

Shirez shoots me a glare. "The natives don't recognize the Imperial Alliance as an authority."

"Why don't they recognize them—*us*?"

What just happened? Did I just call the Imperials *them*? Horror flows through me, and I can only hope Shirez didn't notice.

For a fraction of a second, Shirez looks surprised.

Shaav, you have to stop thinking such rebellious thoughts...

"These people are stubborn and powerful," he says. "They wish only to be left alone yet they are constantly creating trouble for the Imperials."

"So why doesn't the IA just crush them?"

"They can't be *crushed*, as you put it. Which is why the IA tries to—"

A bolt of plasma hits our transport, and once again we are jerked about as if someone wanted to shake us to death. By the stars, we're under *attack*? After another moment, the movement stops.

"Captain, contact the Nav'ae Kir," Shirez demands.

"Sir, can't we just talk to an official—"

"I said *contact the Nav'ae Kir*, Captain. I expect you to follow my orders."

"Who's the Nav'ae Kir?" I ask.

Shirez sighs, obviously annoyed by my ignorance. "He is the current leader of the planet. *Nav'ae Kir* is a title."

The pilot nods to Shirez. An image appears on a small holoprojector.

"Nav'ae Kir Kejam, may I ask why you're attacking us?" Shirez barks. His hand is clamped around the back of the pilot's seat in irritation.

"Identify yourself," the Nav'ae Kir returns flatly. From the projection, the Nav'ae Kir looks sort of like a robot. He's armored from head to toe, and a helmet covers his face.

"Prince Shirez Melohem from Sector 14036 of the Imperial Alliance. We have no intention to harm you or your people."

"What other intentions does your Emperor have?" the Nav'ae Kir asks.

"We have come with the Imperials for the Trials–"

"The IA is made of unworthy scum. The only reason we are dealing with your kind is for the handsome reward. If you are who you say you are, Shirez Melohem of Sector 14036, what are the access codes?"

I cannot tell if the person–or creature–behind the mask is a man or woman.

Shirez rolls his eyes. "One-one-eight-zero-seven-four."

The Nav'ae Kir shows the slightest bit of annoyance, but its voice remains neutral. "You may proceed."

The fighters swarming the transport stop firing and become more of a guarding squad than anything else.

Looking down at the Earth-sized planet, I realize how bare the place looks. There are entire plateaus the size of continents. They rise above deep valleys that are thousands of miles across. These 'continents' have green, purple, and blue areas, where I guess they grow their food and get their water. The inner parts of the 'continents' shine like tiny stars. It's clear the majority of civilization lives there. I wonder if we will be competing in the farm-land-like area, or if it will be in the barren areas shaded with a few specs of green here and there.

"Why would the IA choose this place?" I ask.

Shirez shakes his head. "You'll find out soon enough."

Upon landing, the Nav'ae Kir greets us. I still haven't figured out if it's a male or female yet. Its voice is so mechanical I'm finding it hard to believe it's even alive. So I just assume it's a man.

The Nav'ae Kir approaches us and stops in front of Shirez. His armor is black and shiny. His helmet covers his face and has a large frill on top, leaving only a dark slit across the mask to see out of. He isn't protected by any guards. I wonder if he's just stupid or he's actually good enough to fight off whatever danger he could face out here. Something tells me it's the latter.

"We do not greet your coming with joy," the Nav'ae Kir says. His voice is deep, and husky. "In fact, I greet you only with disgust. You have been promised food and shelter on my world, and I shall give that to you with great reluctance."

Shirez clenches his jaw but bows politely. "Thank you, your highness."

"Do not call me that which you call your Emperor," he hisses. "I want nothing to do with him. You shall call me as I am. Just another being in the galaxy."

"Of all the places in the galaxy, the Imperials chose here," I mutter.

Dragon looks at me, impartial to my words.

I whisper, "I've never seen anyone treat an Imperial with such little respect."

"Trust me, I've seen worse," he replies.

We're brought to our hotel room. After about five minutes, a knock comes at the door. A partially armored man stands before me. He doesn't say anything, but hands me a small scroll and seems to glare at me as he steps away and leaves.

"Who was that?" Liam asks.

I shrug and hold up the scroll. "I don't know, but he gave me this."

Xana furrows her brow. "What is it?"

I open it. "*Congratulations for making it to the final Galactic Trial.*"

"Is this supposed to be a souvenir?" Luci asks.

"For those who lose the Trials, this will be their only remembrance of the 'glory' days," Liam replies. "By the way, I cracked the code on the flight."

"Let's hope this one is more helpful," Xana mumbles.

"Okay, here we go." Liam takes out the crystal and opens it.

> "Take a left then take a right,
> One hundred meters through the night.
> Into the depths of your soul,
> Your destiny lies upon the Scroll.

> To all that are good, you are the defender,
> Yet the win requires ultimate surrender.
> The freedom of life will not always be,
> The prison of death is bound to eternity."

"We've got to take it in pieces, as we usually do," I say. "'Take a left, then take a right, one hundred meters through the night.' Do you think those are actual directions?"

"I'm not sure," Dragon replies.

"Does that refer to the scroll we just got?" Liam asks. "The one saying '*Congratulations for getting this far but if you die no one's going to miss you.*' That one?"

Seth slaps him on the shoulder. "Very funny, Liam."

"Ow, dude, that kind of hurt," Liam grumbles.

I look at Dragon with a sense of remembrance. "Dragon, the Scroll. From Virana!"

His face lights up. "Yes, the one our Masters had us memorize!"

Liam rubs his eyes. "Okay, you completely lost me."

"There was a set of directions that lays out the entire Island of Virana," Dragon says. "There's a single section of it written in poetic form. It's called, The Scroll."

"Okay, good, so how does it go?" Luci asks.

I look at Dragon. "I have no idea. I forget."

He smiles. "I think it was something like this:

"One hundred steps left,
Fifty more to the right,
See the moon in the darkness,
And a cave in its light."

"I kind of forget the second part," Dragon adds.

His words jog my memory, and suddenly I remember.

"Follow it forward,
Walk five meters west,
Only one of these paths,
Will bring an end to your quest."

Dragon nods, a wide grin on his face. "Nice one, Jaina."

I timidly meet his gaze. "Thanks."

"That makes it easy!" Seth shouts triumphantly.

"Are you sure? How could anyone *else* know the Scroll from Virana?" Xana asks.

Avan shakes his head and takes a seat on the couch in front of the giant window. "Maybe they don't."

"How could any other team win?" Liam asks.

"I'm not sure," I ponder. "But it's worth a shot, don't you think? I mean, the other scroll is worthless! Both poems start similarly. Who cares if we're the only ones who know the Scroll? That means we're at a *huge* advantage."

"Okay, so we're going to assume the Scroll is the one from Virana?" Kavi asks.

"Why not?"

"Good. We've got that figured out then," Luci says. "What about the last part? 'To all that are good, you are the defender, Yet the win requires ultimate surrender.'"

Dragon swallows hard, catching my gaze for a fraction of a second then focuses on the ground. "It doesn't sound good."

The faces of my teammates are grim, and I wish Luci hadn't brought it up.

Seth clears his throat and looks Dragon in the eye. "What are you thinking?"

Dragon glances at him then clenches his teeth and shakes his head. He takes a deep, unsteady breath, then says, "I don't know."

"They wouldn't ask us to..." Kavi stops herself. "Would they?"

"They could," Seth breathes. "It's been done before."

"Stop it," I retort. "It's not going to come to that. Now come on, it's time for bed. We'll need all the rest we can get tomorrow."

They disperse into their rooms, turning out their lights and closing the doors behind them. Only Dragon remains, staring forward out the window at the city, glowing against the night sky.

"You coming?" I breathe.

He looks at me like he's not sure why I'm still here. "Yeah. I'm just..." He gazes back out the window, then stands up and moves toward his room. "You're right. Let's get some sleep. Goodnight, Jaina."

He turns off the light and closes the door behind him, leaving me alone in darkness.

chapter

TWENTY-TWO

We're on the drop ship.

My body trembles. Agitation courses through my blood and rises into my throat. I'm nervous. So, so nervous. If we win, our lives will mean so much more to the IA. If we lose, we're nothing. Sent into a Reconstruction Camp as slaves to the IA. I strap on my armor.

With one easy jump, I'm in the arena with the rest of my team. The transport flies away. The final Trial has begun.

We press forward.

Half-a-meter deep water covers the ground and soaks my boots and pants. The trees are tall with thin, white trunks, yet their branches are spread out and sturdy. They have long, spindly roots, reminiscent of hands with too many fingers. A dark shadow is cast across the planet, and the sun doesn't really shine. The sky is grey and purple. A storm is coming.

Kavi taps Dragon on the shoulder. "Hey, shouldn't we have started following the directions the moment we got into the arena?"

"It would be too easy that way." His voice is soft, like he expects something to jump out at us any moment. "There's got to be someplace where the Scroll obviously starts."

"What if it's *not* obvious?" Liam asks, stepping beside me.

"Either way we'll have an advantage over the other teams," I reply. "We know the Scroll and they don't."

"Isn't that a little arrogant to say?" Xana says.

I lower my eyes in embarrassment. "I guess you're right, but it's probably true. Who else would know what the Scroll is?"

"A select few, Jaina," Dragon murmurs. "Even though it's for Virana, it's a famous poem."

"I don't understand how a poem like that got famous," Seth interjects. "*I* could have written it."

Kavi sneers. "I doubt that."

The only sound is the shushing of the trees and the quiet splashes of our footsteps. My feet are soggy, but at least the water is lukewarm.

"I can't decide if this place is a swamp or a jungle," Dragon remarks.

Avan snorts. "I'd call it a wasteland."

It's the first time our team has traveled together. Dragon and I are kind of in the lead, but we're not ahead of everyone.

"I really don't like this place," Luci breathes. "It gives me chills."

I shake my head. "As long as there're no man-eating plants, I think I'm okay."

"If you get over the fact that death could be looming around every corner, it's actually pretty cool," Liam says.

"Yeah, until you're the one getting eaten." Dragon laughs. "But, if we survive, this is a great place to brag about."

Liam rolls his eyes. "Just watch, there'll be something *way* worse than those plants. Each Trial is worse than the last, so it's only natural for this to be the awful one."

"I love your optimism," I grumble.

He only laughs, and we continue walking.

Thunder rolls in the distance. The clouds are still far off, but the storm is rapidly approaching. A light rain begins to fall, trickling down tree trunks and making tiny ripples in the water. The scenery isn't much different in any direction. The only way to tell time is through the soreness of my feet which have grown numb over the last few kilometers.

"Should we find some place to stop?" Avan asks.

"That might be a good idea," Xana says. "I know it's been dreary all day long, but I think it's getting darker."

"There's a ton of caves around here," I suggest.

"Which is why I don't think it's a good idea to sleep in one," Dragon returns. "There are too many to choose from. And fifteen teams are competing in this Trial. Who knows who or what we'll run into."

Liam crosses his arms. "Are you saying we try to sleep on the land? Because if we tried that, we'd drown."

The sky steadily grows darker. The days don't last long here.

Dragon turns to Liam, his eyes narrowed in irritation. "No, Liam, I'm suggesting we find higher ground and sleep *there*."

"Where are we going to find high ground?" I ask.

Dragon shoots me a glare. "I'm getting to that. We'll have to look for it."

"Yeah, that's what I thought," Liam mutters.

Dragon turns to him, his left hand clenched at his side while his right rests conspicuously on the hilt of his scimitar. "Are you messing with me?"

Liam steps forward. "Are you messing with *me*?"

Dragon runs his fingers through his hair. "I'm sick of putting up with you. Now shut the hell up and I'll restrain myself."

"What?" Liam snaps. "You gonna kill me?"

"Liam," Luci cuts in. "Please, just stop."

"I've done worse," Dragon replies darkly.

"Oooh," Liam taunts. "I'm *real* scared now."

Dragon's face contorts with anger, his jaw tightens with disgust and his body tenses preparing to fight. He takes a threatening step forward, but I step in front of him.

"Dragon, please," I whisper. "Don't. That's just what he wants."

"What the *shaav*!" Liam cries as Luci grabs hold of his arm and prevents him from coming closer.

I put my hand on Dragon's shoulder. "Take it easy."

"Hey, guys, what's that?" Xana cries suddenly.

I follow her gaze and blink twice to make sure I'm not seeing things.

In one of the tall, rubbery trees, a mess of purple and green leaves hang around the top of the trunk. The longer I look at it, the more of it I see. It's large. Big enough for a few people to fit in. *There's an idea.* "Well, it's not high ground, but I think it could work," I say.

Dragon turns and hits Liam's chest with the back of his hand. "See that?"

Liam grits his teeth. "Don't rub it in."

We make our way toward the tree, then climb to the mess of branches near the canopy. When we reach the top, Xana, who's the smallest and lightest of us, tests the flooring. She doesn't fall through when she steps down on the material, so she jumps a few times. Nothing happens, so the rest of us follow behind her.

It turns out that our nearly perfect resting place is a nest. Whatever kind of bird builds a nest this big is either extremely large, or has some serious spatial issues.

Soft golden leaves make the bottom of the nest much more comfortable than the dirt on a cave floor.

"Well," Liam says. "Now that we've all gotten to the top of this tree, only to discover it belongs to a giant bird, what are our options?"

Dragon hesitates. "It's fairly shielded from wind and rain. It's big enough for all of us if we're willing to squeeze in. The only downside is it could belong to a predator that might return. What do you guys think?"

Xana yawns. "I think we should stay here. We've been walking for six hours already."

I nod. "I agree. It looks abandoned, anyway."

"What if it's not?" Seth asks. "I mean, I'm all for staying, but what if it's not abandoned? It could come back and eat us."

"But I'm exhausted," Xana says. "I want to stay here."

Avan takes a seat in the soft bed of leaves. "Yeah, who knows how long it'll take to find another place to stay?"

"Whatever comes our way, we can fight it off," Xana adds.

Dragon shrugs. "Looks like we're staying."

"Not everyone voted," Liam interjects.

"Five people voted in favor of staying."

"Don't Kavi, Luci and I count?" Liam asks.

Dragon raises an eyebrow. "You *do* know how voting works, don't you?"

Kavi shoots Dragon a reassuring nod. "It's okay, Dragon. I'm with you."

"Me too," Luci says.

Dragon turns to Liam. "Make that seven."

Liam rolls his eyes. "Fine, whatever. Let's stay here and get eaten before morning."

Dragon looks at me, his jaw clenched in resentment as Liam shuffles away to the other side of the nest in defeat. "*Shaav*, I hate him."

"I can tell." I smile, but can't help feeling sorry for both of them.

"Why is he like that all of a sudden? He seemed all right before, but he keeps getting worse."

I cross my arms. "I don't know, but you're fighting back more than usual, too."

"Sorry," he breathes. "I couldn't stand him any longer."

"Should we go to sleep now?" I ask. "It's getting really dark."

Dragon sighs. "Yeah, we probably should."

"I can guard first if you want."

"Okay, I'll go after you." He doesn't look away from me, and I gaze back. I feel Kavi giving me that curious stare out of the corner of my eye, but I ignore her.

"Guys?" Kavi finally says. We look at her, but she only giggles.

"You should go lie down," I tell Dragon. "I'll wake you up in an hour."

―――――――

The trees rustle below us and I open my eyes. Despite being fast asleep, I'd been waiting, listening for that specific sound I hoped wouldn't come.

After guarding the nest for an hour, I woke Dragon. Everything seemed fine.

My teammates lie around me, all of them sleeping. No one's on guard. Why isn't anyone awake?

Voices pierce my mind, and I peer out of the nest and down at the ground. A girl with pale skin and deep, sunset-red hair stands next to a boy with deeply tanned skin. His black hair is closely cropped, and looks out of place next to her long, wispy locks falling gently down her back.

She holds a sword in both hands, and the boy carries a pistol, ready for anything that might come their way.

"This is pointless," she complains. "I don't trust him."

"He's our leader, Mariia," he replies. "He knows what he's doing."

"How the *shaav* does he expect us to find them? We should be looking for the crystal, not another team."

"They're the only ones who know how to get there, okay? They're our biggest threat."

"And why would you think that, Marco?"

"I don't know, but all we have is his knowledge, and he seems to know a lot," he replies. "I trust him, and so should you."

She shakes her head. "All right, fine, I will. I just–" She freezes and raises her sword. "Did you hear that?"

"Come on, let's get out of here," Marco says quietly. The two take off into the forest.

The trees rustle to my left. A large animal stirs in the branches of a tree near us.

Frozen with fear, I hold back the sudden sense of panic gnawing at me. *Don't panic, Jaina. It will be okay.* I fall back under cover of the nest and shake Liam, who is now awkwardly pressed to me.

"Wake up," I whisper to him, pushing him away.

"What is it?" he replies sleepily.

I press my finger to my lips. "There's something over there."

His muscles tense and he looks over the rim of the nest. "Where is it?"

I point. "Right there."

The moment his eyes lock onto it, he lowers himself back below the nest. "*Shaav*, what is that thing?"

"I have no idea. It looks like some sort of bird."

"It's too big to be a–" He glances down at the nest then back to me. "It's got gold feathers."

I look back at the bird then back at him, wondering what that has to do with anything. "What?"

"The soft gold leaves that make up half of this nest." He pulls one out from under him. "It's not a leaf. It's a feather."

Oh no. "We're in its nest. Hurry, wake everyone else up. We need to be ready to defend ourselves."

Liam nods and follows my orders, waking a few teammates up.

I glance out of the nest, searching for the bird. "L-Liam? It's gone."

All is silent. Thunder booms in the distance, echoing across the sky like the explosion of a cannon. A cold breath of wind surges down my back. I turn around and look up. The enormous bird is perched above us. It stares down at me as if I was a worm, writhing and ready to be devoured.

A bullet splits the air and skims the bird's chest. It screeches and its sharp beak stabs at me in the darkness. I reach for my scimitar but it snaps its beak at my holster belt so I jerk my hand away.

"Help!" I call.

The bird faces Dragon and opens its sharp, sword-like beak. A stream of fire shoots from its mouth. He ducks just in time and falls to the bottom of the nest.

Its eyes scan the nest. The moment it sees me, it jumps down and digs its talons into my shoulders.

Its golden claws pierce my skin. I cry out as blood oozes from the wound. In a single leap, it jumps out of the nest, pulling me with it.

I scream as the bird and I plummet to the watery ground. It barely softens its landing, letting me hit the water hard. I can't breathe, and my vision clouds. The pain grows in my shoulders, as the bird tightens its grip.

The image of the gold and red fire bird ripples above me. The fire bird is drowning me. I want to cry out in anger and call for help. With a final reserve of strength I thrash about, hoping to make it slip and let go...anything. Seeing my gauntlet strapped tightly to my arm, I raise my wrist. With the single press of a button, a ball of fire explodes from my wrist and hits the bird squarely in the stomach. It backs away with a roar and releases me.

I pull myself above the water and retrieve my scimitar. The fire bird lunges toward me, and with all my strength, I bring my sword across its neck. Its head frees itself from its body and splashes into the nearby water. Its body stiffens and collapses into the morass.

"Jaina, are you okay?" Kavi calls from the nest.

"Mostly," I pant.

"We'll be down in a minute. It's almost morning anyway," Seth says.

"I'll be right here." I stumble forward and fall to my knees in front of a tree. I rest my palm on the trunk, unable to stand on my own. Fatigue courses its way through me, turning my body cold.

Despite the darkness of the sky, the sun is rising behind the clouds.

I'm soaking wet with blood, sweat, and water. I'm cold, too.

"Dragon, what was it?" I ask as he approaches me from the tree.

Avan replies instead. "It was a fire bird. A phoenix."

I look at Dragon, and he stares back at me as if he'd been stunned. "What's wrong?" I ask.

He snaps out of his daze. "Nothing. That was... impressive."

Not entirely sure how to handle the compliment, I reply, "Oh...thanks."

All of a sudden, he becomes distant. He doesn't say much else, except for orders. Maybe he got bad sleep last night. I hope that's all it is.

Luci gives me some medicine and takes a look at my punctured shoulders. "I should wrap them up."

I'm dizzy and weak, but I think it's from the sudden loss of adrenaline rushing through me. "I'll be okay. Won't a bandaged shoulder make it harder to fight?"

"No, Jaina. Let me take care of you," she insists. She works fast and skillfully wraps my arms so I can still move freely.

We wander through the arena, hoping to chance upon some sign that the crystal is near. We come out of the dense forest onto a higher rise of ground, where the ever present water has drained away. We're in a valley. Plateaus surround us, rising high into the clouds. The land between them is barren, and devoid of plant-life, consisting of only gravel and black sand.

Caves line the base of the cliffs in an eerily symmetric fashion. A claustrophobic sensation wraps itself around me, and I can't help feeling a bit trapped.

From around a rocky formation at the base of the plateau, two teams emerge, closing in on each other. They're oblivious to our presence as they begin to fight.

"*Na'lav,*" I breathe. "This isn't good."

"Okay, so what's the plan?" Luci asks.

Dragon looks at her, then to me. "I'm not really sure. Jaina, have any ideas?"

The only noise is that of the battle raging a few meters away.

"I say we just do it," Avan says suddenly. "We've got to get past them. We're strong enough. We don't have to fight unless we're attacked. My hope is they'll be too busy fighting amongst themselves to notice us."

I glance at Dragon, but it's clear he's waiting for me to make the decision. "All right," I say. "Let's do it."

Dragon smiles. "This might work. Just be ready for an attack. We'll still try to go as quietly as we can. Jaina and I will scout ahead. We'll move along the perimeter. Make no move to follow us until we order you to."

"Good luck," Avan wishes.

We dash behind a large boulder on the other side of the battlefield. My body feels warm with the sudden rush of adrenaline.

I motion for Kavi and Seth to join us, and they, too, arrive unharmed. Once they are situated, I scan the nearby landscape for the next place to take cover.

"How about there?" Dragon points to a stash of large boulders.

"Aren't they a little far away?" I ask.

"It's the closest thing we've got," he says.

We sprint to our chosen cover. I think we've made it without being noticed when I hear footsteps. I look up and see someone from another team scrambling up the large pile of rocks above us, either trying to run away or catch his breath.

"What do we do?" I mouth to Dragon.

He only looks back at me, a determined, fiery look in his eyes.

The boy lands on the ground, his back to us. Dragon and I activate our scimitars, and the boy jumps around, to face us.

"*Zehma!*" he shouts in his language. His green skin turns a shade lighter than it should, making him look sickly even for his species.

Two more of the pale green Lirens approach us and pull out their swords.

"You bring any more of your kind with you?" The second Liren asks in a heavy accent.

We don't reply.

The Lirens come at us, their swords arcing and diving fast and furiously. I block their attacks. They aren't as hard to fend off as Azad was, but their advanced styles of fighting are unsettling.

The Lirens try to strike us down and force us into the open. *Na'lav.* The rest of their team is going to find us.

Dragon slices a girl across an unarmored section of her belly. She stumbles back, clutching her wound to keep her organs from spilling onto the ground in an unpleasant mess. He drives his scimitar into her chest, then kicks her away as if she was merely an obstruction in his path.

The Liren in front of me lunges forward, aiming for my stomach. I jump out of reach and slash him across the face. The tip of my scimitar meets his left eye, leaving a sickening gash in the soft tissue. I force myself to look away before I vomit.

I search for Kavi and Seth. They remain where they were, like they're not entirely sure what to do. I signal for them to keep moving. Dragon and I can't hold everyone up. We're putting their lives at risk.

We can't hold them off much longer, but we have no choice.

A small human girl arcs her sword at me. It looks much too large for her to be able to lift it on her own. I duck as it sweeps near my head, then raise my scimitar and hit her with a powerful slash. Her sword drops to the ground along with her dismembered hand. She screams and backs away, staring at the bloody stump where her hand should be.

A silvery point bursts out of her belly, dripping with blood. She drops to the ground as a Liren pulls his blade free from her back.

"Come on!" Kavi's voice is closer than it should be.

I whip around and find her about a meter behind me, fighting another Liren.

"Kavi, what are you doing? I ordered you to continue!"

"You think I'm going to let you two die?" she cries.

I take on a new opponent and match him blow for blow. I can't quite tell his age since he's not human, but I guess he'd be around fifteen. His eyes shift around nervously. Although his fighting skills are good, they don't come close to matching mine. I could easily kill him if I had to. Instead, I spin around and hit him hard in the head with the hilt of my scimitar. He falls to the ground, unconscious.

I don't want to kill *any* of these people. After scanning the battlefield for a higher perspective, I scramble up a rock wall to the top of a small ledge in the cliff side. I take cover behind a pile of fair-sized rocks and activate my gauntlet. Pressing a few buttons, I turn on a targeting system and set my weapon to stun.

"This better work," I mutter to myself.

I aim for one of the Lirens. I flip my wrist, and a bolt of electricity springs from my gauntlet. She drops to the ground like a stone. Thank the Emperor that went as planned. I search for Dragon. The boy across from him fights furiously. I don't hesitate. I fire before Dragon has the chance to strike him down. The next moment, the boy is sprawled upon the ground.

Dragon looks around, confused, until his eyes rest on me. I smile and he nods. I hardly notice the trembling of my hand as I take down a few more targets. I prepare to flip my wrist and fire. Before I have the chance, my target's opponent swings her blade around, slicing a severe gash across his belly then lodges it into his chest.

I look away. *Stay calm, Jaina. Breathe.*

Dragon lowers his scimitar. He says something to the last of the Lirens, and they quickly scurry off. I stay where I am, feeling like I actually did some good by saving people.

I hurry back to our team. "We should get moving before they wake up."

Liam nods at me, suggesting a bow. "I'm impressed, Jaina. You took out both teams and left us the victory. Nice."

"Does anyone else have the feeling that we're being followed?" Luci asks.

"That's your imagination," Liam mutters.

"Why is someone always following us?" Avan protests.

"Yeah, why can't *we* follow someone for a change?" Liam asks.

Seth scoffs. "Because we're not stupid."

Dragon turns to Liam. "Have you noticed what we've done to our enemies every time we've been followed?"

"Why do you think we're being followed, Luci?" I ask.

She shakes her head, as if pleading me to understand and looks at Dragon. "Trust me," she begs. "You know I'm right."

"Why do I get the feeling that you and Luci talk in code?" Liam asks.

"Calm down, Liam," Luci orders.

One of the stunned Lirens near Avan moans.

Avan scoots closer to Kavi and shudders. "We should get out of here."

"Come on, let's go," I say.

The Trials are nothing like what I thought they'd be. Killing someone should be a form of overcoming weakness, yet I've gone out of my way to save people. It seems all wrong but completely right.

The sky is dark, but it's the soothing darkness I welcome into my heart. After mindlessly wandering around for most of the day, we finally stumble upon a cave on higher ground. It's fairly hidden and definitely better than a phoenix nest.

My team rests around the campfire. I'm not really listening to them, but I enjoy hearing their voices. I realize I'm smiling as I stare into the dancing flames. I look up and see Dragon gazing at me. The moment our eyes meet, he glances away.

He will betray you.

My smile fades and the warm fire suddenly becomes too hot, too much like the lava. I stand up, wander outside the cave and take a seat on a large rock. Gravel crunches and buckles under my feet. Not wanting to think, I kick some of the stones into the water. Trees grow out of the water, and small fish swim around the roots. The moss on the ground glows a soft blue and green and lights up the water.

"Mind if I join you?"

"Be my guest, Dragon," I say, staring over the nighttime landscape. Stars dot the sky like a million eyes, watching and waiting to see what I do next.

He sits next to me in the darkness, and his arm is pressed against mine.

"What do you think?" he asks.

I continue gazing at the sky. "About what?"

"The Trials are almost over. If we lose, we'll all be separated. And if we win, we'll be separated anyway," he says. "Has it been worthwhile?"

I smile sadly. "It's changed me. For better or worse, I don't know, but I'd never give back a minute of this."

He continues to speak softly, and it's hard not to get lost in his eyes. They're too distracting. "Anyway, what would *you* like to talk about?" he asks finally.

I wish I could tell him how I feel...Maybe I'm a little more rebellious because of him, but I'm not stupid. Even if the Imperials aren't supervising us here, what good would it do to tell him?

"Can we go over the crystal hint and the Scroll? As long as we're together, I won't need to memorize it, but..." I let the silence finish my sentence.

"No, of course. Never know what could happen in the next few minutes here. Might as well be prepared. The Scroll goes like this," he says.

"One hundred steps left,
Fifty more to the right,
See the moon in the darkness,
And a cave in its light."

"Got it?" He asks.

I nod.

"Can you repeat the whole thing?"

"I can try." I remember all the rhymes, but I have to rephrase myself a few times before I get the entire thing right. "How's that?"

"Better than I could do. I didn't memorize it until I was ten, and it seriously took me an entire day of repeating it over and over." He laughs.

"Did Shirez make you memorize it?" I ask.

"No, I actually memorized it because I thought it was pretty." He laughs again. Even in the darkness, I can tell he's blushing. "Please don't tell anyone I said that."

"It's cute." I can't help smiling. "But I won't say a word. My lips are sealed."

"Thanks."

He glances at my lips, then back into my eyes. My stomach shifts in place, and I try to keep my breath steady. He moves closer ever so slightly and gently touches my hair. His fingers trail down my cheek. I take his hand in mine. His face is only a breath away. If only he knew how much I want him.

He presses closer. My eyes start to close, and his nose brushes mine. My hands touch his chest as his unsteady breath falls gently over my lips.

"Dragon." My voice stops him from coming closer. I try to pull myself out of my daze. *Shaav, Jaina, you ruined it.* I instantly regret my decision and want to tell him I didn't mean it.

He hardly pulls back, but it's clear I've prevented any chance of getting a kiss. I realize my hand is still on his chest, and I wish I could keep it there, but I jerk it back, seeing how wrong it is.

"What's wrong? Are you all right?" he asks, surprised.

"Yeah, I'm-I'm sorry. I'm," I pause and look at him. "I'm fine."

No, Dragon, I'm not fine. I just destroyed the moment. I find myself cursing in my head and wanting to kick something. I always have to ruin it. I wonder if he was actually going to kiss me.

"Sorry," he says, focusing on the ground, his arm still around my shoulders. "That was wrong."

So he *was* going to kiss me?

"Dragon, can I ask you something?" I ask as a distraction.

"Yeah, go ahead."

"When you came back and we were in language class together, did you recognize me?"

He raises an eyebrow and smiles. "You looked a lot different after ten years but something about you never changed. I guess that's what told me it was you. What did you think when you first saw me?"

I want to laugh and hide in embarrassment at the same time. "I wasn't sure who you were. I thought you were..." I hesitate, trying to find the word for it. "I thought you were cute, but you frustrated me."

"How did I frustrate you?"

"I don't know...I couldn't figure out who you were or how I knew you. I was so used to being at the top of the class and when you came along you took that away."

He smiles but says nothing.

"Hey, at least I told you the truth!" I roll my eyes.

"I know." He smiles slyly. "Were you jealous?"

"You're a born fighter. You're a better leader than I could ever hope to be. So I'll readily admit I'm jealous. I'm still jealous. But in a good way."

"It's good to be jealous sometimes. Especially if you're used to being at the top."

I look up at the stars and the single moon, so similar to the one orbiting Earth. Everything appears to be at peace. And at the heart of everything with Dragon, I feel at peace, too. I glance at him a few times, trying hard not to stare, but can't help myself. I let my eyes trace the line of his strong jaw, then rise to his kissable lips. What would it feel like to kiss him?

I'm crazy. I'm in love with him, and maybe a little obsessed. I've got every reason to be. Who has the right to tell me I can't love him?

The rest of the IA does. Love can only end with tragedy in my situation.

I look down at the glowing moss in the water. Dragon and I won't work. I've always known that. I'll either die in this Trial, lose this Trial and be sent to a Recon Camp, or make it to the Crystal City where the IA will choose a perfect genetic match for me. What are the chances they'll choose Dragon over everyone else?

I can't lose him. Not now, not ever. I can't go through that again. At least if I die, I won't have to live without him.

"What are you thinking about?" he asks suddenly.

"Nothing."

He looks at me curiously. "We should get some sleep. I've got mixed feelings about tomorrow."

He slinks back toward the hideout as I stare up at the starry night sky. So peaceful. If only it could last.

chapter

TWENTY-THREE

Clashing swords. Echoed screams. Distant rolling thunder like the laughter of giants. As I come to the surface from the ocean of sleep, the sounds I thought were part of distant dreams do not cease, but grow louder. I pull myself out of the darkness with a forceful jerk and sit up.

I crawl over to Kavi. "Kavi. Kavi, you have to wake up."

She opens her eyes with a jolt. "What's wrong?"

"We have to get out before the other teams get here."

"What are you talking about?" she asks.

"Wake the rest of the team." I dump the ashes from our dead fire into the water around our island and run back into the cave to see everyone awake.

I'm about to speak, but Dragon interrupts me. "No need to explain, Jaina. Let's just get out of here."

We run to the west, away from the battle.

"Do you think we can outrun them?" I ask.

"We'll outrun them all right," Dragon replies. "They're too busy fighting each other."

As I run, water splashes up my legs and soaks me. I keep my eyes on the ground to prevent myself from tripping over a tree root. A sound makes me look up, yet even before my eyes process the image, I know who it is. My blood hardens to ice, and my heart screams for me to run.

"So we meet again," Azad says darkly. His eyes are only on me, staring deep into my soul.

My heart stops dead at the sound of his voice.

His lips break into a grin, yet his eyes only glare. "Surprised?"

"Why are you here, Azad?" Dragon snarls, retrieving his scimitar.

I'm too afraid to move. Seven others stand around Azad.

"The IA thought I was worthy of a second try. They reassigned me as team leader for this team," Azad says. "And I *will* have revenge."

"Let it go, Azad," Dragon shouts. "It's pointless."

Azad clenches his fist, crushing the air in front of him as if pretending it were Dragon's skull. "Of course you say that! You think you've won! I'm about to prove you wrong!"

"I can't let you do that."

"You'll die trying."

Dragon charges at Azad in a focused fury.

Breaking out of my shock, I activate my scimitar. A girl pulls out her sword. Her hair is redder than blood. She's the girl I saw yesterday morning. Mariia.

She makes a forceful move to impale me, but I spin to the right and avoid her blow.

"You think I'd be that easy?" I jeer.

She scowls. "You don't put up much of a fight."

I swing at her throat. She ducks, but my blade catches her forehead. Mariia growls with rage and wipes the blood from her eyes.

I glance at Dragon, hoping he doesn't need backup.

A sudden pain shoots down my leg. Mariia's sword slashes furiously at me. The tip of her blade is tinged with my blood. A slow stream trickles from a gash on my hip.

With renewed strength, I lunge forward and high kick her chin. She hits the ground and doesn't move.

Marco, the other boy I saw yesterday, slashes Xana across the face. She backs away and brings her hand to her cheek. He punches her to the ground, knocking her out. He grabs her arm.

I don't have time to watch what happens next because another girl springs at me so fast I barely block her blows. Sweat streams down my back, my fatigued muscles protest every movement. I move forward, gaining ground, then retreat.

She brings her sword near me, and I prepare to block. Suddenly, she changes the path of her blade. As it should slide gracefully over my stomach, a hand closes around the back of my shirt and spins me around. My back is pressed up against someone, and I'm held there, unable to move. An electrified dagger rests only centimeters from my throat. Though I'm not facing him, I know its Azad. He holds me tightly to him. His other hand grips a gun aimed squarely at Dragon.

The battle has stopped.

Stopped dead.

Dragon lowers his scimitar.

"Looks like I win," Azad hisses from behind me.

The icy fingers of fear play at the back of my neck.

Dragon raises his hands in defeat. "You got your victory. Now release her."

"You think it's that easy? After what you did?" Azad snaps. His breath trickles down my back and causes every hair on my body to stand on end. "I think I'll enjoy this victory as long as I can."

Azad's teammates grab Dragon by the arms as he lunges forward toward us. They easily hold him back.

"She's important to you, isn't she? It wasn't so long ago our situation was reversed," Azad taunts. "If you make any move to attack us, Altair, I'll kill her."

Dragon's expression changes from one of fury to severe pain. Like a caged animal, he tries to shake Azad's teammates away, but they hold him tight. How I want to struggle and pull away, but I'm afraid he'll shoot Dragon.

"Back away," Azad purrs softly.

"Let her go."

"I said back away!"

"You don't have to do this! Azad, please..." Dragon breathes.

"I will do anything it takes to claim my revenge." He sneers. "And until you've felt the same agonizing pain I did, do *not* ask me to forgive you."

My body is soaked with water. My hands are cold, but my wounded hip is on fire. I can't move.

Out of the corner of my eye, two of Azad's team-mates drag an unconscious Xana through the water and into their ranks. By the stars, he's got two of us.

The thought suddenly strikes me. Is Dragon going to *leave* us? Allow Azad to take us? Azad's teammates force Dragon to step back.

"If you try to follow us," he continues, "I'll hurt her. If you make any offensive move toward us, I will cause her so much pain. I'll make her scream so loud you'll hear it from the other side of the arena. Do I make myself clear?"

"Azad, please. Don't do this," Dragon begs.

"I'll do whatever the *shaav* I want!" Azad shouts, and each word hits me like a knife, twisting in my heart.

The rest of my team backs up behind Dragon as Azad's squad drives them from their ranks. Dragon glances at Xana's limp form in Marco's arms. My eyes meet Dragon's. I want to scream. I want to pull away from Azad, but I'm powerless. Dragon looks at me long-ingly but is forced back another step.

"Jaina," he whispers. "Jaina, I'm sorry."

"Now go, get out of here," Azad says, putting his gun back in his belt. With his second hand free he twists his fingers around my arm. I take a deep breath, holding back the nausea taking over me.

Dragon glares back at Azad as if his only goal in life is to slit his throat. The rest of my team looks at me, hor-rified. Are they going to leave me and Xana with Azad?

"Don't hurt her," Dragon pleads, his voice cracking with helplessness. "Azad, please."

"You'll regret what you've done," Azad replies. "Go."

Dragon, don't leave me.

By the stars, Dragon, don't leave me with him.

Sheer terror rises in me as my team backs down. Before I know it, they're out of sight. All of my hope drops like a stone in the ocean.

Then I hear his voice.

I'll always be there for you.

I know he'll come for me.

———

My cheek rests against the cold, rocky floor of a cave. My hands are bound behind my back, and I'm unable to breathe through my mouth because something is stuffed inside it. I try to scream, but gag instead. I try to wiggle free, but it's no use. My ankles are bound, too. Even if I can't escape, I'll fight with every ounce of strength I have.

A small girl leans against the rocky wall a few meters in front of me. Her blond hair is matted with dirt and pieces of wood, like she'd been dragged through some bushes. She groggily turns her head my way. Xana.

I roll myself over and sit up, pressing myself against the stone wall.

Xana's hands and feet are bound like mine, and a gag rests in her mouth.

I try to tell her we should attempt an escape, but all I end up saying is, "Mmm hmm mm!"

She shakes her head sadly and gestures to a guard I hadn't noticed outside. "Mmm mm mm," she replies.

"Stop making noise back there," calls the guard.

I roll my eyes, wanting more than anything to snap back at him.

Azad and the rest of his team enter the cave triumphantly with a cooked slab of meat. My stomach rumbles, and dizzying hunger takes over.

"So how are our little rebels doing?" Mariia asks harshly.

"Pretty well, I think," the guard says.

"They've been behaving themselves?" Azad asks.

"I guess."

"Are you going to interrogate her or what?" Mariia asks in a hushed tone.

"Yes," Azad replies. "But you'll have to leave us."

My heart skips a beat. Not only am I being held captive by Azad, but I have to speak to him? Alone? My stomach heaves at the thought, and I keep my eyes on the ground.

"What are we going to do about the other one?" Marco asks.

Azad's eyes rest on Xana. "I don't care. She's not as important. Stay with me and watch her while I interrogate."

Marco acknowledges the order and moves over to Xana. He kneels beside her and grabs her chin, whispering something to her I can't make out.

I watch the shadows of Marco's and Azad's teammates slowly exit the cave. Only one remains, tall, long, and dark. Azad's footsteps echo across the floor. The closer he comes, the colder I feel.

"Jaina Indera."

My stomach twists at the sound of his voice.

"You *are* quite the fighter," he says, leaning against a large boulder to my right.

My body shakes with fear. I stare forward at Xana. Her eyes are on me as Marco continues speaking to her.

Azad kneels next to me. I feel his breath as if it were a spirit trying to drag me into his cold darkness. "It's unfortunate it has to be this way. We could have made quite the team. I know who you are, even if you don't know it yourself." He retrieves a silver dagger from his holster belt.

He touches it to my cheek, then twists it under the gag covering my mouth. I turn my head away, seething with anger and fear. A swift flick of his wrist cuts the gag and releases the pressure from my lips.

"Cooperate, darling, and I won't hurt you," he says.

I clench my jaw tighter, wishing I still had the gag so I couldn't tell him anything.

He removes my scimitar from his holster belt and activates it. I try to meet his gaze unflinching, but surely he can see the icy dread in my eyes.

He studies the hilt. "This is yours?"

I nod.

"It's beautiful," he murmurs. "The only one of its kind."

"How would you know?" I ask.

He shifts his gaze back to me. "You're the one. The Light. Anyone who's heard the Prophecy knows it's you."

I stare at him in confusion.

Azad smiles. "Of course, you wouldn't understand. They've been instructed *not* to tell you. They think it will make things easier when they decide to pull you out."

"What do you want?" I ask through my teeth, tired of his nonsense.

"Revenge." Azad points my scimitar at my throat. It scratches at my skin, light enough so I'm not cut, but hard enough that it hurts.

I shake my head, almost feeling pity for him. "How could someone like you let something as trivial as popularity get you so worked up?"

Azad smiles, but his green eyes darken with hatred. "That's what he told you, is it?" He laughs. "By the stars, Jaina. That has nothing to do with it." He keeps his emotions hidden safely within him.

"Then...what *does* it have to do with?"

He flinches, as if remembering something painful, then looks back at me. His eyes become clouded, and he hides his pain behind a mask of hatred. Azad's face hardens. "If you tell me what I need to know, I won't have to hurt you."

I hesitate then ask, "What do you need that I have?"

He drags the scimitar down my throat and across my shoulders. "The Scroll."

I look away, both afraid and angry. "I don't know it," I tell him quickly.

He presses my scimitar harder into my throat. "Don't lie to me, Jaina."

"I don't know it," I insist, pulling away from him.

He only presses closer. When I say nothing, he takes a deep breath and pulls me up, forcing me to stand and presses me into the large boulder behind me.

"Do you think I'm stupid, Jaina?" he asks harshly. "Do you think I've come across the galaxy on this journey to be lied to? What have you to lose?"

I swallow hard, my body shivering with fear. "More than you know," I manage.

Azad raises an eyebrow. "You mean Altair." He sighs. "If I told you all he was keeping from you, you'd despise him. Oh, Jaina, you would hate him with such passion if you knew what he's done to me...and what he's doing to you."

I don't answer, scanning his face for any trace that he's lying. I find none.

Azad softly strokes my cheek and stares deep into my eyes. He touches a strand of my hair and twirls it around his fingers. "He killed her."

My stomach wrenches as he drags his fingers over my throat.

Azad smiles sadly. "Yes, Jaina. He killed her. My sister."

My breath catches, and automatically I shake my head. Dragon wouldn't kill a girl unless she attacked him. He wouldn't.

"She loved him, you know." He breathes the words against my throat as he runs his fingers through my hair.

I jerk away, but he doesn't let me go far.

"She loved him with such intensity that despite my warnings, despite how she *knew* he didn't love her back, she would have done anything for him," he spits. "He murdered her. She was all I had. And your beloved Altair took her from me!"

"You're a liar," I hiss. "He's...he's not a murderer."

Dragon wouldn't do something like that. I've seen how he protects me, but he doesn't kill without first being provoked.

His whole body is pressed to me and I shudder. "I thought you knew Dragon keeps things from everyone."

"I don't believe you," I continue, more to convince myself than Azad.

"If only you knew," he whispers into my ear. His breath dances on my cheek, enveloping me in coldness. His hand touches my waist and rises up to my ribs. Azad's lascivious grin makes my stomach burn with panic.

I pull away, repulsed by his touch. I moan and grit my teeth to keep from biting him or lashing out with all my strength.

"If only you knew what he's getting you into." He holds my gaze with an icy glare, then storms out.

No. Dragon wouldn't. Azad's trying to break me. I won't listen to him. I can't believe him.

I gingerly lower myself back to the ground so I don't lose balance on my bound ankles. Marco has left

Xana alone, but her eyes hold all the fear in the world as she looks at me. Her gag has been removed as well, yet she doesn't say anything.

What if Azad's telling the truth? I've always known Dragon keeps things from people. What dark secrets lie in his past?

———

Cold envelopes me as the beginnings of a sunset turn the sky a greyish-purple. My body shivers in the cool air. I'm still wet from the battle, and dried blood is caked on my arm. The tendrils of hunger course through my veins.

Dragon, I need you.

Thinking of him hurts more than my bruises and gashes. The constant longing for his presence eats away at me. We have to get out of here. I can't stay a moment longer. Sure, we'd be alone in a forest where fire birds roam free, but it would be a hell of a lot better than sticking around here.

Carefully, I wiggle my ankles, trying to bring back sensation to my feet. If only I could somehow cut the rope.

I flex my wrist and–

I freeze.

My gauntlet.

It's still around my wrist. I have a blade inside my gauntlet.

My throat constricts in anticipation, but if I activated my dagger, it would only stab me in the wrist, and there's a chance it'd miss the rope. And if I stabbed myself in the wrist, I would scream my *shaavez* head off. Azad's team has to be nearby, so they'd definitely hear me. They wouldn't risk leaving us here unguarded.

A sharp rock rests nearby. Maybe I could cut my feet loose and go from there.

Cautious not to make noise, I scoot myself over to the rock. I keep an eye on the cave entrance, but it doesn't look like anyone's around. I raise my feet and begin to saw away at the rope. The tearing fibers are loud so I stop to make sure no one's noticed. But all remains silent. Even Xana hasn't turned my way.

I continue to saw away at the rope, and the pressure begins to fade from my ankles.

Finally, the last few fibers give and my legs are free. Blood rushes into my feet, and I sigh in relief. I flex my toes and point them. I stand and rush over to Xana.

She looks at me and jolts back in surprise, her eyes wide with amazement. "What are you doing?" she whispers.

"Xana, we have to get out of here," I breathe.

"There's no time, they're coming back. You have to go without me."

I shake my head. "I'm not going to leave you."

"You have to," she snaps. "Get out of here, Jaina. They're going to hurt you so much if you don't tell them... I don't know it so I'm safe. Bring Dragon back to rescue me if you can."

"Xana—"

"I'll be okay," she insists. "You have to do this if you want to save me. Now hurry!"

Voices grow louder not far away. *Shaav*, they're coming.

Reluctantly, I make my way to the entrance of the cave and peer outside. The voices die down, and all that's left is the echoed cries of birds and animals unknown to me.

I step into the light.

An unnatural silence fills the air and it sends a tingling coolness through my body.

A sudden hit in the side catches me off guard, and I'm pushed to the ground. The boy lifts his leg to kick me in the stomach, but I roll to the side and sweep his legs out from under him. He hits the ground and growls in anger.

I struggle to get back on my feet, but it's difficult with my hands still behind my back.

The boy scrambles to his knees and crawls over to me. He straddles my waist and brings his fist across my jaw. My body starts to go numb, and my vision blurs. Pulling myself out of my daze, I struggle beneath him.

"Next time you'll think twice about trying to escape!" he hisses, then pulls a knife from his belt. He presses it to my throat, fuming rage in his eyes.

"Charon," calls a gruff voice I recognize all too well.

The boy looks up, and I turn my head to look at the newcomer.

Azad's gun is aimed directly at me, yet his words are directed at the boy.

"Get off her," Azad continues sternly, then he moves closer. "Get up. Now."

"She was trying to escape on my watch," Charon argues. "Let me teach her a lesson."

Azad grits his teeth. "I *said* get off her. I expect my orders to be followed."

Charon grumbles to himself, then stands. "You're selfish. You keep her all to yourself. How could they put you as our leader?"

Azad's expression contorts into a furious, bloodthirsty glare. He raises his weapon and fires. The sound echoes across the landscape. Charon stumbles backward, blood oozes from his forehead, and he collapses to the ground.

Azad *killed* him.

One of his own people.

"I didn't like him anyway," Azad mutters, then looks into the forest. "Marco, Mariia, hold her back."

His team approaches from the surrounding trees, and Mariia and Marco pull me to my feet. I struggle against them, but they hold me firmly.

"You ready to talk, Jaina?" Azad asks, fingering the sharp edges of his dagger.

I swallow my fear and bury it deep within me.

Azad smiles, as if sensing my dread. He approaches me, his eyes full of a dangerous, predatory coldness, full of promise that he'll bring me pain.

"You're going to tell me, Jaina," he says. "How and when I get it out of you is your choice."

I grit my teeth, and in the most defiant voice I can muster, I reply, "I would rather die."

Azad runs his fingers through my hair. He tightens his grasp and holds my head at the angle he wants it. I try to pull away, but it's useless. He touches the knife to my cheek.

"I can do a lot worse than that," he whispers, studying my lips. "I'll take pleasure in bringing you to your knees. I'm giving you one last chance to tell me."

My eyes meet his. I could tell him. If I only said the words, my pain would be gone.

But my team needs more time. Maybe they'll find the crystal and win this last Trial. If I tell Azad, it'll put my team in danger. It'll put their lives at stake.

They trust me.

And I trust them.

"I don't know it."

"Wrong answer." He presses the knife into my cheek, and I jerk back as the tip pierces my skin. "I cut you here, didn't I?"

The harder I struggle, the tighter he holds my hair. He drags his blade in a line over my face, carving a long, bloody gash. I want to scream out but I know that would bring him satisfaction so I keep my lips pressed together.

His hand falls from my hair to my waist, and he traces the space between one of my ribs with his fingers. "And here, yes?"

My jaw tightens. I back away from him, but Marco and Mariia press me forward.

Azad drags the knife over the soft area between my ribs, and I take a hard gasp as he widens the gash. He slashes at my arm, and a burning heat sears through my body. He nods in approval.

"Had enough?" he asks.

"That's all you've got?" I spit back, my voice shaking.

He clenches his teeth and brings his elbow violently across my cheek. My body shudders with the force of the blow, and a choked cough of agony escapes my throat. A salty, coppery taste fills my mouth, and I spit a blob of dark, red saliva onto the ground. *Shaav*, I should've known better than to provoke him.

He grabs my hair again and tilts my head up toward the sky. Azad holds the dagger to my throat. "I should kill you. But you don't deserve it," he hisses.

"Sir," calls one of his teammates.

Azad's gaze remains locked on me. "What is it?"

A girl, maybe only fifteen, approaches him and takes his hand, pulling him off to the side. She stays close to him, and he gently puts his hands on her shoulders. They speak in whispers I can't hear.

He nods, then glances at Marco. "Get her outta here," he yells. "We'll continue tonight."

Marco and Mariia pull me backward and lead me into the cave. Xana's eyes follow me as they force me to sit.

"You try to pull anything," Mariia says, "and you're dead." By the severe look in her eyes, I know it's true, no matter what Azad orders.

The light of the fire dances across the cavern walls. I lean my head against the large boulder behind me. My arms ache from remaining in the same position too long, and every movement I make brings on a dull pain. At least the cuts have stopped bleeding.

Azad's team sits in the mouth of the cave around the fire. It's too far away for me to feel its warmth, yet close enough to smell the half-burned meat on which his teammates feast.

I'd give just about anything for something to eat. Or even a drink.

Xana hasn't moved much since I tried to get her to escape. She only stares at Azad's team, watching and listening I guess. I wish I were close enough to talk to her without drawing Azad's attention.

My mouth is dry, like I've been making-out with tree bark. My head bobs forward, but I fight to stay awake, too afraid of what would happen should I fall asleep. I can't afford to let my guard down.

Azad's merciless gaze rests on my frame. He directs his anger and hatred through his glare, and it's clear he's doing everything he can to keep from ripping me to shreds. I meet his look, hoping he'll stop staring, but he persists, lustfully examining my body like I'm his to do with as he pleases.

I turn away when it becomes too awkward. He's trying to intimidate me. It's working.

His teammates walk outside as if on cue, leaving Azad and Marco sitting alone before the fire. Did he tell them to leave so he can torture me more? My stomach knots with the thought.

He tosses a bone into the fire, then turns his bright green eyes to me. He says something to Marco and nods. Marco approaches me, and kicks me in the thigh. I stifle a hard breath and close my eyes. He moves behind me and pulls me to my feet.

Azad kneels by the fire and picks something up. As he comes closer, I realize the object in his hand is a dagger. The entire top half is red hot. He must have been resting it in the flames.

Nausea overcomes me, and blood pounds in my ears. My hands quiver behind my back, and I clench them into fists.

His shadow looms before me, angrily, hatefully. "Tell me The Scroll," he demands. "Or I will proceed with your interrogation."

A soft whimper escapes my throat as I glance again at the blade in his hand. Cold, icy fear burns through my veins. My body begs me to tell him. To end the pain and prevent further harm. But would Dragon give in? Or would he resist?

The answer is clear.

With a final reserve of stupidity, I look into Azad's eyes and shake my head.

Marco jerks me backward, pulling my back to his chest.

Azad bows his head low, then moves in. "You're terribly defiant. Like your mother."

"How would you know my mother?" My voice is low-pitched and rigid from the lack of water.

"I know more about you than you think," he replies gruffly. "But that's not important at the moment." He brings the tip of the dagger near my face. Heat radiates in powerful waves toward me and I clench my jaw tight to restrain from talking. Azad closes his powerful fingers around my arm.

"Gag her," Azad orders.

Marco pulls out a long cloth and dangles it in front of my face. He forces it into my mouth and ties it tight behind my head. I move to pull away, but Azad keeps my arm in his grasp.

He smiles seductively. "You're not going anywhere, my love."

When Marco's done, Azad grabs my blood-encrusted sleeve and tears it from my arm, revealing my shoulder. Azad runs his fingers over my skin and I tremble beneath his hand. "So beautiful," he breathes. "It's a shame I have to ruin it."

He raises the dagger, letting me rest my eyes upon what will bring me pain. The heat from the dagger dries my eyes.

Marco grips my hair, keeping my head still. I let out a short gasp as I try to pull away, but it does no good.

Azad leans close, and touches his lips to my neck. I shiver and turn my head away as far as Marco lets me.

"Try not to scream," Azad whispers.

He pulls away and presses the dagger into my shoulder.

My breath is torn from my lungs as he drags the searing knife through my skin. Tears well in my eyes, and I kick furiously at the ground, doing everything I can to break free. Marco holds me steady, one hand gripping my right arm, his other in my hair.

I feel Azad cutting into my skin. Deep gashes I know won't be easily healed, if healed at all. I clench my jaw, fighting him with every ounce of my being.

My body begs me to tell him. My life is more important than this. I don't deserve this.

Pain shoots through every nerve in my body, and I bite down hard on the cloth in my mouth. A scream of pure agony wells up in my throat, yet I let it out as a moan of anger and hatred. A cry of resistance.

I won't let him win.

Tears stream my face, and Azad lifts his dagger from my shoulder. There's not much relief, but I welcome it. My body trembles as every muscle tightens, anticipating more.

Yet none comes.

It's impossible to see through my river of tears, and I close my eyes to blink them away. Every centimeter of my skin is covered in sweat.

Azad throws his dagger to the floor, then runs his fingers over his work. My shoulder ignites with fiery agony as he traces the deep grooves in my flesh.

He nods to Marco.

Marco cuts my wrists free from the rope, unties my gag, and releases me.

My legs wobble beneath me, and Marco pushes me to the ground. I glance down at my shoulder in horror.

Four deep gashes are sliced into my arm. The blood that should be leaking from it is burned, and the skin around it is scorched black. Each cut is slanted. The first two lines create a triangle without a bottom, the second line longer than the first. The last two lines form a "V."

My palms rest on the ground, and I attempt to press myself up, but all strength fails me. My shoulder sears with pain as I try to move it. I glance up at Azad. There's a murderous glare in his eyes. Sickening realization makes me go cold.

They're his initials.

AV.

Azad Viraak.

"Why won't you just give in?" he asks. "It would be so much simpler."

All that escapes my throat is a weak groan I can't control.

He presses a button on his gauntlet. A terrible heat radiates through me. I move uncontrollably and hear someone screaming. Me.

My eyes fling open and closed involuntarily. In my glimpses of the world, I see my body covered in blue flashes of light. The pain is searing. I gasp for air but my throat opens and closes on its own.

Azad releases the button.

The pain stops.

My body goes limp and my stomach starts to knot then untie itself. I breathe a few times, coughing and gasping for air.

"Tell me the Scroll," Azad demands. He stares down at me like a lion before his prey. His body is a wall before me. Impenetrable and constant. In this moment, nothing exists but the two of us.

He is my pain. My suffering. He is all that's real.

Dragon is my joy. My happiness. In my thoughts, but far out of reach.

I wonder if Azad has any soul. There is only rage in his eyes. Pure, undying hatred he will never let go.

He presses the button again.

The heat is unbearable. I feel like I'm being burned and frozen solid at the same time. I cry out, wanting more than anything for it to stop. *Tell him, Jaina. Tell him*, a voice says to me, through the chaos of my mind.

The pain stops once again. Every movement causes another wave of agony to wrack my body.

Azad steps closer and shakes his head. "Do you think he loves you? Do you honestly think he feels the way you feel about him?" He nudges me with his boot. "He'll leave you for dead when he's gotten all he wants."

I know why I'm doing this. I know why I feel this pain.

"You're...you're wrong," I breathe.

I try to pull away, but I can't move far enough out of range.

The pain returns and I scream. I clench my teeth, but the electricity is searing in my mouth as well. My muscles contract and tighten while the heat burns me from the inside. I cry out and smash my fist into the ground. It hurts too much. I must give in.

"Please!" I beg through my screams. "Please, stop!"

The heat fades, and I find myself lying on my stomach. My fist oozes blood onto the stone floor.

I let my tears cascade from my eyes. Holding them back takes too much effort.

"Please," I sob. Pools of salty water form on the ground before me. The hatred and embarrassment bring on more pain. He's broken my defiance. Broken everything I've held onto.

He grabs my wrist, flipping me onto my back. "Are you done? Or shall I continue?"

I nod, biting my lip, crying like a child. He kneels over me, one knee on the ground and the other across my waist.

"Should I continue?" he threatens. "The next one's going to be fun."

"No!" I cry, grabbing his hand. "Please! No more! I'll...I'll do anything!" I try to breathe steady, but my body trembles, still recovering from the pain.

He takes my hand gently and examines the bloody gash in it. "Tell me and I won't hurt you."

He strokes my hair softly and I cringe. I'm defeated and insignificant. Powerless against him. There's no point resisting anymore.

"One hundred steps left,
Fifty more to the right,
See the moon in the darkness,
And a cave in its light."

I stop, hearing echoes of doubt ringing in my head. My tears continue to fall, and my body shudders with agony. This can't be right. Dragon has risked his life for me and how am I repaying him? Yet I can't take any more of the pain. Just remembering it sends another wave of sobs through me.

"Shh," Azad says, gently smoothing out my hair. "Continue."

I swallow my despair and do as he says.

"Follow it forward,
Walk five meters west,
Only one of these paths,
Will bring an end to your quest."

"Thank you, my dear," he whispers.

I look up into his dark green eyes. "Will you...will you let me go?"

"No."

Rage bursts from me. I told him all I know. "But you said–"

"I said I wouldn't hurt you," he says sternly. "I never said I'd let you go. Don't you enjoy spending time with me?" A sinister smile flashes across his face.

"I don't know the way," I tell him desperately. "I don't know where to start following the directions."

"I do," he says triumphantly. "We leave in an hour."

My anger rises to the point of explosion, yet I'm trapped in my own body, unable to move. All I can do is close my eyes. I can't look at him anymore.

Azad basks in my agony and leans over, his lips near my ear. "Do not betray us, Jaina."

chapter

TWENTY-FOUR

The sky glitters with stars as we trudge on. I don't try to struggle. It won't do any good.

Xana is kept behind me, Marco at her side. Even though she's not gagged anymore, the fear of angering Azad keeps me from speaking to her. Maybe that's why she hasn't spoken to me, either.

Every motion hurts, and I have to concentrate just to stay on my feet. Exhaustion needles its way into my mind, and hunger gnaws into my stomach. My shoulder burns with shooting pain, and I cup the injury with my palm. Despite how much it hurts, I trace the lines. Will his name always be engraved in my skin?

AV.

It tingles and aches every time I try to move it. If I live to the end of this Trial, what will Dragon do when he sees this? It's not like it'll matter. I might not see him again, anyway.

I want my team back. I miss Liam, his annoying comments and his arrogant idea that he's the cutest thing alive.

I miss Kavi and Seth, and how they constantly annoy each other. Well, maybe I don't *miss* that but I'd much rather hear them bicker than be here.

I miss Dragon. I miss talking to him. I miss his thoughtfulness. I miss his stare and his deep, endless eyes. I miss his touch. I'd do anything to get him back.

"We're here," Azad says.

Before us is a gate. Its stone walls rise six meters into the air, towering over us. Azad opens the gate hesitantly, as if expecting something to jump out at him.

He nods to me. "Come on, Jaina."

I walk through the ranks of his team and stop at Azad's side.

He takes my left arm. "Lead the way." He jerks it upward slightly, and agony shoots through my body. It sickens me, having him holding my arm as if I were *his*. His touch feels foreign and intrusive against my skin.

"One hundred steps left," I breathe.

There's no ceiling to the long, maze-like passage in front of us. The path is wide enough for an entire team to walk side by side, and the ground is covered in water up to our knees.

The night is dark as hell, and if it weren't for the moon, we wouldn't be able to see a thing.

I wish he'd let go of me.

I'm too weak to make a run for it.

His hands are warm, and I realize he's nervous. I feel his heartbeat through his touch. For the first time, I see him as a boy, probably not much older than I am. Is he afraid I'll lead them the wrong way? Is he scared he might not make it into the Crystal City?

We reach a fork in the path. Two roads lie before us.

Azad sighs. "All right, next?"

"Fifty more to the right."

Trees grow along the path. It's as if someone grew a jungle inside their own home. The moon appears from behind a large tree, its light shining upon a large rocky formation.

We continue forward until the walls enclose us in a large circle. The only way out is up. Caves surround us.

"See the moon in the darkness, and a cave in its light," I say aloud with slight amazement. The moon shines directly above a cave before us.

Azad nods, then turns to his team. "Secure the area."

They disperse across the small expanse, leaving Marco, Xana and Azad. Marco stares blankly forward, like he knows looking at me and Azad would be wrong. Yet Xana keeps her gaze locked on the two of us.

Azad smiles at me. "Not so bad." He pulls me closer to him, and I try to step away, but his strength is too great.

"Get your hands off me," I manage under my breath.

He jerks me forward, pressing me to his chest. His hand trails to the small of my back, keeping my body against his. "I'll do as I please, Jaina," he hisses. "You will give in to me...eventually..." he says in a softer tone. His mouth is so close to mine I feel his breath on my lips, and the horrible image of him kissing me runs cold through my mind.

I shake my head in horror. "Never."

"We'll see about that!" He slaps me hard across my cut cheek, and I gasp with the pain. Azad pulls me back to him and groans viciously through his grin. "Mmm, yes, you're mine," he whispers, touching the AV on my shoulder.

I press my lips together, sealing them shut. My stomach drops at his words, and I struggle to swallow the nausea building up within me.

"Stop," Xana manages to say from behind me. "Please, just let her go."

Azad snarls and lets me go. He approaches her and draws his knife. She tries to back down, but Marco holds her in place. "You saw what I did to her," Azad threatens, grabbing Xana's arm. He drags the knife harmlessly over her skin, but it makes his point. "Don't make me do it to you."

Xana swallows hard as tears well up in her eyes. She bites her lip and nods.

"We're clear," Mariia says, returning with the rest of his team.

Splash.

I hear it only meters away. There's forest all around us, and water knee-high. I can't pinpoint what made the sound.

Azad retrieves his pistol, and shoots toward the sound. Nothing happens. I scan the trees wondering what would happen if *another* team captured me. At least I wouldn't have to worry about Azad. There's a look of worry in his eyes.

"You sure we're clear?" Azad asks. "Well, get to it! If someone's there, kill them."

Mariia and the others pull out their swords and fan out to the surrounding area again.

"Marco, you're with me," Azad says.

The four of us move into the cave. The darkness engulfs us like a liquid. I turn around, wondering who could have been following us.

I'd rather not get my hopes up, especially if it was nothing. But a glimmer of faith rings in me. Could it have been...

No.

If it was, they would have come for me right then and there. It's better they remain safe. We move deeper into the cave without a word.

Azad's glowsaber is the only light in the long, dark passage. The water is cold around my knees.

Though I'd like nothing more than to never speak to Azad again, I can't resist asking what's on my mind. "Shouldn't your team be back by now?"

"Not if they found something. What's next?" he asks harshly as we approach a set of three passages.

"Follow it forward, walk five meters west," I tell him. We take the path to the West and find two more tunnels to take.

"Only one of these paths will bring an end to you quest," he says softly. "So this is what it comes down to. Which path do we take?"

I could choose the wrong path and kill him. Probably kill myself, too, but maybe it would be a worthy sacrifice. But Xana's with me. I can't risk her life, even if it means Azad's death.

I shake my head, unable to choose. "I don't know."

"If you are the Light, which I believe you are, you will choose the right path."

I look from one path to the other. One of the paths is lighter than the other, but that could be a deception.

Most people would choose the path that's more lit up, so could that be the path that's wrong?

"I-I don't know."

"I said choose," he curses impatiently.

"Azad," Xana breathes. "She doesn't know."

"Shut up!" he snaps back at her, then squeezes my left arm tight.

"I can't!" I cry, beginning to panic. "I don't know the right path!"

"Just choose one for the galaxy's sake!" His voice echoes through the cavern.

I stare blankly down both paths and close my eyes. *Calm. Stay calm.* I picture the two tunnels in my mind. If I'm the 'Light,' I'll choose the right path. But what if I'm not? Hell, I don't even know what that means.

"Right," I say.

He approaches the right path.

Without thinking, I grab his arm and stop him. "Wait."

Azad glances down at my hand on his arm. His expression softens. "Yes?"

"It's left."

He furrows his brow. "Left?"

I look back at both paths. "No, it's right."

"Make up your mind."

"Right."

He looks into my eyes and forces me to meet his gaze by tipping my chin up. "You're sure?"

"Yes."

Azad nods. He takes me by the arm and pulls me in after him. I'm surprised he doesn't make me go first. I shoot a glance backward, hoping my team is coming.

We enter a chamber and there in the moonlight, is the crystal. A pool of water surrounds the island where the pedestal sits. It's black, and dark as Azad's presence, reflecting a glimmer of light from the moon.

A hole in the ceiling lets the moonlight through, allowing Azad to shut his glowsaber off. Marco and Xana stand to the side.

The room is mostly rock and dirt, and a few formations look like metal. Roots protrude from the walls. The water is a little deeper here, measuring up to the top of my knees. Glowing moss lines the bottom, and fish swim around us.

Azad pulls me forward to the pedestal and forces me onto my knees. "Read it," he orders.

> "It's the spark that keeps you moving,
> The final rope to which you hold,
> Hope is a lie, because in the end,
> There's only the dark and the cold.
>
> Take from others all you prize,
> Through fire you'll prevail,
> The sacrifice for victory,
> Is the same, should you fail.
>
> When the lies have finally burned away,
> For revenge the silence cries,
> When flames of rage have torn us down,
> From the ashes we shall rise."

The words make me shiver.

There's an uncomfortable silence after I finish. Azad touches my shoulder and helps me to my feet.

"You know what they're asking for?" Marco asks.

Azad nods. "There's only one thing it could be."

My worst fears are confirmed. My blood runs cold in my veins and I shake my head, backing away from Azad. "No," I say. "No, that's not what it means."

Azad raises an eyebrow. "That's *all* it could mean, Jaina. This is what the IA demands. We must show no mercy."

"That doesn't make it right."

"So, he finally turned you. What'd he do to convince you? Did he tell you he'll be there for you? That he'll come for you?"

My heart sinks. He couldn't know what Dragon's told me.

"Don't listen to him," Xana says.

Azad ignores her and studies me with a mixture of pity, wanting, and viciousness. He shakes his head and smiles. "Yes, you know what I mean. Did he kiss you?"

My stomach wrenches, and I'm unable to meet his gaze.

Azad laughs. "Mm, yes, he did. And you fell so easily for his sick little act."

"Shut up! It doesn't matter what he said!" I snap. "They wouldn't make us kill one of our own..."

His lips form a nightmarish grin. "Not one of our own," he says, then turns to Marco, who's holding Xana's arm. "Give her to me."

"No!" I cry. "No, you can't do this!"

"Yes," Azad says sternly. "I can. Marco, give her to me!"

Marco hesitates. "What if she's right?"

Azad's glare is so hateful I'm afraid Marco will incinerate on the spot. "Would *you* rather volunteer?"

Marco swallows hard and loosens his grip on Xana. Her breath becomes quick as she backs into the wall. "Wait," she says. "Can't we just take a moment to think about this?"

"I've thought about it," Azad growls and steps closer to her.

I throw myself in front of him and put my hands on his chest to stop him. He grabs my arm and holds me to him.

"Please!" I beg. "It has to be something else!"

Azad shakes his head and gently touches my cheek. "No, Jaina, it doesn't. This is what they want."

"Then sacrifice me instead." I say the words before I know what they are. But I don't take them back. "Please."

"I'm sorry," he breathes. "But I still need you."

He tosses me to the side and Marco catches me as I fall. Marco grabs both of my wrists and shoves me into the wall so I have no way to escape.

Xana makes a dash for the exit but Azad catches her hand and throws her into the water. She struggles to get back up and get away, but Azad is too fast. Seizing her arm, he pulls her to her feet and drags her over to the pedestal.

"Jaina," Xana whimpers. She struggles and lashes out at him, but to no avail. Her strength is no match for him. I can see her face clearly from where Marco holds me. Tears stream down her cheeks and she trembles with fear.

"Azad, please!" I shout. "You don't have to do this!"

Azad grips her hair and forces her to kneel before the pedestal.

My stomach wrenches, and I look at Marco standing in front of me. "Please, stop him! You know this is wrong! He's crazy!"

Marco takes a shaky breath, but says nothing.

Azad tilts Xana's head up toward the ceiling and pulls out his dagger.

Time slows. Something has to happen. My team has to arrive and save us. The moment Azad lowers his dagger, someone will interrupt him, or a knife will come flying at his back. It *has* to happen that way.

"Any last words?" Azad asks her, holding the knife to her neck.

Xana closes her eyes. "Jaina," she sobs. "I-I should've been kinder. Tell Liam I'm sorry."

Azad slides the dagger across her throat.

No one comes.

Her eyes open and grow wide. A soft gurgling sound fills my ears. It lasts a few seconds then finally fades.

No one came for us.

Xana's eyes roll back in her head.

No one came for us.

An animal-like scream tears through my throat. Every muscle of my body trembles in shock, and Marco forces his hand over my mouth to mask the sound.

Azad takes a white cloth and covers the slit in her throat. When it becomes soaked with red liquid, he kicks her body to the side and squeezes the blood from the cloth over the sacrificial bowl.

The black crystal rises.

Azad takes it and puts it in his holster belt.

Tears stain my cheeks and my body goes limp. Marco lets me go and my legs give out beneath me. I sit in the water, my knees pulled up to my chest and cry into my hands. My stomach tightens and convulses, trying to purge the scene from my mind. I gag, but there's nothing to come out.

Death is supposed to be honorable.

Not like that.

Not like that.

"Sir," Marco begins. "What should we do with the body?"

Azad waves his hand. "Leave it."

Marco looks down at me, and furrows his brow. "Shouldn't we–"

"I said leave it," Azad barks.

But Marco persists. "It's wrong to just leave them–"

Azad snarls in disgust and points his dagger to Marco's chest. "You weak *shariin*. Don't you *dare* talk to me about right or wrong."

"Azad!" Dragon calls.

He runs down the corridor, with his scimitar activated.

"Dragon!" I call back, not quite believing he's here. Hope rises in me at the sound of his voice. He's alive!

"*Shaav* you, Altair!" Azad snaps back. "Marco, kill him!"

Marco retrieves his sword and charges for Dragon with frightening speed. I jump to my feet, hoping I can reach Dragon to help him. But I don't have my scimitar. Azad steps in front of me. Marco's sword is a flash of light, up and down. Dragon's isn't much different, but he's losing ground. The two of them take their battle into another corridor.

Azad puts his hand to his holster belt and pulls out my scimitar and his sword. I can't defend myself.

"I can play fair." He tosses my scimitar to me.

The hilt is stained with the blood from his hands. Xana's blood. Tears threaten my eyes once more, and I activate it in my right hand, careful to keep my left shoulder out of the way.

"You murderer." My voice is deep with rage. "You sick, disgusting murderer."

A deep throaty laugh escapes his grinning lips. "I only did what you couldn't."

I let him make the first attack and block each and every one of his moves. He's not fighting his hardest, I can tell. I try to lock our blades.

"You can't win, Jaina," he continues. "Not in the end."

I refuse to believe him. Even if he's right, remorse won't help me now. Our blades unlock, then clash again. I pull my blade away and take a long powerful sweep at his throat. He ducks and trips me. I fall and struggle to keep my head above the water. Azad moves closer, his sword raised and ready to fall. I jerk to the right at the last moment and stand once I'm far enough away.

I attack him faster, with more power than before. Our blades lock once more, and water splashes around us in a frenzy of activity. I lunge at him and block whatever he has to throw at me. I jab at him and it skims his arm. Blood oozes from the dark gash. His eyes burn with rage.

"The three of us are more alike than we want to admit," he says.

"I'm not like you," I cry. "You're a liar and a murderer! Someone like you only deserves to die!"

Azad's eyes are dark and ruthless. "Then you'll have to kill your lover along with me!"

I take another swing at him but miss. He lunges at me, and I back away avoiding his blade by a mere centimeter. Sweat streams down my back. I *must* do this. For Xana.

I watch his every move, searching for some weakness. He swings, and I duck but he changes the path of the blade at the last moment and skims my thigh.

He smiles. "Now we're even, love."

My blade comes alive with fury, a part of me moving to my will.

Azad becomes more dangerous, his attacks harder to block.

His sword glimmers in the moonlight as it moves downward, close to my stomach. I back away but not far enough. I hear the ring of his sword as it slashes through my skin. Agony sears in my left leg and I find myself kneeling in the water.

Azad runs at me, sword overhead. I block his attack at the last moment, holding my blade with both hands. He presses into me with all his force. My branded shoulder screams with pain. I feel like it's being torn apart, a crack spreading through my skin and up my neck, splitting me into pieces.

I'm not strong enough.

Clearing my mind, I concentrate on my goal. Azad presses harder into me, and I know I can't hold on much longer.

I lean away from him and grit my teeth as I hold back all his strength with my own. I close my eyes, knowing I'll give out at any second. A soft light flashes in my mind. A warm glow that gives me a final reserve of strength, spreading through my body. I press against Azad's force and I bring myself to stand.

With one swift move, I loosen my grip on my scimitar and let it fall as Azad's strength pushes it away. I spin toward him, my back to his chest, and reach into his holster belt. I close my fingers around his dagger and step away.

Azad closes the gap between us and raises his sword. I thrust myself forward, and a sickening squelch fills my ears. Azad drops his sword in shock. It falls, then splashes into the water. He takes a step toward me, but doesn't look down.

He knows what I've done.

His blood oozes onto my hand.

His breath falters, and he knits his brow, his face contorting in agony. I try to pull away from him and leave the dagger in his side, but he grabs my left shoulder with such a force I can't escape him.

"Oh," I gasp in pain.

He presses his thumb into my wound and smiles darkly. "Look at me, Jaina. Is this what you wanted?" He pants.

I keep my eyes on the ground.

He forces his fingers around my jaw and tilts my head so my eyes meet his. "Look at me!" he demands. "Are you satisfied?"

Warm, sticky liquid flows steadily onto my hand, and my stomach convulses with fear. He rests his other hand on mine, letting both of ours be drenched with blood.

"I'm sorry," I whisper. My voice is shaking and so are my hands.

"Don't be. You haven't won yet."

"You're my only enemy," I say. "I've defeated you."

His hand brushes the cut on my cheek. I flinch at his touch but don't pull away. "I know my destiny, and I know yours. I'll return. And when I do, don't expect mercy from me." His strength is so great, it's hard to believe he's injured. He pulls my body against his and touches his nose to my forehead. He's too strong to resist. "You're mine, Jaina. You're mine, and you always will be. As long as you wear this," he brushes the AV with his fingers again, "you belong to me."

"I'll never be yours," I whisper. "You were wrong about everything. Dragon isn't a liar. He's not a murderer. Admit you were wrong."

"He's everything I've said he is. The only reason he pretends is because he knows who you are." He starts to lose balance, and for some reason, I help him stay upright.

He gasps in pain, and I back him into the wall. I retrieve the dagger and pull away to the other side of the room. He moans and collapses onto the ground.

A shadow crosses his face. "He'll hurt you. He doesn't love you. And when he does, think of me. Everything he's told you is a lie."

"He won't."

"He'll betray you," he says, smiling slyly. His eyes are dark with fury, yet it's clear he's running out of energy.

"No." I refuse to believe it. "Tell me it's not true."

"Until we..." he gasps. "Meet...again...my love..."

His eyes close.

I've won.

He's dead. He has to be dead. I've pinned myself to the opposite wall, hyperventilating. Dizziness takes over me as everything sinks in.

I killed him.

By the stars, I *killed* him.

I don't know if I should be relieved, or afraid. Tendrils of blood streak the water, reaching out to me as if looking to avenge Azad. I don't take my eyes off him for a few more moments.

I can't make myself get any closer. He looks as if he's still breathing, but I can't tell. Even in death, would Azad lie to me? Dragon will betray me?

Forcing myself to snap back into the present, I glance at the pedestal. I need the crystal. It's in Azad's holster belt.

My hands tremble as I move back over to him and go through the pouches on his belt. I imagine his jade eyes shooting open. I imagine him snatching the dagger from my hand and slitting my throat as he did to Xana.

My hand closes around the black crystal. Azad's hand twitches.

I nearly scream and my heart makes a move to jump out of my throat. Pulling the crystal from his pocket, I back up to the opposite wall.

My heart is pounding in my throat. I look down at my bloody hands. I gag.

Breathe.

Just breathe.

My eyes rest on Xana's lifeless form. There's nothing I can do for her. I contemplate dragging her out, but Dragon needs my help.

Dragon.

I have to get to him.

I take one last look at Azad before I leave. He *is* still alive. How long that will be true, I'm not sure, but I don't want to hang around to find out.

I run through the corridor we came from and down more passageways. I've got to get out of here and find Dragon. I approach a chamber full of light. The clashing of swords fills my ears and I step inside in time to see Mariia slash Dragon in the chest. I cringe as it happens, and he backs away, touching the wound and examining the blood. He regains his stance and blocks another of her blows.

Marco lies dead a few meters away from the two of them, a bright splotch of blood staining his stomach.

I pull out Azad's dagger and aim. I'm good at this. I can do this.

Mariia's about to strike him down. Dragon prepares to block, but from his hunched over stance it's clear he's in pain.

I can't tell if he's seriously hurt, but I don't have time to wonder. We have to get out of here. I throw the knife.

Mariia brings her sword down but crumbles to the ground as my dagger digs into her thigh. She screams and lets go of her sword.

"Dragon!" I shout.

He moves in time to prevent her sword from falling down on him. She falls to the ground, and he drives his scimitar into her stomach. I hear her sharp intake of air and her quiet sigh as he pulls it from her.

Azad's words resurface in my mind, and the picture of Dragon murdering Azad's young, unarmed sister makes me jump with surprise. Before, the thought was outrageous. Unbelievable. But now...he just killed an unarmed, injured girl.

The thought fades as he approaches. Dark rings encircle his eyes, and his handsome face seems to have sunken in with exhaustion.

"Jaina..." he says my name in a whisper, as if the word is too sacred to say aloud. He studies my face, then pulls me into his embrace. "Jaina, by the stars, I'm so sorry."

I sink into his touch. The arms I have longed to fall into don't disappoint me. He presses me to his chest, and I want to cry with relief.

"Dragon," I breathe against his warm shirt. I open my mouth again, wanting more than anything to tell him I love him. Instead, I say, "I missed you."

"Jaina, are you all right?" He pulls away. "Are you–"

I shake my head as tears blur my vision. "Xana..."

His eyes widen and his face grows dark with anguish. "There's nothing we can do."

"I know," I breathe. "Where's everyone else?"

"They're waiting at the entrance of the cave."

I take a step away from him, but he grabs my hand.

There's a worried look in his eyes. He looks down at my hands, rubbing his fingers over my own. "Who's blood?"

I follow his gaze and shift uncomfortably. My hands are streaked with red, like someone spilled paint over them.

"Who's blood?" he repeats, sternly.

I lower my head, not wanting to think of him. "Azad's."

Dragon blinks twice, stunned. "He's dead? You killed him?"

I nod. "I think so."

"You *think* so? Or you *know*?"

I shrug. "I think so."

"What happened?"

"I stabbed him."

He hesitates then says, "Come on, let's go."

We run through the maze of tunnels. Dragon stays by my side.

"Why are they in the mouth of the cave?" I ask as we round a corner in the dark corridors. "Why didn't they come with you?"

"They followed me in, but we were ambushed by Azad's team," he says. "I got out in time to come find you. Do you have the crystal?"

Dragon grabs my hand and pulls me into a tunnel to the left. We reach the mouth of the cave.

"Jaina!" Kavi shouts. "You're alive!"

I shoot her a half-smile. It's all I can bear to muster.

"Where's the checkpoint?" Dragon asks.

"It's somewhere in this maze," Seth replies.

"Can you lead us to it?"

"I better lead. It's not far away at all," Kavi says.

Dragon nods. "We have to hurry."

I hardly process what's happening. I'm running to the checkpoint, but my limbs don't want to continue. Hunger takes its toll on me. Seth activates the checkpoint, and a helitransport appears above us.

Liam starts climbing the ladder after everyone else is in the transport besides Dragon and me. He shouts something about Xana but Dragon orders him not to worry about it. Another team appears not too far away.

I look at Dragon, and he looks back at me. The moon is high in the sky, but dawn is approaching. He makes me climb up first, and he follows not far behind. I reach the top and enter the shuttle.

The moment we begin moving, I start feeling dizzy, so I can't stand.

"You okay?" Dragon asks, grabbing hold of me.

I bring my hand to my forehead and close my eyes, but the dizziness doesn't go away. "Yeah, I'm just really dizzy," I reply.

"Jaina, you should sit down," Liam says.

Someone says something else about Xana but I can't catch their words.

I sit down and feel better for a moment until world goes completely black.

I wake up with a bright light in my eyes. For a moment, I actually think I'm dead, but as the world forms around me, I'm relieved that's not the case.

I'm in a bed. It's not very comfortable as far as beds go, but it's better than sleeping on a cave floor. Blue curtains enclose me in a small space.

I can't remember much of what happened after I grabbed the crystal...after I killed Azad.

Shirez stands a few meters away and is speaking to a doctor, but when he sees I'm awake, he approaches me.

"Did we win?" I ask.

Shirez nods. "You did."

"Is everyone else all right?"

He nods, but doesn't smile. "The doctors tried to revive Xana from the arena once you got out, but she was too far gone."

My jaw tightens at his words, and hate burns through my veins. It was Azad's fault.

"You were in the worst condition of everyone who survived," Shirez says. "So if you feel okay, the rest of your team feels much better."

I manage a laugh. "That's nice to know." My smile disappears as more of the past returns to me. Is Azad still alive? "What about the other teams?"

Shirez sighs. "It's best we don't talk about that now."

I swallow the fear that's been climbing my throat since the moment I thought of him again. "Am I allowed to get up now?"

"Yes." Shirez glances at my white hospital gown. "But you may want to change out of your current clothes. I brought you this." He hands me black pants and a soft, gold shirt.

"Thanks."

Shirez leaves the room, and I make sure the curtains are attached to the opposite walls, just in case someone decides to come in. I see my cuts and scars have almost completely healed. All but one.

His initials remain deeply engraved in my arm. My flesh is still bright pink where he wrote them. They won't leave me. Ever.

Moving my shoulder sends shudders of pain through my neck and down my back, but it's nowhere near as bad as it was before.

I put on the clothes Shirez gave me. The shoulders of the shirt are open, and the impulse to cover his initials is overwhelming. I place my palm over them so no one else can see.

There's a small waiting room, and Kavi sits alone on one of the fluffy couches.

She stands up and rushes in to hug me. Her arms wrap around me with such force the air is squeezed from my lungs.

"By the stars, Jaina, I'm so glad you're okay." Her voice trembles as she speaks.

"Where's everyone else?" I ask.

"Shirez had them all get on the ship to the awards ceremony," she replies. "Don't worry, it's not going to take off without you. He just wanted them to be ready." Her eyes meet mine, and by the glossy look in them I can tell she's been crying.

Shirez strides into the room. "So it's awards, then the Crystal City," he says softly.

The Crystal City. I forgot. I smile at Shirez, but I don't feel like smiling at all.

I gaze out at the stars. The small hallway of the transport is empty except for me. When we first got on board, I thought I'd wander around a little to think, but the view here was too spectacular to pass up. The windows are much larger than the ones on previous ships. Though we've broken away from the planet, we still haven't entered light-speed. A nebula, probably a few light-years away, lights up the sky.

Azad's voice won't leave me. *"I'll return. And when I do, don't expect mercy from me." "You're mine, Jaina. You're mine and you always will be."*

Is he dead? And if not, could I ever see him again? *"He'll hurt you. He'll betray you."*

But Dragon didn't betray me. He wouldn't. He *won't*.

Though, if Azad's dead, why would he lie? Those were his last words. Would he want the last sentence he ever said to be a lie? He wanted revenge on Dragon so badly...

The door to my left slides open.

His tall, comforting frame rests in the doorway. He studies me then quickly moves closer.

Dragon pulls me into his arms, and he sighs. "By the stars, Jaina. You really like putting yourself in horrible situations."

"You think I do that intentionally?"

He runs his fingers through my hair, resting his cheek on the side of my head. "I was so scared," he whispers. "I couldn't sleep with you gone. Every thought I had was about you."

I sink deeper into his arms, resting my head on his shoulder and pressing my nose to his neck.

He lets his hands fall to my shoulders, and I gasp with the pain. He pulls away. "I'm sorry, did I hurt you?"

I shake my head, not wanting him to see what Azad has done. "No, it's all right. I'm fine."

He directs his attention to my shoulder. I feel naked before him with the slight revealing of my arm, but I let him look. I turn away from my shoulder, not wanting to see what I already know is there. I focus on him. His face contorts in anguish as he gently touches my skin. I flinch, and he quickly pulls away.

"He...he did this to you?" he asks, but it's clear he knows the answer. "I'm so sorry. I should have come sooner. I shouldn't have–"

"It's okay." I brush a strand of his beautiful, sandy-brown hair from his forehead. "There wasn't anything you could have done."

He stares down in horror at my arm. "How did he–"

"Please, Dragon," I breathe. "It doesn't matter."

Dragon swallows hard, and I press my forehead to his cheek.

"I'm sorry," he whispers.

"It wasn't your fault," I insist. "Don't blame yourself for this."

He sighs. I rest in his embrace, letting everything sink in. I love him, yet the odds are against us. We won. And it's such a horrible thing. It cost Xana her life. And will cost me my love.

"What are we going to do? In the Crystal City, I won't see you," I say, trying hard to hold back the raw sorrow in my voice.

"I'll come for you, Jaina." His lips are so close. I let my eyes close and feel my nose brush his. "I promise." He speaks so softly, his warm breath dances across my cheek.

His lips gently brush mine, and I can no longer defy the raging emotions in me. His hand glides across my cheek, and his fingers trickle through my hair. I tremble from his warm, soothing touch. He kisses me again, a true, deep kiss I know I can never forget.

He moves his hand up my waist, sending warm shivers through my body. I press myself closer to him, constantly wanting more. And yet, through my wanting, I am content.

Our lips part for an instant, and his breath trembles as he takes in the air near me. He holds me close to him.

"I promise I won't leave you," he breathes against my skin. "I'm sorry I didn't–"

Before he can finish, I press my lips to his. I feel his heart pounding in his chest to the same rhythm as mine. Dragon intertwines his fingers with my own, and I squeeze his hand, never wanting to part from him. If it were up to me, I'd stay here in this moment forever.

Someone clears his throat. "Altair?" Shirez asks.

I pry my lips from Dragon's and take a step back, breaking our embrace. Shirez leans against the doorway, and I feel my cheeks burn bright red. Shirez looks from Dragon to me, his eyebrow slightly raised.

"Yes, sir?" Dragon asks, his voice unsteady.

"I hate to be interrupting anything–"

"No, it's okay, we were just..." Dragon turns back to me.

I try hard not to laugh and cry at the same time. I'm going to miss him so much.

"No need to explain. I've seen quite enough," Shirez replies. "I need to speak with you, Altair."

"Yes, sir, I'll be there momentarily," Dragon replies.

Shirez rolls his eyes, then walks out.

Dragon turns to me, his cheeks flush red.

I laugh, but the thought of leaving him casts a shadow over me. I look down at the floor. I can't cry in front of him and I do my best to restrain the tears in my eyes. "I'll miss you, Dragon," I choke out.

"We'll see each other again," he promises, then kisses me once more.

"I'm so afraid."

"I am, too."

"Don't leave me," I say. I kiss him a final time, and he strokes my hair.

He starts to move away. "This won't be forever, Jaina. I promise." He takes a deep breath, turns from me, and walks toward the door. At the last moment, he looks back at me. "I promise, Jaina."

The door slides shut behind him, and I'm left staring out at the nebula, longing for him. It doesn't matter what Azad said.

Dragon will come for me.

I trust him.

END OF BOOK ONE

Acknowledgements

First, I'd like to thank my mom, for her constant support. She read through all eight drafts, and helped me edit far more than she had to. I'd like to thank Nicole Zoltack for being an awesome editor, and helping me along the final stages of creating this book. I'd also like to thank Kate Agan, Chanel Gray, Amanda Leong, and Terri Wallace, for being my four most favorite critique partners ever!

Thanks to Angela Brown, PK Hrezo, Elisabeth Kauffman, Alyssa McKendry, Reiko McKendry, Ryan McKendry, Sandie Nelson, and Prerna Pickett for beta reading for me, and giving me really great feedback to work with.

Thanks to Margaret Agan, Jenna Blackburn, Alex Cavanaugh, Cameryn Celestina, Sydney Harper, Nick Hight, David Powers King, Hannah Loomis, Jesse McKendry, Francesca & Gabriella Rapposelli, Pallavi Shamapant, and Grayson Zillich, for constantly supporting me and helping me choose the cover design for this book.

I'd like to thank my CreateSpace team for being so easy to work with and bringing *From the Ashes* to life.

Finally, thanks to everyone in the blogosphere, and all of the amazing people in my life who have kept me inspired, and made this book possible.

21631330R00271

Made in the USA
Charleston, SC
24 August 2013